THROUGH GLASS DARKLY

Book Three
Between Worlds Series

TRACEE FORD

THROUGH GLASS DARKLY
BETWEEN WORLDS SERIES
BOOK 3

This book contains mature themes and disturbing subject matter
and is intended for adult readers. Reader discretion is advised.

DEDICATION

For David, my north star, my constant, and the most inspiring
person in my life.

For Bennie, my dearest friend. I will forever cherish the stories
we told one another, the grade school puppet shows we
performed, the skits we directed, and all the beautifully creative
things we shared growing up. I love you, old friend. This book
exists because of those early creative adventures.

For those directly impacted by the events of 9/11, especially the
first responders who made the ultimate sacrifice, I honor you
with this book. You inspire me. You move me. You bless me.

THROUGH GLASS DARKLY

ACKNOWLEDGMENTS

This book was shaped over time, and I am grateful for the patience, understanding, and quiet support that made its completion possible.

To those who offered encouragement, space, and steadiness along the way…thank you for staying present while this story found its way to the page.

I am also thankful for the careful revision and refinement that helped bring clarity to the final manuscript. Any remaining imperfections are entirely my own.

Table of Contents

1

Henry

Henry stood in the barn feeding the horses, enjoying the warm summer breeze as it drifted through. Suddenly, a high-pitched scream pierced the air, coming from the farmhouse. His face darkened with a scowl as he quickly strode toward the place he had called "home" for the past few months.

Before he could reach the house, his foster sister, Candy, burst through the back door and ran toward him. She threw herself into his arms, her small body trembling against his. Concerned, Henry gently pushed her back, his hands gripping her shoulders. He needed to see her face.

Blood trickled from the corner of her mouth, and her swollen bottom lip was already bruising. Her mousy brown hair was disheveled, and she wore only a shirt and underwear. Henry's gaze met her frightened eyes as her hands, resting on his bare chest, clenched into tight fists.

"What happened?" he asked.

"He's doing it again!" she exclaimed. "I told him to stop. I told him that I didn't want to do it anymore, but he doesn't listen." Her eyes overflowed with tears.

"Candy, what are you talking about? Who did this?"

"Mike!" she shouted.

"Mike did this?" He tried to wrap his mind around what it all meant, but he simply could not.

Candy wheezed desperately, trying to catch her breath. She grabbed Henry's arms and shook him. "You don't know who he really is," she continued. "Please, Henry, don't let him hurt me anymore," she begged. "They like you. They'll listen to you. I know they will."

Suddenly, a shout came from the house. "Get back here, girl!" Mike shouted, his Southern accent thick and distinct. "I'm not finished with you yet!"

The revulsion in Candy's eyes burned into Henry's memory, and he knew he would never forget the dread and terror coloring her expression. She ducked behind him, her fingernails digging trenches into one of his arms. Henry squared his shoulders and planted his feet on the ground, steeling himself for the confrontation. He watched as Mike flung open the back door and raged toward him.

"What's wrong, Mike?" Henry asked calmly.

Mike pushed his index finger into Henry's chest. "You stay out of this, boy. It doesn't concern you." He reached around Henry and tried to grab Candy, but she turned and ran toward the woods, shrieking and pleading for mercy.

Mike's fury surged, his finger still pressed hard against Henry's chest. His glare burned into Henry, as if accusing him of ruining some flawless master plan. "I'll deal with you later," he growled before spinning around and running after Candy. Henry stood frozen, his eyes following Mike until the man disappeared into the dense line of trees at the edge of the property.

Through the humid summer air, Candy's desperate cries

and pleas carried back to him, mingled with Mike's chilling, mocking laughter. Henry did not need to see beyond the trees to know what was happening. He could feel it in his gut.

The instinct to protect life swelled within him, driving him into action. He turned and sprinted into the house, his heart pounding with urgency.

"Holly!" he shouted.

"Down here," she called from the basement, her voice pleasant and serene.

Rushing down the basement stairs to the laundry room, he saw Holly busily folding laundry. "Holly, you have to help me," he began, panting, his heartbeat pounding like a drum in his ears.

She gently put the towel down on the table in front of her and turned her full attention to Henry. "What's wrong, sweetheart?" She raised her hand to his cheek, her eyes filled with compassion and understanding.

"You've got to help Candy," he pleaded. "He's hurting her!"

With an oblivious countenance, she said, "Oh, Candy's fine. She and Mike play like that all of the time."

"Play?" He shook his head in disbelief. "I just watched Mike chase her into the woods. Didn't you hear her screaming? I know what he's doing to her. Help me go get her!"

Immediately, her expression changed, and her hand

dropped from his face. A blank stare colored her expression. It was as if she had turned into a robot. "You're overreacting. They're just playing."

"What? Are you serious? Are you high? Are you deaf?" he bit out.

"Really, Henry, there's nothing I can do." She shrugged as she turned back to the laundry.

"Nothing you can do?" he shouted. "We're your foster kids, damn it!"

"Watch your language," she instructed, bringing her eyes to briefly meet his again.

"You have to do something! Your husband is out there raping her!"

Holly kept folding the clean towels as if she heard nothing else. Then she spoke quietly. "Henry, let me give you a brief education on how things are really done here. We agree to look after all of you and give you clothing to wear and a bed to sleep in. We'll continue to do that, but you'll have to do your part too. You'll have to keep quiet about the things that you hear and see in this house. That's what families do. They protect each other."

"Then go protect Candy!"

Ignoring him completely, she went on. "You have to keep doing what you're told. If you do, then we will give you a good life here. If you fail, you'll pay the price. There are different punishments for different offenses."

15

"So, raping her is punishment? You just said they were playing," he retorted.

"Really, Henry, this doesn't concern you," she said, shaking her head.

"She came to me, Holly. She was screaming. She was terrified. I know what I saw! Please, I need to help her!"

The rage of injustice consumed him. He would call the police. Surely, they would help. He turned on his heel and started up the stairs but was quickly met by Mike, who stood at the top of the staircase. He met Henry on the landing and grabbed him by the collar.

"Time for your first lesson, boy!" he thundered as he dragged him out the kitchen door.

"Now go easy on him, Mike," Holly called out. "He didn't know any better. I just explained everything."

Yelling and fighting proved to be futile for Henry. As they neared the barn, he glanced at the upstairs windows of the farmhouse. The two other foster children looked down at him. To think they all knew about the abuse and assaults but told him nothing. They had given him no warning at all.

When they reached the barn, Henry saw shackles hanging from a rafter in a corner of one of the horse stalls. He dug his heels into the ground as Mike continued pulling him forward. Henry tried to fight back, but it was pointless. He was no match for Mike as he locked Henry's wrists in the shackles.

The hope he had for a stable home was shattered. Henry hung helplessly, exposed and vulnerable. Then he felt searing pain in his back and felt the flesh ripping from his body. He had been struck with baling wire. After the twelfth strike, he quit counting.

Even when Henry's voice was nearly gone from wailing, he still cried out for help. The neighbors lived too far away. Candy was likely still in the woods or hiding in the house by now. The other foster children did not dare intervene, knowing that they would receive a similar punishment.

Once the beating stopped, Henry hung from the shackles, smelling his own blood and sweat in the air. Mike walked around and stood in front of him.

"Understand something," he began as he tossed the blood-soaked baling wire to the ground. "No matter how much bigger or stronger you think you are, you will always be weak." Mike backhanded Henry as he continued. "You won't interfere, and you will keep that big mouth shut. Now, I'm going to let you hang here until supper. You can think about things. Plot your revenge even, but eventually you'll realize that you can't do anything. You're nothing. You're helpless, and you belong to us now. I will send Candy out to dress the wounds on your back. I will not take you to the hospital, so you'd better hope you heal up."

Henry had been bounced around foster homes since the age of five. Each time he moved to a new home, his resentment toward his mother worsened, which caused his behavior to deteriorate. He did not want to be in the hands of the state welfare system, but he had no choice.

His delinquent and unruly behavior had cost him dearly. However, he never caused problems at school. Bordering on genius, Henry had always risen to the top of the class quickly.

All he had ever wanted was a home. Finally, by the age of fifteen, his attempts at running away led him to placement with Michael and Holly Henson. They had been foster parents for years and had a reputation for doing well with problem children. Upon his arrival, there were three other foster children with the Henson family.

Mike and Holly had made a good impression. They had been gracious and kind. They had the respect of the community and the educational institutions in the area.

Henry's time in the system had taught him some vital survival skills. Observation had always proved to be the most valuable. He had quietly sized up the situation in the Henson home. Holly seemed busy running the children to school activities. Mike was a hard-working farmer and diligently trained the children to do chores in an effort to teach responsibility. Holly did not seem to play favorites with the children. Mike, on the other hand, had seemed to dote on the fourteen-year-old girl, Candy Rankin, the only female foster child in their care.

For the first month or two at the Henson farm, Henry had kept to himself, appearing shy and retiring. He had noticed that his foster siblings did the same. There was Kyle, age seven, and Miller, age fifteen.

Miller, a lanky redhead with green eyes and freckled cheeks, had been removed from his parents when he was only two. Like Henry, he had also been bounced around to various foster homes. When Miller was only twelve, he had assaulted his foster mother by punching her in the face. He ended up in juvenile detention for thirty days. Then the case manager placed him with Mike and Holly. He had been there ever since.

Candy was a striking young girl with porcelain skin and light brown hair. She was failing school and was withdrawn and awkward. She had been placed with the family at age twelve after watching her father kill her mother and then himself.

A handsome young man with tanned skin and deep brown eyes, Kyle often acted out at school, sometimes intimidating or bullying other children. At times, he even frightened his peers. Kyle had been in the system since the age of three. He had disrupted his placements along the way too. He had often thrown violent tantrums in placements and at school. He had also been caught setting a couple of fires in the boys' bathroom at school. From listening to conversations between Holly and Mike, of all of the foster children, Kyle needed the most help. By far, he required the most attention.

As the weeks passed, Henry became more comfortable. He fell in love with the farm. The one chore he always looked forward to, however, was caring for and feeding the horses.

He often spent hours watching them in the pasture. In

those times, Henry felt truly happy. He envied their freedom.

Henry began to flourish in Mike and Holly's care. Six and a half months had come and gone. He was getting raises in his allowance because he took on extra chores. He helped with the heavy tasks because he was bigger than the other boys. He received extra privileges because of his grades and behavior. Mike had even taught him how to ride.

Henry had found his potential and tapped into his inner strength. He had made friends at school. He had become involved in track and had enrolled in advanced college prep courses.

During his short time on the farm, Henry had grown noticeably stronger. The demanding manual labor had sculpted his muscular build, enhancing his already striking features. With dark hair that had grown longer and crystal-blue eyes, he possessed a stunning appearance. His sun-kissed skin, tanned from long days spent outdoors, only added to his allure.

At school, many girls showed interest in him, but none of them captured his attention. None were challenging enough to intrigue him.

In just one day, everything changed. As he hung in the barn waiting in agonizing pain, he realized that his hell was just beginning. The peace and favor he had felt before was now shattered. His belief in this new life was shattered in a matter of hours.

As the years went by, Henry watched his foster siblings as they were abused and violated. He could not believe all of the things that had been hidden from him. How had he missed it?

Holly sexually assaulted Kyle and Miller repeatedly. However, she steered clear of Henry. Mike continued to assault Candy. Existence in such a hellish place together nurtured not only a friendship between Henry and Candy, but eventually and inevitably, a physical one. It was not long before Candy confided in Henry with unbelievable news. She told him that she was pregnant. Neither of them was sure who the baby belonged to. Still, Henry took responsibility, and because of Candy's delicate condition, he would not allow her to be victimized further.

After supper one night, Henry walked out to the barn. He had thought of a thousand ways he would confront Mike. He wanted to beat him to death but knew better.

Mike stood in the loft, throwing hay down into the horse stalls. With his arms folded, Henry looked up at him. His body filled with anxiety, but he kept his composure. He climbed the ladder and squared his shoulders. The pit in his stomach grew, but he was not going to back down.

"Candy's pregnant," he blurted out.

Mike stopped, frozen by his words. "What?" The blood rushed from his face as reality set in, his eyes wide and wild.

"She's pregnant. You'd think you would have been smart enough to use a condom," Henry bit out.

"How does she know she's pregnant?"

"She's not an idiot, Mike. She's missed her period, and she took a pregnancy test. It's positive." Pausing for a heartbeat, he then added, "Here's the thing though. It's not a done deal. It's a little more complicated than what you think."

Mike tilted his head with a confused grimace. "What do you mean?"

"The fact is that the baby could be yours, but it could also be mine. We won't know until the baby's born," he said, shoving his hands into his pockets and shrugging.

The blood that had rushed from Mike's face quickly returned. "You've been sleeping with her?"

Before Henry could respond, Mike hurled the pitchfork aside and lunged at him. Grabbing Henry by the collar, he yanked him forward and slammed him down with brutal force. The fragile boards of the loft groaned under the impact before giving way with a loud, splintering crack.

Henry plummeted several feet, hitting the ground hard. Pain exploded through his body, sharp and unrelenting, pinning him in place. He could not move. His mind raced to process the damage. Was it his leg? His back? Maybe both.

Through the haze of agony and tears, his eyes drifted upward to the shattered loft. Mike stood above him, glaring down with a cold, unyielding stare, his shadow stretching like a threat across Henry's broken body.

Mike made his way down the ladder from the loft. Then he stood over Henry. "You can die for all I care," he said as he turned and walked out of the barn, leaving Henry to perish.

Unsure how much time had passed, Henry felt a warm hand on his cheek. He opened his eyes slowly. Candy's face came into view. "I've called 9-1-1. The ambulance is on the way. I told them that I found you lying out here and was not sure what happened."

Now at age thirty-eight, Henry was a brilliant scientist. He lacked empathy, often coming across to others as arrogant and unapologetic. His genius discoveries in the lab, however, made up for his poor people skills. He had played a significant role in new treatments for various diseases and had even contributed to cures for other illnesses.

Henry self-medicated to manage the chronic pain and the mental wounds that haunted him. Heroin and pain pills were his drugs of choice. He typically poured whiskey on top of those if it was a really hard day. Sadly, the haze of addiction was the only place he truly felt safe. No matter how far down the rabbit hole he slid, his habits never impacted the quality of his work. It never impacted his general focus. He had poured himself into his career and become the head of the diagnostic lab.

2

Danny

Daniel Knight sank into the worn embrace of his bed, exhaustion clinging to him like a shadow. The Brooklyn apartment was quiet, save for the hum of the city beyond his windows. Fresh off a grueling night shift, he craved nothing more than the sweet oblivion of sleep. By 7 a.m., his head met the pillow, but the fragile peace was shattered moments later. Something jolted him awake.

Blinking against the intrusion, he rubbed his eyes, the weight of fatigue pulling at him. Lying still, he stared at the ceiling as his stomach growled, a harsh reminder that his last meal had been hours ago, sometime around 3 a.m. A sigh escaped his lips as he threw off the covers and sat up, reluctant but resigned.

Perched on the edge of the bed, he raked his fingers through his thick, dark hair, pondering his next move. Pancakes, he decided. Yes, pancakes would do nicely.

Planting his feet firmly on the floor, he rose, stretching his arms high overhead. His body responded, muscles tightening then easing, as he prepared to face the day, or at least, breakfast.

He heard his cell phone ringing in the kitchen. Groggily, he walked to the counter and looked down at the screen. His shift captain's name popped up, so he took the phone into his hand and flipped it open.

Before he could even say hello, his captain said, "Knight, I need you to report for duty ASAP. We got a situation."

"Everything okay, Captain?" Danny asked, his accent thickened by exhaustion.

"Listen carefully, Knight," he continued. "I want you to get into your uniform right now. I'm sending your partner to pick you up right now."

"Yes, sir," he replied as he walked to the chair where he had tossed his uniform and gun belt. "What's going on?"

"You'll be debriefed in the car," he said, and then hung up abruptly.

After dressing, Danny walked outside and looked up at the skyline. Shock shook him to his core as he saw smoke billowing from the World Trade Center. Sirens echoed from every direction. Moments later, he saw the cruiser turn onto the street.

Aaron was not only his partner. He was also Danny's brother in law. Danny had learned to trust him both as family and as a co worker. They had been paired for a very long time.

The engine whirred as Aaron drove closer. The vehicle stopped suddenly, and Aaron flung the passenger side door open.

"Get in," Aaron demanded.

Without question, Danny slid inside. Before he could

even shut the door, Aaron mashed the gas pedal. Both of them knew it would not take long to reach the sixty seventh precinct. Getting to Manhattan Island would be an entirely different problem.

"What the hell is happening?" Danny asked.

"Not sure. News is saying they think it could be terrorists," Aaron answered.

"Jesus," Danny muttered. "Where's Margie? Is she out?"

Aaron turned toward him. The solemn look in his eye caused a pit to form in Danny's gut.

"She's still in there?" Danny asked, his voice rising an octave.

The radio interrupted them. Dispatch instructed all officers en route to report directly to the World Trade Center. Even with lights flashing and sirens blaring, it would take no less than seventeen minutes to get there.

As they made their way toward the bridge, Aaron spoke again. "Margie called me right after it happened. I told her to get the hell outta there. She said her supervisor was telling everyone to stay put. I told her not to listen. To save herself. Head to the ground floor. She promised me she would. She said she'd call me once she got outside."

"Has she called yet?" Danny asked.

"I'm still waiting," Aaron replied, his eyes fixed on the road.

Danny watched black smoke roll across the New York skyline and shook his head. "How bad is it?"

"It's bad, Danny. It's really bad."

As they tried to navigate traffic, a sudden roar thundered overhead. Aaron slammed on the brakes and shifted into park. They stepped out of the car and looked up.

What they saw could not be put into words. The beautiful September sky split open as another plane smashed into the second tower.

Being a New Yorker came with certain risks. Danny knew that. He had been raised there. Joining the NYPD upped the ante, but never in his life had he expected to see something like this. Planes flying into buildings. It felt like a nightmare.

They climbed back into the car and sped toward Manhattan. Not once did either of them think about their own well being. They were driven by the need to help others. Getting to the towers meant getting people to safety.

Aaron's phone rang. His hands shook as he answered.

"Margie!" he shouted. "Oh thank God. Get away from there. Go as far away as you can. Those towers are gonna collapse. Baby, you gotta get away from there. I know. I'm just glad you're safe. I'll call you as soon as I know more. Tell everyone to get away from there. I love you too."

He closed the phone.

"She made it out?" Danny asked.

"She said there are officers and firefighters everywhere. Ambulances all over the plaza. She passed at least five firefighters runnin up the stairs." Aaron shook his head. "They all need to get away from there. Those towers are gonna fall."

Danny glanced at his watch. It was 9:57. "I'm just glad Margie's safe."

"Your sister is everything to me," Aaron said. "I'd be lost without her."

Danny looked toward the towers. What happened next would be burned into his memory forever. The south tower buckled and collapsed, sending smoke and debris into the sky.

Aaron slammed on the brakes, stopping the car in the middle of the street.

The radio crackled again. Dispatch ordered all units to stay clear until further notice.

"We can run," Danny said. "They're gonna need help down there."

Aaron pulled the car into a vacant spot. They got out and ran toward the World Trade Center, but were quickly stopped by people needing help. All of them were coated in white concrete dust. It looked like a war zone.

They directed people to safety, rendered first aid, and stayed as far from the chaos as they could. The sheer number of people needing help made it impossible to move closer.

When the second tower fell, everyone stopped. Tears streamed down faces. Screams filled the air. Radios crackled with orders to find survivors and report to Ground Zero.

They returned to the car and drove as close as possible before parking several blocks away. The rest of the way, they walked.

Twisted metal, broken concrete, smoke, and embers filled the air. Medical personnel, law enforcement, and firefighters dug through debris as cries and wails echoed around them. It was a sound none of them would ever forget.

The recovery effort never stopped. Hours turned into days. Days into weeks. Weeks into months. Danny and Aaron stayed, sleeping only a few hours at a time and refusing to leave.

Though they avoided the initial catastrophe, they grieved for fellow officers, friends, neighbors, and countless others. Once the cleanup ended, Aaron and Margie moved to Chicago to be closer to her family. She reduced her hours and eventually filed for disability due to her mental health. Aaron took a job as a security guard at a local mall, knowing he could not return to high risk law enforcement.

Danny tried to believe he was okay, but he struggled to remain in law enforcement. Cleaning up body parts, identifying fallen officers, and witnessing the aftermath at Ground Zero pulled him into a deep depression. He battled panic attacks as well.

There were positive outcomes too. During cleanup, Danny met dedicated officers from all over the country. He formed strong friendships with two men from Ohio, Gary Wallace and Rick Barnes. Both were young and new to law enforcement. Gary, the more ambitious of the two, aspired to become sheriff.

As months turned into years, Danny's mental state continued to deteriorate. He confided in Gary and Rick, and they offered him a position as a detective with the County Sheriff's Office.

Danny accepted without hesitation. Leaving New York felt necessary. Columbus offered him a chance to breathe, to reset, to start again.

He was happy to take it.

3

Olivia

Olivia Gregory looked down at the belt around her arm as the needle dangled from her bruised vein. She heard muffled voices coming from the other rooms. The pungent smell of sweat, cigarettes, and pheromones lingered in the thick summer air.

As the high crept into her body, she laid her head back on the mattress. All of the pain started to numb. For the moment, the terrible memories finally began to disappear.

She knew her father, Matthew Gregory, and her stepmother, Robin, loved her. She had never questioned that, but it was the love she had lost for herself that dragged her into these dark and terrifying depths. Being molested by her stepfather still haunted her. Even with all of the wonderful things Robin had taught her about healing and spiritualism, nothing killed the ache of the memories except for heroin.

The inspirational talents she had once used to help stabilize life at Pikeview Manor had all but vanished. With the loss of her faith, her ability to see and speak to the dead had also disappeared. She just wanted the emotional cuts covering her heart to stop bleeding. To numb all of the pain of the past. The nightmares to stop. The flashbacks to cease. All of it. The drive toward escape had led her down a darker path than she had bargained for.

Sometimes, she wondered if she had been crazy to ever

think she could see and hear the dead. Everyone who had known her had always told her that she was tremendously gifted. That the ability to speak to those who had passed was a God given talent. Now it just felt like a fairy story. She wondered if it had all been a delusion.

Now age twenty, she had been a heroin user for a little over a year. When she met Sheridan Billings, he had become a detrimental influence in her life. Her family saw it right away. Not Olivia.

Matt tried to stomp out the budding relationship quickly, but once Olivia graduated from high school, she immediately left her hometown and headed to Cleveland to begin a life with Sheridan. It was not until then that she realized he had been disowned by his family.

Sheridan had introduced her to the circle of drug addicts she currently associated with. Now he was gone from her life. He had been arrested and sent to prison for armed robbery. She had a new pimp who kept her turning tricks and kept her well supplied with drugs.

During waking hours, Olivia lived in a haze of addiction and sex. She was in a constant fog that allowed her to escape everything. The thoughts of home. The memories of her family. The life she once lived.

Still sitting against the wall, letting the intoxicant spread, she heard a familiar voice call to her from another room. It was difficult to find her footing, but she stood anyway, knowing it was time to pay up.

Stumbling into the next room, she saw her current

boyfriend lying on a mattress. Completely naked, he would not be the only part of the package this time. Two other men stood waiting their turn. Her body and her mind were so clouded by the drugs that she did not care what happened as long as she got paid.

4

The next morning, as Olivia lay on the bed watching the sunbeams cut through the room, the dust particles danced in the light. Everything was quiet. On the nightstand beside the mattress, she noticed the fattened envelope of cash. She grinned. Experience had taught her that there was a precise science to estimating the amount of money in an envelope just by its girth. The one she was staring at had at least two thousand dollars in it.

"I must have been pretty good," she said to herself. "I don't freakin' remember," she concluded as she flipped onto her back and rested her hand on her forehead.

She sat up, her bare feet feeling the cold hardwood flooring beneath her. In the far corner of the room stood an oval mirror. It reminded her of the one in her dad and stepmom's master bedroom. She stood slowly and walked to it. As she stared at her reflection, she felt sickened by her appearance. Completely naked, she felt disgusted by how thin and pale she was. She did not even look human. With mascara smeared under her eyes, her blonde hair matted and tattered, and her blue eyes bloodshot, she sat back down on the bed once more.

"So, this is what your life has become?" a voice boomed in her ear.

She looked up again and saw a large man standing before her. He was beautiful. She wondered if she might be hallucinating. She rubbed her eyes and then opened them wider. The figure still stood before her. He had long golden locks of hair and wore something that reminded her of the Roman Empire. A sheath hung from his golden belt.

She met his gaze. His irises filled with fire. His skin was like bronze.

"I'm Validus. I'm your master guide," he boomed again.

"I know who you are," she bit out. She had come to know him through many hours of meditation when she was in a much more stable place. She also knew he was responsible for her health and safety, a guardian of sorts.

"I don't want you to die," he said. His mouth did not move. He knelt before her. "You are too important and can help so many." His hand reached out to touch her cheek. The sensation of his touch against her skin burned a little.

"I don't want to help anyone anymore," she answered in a soft, childlike voice.

He stood with a sternness that reminded her of her father when he was angry with her. "I've done all I can on my own to help you," he admitted.

She tilted her head and scowled at him.

"Olivia," he continued firmly, "your life is going to change. I'm simply here to warn you. There's a price to pay for anyone who ignores the gifts they've been given."

Olivia dropped her head into her hands and ran her fingers through the greasy blonde strands of her hair. "Will you just go away?" she shouted.

When she looked up, she was alone in the room. The hole inside her chest deepened. She fell back onto the mattress and wept.

5

Time passed. Each day was the same as before. It was not long before Olivia realized that her body was changing. The sickness in the morning and the nausea throughout the day told her that she was most likely pregnant. Still, heroin would always be a priority. The last thing she needed was a baby.

She sat in the waiting area of the abortion clinic, preparing to take the next step. With her heart hardened and her spirit broken, she knew that terminating was the right thing to do. In fact, she felt it was the one way she could protect the child from such a destructive kind of life. Olivia did not know how to be a mother. She knew she was barely taking care of herself.

She watched as the large wooden door opened and closed, women coming and going, their choices made and their lives forever changed. Their expressions could only be described as shock. They seemed anesthetized by the conclusions they had come to. Most were not alone. Male partners, best friends, family. They were all there to support such a difficult decision.

Olivia wondered about each woman's story. Was their choice health related? Was the pregnancy a result of an affair? Were they raped? Molested? Whatever the reason, they all held the same lifeless look in their eyes.

As she raised her eyes once again, alerted by the opening door, Olivia saw a little boy with thick dark hair and big, beautiful brown eyes standing in a vacant corner. He wore an entirely white jumper, tube socks, white leather shoes, and a white short sleeved shirt with a pointed collar. For the life of her, she could not understand who in their right mind would bring their child to an abortion clinic.

Watching the little boy carefully, she noticed how perfectly still he was. He was like a statue in a park or a museum. She wondered if she might be hallucinating again. She shot up, just before entering the clinic, to attempt to calm her nerves and numb her emotions once again.

He smiled at her. It was a peaceful grin, and quite unexpected. "They can't see me," the boy said, glancing around the room. He turned his gaze back to Olivia. His mouth never moved as he spoke. "Only you can see me."

Then Olivia noticed a subtle light surrounding the boy. He was a ghost.

"I'm your brother, Bryan. Remember?" he continued.

Olivia immediately felt self conscious. She hugged herself as she remembered his funeral. Watching her dad and stepmom grieve had been excruciatingly painful. His death had been a direct result of the evil in Pikeview Manor. Bryan had appeared to her after his death, and Olivia had tried to bring some comfort to her family by relaying messages.

"Bryan," she said in her mind, "why are you here?"

"I need you to make the right decision. This isn't the right choice. Don't do this," he replied in a hushed tone.

"I have to," she thought as she rested her thin, bony hands in her lap.

"No, you don't. Some of the women in here have to do this, but you don't. Go home. Mom and Dad will help you."

"I can't go home," she thought. "How could they ever forgive me?"

"You're not fooling anyone, Olly. You can't keep this up. Please, listen to me. Your child is special, and it's because she's yours."

"I don't even know who the father is."

"You don't need to know. All you need to know is that she's your child. She deserves the chance to fulfill her destiny." He smiled and faded away.

Olivia's eyes filled with tears as she pondered Bryan's words. In her heart, she knew she could not go through with the abortion. So she got up and briskly walked out of the clinic, never looking back. Still, she wondered what to do next. She had no idea how to raise a child on the streets.

6

A few months passed. The life inside her grew, but Olivia was powerless to stop her drug use. Prostituting herself ended quickly, however. This impacted her ability to obtain them, so she resorted to trafficking for some of the suppliers.

Olivia always landed in the same spot. She stayed with a group of five friends in a rundown house in one of the roughest parts of Cleveland. Justin and Tony ran things. She had met them not long after relocating to the area.

Tony and Justin divided the shipment in an orderly fashion as Olivia waited for her orders. She took a drag from the cigarette in her hand and flicked the ash into a tray.

"So, when will you know what you're having?" Justin asked.

"I've still got some time," she answered.

Tony chuckled, something sinister hidden behind his laugh. "Hope it's a girl," he bit out.

Justin turned his head with a smirk, making eye contact with Tony. Clearly, Olivia was missing something. "I'm lost," she said. "Why does it matter if it's a girl?"

Tony's eyes met hers. "Because girls are much more marketable. They have more value out here."

The explanation sent her mind reeling. With a deeply set

scowl, she took another hit from the cigarette. She did not want her child to live this way. She certainly would not use her daughter to score drugs, and prostituting her out was completely out of the question. "I'm not going to drag my kid into this shit," she said angrily.

"You'd be amazed at what you'll do for this stuff," Justin said, pointing at the fine, white powder.

After that, Olivia distanced herself as much as possible while still trafficking for Tony and Justin. Instead of staying in the old two story house in the ghetto, Olivia migrated to a local homeless shelter. The counselors there referred her to a free clinic for prenatal care, and thanks to public assistance, she agreed to go.

She stood in the exam room looking out the window. The snow poured, a blanket of white covering the landscape. It would be another cold night in the shelter.

The doctor came in and smiled. She was a beautiful middle aged Native American woman with dark, chiseled features and short black hair. Dr. Wolf was compassionate despite Olivia's nonreceptive demeanor. She always offered encouragement.

"Morning, Olivia," she said, entering the room. Her voice was sweet, and she spoke softly.

"Morning," Olivia replied with a nod.

"How are you doing?" Dr. Wolf asked as she took a seat on the rolling stool.

With her back still turned and her arms folded, Olivia replied sarcastically, "I am livin' the dream, Dr. Wolf."

"Still using?" Dr. Wolf asked, the clicking sound of her fingers on the keyboard of her laptop echoing through the room.

"What do you think?"

"Are you eating?" Dr. Wolf continued.

"Yes. They always feed us at the shelter. I have WIC, too. That helps, and of course, the food stamps. I just have to show up to do my hours. That's not so hard. It's not like they drug test me or anything."

"What kind of work do they have you doing to get your benefits?"

"Data entry for some of the caseworkers. They said that it helps that I type so fast."

"Still turning tricks?"

Olivia turned and then walked to the examining table. She hopped up and sighed. "Kind of hard to do that when you look like this," she answered as she made a circular motion over her belly.

Dr. Wolf sighed. "Olivia, you're a smart young woman. You can do better than all of this. I see a lot of young moms, some that use. There's something very different about you. Of course, you're trying to escape from something. Heroin isn't the way to do it. Let me help you. Please."

Olivia shook her head with conviction, tears welling in her eyes. "I don't need any help," she protested as she lay down on the exam table.

"Well, if you ever want help, please come to me," Dr. Wolf said as she gently placed her hand on Olivia's arm.

Her eyes focused on the ceiling tiles. "Can we just make sure everything is okay, please?" Olivia asked curtly.

"Certainly," Dr. Wolf replied.

First, the doctor checked the fetal heartbeat. As she did, she added, "You know that when you and your baby test positive, Child Services will take the baby from you?"

"Probably best," Olivia replied callously, still looking at the ceiling.

"Why don't you just give the baby up for adoption?"

"Thought about it."

"Would your parents take the baby in case you wanted to get clean? You could get the baby back."

"I don't know. I haven't talked to them since I left."

"Maybe you should call them, tell them you're pregnant. See if they want to take the baby," Dr. Wolf suggested as she continued with the exam.

"My dad and stepmom have my nine and seven year old half siblings they're raising. I doubt they'd want a newborn. My dad is fifty and my stepmom is forty. I don't think they will live to get the other two raised."

"Are they in poor health?"

"Oh, hell no. My dad works out every day and runs. My stepmom is a Zumba instructor. She teaches four days a week. They don't stop. And then they're always running everywhere for my brother and sister."

"From experience, most grandparents would rather raise their grandchildren than see them go into foster care. I really think that you should talk to them."

"My stepmom has been a child welfare supervisor for as long as I can remember. If I need help, I know she'd know what to do."

"I really think you should talk to them," Dr. Wolf pushed.

"I just can't, okay?" Olivia replied as tears escaped the corners of her eyes and dampened her hair. Hopelessness swept over her.

7

Olivia walked out of the clinic and onto the sidewalk. She made her way back to the shelter. It was only a few blocks away, and even though it was still snowing, she did not mind it. It reminded her of the happier times in her life.

She mulled over the conversation with Dr. Wolf. She did not want to see her baby go into the system, but she also knew she was an addict. She wanted her child to be safe. Raising a baby in a homeless shelter was not quite ideal either. Having a mom who was a junkie and sex worker was not either. Maybe adoption would be the best option.

The brisk air cut through her, and she closed the front of her coat, her chin and bottom lip covered by the thick knitted scarf the shelter gave her. She stopped at a covered bus stop for a moment. As if under some sort of spell, she pulled a piece of paper from her tattered purse and wrote her dad's name on it along with his cell phone number. She had no idea why she felt compelled to do this, but she did not question it.

After warming for a few moments, she stood again and walked on, shoving her gloved hands into the thick coat. The sounds of passing traffic blended into her thoughts as she realized she wanted to be a good mom. She sort of wanted to get clean. The issue was always the withdrawals. Each time she tried to quit cold turkey, she suffered excruciatingly. Besides that, she did not have the courage to ask Matt and Robin for help. She figured they probably hated her by now.

She arrived at the shelter ready for a hot meal and a semi-warm bed. She was greeted by one of the workers. Smiling courteously, Olivia made her way downstairs, where the private showers were. The hot water was exactly what she needed. It was a rough day, and all she wanted was a little comfort.

8

Twenty one was supposed to be a milestone birthday. It was meant to be celebrated with friends, with cake and candles and maybe a few drinks. However, Olivia celebrated her twenty first birthday shooting up heroin in an alley.

She was nearly eight months pregnant by now. She leaned against the dirty brick wall, waiting for the heroin to move through her body. The numbness would come soon, and she closed her eyes expectantly. Suddenly, it felt like her arm caught fire. The burning sensation spread quickly. Her head felt as if it might explode.

She opened her eyes, terrified by the realization. Fear gripped her as she stumbled toward the light at the end of the alley. She hoped to find the sidewalk soon. She knew she needed help. She needed medical intervention.

Stumbling forward still, she knew the drugs must have been laced with something. Fentanyl, maybe. This seemed to be more and more common among members of their community. She had heard about it from one of her friends still working the streets. She could not understand why Tony and Justin would lace their product, especially since fentanyl was getting such bad press.

Finally, she reached the sidewalk. The glow of the streetlight above reflected on the wet pavement. She tried to stay on her feet as the blazing pain coursed through her. "I'm going to die," she thought as she fell onto the hood of a parked car. It was the last coherent thought she had.

She opened her eyes to utter darkness. A small beam of light floated in the sea of blackness. She knew she had met her end.

9

Matt and Robin were on their way once they received the phone call from the hospital. The social worker on the phone told them that Olivia had overdosed. That was when they learned she was pregnant. Olivia underwent an emergency cesarean section. The baby was premature, with low birth weight, and tested positive for opiates. She was placed on morphine to help wean her off drugs and to help control her pain. Despite the uncertainty of Olivia's outcome, the baby seemed to be stable.

As they drove north to Cleveland, Matt did not say anything. The sadness radiated from him. Robin sat in the passenger seat, also quiet, remembering the last conversation she had had with Olivia.

Robin glanced over at Matt. She took careful notice of his face, fine lines deepening around his eyes. Now at the age of fifty, his hair was still the same tousled mess it always had been, but featured much more gray, especially at the temples. He now had a full beard, the salt and pepper pattern giving him a more rugged appearance.

The changes to his appearance did not matter to Robin. He was still the man she had fallen in love with so many years ago. He had truly become her everything. He had only grown more courageous and stronger through the years, his health holding steady with minimal issues.

Robin reached over and touched his leg in an attempt to provide some reassurance. "This isn't your fault," she said.

"If I would have just…" he started, hands white knuckled on the steering wheel.

"There's nothing you could have done. When she was a senior in high school, I knew things were going wrong with her."

"She was smart. She helped with the kids. Hope and David looked up to her. She was a good girl," Matt sighed, focusing on the road.

"She still is smart. She's just lost. When she met Sheridan, her judgment went right out the window." Robin paused. "I never saw him coming."

"I should have stopped that," Matt said in a tone of regret.

"You tried. Remember? She had to have him. No matter what we said or did, she wanted him. Not a thing on this earth would have stopped that freight train. Her mind was made up."

"When the demon fled from Pikeview, I knew evil would arrive in a different form," Robin continued. "Evil never truly gives up. It just finds other ways to get in. The Darkness used Sheridan to get Olly. To steal everything from her."

Matt paused and then exhaled heavily. "I can't believe she didn't call us. This is how we find out we're going to be grandparents?"

"She was probably scared and ashamed, Matt," Robin

argued. "Deep down, under all that hate and resentment, she is still that sweet, gifted little girl we raised. It's just buried under the hurt and that all consuming pain."

"You didn't turn out that way," Matt continued as he looked over at Robin, his gaze lingering for a few seconds.

"What do you mean, Matt? What do you mean I didn't turn out that way?" she asked, returning the glance.

"When you were molested, you didn't do this stuff. You didn't rebel and run off with someone you hardly knew."

"I've already told you that everyone handles the situation differently. I know that doesn't help you. I used my pain to push forward in a positive way. I truly hoped she would too. I worked very hard with her to push her in the right direction," she concluded.

He glanced back at her once more, taking note of her. He was so thankful to have her. She had been his rock, his teacher, his partner, and his confidant. Her beauty was unchanging. Her hair, now cut into a short bob, reflected Robin's refusal to accept her graying condition, and she went to the salon monthly for professional color. Her face still held a peaceful countenance, even when the storms of life had them tossed about on a sea of uncertainty. This was exactly one of those times. He needed her as his anchor, and whatever the future held, they would face it together.

10

After several hours on the road, Matt and Robin pulled into the parking garage at the hospital. They made their way to the lobby and onto the elevator. They arrived at the ICU nurse's station. Once they explained who they were, a nurse directed them to Olivia's room.

Hand in hand, they stood in the doorway. What they saw left them breathless. Olivia lay in the hospital bed surrounded by machines. Tubes seemed to be coming from every part of her. Two IVs hung from a pole.

Matt dropped Robin's hand and walked to Olivia's bedside. He sat down gingerly and took account of his daughter's condition. Memories of her flooded his mind. When she was born. When she was small. When she was healthy. Before she had endured the damage at her stepfather's hand. Tears filled his eyes as he traced the track marks on her arms. "Look at this, Robin," he said in a whispered tone.

Robin went in and stood on the other side of the bed. She peered down at the marks on Olivia's arms as Matt continued to touch them. She only nodded in response. She really did not know what to say.

"Did she really want to die?" he asked, the brokenness heavy in his voice. He sniffed and brushed a tear from his cheek. He took her hand into his.

"I'm sure she felt like dying sometimes," Robin

answered softly.

A nurse interrupted with a half smile. "Do you want to see the baby?" she asked.

Robin and Matt nodded. They followed her to the elevator and stepped in. The silence among them was deafening.

Three floors up, the doors opened to the NICU. The nurse led them to a room with several cribs. There were more machines and IVs scattered about the room, connected to the tiny beings silently resting.

Rocking chairs sat beside each crib. Some nurses held babies for feeding. Other nurses stood at the station busily charting.

The nurse escorting them stopped at the station and grabbed two key cards. She wrote something on a clipboard and handed them the cards. "This is a secure area of the hospital. No one comes in or goes out without this. So when you want to visit, you need to use the card to get into the unit."

Both Matt and Robin nodded.

The nurse led them to a corner of the room where a baby lay enclosed in an incubator. "This is Olivia's daughter. We're not sure what she wanted to name her, so we call her Baby Gregory," the nurse explained.

Robin's steel exterior quickly fell apart as she peered down at the infant. She grabbed Matt's hand and squeezed.

Memories of her son Bryan flooded her mind, and the pain of losing him overwhelmed her. "How could she do this?" Robin whispered.

A voice from behind startled them. "Dr. and Mrs. Gregory?"

They both turned as a doctor in a white lab coat walked toward them. "I'm Dr. Wolf," she began as she offered a handshake to both of them. "I've been seeing Olivia at the free clinic. I performed the C section. The staff found my appointment card in her belongings when she was brought in, so they called me. Of course, I came as soon as I could."

"What's the plan right now?" Robin asked.

"Well, the baby is addicted to heroin because Olivia used consistently during pregnancy. So to keep the baby comfortable..."

"You're administering morphine," Robin interrupted.

"Yes. It keeps the baby relaxed and helps with the withdrawals. We'll start weaning her off in a day or so. We encourage physical contact with the baby if she can tolerate it. It will help with bonding and..."

"And develop secure attachment," Robin finished for her.

"You seem to have a lot of knowledge about this. Olivia mentioned you worked in child welfare."

"Yes. I've been a supervisor for years but was involved with investigations prior to that. I've seen my fair share of drug addicted babies, Dr. Wolf. Anything else we should know?" Robin asked.

"Well, as I'm sure you're aware, with drug addicted babies, she's feeding a little slow. She cries a lot too and spits up a little more than other babies. She's got the typical tremors also. Her scores have been averaging six to eight, which is more than what we'd like to see, especially with the morphine treatment."

"Is she going into foster care?" Matt asked.

"We've called Child Services. It's required," Dr. Wolf replied. "A caseworker has already been here, and we told them you'd been called and were on your way. They should be back in a couple of hours to speak with you."

"Can I hold her now, please?" Robin asked.

"Yes, of course," Dr. Wolf replied.

Opening the incubator, Dr. Wolf reached in and carefully lifted the swaddled baby into her arms. She handed her to Robin.

Robin walked to the nearby rocking chair with the baby and sat down. Smiling down at the little bundle in her arms, she patted her diapered behind through the thin blanket. "She's like an angel."

The baby's eyes were closed in a dreamless sleep. She sucked madly on a pacifier as Robin continued. "Sweet girl," she whispered. "I'm your Mimi, and this is your Pap. Welcome to the world, little one."

Matt knelt beside the rocking chair and touched the baby's tiny hand. "How much did she weigh at birth?" he asked, looking up at Dr. Wolf.

"Well, Olivia was due in another month, so although she is considered a bit premature, her weight was really good. She is five pounds and four ounces. She's seventeen inches long. Her lungs seem to be strong. Her vital organs are alright too. We could have gotten the date wrong as well. It's possible to mistake the due date with homeless moms who do not get prenatal care right away."

Matt nodded and then turned his attention back to the baby. Her face reminded him of Olivia's at that age. Tears filled his eyes once more. He smiled through the sadness at the beautiful life in Robin's arms. He put his large hand on the baby's hat, the pink hat covering the locks of blonde underneath.

The hours passed as Matt and Robin got to know the little person that Olivia had carried inside her. They took turns holding her, rocking her, and feeding her. They talked to her. Although she slept a lot, they tried to make sure someone was holding her at all times.

Finally, the child welfare worker made an appearance. She explained that the agency would have to take the baby from Olivia for a few reasons. The first was that Olivia's living situation was entirely too unstable. Secondly, Olivia had used drugs during pregnancy, which constituted abuse of the child. However, Robin made it abundantly clear that the baby would not be going into foster care. She explained that she and Matt intended to file for custody immediately.

She wanted to ensure that the baby would stay out of the system.

In the days that followed, Robin and Matt conferred with their attorney. An emergency motion for custody was made in their home county. An emergency hearing followed. The judge gladly granted temporary custody to the Gregorys. The hope was that Olivia would pull through, get clean, and eventually be a mother to the baby.

Matt and Robin waited for an absolution as Olivia's life hung in a delicate balance. She remained in a coma. Little did they know a battle raged within her that would have an everlasting impact on her life. It did not matter if she lived or died. Either way, everything would change.

11

Olivia stood in the darkness. Small glimmers of light danced against the black backdrop. She didn't know where she was. The last thing she remembered was the hood of the car.

She took a moment to look around, trying to make sense of her surroundings. Examining her hands and arms, her skin gleamed white, glowing with warm, soft light.

"I'm dead," she thought.

"You're not dead yet," a voice called out. It was familiar and slight.

Olivia spun around. In the distance, she saw an apparition, small in stature. The dress was white, and a beautiful red bow hung from long, dark hair. Instantly, Olivia knew she was in the presence of Emma.

Emma was the ghost child she'd crossed over at Pikeview Manor. She had been a close friend and ally when Olivia needed one. "Emma," she called.

Suddenly, the apparition stood directly in front of her. "Hi, Olly," she said sweetly.

Staring into Emma's gaze, Olivia realized they were the exact same height. Out of the corner of her eye, she saw an oval mirror. She turned and stared at the reflection. Olivia was once again a child.

"How's this possible?" she whispered.

"You're known as you were known," Emma whispered. "This is how I remember you," nodding at the looking glass.

"But I'm not a child anymore."

"To me, you are and always will be."

"Where am I?" Olivia asked.

"You're in the In-Between."

"In between what?"

"You're between worlds. This is the place where you must go before you get to the light."

"So I am dead."

"Not yet. The Creator sent me here to find you," Emma replied.

"Why?"

"Look closer at the glass in the mirror, Olly," she continued.

"It's so dark," she protested.

"It always is until we cross over. The glass is filled with shadows from our human life, but when we go through the In-Between and prepare to pass into the light, everything becomes clear."

She turned to Emma. "I don't want to die," Olivia said, her lip quivering and her eyes filling with tears.

"Then you have to do this with me," Emma said. "Please, look into the glass."

Olivia's eyes shifted back to the mirror. Her childlike reflection disappeared, and she saw her childhood home appear. Pikeview stood majestically against the wooded background. Emma took Olivia's hand and led her through the glass.

They stood in Olivia's old bedroom. It was exactly how she remembered it.

"Why are we here?" Olivia asked.

"Because this is where it all started for you. This is where everything changed. You made a decision to be someone else. It isn't the person you've turned out to be."

"I don't understand."

"You will," Emma assured her.

As they stepped out of the mirror and back into the darkness, Olivia watched as a white light appeared in the reflection. Her entire life played out like a movie. She watched her birth and her first steps. She watched her father taking care of her. The first time she met Robin. The feeling of excitement when she saw her room at Pikeview for the first time.

It was clearly a life review, and this made the anxiety rise inside of her as she anticipated what would surely come next. The molestation. The heartbreak as she watched the wandering souls find her. The crossing over. When they went through the tunnel at the In-Between, they emerged as pure light. It was the most miraculous and inexplicable thing she had ever seen.

A smile made its way to Olivia's lips. As she watched soul after soul transform through her guidance and assistance, she realized how valuable she had been. She had played a key role. She had helped people who had lost their way.

Then she saw Sheridan. She watched as their relationship took shape and the darkness covered him. It enveloped him, swallowing him whole. She remembered feeling alone as she put the first needle into her arm. It was like a horror movie now. All of her aspirations disappeared as the path twisted into the devastation she had felt during the overdose.

"I don't want to see anymore," Olivia protested.

"There is no more," Emma explained. "It's unfinished. You have gone your own way. Sheridan was sent to take away your gift. The Dark Ones roam the earth looking for souls they can influence. They take the pure of heart and bend them into something unnatural. Dark Ones use humans to steal the souls of other humans. They extinguish light by clouding the souls of good people who love life. They work tirelessly to extinguish the hope that each gifted human has. They fail miserably most of the time, but for each failure, they triple their successes. Sheridan was the perfect pawn. He had been abandoned by his family. He was vulnerable. He was an impeccable recruit."

"So, he was possessed?"

"Oh no. He was simply a hostage in the game."

"So, now what? I go to hell?" she asked.

Emma smiled and shook her head. "I want you to meet your spirit guides."

"Guides?"

"Well, Validus is your master guide," Emma said as he stepped through the looking glass. "You've met him, though. He plays one of the most important roles. Meditation allows him to bond with you. You've never been alone because he's always been there. He also manages your other guides."

Bryan appeared in the mirror and stepped into the space. Still wearing his white attire, he smiled and put his hands in his pockets. He stood beside Validus. The size difference between the two was astounding. Bryan looked so small in comparison to the gladiator-like master guide.

"Bryan is your moral guide," Validus interjected. He still didn't move his lips. "That's why he appeared at the clinic. His occupation is always to show you what is right, even if only subtly. When you face ethical decisions, he's there in the shadows watching and attempting to guide you in the right direction."

Loud footfalls came from the mirror. A tall man with dark skin stepped through. He wasn't as big as Validus but was equally robust. His head was shiny and bald. He wore a golden crown with precious gems etched into it and a white robe trimmed in gold. His wings were silver, and his eyes were pure gold.

"I'm Madrich," he said with a bow. "I suppose you could call me the gatekeeper. I help you navigate your mediumship duties. I ensure that you aren't bombarded day and night with wandering souls begging for passage to the In-Between and into the light. I ensure your privacy from the wanderers. But when you're ready to consult, I allow the souls to have an audience with you. I ward off the thousands of voices that call to you for assistance. I also help you with discernment. If it weren't for me, you might go insane," he concluded with a chuckle.

Olivia smiled, as did the others. "Thank you," she said with a reverent nod, tears streaming down her cheeks. "All of you are amazing."

"You have a choice," Validus started. "The Creator has given you a profound gift, Olivia. We have watched you squander it for some time now. You took it for granted. Our Creator is filled with forgiveness, however. If you want that forgiveness, it will be given. The most wonderful part of your human life is that you can change. Not everyone is afforded a second chance, especially when they've made it to the In-Between."

Emma spoke up. "The Creator believes in you. We all believe in you." She stepped aside and revealed a vast number of light beings behind her. They stretched as far as the eye could see. Some of the beings were faceless, while others were souls Olivia recognized.

"You have the chance to change everything and make everything right," Madrich added.

"You have a daughter who will be lost without you," Bryan interjected. He nodded toward the mirror. In the reflection, Olivia saw Robin rocking her baby in the NICU. Matt sat close by, waiting for his turn.

"I'm so sorry," she whispered.

"That's all it takes, being sorry," Emma whispered as she took Olivia's hand.

As the tears continued to cascade down her cheeks, she asked, "What do I have to do? How do I make this right?"

"Go back. Get help," Bryan answered. "You have to heal yourself. We will help you as much as we can, but this is a battle you must fight."

"In your quest for healing," Validus said, "find your soul's mission. Your father's was medicine. He is a natural human healer. Robin's mission was to be a guardian of children, providing protection and safety when they had no one else to defend them. Only you can solve the riddle of your soul's destiny. Meditate often. Commune with us. We will help you find the answers you seek."

Bryan spoke up again. "Once you discover what your soul's mission is, do it with all your heart. Find yourself. Love yourself. Raise your daughter to love herself and to love others. The answers will come."

"That's all I have to do?" Olivia asked. It was almost too simple to comprehend.

Emma's lips curled into a smile. "It's a very easy thing, Olivia. As easy as taking a breath."

"That's the great thing about the Creator," Bryan said.

Validus nodded in agreement. "Simple, but uniquely complex." He stepped out and stood before Olivia. He looked down into her eyes. He placed a strong hand on her shoulders.

"A warning. If you choose to go back down the road leading to addiction, a path that will ultimately destroy your life, there will be no reprieve. The choice to throw away the chance you've been given comes at a high price. The Dark Ones become what they are because they were given chances, and they chose wrong. They are human souls transformed by the Living Darkness to do its bidding."

"So, there is a hell?" she asked.

Validus didn't answer. Instead, he continued. "You can do great things. I've seen it in each one of the lives you've lived. This life, by far, has been your most challenging. You just have to persevere. Not give up."

Olivia threw her arms around Validus's waist. "Thank you," she whispered. He felt like a giant against her tiny frame. "I owe you all my life."

As she broke the embrace, the others gathered around

her, forming a circle. Madrich spoke softly. "We love you just as much as our Creator," he said. "We have always been with you. Every single life. We've been there to guide you."

"As you grow older, and through meditation and research, you'll learn more about your past lives. For now, your focus is your healing and your daughter."

Emma took Olivia's hand. "I am going to help you leave the In-Between." She paused. With a serene countenance, she said, "Live a good life. You once helped me, and now it's my turn to help you."

"Thank you so much, Emma. You've always meant so much to me," Olivia said, looking down at her.

"I want you to know that I've been given a tremendous gift in the light. I help children cross over. So, when you helped me cross over, you allowed me to help others. Thank you so much for that, Olly."

Suddenly, Olivia felt a pulling sensation, and a bright light flooded her vision. It wasn't the soothing beams that she remembered in the In-Between. She squinted. Then she felt intense pain throughout her entire body. She was back in her physical body again. She was flooded with the ache of withdrawal.

She opened her eyes completely as she struggled to focus on her surroundings. Matt stood next to her bed, her hand in his. The ventilator was still in her throat, and she couldn't speak. When she gathered enough strength, Olivia pointed at it. She wanted it out.

He nodded. "Robin is already at the nurse's station asking for help."

As the nurse worked to remove the ventilator, she realized how utterly exhausted she truly was. For years, she hadn't rested. She struggled to stay awake but drifted back to sleep.

No longer among the dead, the road before her would be devastatingly difficult. To solve the mystery of her life would be one of her greatest quests. Overcoming her addiction would be her greatest challenge.

12

Olivia sat up in the bed. The bag of morphine hung from the IV pole. She felt the ache of withdrawal and the burning sensation throughout her body.

Robin sat in the chair across the room. She smiled appreciatively. She was beyond thankful that Olivia had pulled through.

Matt stood in the doorway of the room, leaning against the frame. He folded his arms. Olivia wasn't sure if the grimace on his face meant he was angry or disappointed. Either way, she couldn't blame him.

"Is she okay?" Olivia asked as she looked down at her hands and nervously picked at her cuticles. The tremors came and went for the most part. She was just thankful to be back among the living. She knew she would be at risk for health problems. Whatever she faced, she'd do it courageously.

"She's doing better," Robin answered with a positive hint in her tone.

"I'm so sorry I did this to her," Olivia said as her bottom lip trembled with emotion. She still wasn't able to look up from her hands. Guilt clung to her like thick chains. She fought the urge to sob. Keeping her composure was the least she felt she could do.

"She's a trooper," Matt added. "Your little girl certainly

has your determination."

"Am I allowed to even see her or hold her?" Olivia asked, finally mustering the courage to look up at Robin and Matt.

"Of course," Robin answered.

"Is she going to go to foster care?"

"No," Robin quickly replied. "We took care of that right away. We have temporary custody of her until you can handle things. Until you can get back on your feet. We're going to help you get well. Once you're well, we'll go back to court so she can be back with you."

Olivia couldn't contain herself any longer and cried into the palms of her hands. Relief swept over her like a wave. Finally, after a few moments, she composed herself.

"What's her name?" Olivia asked, making eye contact with both of them once more.

"Well," Matt began, "we wanted you to name her."

"Really?" Olivia asked. She couldn't hide the astonishment in her voice.

"She's your little girl," Robin said. "It wouldn't be right if we named her."

Olivia nodded and brushed the tears from her face. "Thank you both. I'm so sorry," she choked out. "To both of you. To her. She'll probably be fucked up for the rest of her life because of me. Because of the drugs."

"Shhh..." Robin replied as she stood and walked to Olivia's bedside. She sat down and took her hand. "Listen to me. Early intervention can help a lot in these situations. We know what to look for. What to expect. So, we can take the necessary measures to ensure that she is okay. She may struggle in some aspects, but we can get ahead of most of it. And remember, none of us are perfect. We all fail in our own way. We all get lost."

"I have put you two through so much," Olivia whispered as she felt Robin's warm hand on hers.

"Just get well," Matt said, still standing in the doorway.

The conversation was quickly interrupted by the NICU nurse. They were easy to pick out of a crowd. They always wore the purple scrubs. She wheeled the incubator into the room and placed it at the foot of the bed. She smiled sweetly.

"I'll let you have some time with her," the nurse said pleasantly before leaving the room.

Olivia looked at the incubator and then at Robin and Matt.

"Well, meet your daughter," Matt encouraged her.

Robin stood and stepped aside. Olivia pushed off the covers and stood to her feet slowly. Pain shot through her body like electricity, but she ignored it. Still weak, she shuffled toward the incubator, gripping tightly to the footboard of the hospital bed.

She looked at the little bundle inside the enclosed

plastic. Swaddled tightly, the baby wore a little pink knitted hat and enthusiastically sucked on a pink pacifier. To Olivia, she looked like heaven.

Carefully, she lifted the lid, gently pulling the baby into her arms. She was perfect. Olivia traced invisible lines on her impossibly soft skin.

"Amelia Doris," she said quietly.

"You're naming her after Grandma," Matt said as he beamed.

She nodded. "And 'Amelia' means 'winning one.'"

13

Olivia's road to recovery began with an unwavering decision: to reclaim her life, for herself and for Amelia. Her journey started at an inpatient rehabilitation center in Columbus, Ohio, a sterile yet hopeful place where transformation felt both distant and possible. Walking through the doors that first morning, she briefly wondered if she would turn around and leave before anyone noticed. The plan was for her to stay six months, long enough to rebuild her fractured foundation, while Amelia remained lovingly cared for by Matt and Robin at Pikeview Manor.

The first month tested Olivia in every way imaginable. The physical pain of withdrawal was excruciating, a relentless ache that seemed intent on dismantling her entirely. The Suboxone offered a measure of relief, but it could not quiet the emotional storms that surged within her. At times, she felt as though her body and spirit would shatter under the weight of her suffering. More than once, her mind whispered that relief could be found the same way it always had been. Yet even in her darkest moments, she clung to a fragile thread of hope, fueled by the thought of being a mother to Amelia.

By the third month, a sense of rhythm had begun to emerge. The doctors began weaning her off Suboxone, a process that required both patience and resilience. As her body adjusted to this new normal, her focus shifted toward the deeper work of healing. Individual counseling became a daily ritual, an excavation of the buried pain she had carried since childhood. In those sessions, she confronted the long-lingering wounds of sexual abuse, untangling the web of shame, anger, and sorrow that had ensnared her for years. Some days, she sat in silence longer than she spoke, unsure where to begin. Some days, the emotional weight threatened to pull her under, but she pressed on, determined to find peace, not just for herself, but for the life she was determined to build with Amelia.

Group therapy, held every other day, brought its own challenges but also surprising comfort. In the shared vulnerability of others' stories, Olivia found a sense of connection she had not felt in years. These sessions often began with a prayer, a practice she had long abandoned but now tentatively rediscovered. Learning to pray again was like rediscovering an old friend, a source of solace and strength she had not realized she missed. Meditation followed, teaching her to still her mind and observe her thoughts without judgment. Through mindfulness techniques, Olivia began to reclaim her sense of agency, grounding herself in the present moment rather than being haunted by the shadows of the past.

Yoga became another cornerstone of her recovery, a physical practice that taught her to inhabit her body in a way that felt safe and empowering. Each pose was an act of reclaiming the space within herself, a way to integrate the fragments of her being. The stretching and breathing opened pathways not only in her muscles but also in her heart, allowing long-held pain to release and make room for something new.

It was during these moments of stillness and surrender

that Olivia felt the presence of her spirit guides. They did not arrive with fanfare but slipped in quietly, like whispers carried on the wind. Their presence grew undeniable. They came to her in meditation, in dreams, and even in moments of quiet reflection, offering guidance and reassurance. At times, she questioned whether what she felt was real or simply something she needed to believe. Sometimes it was a subtle nudge, a thought that was not hers yet felt profoundly true. Other times, it was a feeling of warmth or light, as though invisible arms were wrapping around her, holding her steady.

Her spirit guides were once again trusted companions on her path to healing. They reminded her of her inherent worth, whispering truths that countered the lies she had internalized over the years. They encouraged her to forgive, not to excuse the actions of those who had hurt her, but to release herself from the chains of resentment and anger that kept her tethered to the past.

By the time Olivia reached the halfway point of her stay, she was no longer merely surviving; she was beginning to thrive. The therapies, spirituality, and mindfulness practices she embraced were not just tools, they were lifelines, each one helping her reclaim a part of herself she thought she had lost forever. With every step forward, Olivia felt more aligned with her true essence, guided not only by the professionals at the center but also by the unseen forces that seemed intent on helping her heal.

Though the road ahead was still long, Olivia felt a growing sense of peace. It was not confidence so much as commitment. She was no longer defined by her pain or her past. Instead, she was a woman on a journey, a mother, a survivor, and a soul rediscovering its light. And for the first time in years, she believed in the possibility of a future filled with love and joy.

14

During Olivia's time in treatment, she joined a program that trained K-9s for the Ohio State Police. The dog assigned to her was Nigel, a stunning two-year-old black German shepherd who had started his career as a therapy dog at the facility. Their bond was immediate and profound. Nigel stayed by her side around the clock, twenty-four hours a day, seven days a week, and quickly became her steadfast companion during one of the most challenging periods of her life. Olivia adored him, finding comfort and inspiration in his loyalty and intelligence. She was proud of the promising future he had as a police dog and felt motivated by his unwavering presence.

One day, as Olivia sat in the chapel meditating, she reflected on everything she had learned during her time in the program. Her mind wandered to her experience in the In-Between and her ongoing search for her soul's mission. She gazed up at the vibrant stained-glass windows and smiled. Then, looking down, she saw Nigel resting quietly at her feet, his bright eyes meeting hers as he tilted his head. In that moment, a deep sense of peace washed over her, and clarity emerged. She realized her purpose. She wanted to help people, and she wanted Nigel to be part of that mission too.

Excitement surged through her as she stood and briskly walked down the hall to her counselor's office, with Nigel following closely, his tail wagging in anticipation. Without knocking, Olivia pushed the door open, finding Dr. Meredith sitting at her desk.

"I know what I want to do!" Olivia exclaimed, her hands clasped together.

Dr. Meredith looked up, smiling knowingly. "Well, aren't you going to wait to share it in group?"

"I can't," Olivia said, practically bursting.

"All right, then," Dr. Meredith replied, gesturing for her to take a seat. "What have you decided?"

"I want to be a K-9 handler. I want to become a cop."

Dr. Meredith's face lit up as if she had been expecting this. "That's fantastic. You know, my partner works at the Ohio State Police office and helped get us involved with the K-9 training program here. I'll talk to her and see what we can do about getting you information on the program. How does that sound?"

"Really? You'd do that?" Olivia asked, her voice filled with hope.

"Absolutely," Dr. Meredith replied warmly. "I'll ask her to visit and talk to you about the program and what steps you'll need to take."

A few days later, Olivia sat in her room journaling while birds sang outside her window. Nigel lay curled at her feet when Dr. Meredith appeared in the doorway.

"Hi there, you two," Dr. Meredith said.

"Hi," Olivia replied, setting her notebook aside.

"I have someone here to meet you. Can you come down to the conference room?"

"Of course," Olivia said, standing. Nigel followed as they made their way to the room.

Inside, a woman in a police uniform stood up from the table and extended her hand. "I'm Lieutenant Linda Montgomery," she introduced herself with a warm smile. "You must be Olivia Gregory."

"I am," Olivia said, shaking her hand. "And this is Nigel." She glanced at the dog, who looked up attentively.

"I remember him," Linda said with a chuckle. "I was there when he was born. I'm glad you've bonded with him. We knew he'd make a wonderful therapy dog."

"I love him," Olivia said, stroking Nigel's soft fur. "He's so smart and easy to train."

Linda's expression grew serious but encouraging. "Dr. Meredith told me you're interested in OPOTA training and becoming an officer."

"Yes, I am," Olivia affirmed.

Linda explained the recruitment process, detailing the written and physical exams, as well as the requirement to live on campus during training. Olivia was not worried. She and Nigel ran the track daily, and her health was the best it had been in years. Academically, she felt confident as well, knowing she had always excelled in school. This time, her determination was focused on a goal that could reshape her future.

As they talked, Olivia opened up about her past, sharing her struggles with heroin and prostitution. She explained that while she had never been charged with a crime, her battle had left scars that she was working hard to heal. Olivia also spoke about her daughter, Amelia, and her unwavering commitment to providing a stable, loving home. Winning Amelia back was her ultimate goal, and she was determined to create a life they could both be proud of.

Lieutenant Montgomery listened intently, nodding with understanding. "You've already overcome so much, Olivia. I'll help guide you through the process. With your determination, I have no doubt you can succeed."

Olivia left the meeting feeling a renewed sense of purpose. For the first time, her future felt tangible, an opportunity to turn her struggles into strength and to build a life of service and love, with Nigel by her side every step of the way.

15

In mid-June, Olivia was released from the clinic and moved into the dorms at the K-9 training center. Walking through the doors felt strange. It was freedom, but it was also accountability. She had no margin for error anymore. After completing an intense six-week training course, she graduated at the top of her class. The result should have felt like a celebration, but it landed in her chest like a weight. Now she had to keep it. Impressed by her performance and the recommendations of high-ranking officers in the program, the Franklin County Sheriff's Office promptly hired her.

Although Robin and Matt were only two hours away, the distance was enough to make Olivia feel isolated at times. She told herself she could handle it, because she had to. Fortunately, Linda and Dr. Meredith ("Shay") stepped in to provide unwavering support. Shay's daughter, Sarah Hotch, who worked as a daycare provider, even offered to help care for Amelia when Olivia regained custody. Olivia didn't miss what that meant. People were placing their names beside hers. Trust like that was not free.

The trio, Linda, Shay, and Sarah, lived in the Worthington suburb, where they helped Olivia find a small cottage to rent nearby. The house was perfect for her, a charming, one-story home with two bedrooms. The rent was affordable, and the landlord, a close friend of Linda and Shay, ensured the property was always well maintained. Living just a few doors down, he personally took care of tasks like mowing the lawn and addressing any maintenance needs. Olivia appreciated it, but she also knew it was temporary in the way all kindness could be temporary. One wrong choice and she would lose more than a house.

The generosity of Olivia's friends didn't stop there. They provided hand-me-down furniture and worked together to help her set up a cozy nursery for Amelia. The nursery made her throat tighten. It looked like a promise she was still working to earn. For the first time in a long while, things were beginning to fall into place, and Olivia felt a sense of stability and hope for the future. Even hope came with rules. She kept reminding herself not to treat this life like it was guaranteed.

From September to December, Olivia concentrated on her outpatient treatment and her career. Every week was structure. Meetings, appointments, work, and the quiet discipline of staying clean when no one was watching. The judge allowed Olivia to see Amelia without supervision and granted her time every other weekend for overnight stays. Olivia did not take that lightly. She knew the court was not rewarding her. It was measuring her.

Each time Olivia saw her daughter, she realized how much she'd missed out on. Still, she knew that her recovery had been paramount. It was the only way she could possibly establish a stable life for not only herself but also for Amelia. She had wanted this future for so long. Now she had to live like it could be taken away, because it could.

16

As Christmas approached, Olivia and Sarah decorated the small cottage with colorful lights, giving the space a festive and cheerful glow. Linda and Shay gifted Olivia a beautiful Christmas tree, which she proudly displayed in the front window. She adorned it with handmade ornaments, creating a simple yet heartwarming scene that filled her with gratitude.

The white brick fireplace was decorated with pine garlands and cheerful snowmen figurines, while a single stocking hung from the mantel. For Olivia, the stocking symbolized hope, hope that Amelia would soon return to live with her full time. Deep down, Olivia knew it was time to pursue this aspiration.

During one of Robin and Matt's regular visits, Olivia decided to broach the subject. The family gathered in the cozy living room. Hope and David were sprawled on the floor, playing with Nigel and Amelia, while Robin sipped coffee on the couch. Matt leaned back in the recliner, watching the children with a smile.

"The house is just adorable," Robin complimented. "You and Sarah did such a great job making it feel like home."

"It's Amelia's first Christmas," Olivia said softly, her gaze lingering on her daughter.

She watched Amelia pull herself along the furniture,

cruising with tiny, determined steps but not quite walking yet. It was hard to believe that in just a few weeks, her baby would turn one. Nigel, now tired from playing, lay on his side. Not content with his rest, Amelia crawled over to him and gently rested her head on his belly. The loyal dog offered a gentle lick as her little hands opened and closed on his soft fur.

"She loves him," Olivia remarked as she moved to the floor to sit with them.

"She's always been taken with him," Robin agreed, smiling.

Olivia took a deep breath, her heart pounding. She reminded herself to stay steady, to say what needed to be said without fear.

"I want her back," she said suddenly.

The room grew quiet. All eyes turned to her as she continued, her voice steady but full of emotion. "I'm working now. I have a house. My income is more than enough to take care of us. I have someone to provide daycare for her. I have good insurance. I don't use welfare anymore. I can support us. I want her back."

Matt smiled reassuringly. "We think you're doing great."

"I am. I know I am. And I know it's time."

Robin set down her coffee and leaned forward. "We can talk to the attorney and see about getting everything in motion. Your dad and I were actually planning to discuss this with you."

"I know I'm ready," Olivia said, her voice firm. "I keep to myself. I go to work and come home, that's it. I don't party. I don't go out. I make time for my counseling, my group meetings, and my meditation. I feel good. I feel strong."

Robin's eyes softened. "You've really come a long way, Olly."

Matt nodded in agreement. "We're very proud of you." He moved to the floor and leaned against the empty recliner.

Olivia smiled and looked down at Amelia, who had fallen asleep on Nigel's side. Her voice trembled with emotion. "She's so beautiful. I'm so thankful nothing's wrong with her."

"The doctor says she's perfect," Robin said gently.

"I can't take any credit for that," Olivia whispered.

"Of course you can," Robin countered. "You're both miracles. You've worked so hard, and she knows it. Even though she's just a baby, she knows."

"Can I go ahead and keep her with me, then?" Olivia asked, her voice tinged with both hope and hesitation.

Robin exchanged a glance with Matt.

"You're finally surrounded by some pretty amazing people, Olly," Matt said. "They've proven to be great supports for you. We just want you to keep it that way."

"Dad, I know I messed up. I just want to be with my daughter. I'm not interested in anything else. I promise, I'm not seeing anyone. I don't want to."

Robin interrupted gently. "Honey, we don't want you to spend your life alone."

"Oh, yes, we do," Matt joked, earning a smile from Olivia.

"You don't have to worry about that, Dad," Olivia said, shaking her head. "I don't trust men, and honestly, I don't want to."

"That doesn't mean we're all bad," Matt protested with a laugh.

"Dad, there's no one out there like you," Olivia said sincerely.

"I'd have to agree with that," Robin added, grinning.

Matt chuckled and reached out to touch Olivia's hand. "Here's what we'll do. I'll gather up Amelia's clothes, toys, and anything else she might need. When we come back next weekend for Christmas, we'll drop her off. After the holidays, we'll talk to the attorney and set up a court date."

Tears welled in Olivia's eyes as she bowed her head, the weight of gratitude washing over her. "Thank you for everything. For paying for my rehab, for taking her in, for helping me with her. I'm so sorry for all the pain I caused. I appreciate you both more than you know."

Matt smiled warmly at Robin, then turned back to Olivia. "We love you, Olly. We'll always stand by you. Never doubt that."

Olivia nodded, her heart swelling with both relief and joy. She looked down at Amelia, still peacefully sleeping on Nigel, and allowed herself to feel a glimmer of hope for the future, a future she was finally ready to embrace.

17

The custody hearing was scheduled with surprising urgency, a development that left Olivia both anxious and hopeful. She stepped into the courtroom, prepared to fight for Amelia, her testimony a heartfelt recounting of the strides she had made in her life. With unwavering honesty, Olivia detailed her journey of self-improvement, sharing how she had worked tirelessly to create a stable and loving environment for her daughter. Witnesses took the stand in her defense, friends and professionals who vouched for her transformation and dedication as a mother. Their words painted a picture of a woman who had overcome adversity and was ready to reclaim her role in Amelia's life.

The judge, though reserved and measured, acknowledged the sincerity in Olivia's progress. After carefully weighing all the evidence and testimonies, he made the life-changing decision to award full custody of Amelia. The room buzzed with quiet relief and joy as Olivia realized her deepest wish had been granted.

Amelia adjusted to her new living situation with remarkable ease, a transition made smoother thanks to Sarah, Olivia's closest confidante and steadfast supporter. Despite being only a few years older than Olivia, Sarah had a wisdom and maturity that belied her age. The two women had formed a deep and unshakable bond, their connection more like that of sisters than friends. In many ways, they were kindred spirits, drawn together by their shared values and a mutual understanding of life's complexities.

Sarah had been married to her husband, Paul, for a few years. Though they did not yet have children of their own, their household was warm and inviting, a reflection of their loving partnership. Paul had a prestigious job downtown, his steady income allowing Sarah the freedom to focus on her passion for running a daycare business from home. She poured her heart into nurturing the children she cared for, her natural warmth and energy making her a favorite among parents and little ones alike.

With her golden blonde hair, luminous brown eyes, and sun-kissed tan complexion, Sarah exuded a natural radiance. She stood a little taller than Olivia and shared the same strong, athletic build. Her dedication to health and fitness was evident in her daily life, whether she was practicing yoga, leading a high-energy Zumba class, or experimenting with new healthy recipes in the kitchen. Sarah's commitment to wellness inspired Olivia, who found herself adopting similar habits and prioritizing her own well-being.

Olivia often shared her innermost thoughts with Sarah, things she could not discuss with anyone else. Sarah listened without judgment, offering comfort and insight when Olivia needed it most. In fact, apart from Olivia's family, Sarah was the only person who truly knew the entirety of her story.

In the quiet safety of that knowing, Olivia allowed herself to feel how calm life had finally become. It was a feeling she did not take for granted. She understood that peace was not something the world promised to keep, especially in the work she had chosen. But she also knew she was no longer fragile. Whatever the world asked of her next, she was ready to meet it.

What made Sarah even more intriguing was her deep spiritual side. A self-proclaimed mystic and experienced past-life reader, Sarah often spoke about the mysteries of past-life regression. She wove these conversations with reminders about the importance of living in the present, balancing the allure of past-life exploration with a grounding sense of mindfulness. Sarah promised Olivia that, when the time was right, she would guide her through the process of uncovering her own past lives. Until then, she encouraged Olivia to focus on the here and now, building the future she had fought so hard to secure.

18

The snow melted away, and soon it was mid-April. Unfortunately, being a rookie meant that Olivia wasn't exempt from working weekends. She hadn't yet found her place at the precinct. The narcotics department and major crimes approached Olivia several times offering a place with them simply because they needed more K-9s in the unit. However, Olivia agreed with the sheriff that it was best for her to start slowly to avoid burnout.

Olivia prepared for work, putting her uniform on along with the ball cap with the sheriff's crest on it. She dropped off Amelia at Sarah's and checked in at the precinct. Saturdays were typically a wild card of a day. Things could go one way or the other. It was either crazy-busy or as quiet as a morgue. She had learned that some calls passed without consequence, and others stayed with you long after the shift ended. She didn't dwell on it. It was simply part of the work.

Once she settled in and caught up on some paperwork, she and Nigel got into the patrol car and headed out. Nigel's company was peaceful, and Olivia often found herself conversing with him while on patrol. With him by her side, she never felt alone and always felt protected. The situation certainly wasn't one-sided. She provided a loving home for him, kept him fit and healthy, and loved him unconditionally.

She made her way to the rural part of her route and turned onto the country road. She noticed a man standing at the edge of the field looking up into the trees. A teenager in pajamas stood beside him. Olivia thought this was very strange. Although it was mid-April, it was still rather chilly for a youngster to only be wearing pajamas.

Before she could even pull the car over, the farmer flagged her down. Once parked, Olivia got out of the cruiser. She left Nigel in the car. Her focus narrowed automatically as she took in the distance, the man's posture, and the direction of his gaze before following him into the field.

She looked around for the girl in the pajamas, but didn't see her.

Olivia met the farmer in the field. He pointed up at a tree in the distance. A girl hung from a branch, a noose tied around her neck. For a brief moment, Olivia's mind resisted what her eyes were registering. As they got closer to the body, Olivia quickly realized this was the girl in the pajamas, but she wasn't wearing a stitch of clothing.

Out of the corner of her eye, Olivia saw the young girl in the pink pajamas reappear. She heard Nigel barking from the patrol car and ran back to the car. She grabbed him by his lead and rushed back to the farmer's side.

Nigel turned his attention toward the apparition who was still standing at the edge of the woods. He barked wildly.

"Nein!" she commanded with a correction to his lead.

He stopped, but the tension in the lead told her that he really wanted to disobey. He was understandably spooked.

Emma and Madrich appeared beside the girl. That's all

it took for Nigel to start barking again.

"Nein!" Olivia commanded again.

Nigel settled reluctantly.

Olivia locked eyes with the ghost. *I'm Olivia. I'm here to help you, but you'll have to wait while I talk to this man. Do you understand?*

Emma spoke for the girl. Without any movement from her lips, she said, *She doesn't understand, but she will. Madrich and I will help her.*

Turning her attention to the farmer, Olivia began. "I'm Deputy Gregory. When did you find her?"

"Well, I came out here to look over the land. You know, to check on things. That's when I saw her," he said, looking up.

"Do you know the girl?"

"Never seen her before in my life," the farmer replied.

"How long has it been since you've been out this far on your land?"

"Oh, 'bout a week or so."

"I'm going to call this in and get some people out here, Mr...?"

"Watts. Edmond Watts."

"I need to prep the scene for our forensics team. If you

could give some distance, I'll take a formal statement in a moment."

"Absolutely," the man agreed as he walked toward the road.

As she walked with Nigel back to the cruiser, Olivia spoke to the girl again telepathically. *I'll be back.*

She put Nigel into the car. He couldn't be on the scene per the regulations of the department. Once he was settled in, she called the situation into dispatch. After that, she walked to the trunk, popped it open, and grabbed a duffel bag with crime scene tape, a hammer, and stakes. She walked back through the empty field and to the tree where the girl hung.

As Olivia put the scene tape up, she tried to find out what she could from the ghost.

What's your name? she asked as she hammered in the first stake.

"Jody," a small voice replied.

When Olivia looked up, Jody stood close enough to touch. A bit startled, she continued with her duties.

Do you know how you got here, Jody? she asked as she hammered another stake into the ground.

"He took me from the soccer park."

Who took you?

"I don't know. Can't I go home?"

Emma spoke up. "Jody, I'm Emma, and I'm going to help you cross over, so you have to come with me."

"What do you mean?" Jody asked, her voice colored by panic. "I'm dead?"

Olivia stood to her feet and looked at Jody. She whispered, "I'm so sorry."

Jody sat down on the ground and pulled her legs to her chest as she wept. Olivia watched as Emma sat down and put her arm around the girl's shoulders. Madrich stood still and remained quiet.

Do you remember anything else that happened? Olivia continued in her mind as she finished with the scene.

"No," Jody sobbed. "I just want to go home."

Madrich spoke up. "Let us handle this, Olivia. When she checks in, we'll bring her back."

"No," the child bit out. "I don't want to go."

You have to, Olivia thought.

"I can help you," Jody protested. "I met him at the soccer park. I was playing with my friends. He asked me for help finding his dog. I helped him and then he took me."

Do you remember what he looked like?

"He had on sunglasses and a ball cap when I saw him. After that, I was blindfolded. I remember two voices, though."

"Did they hurt you?" Emma asked.

"Yes," she replied as the sobs grew louder.

I'm so sorry, Olivia thought sadly. *Is there anything else you can think of, Jody? Anything at all. Color of hair, eyes, height?*

"I don't want to be here," she cried.

Emma, Madrich, Olivia thought, *I have to go. Please help her.*

"But my mom and dad! I want my mom and dad!" she shouted.

Olivia knelt on the ground again, putting the equipment back in the small duffel bag. "The light is safe, Jody. Do you see it?"

Jody looked up and around. She focused on a point in the sky. "I see it."

"Go to it. Once you cross over and check in, you can come and go as you please. Your parents probably won't be able to see you or hear you, but sometimes they'll know you're near." Olivia sighed. "You must check in first, though. Emma and Madrich are good. They'll keep you safe. Don't be afraid."

Emma stood with her hand out. "Come with me, little one."

Jody wiped her eyes and stood. Her eyes met Olivia's again. "I'm sorry I couldn't help you more."

"Don't be," Olivia replied. "It's okay. You are just confused. That's normal."

Olivia watched in wonder as the three of them disappeared. Even after crossing over hundreds of souls during her younger years, the process still amazed her.

She walked back to the cruiser and put everything back in the trunk. Opening the driver's side door, she slipped in and sat down, waiting for the teams to arrive.

19

For the past thirty years, Dr. Andrew Bentley had been the senior medical examiner. Olivia had met him during one of his trainings for the precinct. A sweet older man, he had a heavier build. He was bald, with a snow-white beard and big blue eyes. He was always kind to Olivia, offering a warm, comforting smile.

He was the first on the scene. He pulled up in the van, and Olivia got out of the patrol car to greet him. He waved as she walked toward him.

"Deputy Gregory. How are you?" he began.

With a smile, Olivia offered her hand. He took it with a hearty handshake. "I'm good. Sorry to bother you on this gorgeous Saturday," she said, looking up at the blue sky and folding her arms against her chest.

"No bother at all," he said, throwing his hand up. "Do you know what happened here?"

"Not yet. The detectives and the forensics team are on their way."

"I will wait until they get here, then." He smiled. "Gives us the chance to catch up." He put his hands in his jacket pockets and continued. "How have you been, young lady?"

"I'm great," she nodded.

"I hear nothing but wonderful things about you."

Olivia smiled, her face warming as she blushed.

"Sheriff Wallace is very impressed with your work. He says you're really good with people. Says you're friendly and that the community likes you."

"I'm glad. I don't like being adversarial. It doesn't accomplish much. It just makes people mad," she replied.

"How's little Amelia?"

"She is wonderful. I can't believe how fast she's growing."

"You'll blink, and she'll be all grown up. I have four daughters and three granddaughters. I know what I'm talking about."

Their attention was drawn to the sound of approaching vehicles and sirens. They looked down the road as black SUVs and a van barreled toward them, dust trailing behind. The vehicles came to a stop behind the ME's van. The forensics team got out and immediately started processing the scene.

Olivia and Bentley waited for the scene to be cleared. Detective Ronald Salyers walked toward them. He was a middle-aged veteran detective who was semi-retired. He typically worked weekends and holidays. Rather short in stature with a stocky build, his black hair was thinning, and he was terribly out of shape.

Olivia always had the impression that Salyers thought he was better than everyone else, especially her. She also felt like he didn't trust her. During their brief interactions, he barely spoke to her and always shot disapproving glances her way. Because he was fairly close to the sheriff, she figured Salyers knew about her past struggles. She assumed he was judging her pretty harshly.

"What happened, Gregory?" he asked directly.

She explained what she found on her patrol. She also made it very clear that she was careful and didn't touch anything, assuring him that she followed procedure while securing the scene.

"Well, you can go now," he said, throwing up his hand dismissively.

"Please, Salyers, let me stay," she implored.

"Why?"

"Because I've never really witnessed something like this," she began. "This is a big deal. I feel like I could learn something valuable. Besides, maybe Nigel can help."

"First of all," he said, crossing his arms and furrowing his brow, "I'm not letting that dog near the scene."

Bentley quickly came to Olivia's aid. "Oh, come on, Ronnie," he started. "It'd be good for her. You can never learn too much on this job, and she's right. Maybe the dog can be of some use."

With his arms still folded, he said, "I already said that the dog wasn't working the scene. He'll probably piss all over it."

Olivia took his backhanded comment to heart. She quickly came to Nigel's defense. "Detective," she said as she crossed her arms, "that dog is highly trained." She nodded toward the cruiser. "Nigel would never destroy a crime scene."

"You're being a dick, Ron. Ease up," Bentley bit out.

Salyers pursed his lips. "Fine. I guess you can stay. Let me run it by Wallace to make sure it's okay, but the dog stays in the car," he said, pointing toward the patrol car.

"You don't know much about K-9s, do you?" Olivia asked, still offended by his previous comments.

A few moments passed. She watched Salyers get into his car and put his mobile phone to his ear. Then he got back out, a defeated grimace on his face. "Welp," he said as he came closer, "Sheriff Wallace says you should stay. You can only observe, though."

"Yes, sir," Olivia said with a nod.

She made her way across the field, Bentley and Salyers following close behind. She watched as the forensics team processed the area. They took soil samples and photographs. The body was carefully lowered from the tree onto a blue plastic tarp. The child's hands were bound behind her back, so samples of both the noose and the ligatures were collected.

Bentley walked to the lifeless body and knelt, opening his kit. He pulled out the thermometer and pierced her skin. "Liver temp tells me she's been here for about twelve hours.

I won't know the cause of death until I do the autopsy. Preliminary findings? She's been held for a while. The bruising and reddening of the skin on her face and around her mouth indicate that she's been gagged. Of course, the ligature marks around her wrists are evident, but Olivia, note how deep they are. This means she struggled to get out of them."

Olivia knelt beside Bentley and looked closely.

"Hey, I know this kid," Salyers said quietly.

"How?" Bentley asked as he looked up at him.

"Parents filed a missing person's report a few days ago. Jody Stevenson."

20

Olivia sat at her desk as Nigel rested in the crate beside her desk. Hours of paperwork awaited her, but she persevered and waded through all of it.

As her shift drew to a close, she leaned back in her chair. Her head ached. She rubbed her temples and sighed. She watched as Salyers led two individuals to an interview room. Their heads were down, and the man had his arm around the woman. Olivia also noticed Jody's ghost trailing behind.

She also noticed Salyers watching from across the room. Olivia had learned early on which men at the precinct were best avoided, especially those who did not tolerate compassion or deviations from the way things had always been done.

Salyers opened the door for them and then closed it and walked away. Olivia stood and made her way across the room. She felt compelled to talk to the parents of the poor girl who'd been found in the tree. So, she cracked the door, peeked in, and observed the couple sitting on the couch. She opened the door completely and boldly stepped inside. She sat down in a chair across from them. They both wore blank expressions, their eyes hollowed from grief.

"I just wanted to tell you how truly sorry I am for your loss," Olivia began.

The man nodded and spoke up. "Thank you. Are you the one who found her? They told us it was a deputy on patrol."

"Yes sir. I called it in."

The woman began sobbing loudly. Olivia reached over and gently touched her hand. "I am so very sorry for your loss. If there is anything at all that I can do."

The door swung open.

"Gregory," Salyers interrupted. "Will you come with me?" he asked gruffly.

With a kind smile, Olivia let go of the woman's hand and walked out behind Salyers. He let the door slam shut.

"What the hell are you doing, Gregory?" he shouted.

Several heads turned. The busy atmosphere of the precinct slowed, conversations trailing off as Salyers continued.

The cursing and chiding ended abruptly when Sheriff Wallace shouted, "Both of you, in my office, now!"

They walked in, but Olivia remained quiet while Salyers ranted and paced, waving his arms angrily.

"She waltzed in there and just took over!" Salyers bellowed.

He paced once, then turned sharply.

"Started telling the family how sorry she was and offered them help!" he yelled as he looked at the sheriff, his eyes filled with malice.

He turned his attention back to Olivia. "We aren't social

workers here, Gregory! We're cops!"

"I'm sorry, I just wanted to help," she said repentantly.

"Listen to me!" Salyers continued as he jabbed his index finger into Olivia's shoulder. "I'm the lead detective on this case. You run patrol. You're a rookie. You know next to nothing! These people could be suspects! You ever think of that, genius?"

The sheriff stood and walked to the front of his desk. From the expression on his face, he was obviously upset, but Olivia wasn't sure exactly who he was upset with. The blood collected in his cheeks, and he looked like he might explode. Then he shouted, "Shut the damn door, Salyers!"

Salyers turned and shut the heavy door, but before he could fully return to the conversation, Wallace took over.

"First of all, you know my rule about respect. You don't reprimand anyone in front of the entire precinct. It causes problems. And you sure as hell don't put your hands on anyone."

He quieted for a moment, catching his breath and squeezing the bridge of his nose. Then he refocused.

"Poking her in the chest..." he trailed off as he shook his head. "Who in the hell do you think you are?"

He walked to the window in his office and looked out over the city. Then he turned around with his focus back on Salyers.

"Olivia was the first officer on the scene. There's

nothing wrong with her telling the family she's sorry about what's happened. It's terrible. Their child is dead! So, what did she do wrong really? I'll tell ya what she did. She stepped on your ego. She walked in there and showed compassion. I know you, Salyers. You were getting ready to play the bad cop. You planned on backing those folks into a corner. You were gonna try to pin their daughter's murder on them. There's zero evidence to indicate they are even involved! You're always trying to find the easy way out."

Sheriff Wallace took a step toward Salyers and continued, "You jump the gun a lot. Olivia was taking a different approach. A friendlier one. You never do that. You come in with guns blazing every single time!"

"But, I..." Salyers started, only to be interrupted again.

"No! I am backing her on this one," he said, shaking his head with disgust as he folded his arms. "She did nothing wrong! You jumped her ass because she intimidates you. That's all. Just because you've had a badge longer don't make you right! It's the good ol' boys syndrome. That's all it is!"

Olivia's face fell, devoid of reaction. She didn't know what to think or say. She was glad that Wallace was backing her play, but the entire situation was generally uncomfortable.

"She doesn't intimidate me!" Salyers roared.

The room went still.

"She's a drug addict whore!"

Olivia's face warmed with fury and embarrassment. Her suspicions were confirmed. Salyers knew about her past, and now the entire precinct probably knew.

"You're off this case!" Wallace shouted. "You're going to apologize to her right now, and you're on leave starting today! I won't allow this kind of disrespect in my ranks! It spreads like a cancer! You are abrasive. You come across like a real asshole when these families just need someone to lean on. You've been doing this for a long time, and never once have I seen a family openly talk to you. And now this! Treating a fellow officer as if she's beneath you! I will not tolerate it! Do you understand?"

With a hardened expression, Salyers remained apathetic.

"I said, you will apologize to her," Wallace said in a quieter, directive tone.

He bowed his head, and with great reluctance, uttered the words, "I'm sorry."

"Now gather your things, Salyers. I'm writing you up. You're suspended as of today. We'll hash out the details with HR on Monday. For now, get out of my sight," he concluded as he pointed to the door.

Salyers didn't say another word. He turned abruptly and threw open the door. He walked out and slammed the door behind him.

With a disappointed countenance, Wallace walked back to his desk chair and sat down. The red tint in his cheeks and neck began to soften to flesh color again.

"Sir, I can explain," she started.

He put up his hand to silence her. "What you did in your past has nothing to do with now. We ran a background check on you. You already told me about your rehab. I did not break your confidence. I just want you to know that. It isn't every day that a recovering addict becomes a well respected cop. No one's perfect, Gregory. Most of us just don't get caught."

"Yes, sir," she said respectfully.

"We're going to try something, Gregory. I want you to go in there and talk to the family. See what you can find out."

"But I..."

The sheriff, a tall man with a gentle smile, looked into her eyes. His tone even and quiet now, he said, "I want you to build rapport. Get them to talk to you. Ask questions. You will know what to do. I'll watch through the glass, so if you get stumped I can help you. You've already made a connection with this family, and it just might help us."

"I'm not a detective, sir," she protested. "I have no clue."

"You're right..." he interrupted. "You're not a detective, but you have the heart of one. So let's see what you can do."

Olivia looked up and then nodded. "Okay, but I want Nigel with me. He was a therapy dog before he was an officer. He can help break the ice."

The sheriff nodded.

They walked out into the busy office, separating as Olivia walked back toward her desk. She released Nigel from his crate, and then they walked to the conference room, his lead in her hand.

Opening the door slowly, stepping in, and then closing it gently, she smiled. When she sat down, Olivia noticed Jody standing in the corner.

"Sorry about that," Olivia began. "Can I get you two some coffee or water? Anything?"

"No thanks," the man said.

"I don't think we were able to properly meet before," she continued. "I'm Deputy Gregory. This is my partner, Nigel."

He wagged and panted happily as the woman perked up and held out her hand. "May I?"

"Oh, yes. When I first met him, he was a therapy dog."

"He's beautiful," she commented as she reached out to pet him. "And so peaceful."

"I'm Miller and this is my wife, Wanda," the gentleman said.

"I'm really sorry we're meeting under these circumstances," Olivia continued. "And again, I am so sorry for your loss. Will you share with me a little about yourselves and about Jody?"

"I'm her biological father. Wanda is her stepmom," Miller started. He paused, swallowing hard before continuing. "I was nineteen when I found out my girlfriend was pregnant. I had been in foster care all my life and things were rough. The homes I had been in were… well, let's just say it was a bad situation. I worked some minimum wage jobs and met Samantha, that's Jody's mom. She got pregnant and we moved in together. Samantha left me with Jody when I was twenty one. I had no idea what to do, and I didn't have any family. So, I raised her on my own. I did the best I could. Then Wanda came along. It was like a miracle.

"I went to college and got my business degree. I am the administrator for a company here in Columbus now. We gave Jody a good life. I got into some trouble growing up and didn't want to see Jody do that. We took her to church, we monitored her friendships very closely, and we made sure she ran with a good crowd. She is the best kid," he said as he choked up.

"When did she go missing?" Olivia asked.

"Four days ago," he explained. "We couldn't believe she would run away, so we reported her missing. They didn't take us seriously at first. But here we are.

"You said that you kept a close eye on her with regard to her friends. Any of them stand out to you?"

"No. They were all good kids," Miller answered. "She met most of them at church. She hadn't really gotten into boys yet. She was starting to but nothing too horrible. She'd just gotten her license around Christmas time, and we already bought her a car with the understanding she'd have to get a job this spring to help with the insurance. She didn't protest either. Like I said, she is-- was a really good kid."

"Miller, what sorts of activities did she participate in?" Olivia asked as she remembered the inference about the park.

"Well, she loved going to the park down the street. She and her friends played soccer there. That's where she went missing."

"Tell me about that."

"She came home from school like she always did," Miller explained. "She gets home around 3 p.m. She walked down to a friend's house, and then they went to the soccer park. Even though it was a little chilly outside, you couldn't keep Jody away from the field. She called to check in around 5 or so. Then she never came home. We tried her cell, and she wouldn't answer, so we figured she might still be playing. Then we called her friends. Her best friend, Sonya, told us that she'd left the field around 6, but that someone had asked Jody for help finding a dog. Sonya said she figured Jody found the dog and then went home."

"A dog, huh?" Olivia clarified.

With a nod, Miller kept going. "We called the police immediately and they said we had to wait 24 hours. Said that given her age, she was probably joyriding or a possible run away. We argued, but no one would listen."

Wanda spoke up. "When Jody hadn't come home after

two days, then someone took us seriously."

Olivia nodded empathetically.

"It's torture," Wanda continued. "Then the detective showed up today and told us nothing. He demanded we get into our car and follow him to the morgue. The morgue!" she said exacerbated. "We got there, and he told us that they'd identified Jody based on the missing person's report we filed. No empathy. No emotion. Nothing. Just matter of fact, 'Hey we found your dead daughter.'"

Olivia shot a glance at the mirror knowing Wallace heard every word.

"We still had to identify her body," Miller said, his voice quivering. He looked down at his hands. "Then that detective shoved us in the car like we were suspects and here we are."

"I am so very sorry," Olivia said as she reached over and touched Wanda's hand.

Their eyes met.

"Then you came in," Wanda added. She wiped at her face, her voice barely steady. "I hoped you were the lead on the investigation because you were so sweet and seemed to understand what was happening. Then he jerked you out of here. I don't want to work with him. I refuse to."

Olivia took her hand back and gave a half smile. "Ma'am, I will help however I can. A forensic supervisor will be in shortly to make arrangements to get some of

Jody's belongings. We are in the very beginning stages of the investigation, but all I ask is that you be patient with us. Anything that stands out to you, anything at all, please report it. I won't make promises I can't keep," she continued, "and the investigation is a process. Most of the time that process isn't short. It takes time."

"If we'd have gotten a little more compassion from the detective, I think that might have helped," Miller said.

"Well, I'm being as up front as I can be about everything I know. If I hear of anything at all, I will contact you or have the new lead on the case call you. Detective Salyers has been taken off the case." She paused. "Is there anyone that you know who would have wanted to hurt Jody?"

Both shook their heads.

"No one," Miller concluded.

"Thank you so much for talking to me," Olivia said as she stood and smiled. The couple courteously stood. "Someone else will be in shortly to talk to you and finish up with the process."

They nodded as Olivia excused herself, opened the door, and walked into the hallway. Wallace waited for her, his arms crossed with his chin set.

"Follow me into my office," he said as he turned and walked down the hall into the bullpen.

Olivia's breath caught in her throat. She worried she may have said something wrong, and she combed through the conversation as she followed behind Wallace.

They stepped into his office. He sat behind his desk as Olivia stood waiting for the reprimand to begin.

"You're lead on this."

Her mouth dropped. "What?"

"Outstanding progress in just ten minutes with those parents. You gained rapport. Then you won their trust. More than anything else, they respect you. If they did have something to do with Jody's death, you got a way in. They feel completely comfortable talking to you."

"Sheriff," Olivia began, "I don't know how to be a detective. I just…"

"Listen to me," he interrupted as he leaned forward and folded his hands on his desk. "Danny Knight is one of the best detectives I have in major crimes. He'll mentor. He'll work right down in the trenches with you. Sue Barnes. Rick Barnes. All of my detectives in major crimes are pretty good, but Danny is one of the best. I'll let HR know you're being promoted. That'll come is a pretty significant raise, too. Get yourself some professional clothing. You won't be needing the uniform anymore," he said with a smile.

21

Robin and Olivia searched through the racks at the department store.

"I don't have money for this right now," she said softly. "My new rate doesn't kick in…"

Before she finished, Robin interrupted. "It's my treat. You need some nice clothes. The chief said so himself," she started, as she took a closer look at the blouses. "No daughter of mine is going to wear cargo pants and polo shirts when you've been given such an awesome promotion."

"You shouldn't have to buy this stuff. I've gained so much weight," she said, glancing down at herself.

"First off, I'm your mom. Well, stepmom. And I want to do this for you. As far as gaining weight, of course you've gained weight. You're eating on a regular basis instead of starving. Olivia, you were so thin. For your height, it was concerning. Now you're a healthy size twelve."

She nodded. "I know. It just feels strange to me. And for the record, I do consider you to be my mom. You're the only mom that ever gave a damn about me," she added as she looked down at the clothing. "Are you sure you want to go to the salon after this? I don't want you to pay for that either."

Robin stopped. She turned to her and put her hands squarely on Olivia's shoulders. "Look at me," she began.

Olivia's expression was hesitant, but Robin didn't care. She continued. "You have come a very long way. We are celebrating. We are all so proud of you."

Olivia pursed her lips and fought back tears. "I love you."

"You're my girl," Robin said as she smiled and touched Olivia's cheek.

22

After a productive day of shopping and self-care, Olivia had restored her natural hair color to a shiny blonde. She kept most of the length, letting it cascade down to the middle of her back.

Her nails were impeccably manicured, gel nails with white tips that gave her hands a refined, sophisticated look. After a facial and wax treatment, her skin felt as smooth as silk. She felt more confident, her self-assurance beginning to grow.

Wearing dress slacks and shirts would be a change for Olivia. Having grown accustomed to her uniform, it was hard to picture herself in anything else. Still, she welcomed the more polished appearance. Of course, she'd continue carrying her gun, but now on a much lighter belt.

That night, after the excitement of the day and after tucking Amelia into bed, Olivia rested on the couch watching television. Over and over, she played out Jody's crime scene in her mind. She hoped she would be able to help solve the mystery of the young girl's death.

And then there was the crossing. She had crossed many souls over to the other side. However, none were so fresh. Many of them had died years ago, even decades ago. Jody's situation was entirely different.

As she lay with the television's background noise, she worried that she would have to rely on her gifts to figure out who killed Jody. However, she wanted to focus on factual evidence collection and science. She prayed the crime could be solved without her abilities.

Suddenly, Olivia found herself in an unfamiliar place. The room had white tile floors and tan walls. A pedestal sink stood against the far wall, and a large bathtub occupied the other end of the room. She moved toward the sink, her fingertips brushing against the cold porcelain.

A presence behind her made her freeze. Slowly, she turned around and looked down. She saw tennis shoes and a pair of jeans. As her gaze traveled upward, she noticed a wrinkled blue button-up shirt with thick forearms and large, strong hands emerging from its rolled-up sleeves.

Her eyes kept climbing, searching for a face, but there was none. Instead, the most striking blue eyes stared back at her.

Startled awake, she realized she was only dreaming. As she sat up and wondered what it all meant, she heard Amelia cooing and giggling. The clock hanging on the wall chimed to three-thirty. She stood and walked to the nursery.

Olivia reached into the crib and pulled Amelia out. She walked to the white glider chair and sat down. The quest to put her daughter back to sleep began.

As she glided with Amelia in her arms, Olivia contemplated the dream. She didn't understand any of it. She became drowsy as the gliding began to relax her. Amelia was already back to sleep, so she stood and put her back into her crib. She then returned to the glider and continued delving back into the unconscious.

She heard a voice. "It wasn't a dream. It was foreshadowing." It was Validus. "You'll understand more as time passes. Have faith."

23

Henry walked down the long hospital hallway toward his office. Although he'd never admit it, he was excited to see his daughter, Mya. For the past five years, he'd been visiting her on a regular basis. Candy had finally decided to be sensible and had encouraged a relationship between them. He didn't presume to know why, nor did he care. All that mattered was that his little girl was a part of his life again. She was the bright spot in it.

Mya, now fourteen years old, was blossoming into a beautiful young woman. Henry saw a great deal of his personality traits budding up in her. Just like him, she also kept an emotional wall up and often seemed hard and cold. She had a sternness about her that he completely recognized. This made Henry sad. He had hoped that she would be more like Candy.

He approached the glass double doors leading to his office and saw Mya sitting in the chair, earbuds in her ears and her phone in her hand. He pushed the doors open. "Sorry I'm late," he said.

"You're always late," she remarked under her breath.

"Sorry. There was a problem in the lab on the eighth floor," he said as he sat down hard in his rolling desk chair.

"Going to the rescue as usual," she replied smartly.

"Well, that's my job."

She shook her head. "But you hate the people that work for you."

He got up and walked to the vacant chair beside her and sat down. With a sigh, he answered, "I like what I do. I like the puzzles. Figuring out things. Being in the lab keeps me from dealing with people. Turning down a promotion, on the other hand, was not something I was stupid enough to do. Dealing with employees is just part of the headache for that promotion, but I manage."

"So, what is on the exciting agenda this weekend?" she asked sarcastically.

He got back up and walked around his desk. He opened his drawer and pulled out tickets. "Monster trucks," he said as he held them up.

"Whatever," she said, turning her attention back to her phone.

"Shane will be there," he said as he sat back down in his desk chair.

His best friend, Jim, had a son, Shane. Henry knew that Mya had an enormous crush on him and that he was the key to getting her to agree with pretty much anything, especially a monster truck rally.

"Really?" Mya asked, her eyes meeting his and brightening with anticipation.

He smirked. "Yes. Jim is picking him up right now. We're all going together. And we're going to go to a rally every weekend I have you. Jim and Shane will be going with us. We are going to make a month of watching crashing, big-wheeled trucks."

"Well, that's cool, I guess," she replied with a shrug and a smile. Then she focused on the screen of her phone again.

Henry opened another drawer and grabbed a pill bottle. Popping the lid off, he spilled several of them into his hand and then quickly threw them into his mouth.

"Mom says you're going to kill yourself taking those," Mya bit out as their eyes met again.

"Anti-anxiety pills?" he asked rhetorically. "Believe me, I don't take enough to kill myself. They take the edge off."

"I don't understand why you need them. What do you have to be anxious about?" she asked.

"Honey, it's an adult thing," he replied as he threw the bottle back in his drawer.

"Mom also says you're gay," she continued.

That caught him off guard. "Gay? I couldn't have been gay. I helped make you."

"No, she means you're gay now. She thinks you're all bitter or something and you hate women. So she says you're gay."

His face turned toward his computer screen as his

thoughts raced. He was confused.

Mya went on. "She says you haven't had one steady girlfriend since you guys split up years ago. She thinks you and Jim are a couple. I guess she thinks she ruined you."

Shaking his head subtly, his voice deepened. "I can assure you, Mya, I'm not gay."

He looked at her as she sat as still as a sculpture. Her eyes filled with skepticism as she rolled them up to meet his. He could see she didn't believe him. "I'm just selective," he concluded.

"You're gay," she said as she once again turned her focus back to her phone. "It's nothing to be ashamed of, Dad."

He pursed his lips. "Well, I appreciate the vote of confidence."

Henry wasn't gay at all. It was true he'd avoided relationships. Instead, he had a line item in his monthly budget for female companionship. Relationships took work and upkeep. Most of all, a relationship demanded maintenance and true human interaction. Female escorts meant there were no strings attached and no emotional commitments. It was just sex and company with a price tag.

He was preferential, nonetheless. In fact, there was one woman he had gotten to know over the years. He preferred her company to the rest. Whenever he went to dinner, she went with him. Whenever he had to attend a function for the hospital, she went with him. Whenever he needed intimacy, she provided it. She was the only girlfriend he needed, and everyone was sure they were a couple.

Henry lacked a true desire to emotionally connect with anyone. He wasn't about to risk any more hurt in his life. Things were much less complicated without interpersonal relationships. He had no intention of changing that.

His emotional bond with Mya, however, was different. She was his daughter. He felt safe nurturing that bond. Even though she was absent from his life for a significant amount of time, he loved her very much. There hadn't been a day that had gone by when he hadn't thought about her.

Then one day, out of the blue, Candy contacted him to set up a meeting between the three of them. He welcomed his daughter with open arms, metaphorically of course. His past made it very hard for him to show affection. He wasn't the sort of dad to give hugs. Showing emotion meant vulnerability, and that was more than he could give to anyone, even his child.

Henry quickly signed off on paperwork as Mya waited. He looked up for a moment and watched her as she played a game on her phone. He was very proud of her. Her grades were excellent. Her teachers always bragged about her when he met them at the school conferences. When he attended her school activities, he could see she was well liked by her peers.

Despite the turbulence surrounding her conception,

Henry could easily see Mya belonged to him. Her mannerisms were his. Her skin tone and eye color. Most of all, her icy demeanor was most certainly a trait she got from him. He had lost so much time with her, but he tried to remember that the present was all that mattered now.

24

Olivia stepped into the precinct dressed in straight-legged gray slacks, black heels, and a crisp white button-up oxford with a wide collar. Her hair was softly curled, falling neatly over her shoulders. She marveled at how such a simple change in her appearance could make her feel so confident and uplifted.

Beside her, Nigel trotted proudly, his lead secure in her hand, as though he shared her newfound energy. She glanced down at him as they stepped into the elevator.

"Here we go," she murmured, giving his lead a reassuring tug.

When the elevator doors opened, they were met by the bustling noise of the department, phones ringing, conversations overlapping, and the rhythmic clatter of office machines. But as Olivia stepped out, the world seemed to pause. All movement in the room stopped. Eyes turned toward her, and even the hum of typewriters and copiers faded into silence.

She felt the weight of their gazes, her every step observed as though she were walking a tightrope with an audience captivated below. The intensity made her stomach flutter, but she held her head high and continued forward.

A cheerful female voice broke the silence. "Olivia?"

Turning toward the voice, Olivia saw an attractive redhead with a warm smile.

"I'm Sue Barnes," the woman said, extending her hand.

Olivia shook it, offering a polite smile. "Yes, that's me."

Sue was tall and slender, her long legs and athletic build hinting at a runner's physique. Her freckled complexion and striking light green eyes made her appearance effortlessly stunning.

"Danny sent me down to get you," Sue explained.

"Oh, okay," Olivia replied.

"Your office has been moved to the fourth floor with the Major Crimes Unit," Sue continued. "You'll need to pack up your desk and move everything upstairs. I've already asked Rick and Danny to set some boxes by your desk and help you out."

"Rick?"

"Yes. He's the senior detective," Sue said with a playful grin. "But he lets me boss him around. He better. He's my husband," she added with a laugh.

"Oh," Olivia said with a slightly awkward smile.

"Take as much time as you need. Once you're ready, I'll show you to your new office," Sue offered. "If you'd like, I can take Nigel with me. We've already moved his crate upstairs to your new space."

Olivia's smile widened. "That's so thoughtful. Thank you!"

"We'll take care of you," Sue said with a wink, her tone reassuring and warm.

It took about an hour for Olivia to settle into the large office among her new colleagues. Nigel rested in his crate, watching her as she moved things around and organized the space.

As she unpacked another box, Olivia noticed Sue popping her head in. She smiled and then entered the office. "Settling in okay? Is there anything you need or anything I can do?" she asked.

Olivia turned with a smile. "Oh, everything is fine. Thank you so much, Sue."

"Danny should be here in a few minutes. He and Rick were meeting with Wallace this morning to go over the game plan."

"Okay," she said, as she continued busying herself.

"Listen, if you need anything, you just let me know. We're all pretty tight up here. And with Danny, you're in good, capable hands."

Olivia stopped and walked to Sue. "I'm really nervous," she admitted.

"Don't be. Like I said, Danny is great. Of course, Rick is pretty awesome, too, but I am a little biased there." She laughed a little and even blushed.

To break the ice, Sue shared the story of how she and Rick met. She described him as ruggedly handsome, with wavy blonde hair and sea-green eyes. Sue confessed that she was slightly taller than Rick, which had initially bothered her a little, but his charming personality quickly won her over.

Sue explained that she was already part of the investigations unit when they started dating. When their relationship became public, the sheriff decided not to transfer either of them, as Rick wasn't her direct supervisor. Sue recounted how Rick had courted her, winning her heart with his persistence and kindness. It was a sweet love story, pleasant, though not particularly extraordinary.

Now, Sue told Olivia, they had three children: Blake, Ashton, and Cyndy. Like many working moms, Sue was constantly juggling the demands of her career with her responsibilities at home. Her days were packed with karate practice, cheerleading practice, homework sessions, and chasing after a two-year-old, all while balancing her role as a detective. But she explained that Rick was a tremendous help, and their extended family was always supportive, making the chaos manageable.

Deep down, Olivia felt a twinge of envy. She couldn't help but wonder what it might be like to have someone in her life who loved and supported her unconditionally. While she cherished her family, she had never experienced the kind of love Sue described, the kind that made you feel truly seen and valued.

Hearing a knock on the door facing the office, the ladies turned to see a man standing there. Olivia knew it must be Danny.

He stood at an imposing 6'1", his short, slightly messy brown hair adding to his casual charm. His Pacific blue eyes complemented a warm, easy smile, while his broad shoulders and athletic build gave him an effortlessly commanding presence. He was dressed in khaki cargo pants, a blue polo shirt, and sturdy treaded hiking boots. A gun rested on his belt, with his shield clipped beside it.

Olivia couldn't help but notice the contrast. She had expected him to be in a suit. Glancing down at her own attire, she suddenly felt a bit overdressed. He waved casually.

"How you settling in?" he asked in a thick New York accent.

"Slowly," she replied as her cheeks warmed.

Sue sighed and clasped her hands together. "Well, I have to get going." She turned to Olivia, "We can do lunch anytime you want. If you need anything, just yell. I'm right across the way there," she pointed.

As she left the room, Danny came in and sat on the tan couch against the inside wall. "Looks nice," he complimented as he glanced around the office. He held a file in his hand. "So, I have the coroner's report from Jody's autopsy," he continued.

"Okay," Olivia said as she walked to the couch and sat down.

"Cause of death was strangulation. Bentley took photos of the vic," he said, opening the file and showing her a picture. "You can see here, there's bruising around the girl's throat." He handed the image to Olivia.

She examined it carefully.

"Also," Danny continued, "there's evidence of sexual assault, but there was no DNA recovered. That tells us the guy probably used a condom. Trace didn't recover anything useful at the scene either."

"That tells us the primary crime scene is elsewhere," Olivia said with a nod.

"Yes. Exactly. Good," he said with a smile and a nod. He pulled out another picture. "If you look at this picture," he said, handing the image over to Olivia, "you can see there's a tic-tac-toe board tattooed on the vic's inner thigh?"

Olivia looked over the photograph carefully. She saw that there was no "x" or "o." It was just the board. "What does that mean?" she asked.

"I think it's probably some sort of signature. I'm not sure yet, though."

"What do we do first?" Olivia asked.

"Well, you've spoken to the family, right?"

She nodded.

"So that's covered. Forensics is gonna want the kid's computer, phone, and any other electronics. They're takin' care of that warrant and then gonna get that stuff from the family. What we gotta do is narrow down who had motive. We gotta create a suspect pool."

"How do we do that? The family already said they couldn't think of anyone that would want to hurt her."

"You have to look outside the box," he answered, leaning forward, resting his elbows on his knees. "There's a connection somehow, somewhere, but we also gotta consider that this could be random. We don't have enough information yet. If more bodies start poppin' up, then it helps us."

"Helps us?"

"I know. It's a chilling thought."

Olivia nodded.

"The fact is that investigations nowadays rely heavily on forensic evidence. Without it, it's hard to come up with answers. Hard to get a conviction. All that jazz. And it's a double-edged sword. Yeah, we track down leads and follow up, but the magic happens in the forensics lab, so we are extra nice to those folks."

"It sounds terrible that we have to hope for the body count to go up," Olivia stated.

"I don't want any more bodies, but the reality is that the more bodies we have, the more evidence there will be to work with. More leads will become visible. I've seen it a hundred times. Cases like this one with a single incident go cold. I've also seen the reaction of the community when stuff like this happens. They pitch in and help. You get triple the leads, at least in this county. The chances of more evidence being collected also go up." He sighed with a thin smile.

"The important thing is to keep an open mind and not jump to conclusions, whether we have one body or twelve. As a detective, you just gotta deal with what you physically have and go from there. Right now, we have a body, an autopsy report, physical evidence of rape, and cause of death. From what Wallace told me, I can thank you for gaining the family's trust. We just gotta go with what we have. Make sense?"

"Yes," Olivia answered. She couldn't hide her perplexed expression, though. She felt completely out of her element. She was confused and even scared. She wondered if being a detective was just too much.

"Hey, listen to me," Danny began as he turned his body toward hers. "I am gonna teach you everything I know. Some cases are harder to work than others. This one isn't going to be easy 'cause it involves a kid. I don't have any kids of my own, but I have nieces and nephews that I'm close to. I'm also pretty close to Rick and Sue's kids, so the thought of somethin' happenin' to them…" He paused and took a deep breath. "Like I said, some cases give ya nothin' and they go cold. There are plenty that have glaring leads, though. Each one is different, but we will figure it all out. Don't feel overwhelmed, okay?" His eyes met Olivia's.

"I just want the family to have some peace," Olivia admitted. "And all of this is overwhelming. I give out traffic tickets and citations. I've never worked a case like this."

"You'll catch on. I promise."

"I'm wondering…" she trailed off.

"If you've made a big mistake?" he interrupted. "I've been there, but what you gotta remember is that Wallace saw somethin' in you. He saw somethin' that gave him confidence to move you to Major Crimes. Just be patient with yourself. You'll get it. We all want the same thing here. We wanna give peace to the family and bring the killer to justice. That is what keeps us motivated."

Olivia nodded and pursed her lips.

"You just do what ya can. We talk to the victim's friends and teachers. We look for any connections she had. They will have leads, and we'll follow them. It may lead to somethin'. It may not. It's like dumping a jigsaw puzzle onto a table. Sometimes things fit right together right away. Other pieces take months."

25

After a full week of interviewing Jody's friends, teachers, relatives, and anyone else who might have had useful information, Olivia and Danny were still at square one. Frustration over the lack of progress simmered in Olivia, but she couldn't deny that being a detective had its perks. One of the biggest was the schedule: daytime hours with weekends and holidays typically free. According to Danny and Sue, it was rare for Major Crimes detectives working Monday through Friday to be called to a crime scene on weekends or holidays. For Olivia, this meant more time with Amelia.

Every day felt like a gift as Olivia watched her daughter grow and hit milestones, learning to walk and beginning to talk. It was like peering through a window at a world of wonder. She reminded herself daily how fortunate she was to have a second chance at life, giving thanks for the opportunities she'd been given.

Outside of work, Olivia avoided any kind of social life, preferring to spend her time with Amelia and her family. She adored her half-brother and half-sister, David and Hope, and found solace in the company of Shay, Linda, and Sarah. Immersing herself in positivity helped her fend off cravings and stay on track with her recovery. So far, it was working. Her progress was well established, and she was determined never to go backward.

Group meetings provided additional strength, empowering Olivia to remain steadfast in her journey. She had even been discharged from individual counseling because of her remarkable progress.

Her unwillingness to have a social life, however, didn't stop men from showing interest in her. Many of her male coworkers found her attractive. Still, Olivia paid them no mind. Her priorities were her daughter and her recovery.

Then there was Danny. Olivia would have to be blind not to notice how attractive he was, and his charm and respectful demeanor didn't go unnoticed either.

Olivia was also developing a budding friendship with Sue. The two had shared lunch twice that week, and Sue had been candid about the men in the precinct. She explained that Olivia's change from heavy uniform to a more polished appearance hadn't been disregarded, and she should expect some distractions. Sue also gave Olivia a heads-up about which men to avoid, which Olivia appreciated.

Despite the extra attention, Olivia's disposition remained unchanged. She wasn't vain or overly confident. In fact, she still struggled with self-image. Her focus stayed firmly on Amelia and on keeping her life together. Yet, as strong as she remained and as much as she avoided social interaction, there was a part of her that missed physical intimacy. Deep down, though, she didn't truly understand what it meant. Her past experiences had twisted her view of love and connection, leaving her unsure if she'd ever find someone who could show her how to love in a healthy, meaningful way.

26

It was a beautiful May afternoon. Olivia sat in the backyard, listening to the joyful sounds of Nigel and Amelia playing. The weather was perfect, the sunbeams warm as they danced on her face. Closing her eyes, she felt a surge of gratitude. The sound of her daughter's laughter and the dog's barks brought tears to her eyes. Joy filled her heart.

She could hardly believe she'd been working in Major Crimes for nearly a month. With no leads in Jody's case, Olivia and Danny were reassigned to assist Narcotics. Nigel had proven to be a tremendous asset during drug sweeps, finally gaining some field hours, which made Olivia proud.

The peaceful afternoon was interrupted by the ring of her phone. Glancing at the screen, she saw Danny's name. She hesitated before answering with a soft, "Hello?"

"First of all, you need to answer your phone like this: 'Detective Gregory,'" Danny teased. "Secondly, we've got a fresh one. Normally, the weekend detectives would take it, but the scene's a mess, and they said we needed to handle it. Sue's coming with us. Also, dress down. It'll be soggy from all the rain we've had."

"Are you already there?" she asked.

"No, not yet."

"Okay. I need to get things squared away with my daughter first," Olivia replied.

"No problem. I'll meet you at the station in about an hour. Let me know if you need more time to find a sitter," Danny said before hanging up.

Olivia quickly changed into light-washed boot-cut jeans, brown treaded hiking boots, and a cream-colored V-neck T-shirt. She secured her shoulder holster and clipped her badge to her belt. Her hair was tied back in a messy ponytail. After a brief call to Sarah, she was relieved to learn her friend was home and willing to babysit. Sarah even welcomed the escape, complaining about the noise her husband was making while renovating their bathroom.

Within the hour, Olivia and Nigel arrived at the station in her black Ford Explorer, a perk of being a newly promoted K-9 detective. Wallace had assured her the SUV could be used on and off duty, a convenience she deeply appreciated.

Sue stood beside her car, phone pressed to her ear. She wore jeans and a tan scoop-neck tee, her shoulder holster snug against her back. Moments later, Danny pulled into the lot in a black Dodge Charger. He stepped out wearing gray cargo pants, treaded boots, and a white V-neck shirt, his gun and badge on his belt. Olivia couldn't help but notice the NYPD tattoo on his bicep. It was a personal detail she hadn't picked up on before.

As Olivia drove them to the crime scene, Sue and Danny chatted nonstop, their easy camaraderie evident. Olivia felt like a third wheel. The bond between Danny and Sue was undeniable, their friendship solid. It left Olivia feeling a bit isolated. She'd turned down multiple invitations to spend time with Sue's family, knowing Danny would be there.

Isolation had become her default.

They arrived in rural Franklin County, where a cruiser, the coroner's van, and the forensic team's vehicle were parked along the roadside. Olivia parked behind them, and the trio stepped out. She followed Danny and Sue into a field lined with budding corn. Yellow crime scene tape fluttered like a beacon at the tree line. Deputy North greeted them as they approached.

"What's the story?" Danny asked, grinning. "Don't you people have better things to do on weekends?"

"Boys, I'm missing my son's ballgame," Sue added with mock annoyance.

"Shut up, you two," the deputy replied, smiling despite himself.

"Got a call from Mr. Timothy," North began. "He was out walking the property and saw something hanging from one of his trees. When he got closer, he realized it was a girl. Naked. Hanging from a noose." He pointed toward the woods. "Bentley's with her now."

As Danny and Sue continued speaking with Deputy North, Olivia scanned the area. A chill ran down her spine. She felt the girl's presence. Her spirit lingered, hidden but near, a silent witness to the tragedy.

Moving toward the woods with the bustling activity, Olivia finally noticed the young girl standing in the distance. With mousy brown, shoulder-length hair, her shoulders appeared slumped. She wore a pair of jeans, a black hooded sweatshirt, and a pair of Converse-style tennis shoes. Emma and Madrich stood beside her. When Olivia focused on what was being said, she heard, *Olly will help you, but you need to let her do her job first.*

Olivia walked further into the forest. Emma, Madrich, and the girl stood even farther away now. She smiled at the girl and clairvoyantly communicated with the victim. *I'm Olivia. What's your name?*

Mya, she answered sheepishly. *How can you see me? What's happening?*

Olivia thought, *I have a gift. I can see people after they've died. I help them move on.*

So, I'm dead? she shouted.

The terror in her gaze caused Olivia's heart to sink. Too many times, the ghosts didn't realize their life had ended. She had never become immune to their reactions.

Mya, what is the last thing you remember? Olivia inquired as she took careful account of the girl.

I was at a monster truck rally with my dad. I went to use the bathroom. When I was washing my hands, someone hit me over the head, she explained. *When I woke up, I was blindfolded. I was blindfolded the entire time.* She paused, trying to think. *I remember feeling a lot of pressure around my throat. I remember I couldn't get any air.*

Do you remember anything before or after that?

I remember that when I woke up, I didn't have any

clothes on and my hands were tied behind my back. She stopped, tears welling in her eyes. *I remember them… hurting me… a lot.*

It's okay, Mya. You're safe now, Olivia assured her.

Mya looked up again, composed but sniffling. *I remember being in this really dark place, but there were all kinds of lights. And then Emma came. She talked to me for a while. I thought I was dreaming or something. Then we ended up here.*

"I'm so sorry this has happened to you," Olivia remarked compassionately. "How old are you?"

"Fourteen."

Olivia shook her head. She realized the murderer was establishing a pattern. The last body was discovered less than a month ago. The ages were also a huge red flag.

Mya, Olivia continued, *Emma and Madrich are going to take you through to the other side, but you have to be willing to go. You have to be able to move on. I'm so sorry your life was cut so short, sweetheart. I wish there was more that I could do.*

But my mom… my dad… You don't know what this will do to them. I've been so awful to my dad, too.

It's okay. He'll forgive you. You can visit him whenever you want, but you must go with Emma and Madrich now.

Mya nodded reluctantly.

She's not afraid, Emma said without moving her lips. *She's been in the In-Between with me up until now.*

Olivia thought, *I have to get back to work. If there's anything else you can think of that might help, Mya, please check in with me.*

How do I do that? Mya asked.

I will teach you, Emma said.

Mya shook her head. *I don't understand any of this. This can't be real.*

You'll understand in time, Olivia thought.

They all disappeared, and Olivia turned back toward the scene. She walked to Danny and Sue, who stood talking to the officers. Bentley knelt beside the body. Mya was completely nude and lying on the plastic tarp. Relief swept over Olivia. She was grateful Mya had left when she did. She didn't want the poor girl to see herself like that.

"Another tic-tac-toe board is tattooed on the inner thigh of this one," Bentley said, looking up at the detectives.

They knelt beside him as he pushed Mya's legs apart. A finely branded marking glared up at them. In the upper right-hand corner of the board was an X this time.

"What the hell does this mean?" Danny asked.

"Game on," Olivia said matter-of-factly. "He drew a blank board first. He's made the first move. This is a game to him."

Sue looked over at Olivia, clearly pleased. "Very good. And what does this tell us?"

"Eight victims possibly?" Olivia answered, glancing over at Danny.

"Maybe. He could also start another board on a ninth victim," Danny added. "One thing is certain. This bastard is tryin' to make a name for himself."

Olivia shook her head slightly. "Not necessarily. He may just be targeting us. He might be mocking the police. He is hanging the bodies in remote locations in the county. They've been found by chance. The act of hanging the children, though... it's a display."

"Good, Gregory," Danny said with a smile. "You're starting to use critical thinking. You're tryin' to work it all out in your head. That's good."

"I am sending this stuff to Lauren Harris," Sue interrupted. "Well, Lauren Harris Bennette now. She got married a while back."

Olivia stood. "The forensic psychologist? The writer? I love her work. I've read every single one of her case studies and novels." She paused. "Why would we be consulting with her this early in the investigation? I thought there had to be at least three dead bodies before she'd confer with us."

"She still consults for the FBI and the Ohio State Police. Even local jurisdictions sometimes. She is the best profiler in the entire world," Danny agreed. "And you're right, Olivia. She usually doesn't talk to anyone until there's at least three bodies."

Sue nodded. "Well, I have a bad feeling about this case. I still want to send her what we've got. Maybe she'll make an exception."

"Okay," Danny said with a shrug. "It's up to you, Sue."

Bentley sighed. "I agree with Olivia. It's too early."

"Like I said," Sue continued. "This is preemptive. It doesn't hurt to ask her to take a look. Maybe do us a favor. She worked with Franklin County a lot in the past. Maybe she's got a soft spot for us."

A forensic technician interrupted the debate. "Detectives," she said, "we have a facial recognition of the victim."

The four of them walked to the van, which resembled a high-tech computer lab. Wires snaked across the interior, connecting various devices, while locked cabinets lined the walls. A small desk was positioned in one corner, completing the setup.

From where Olivia stood, she had a clear view of the laptop screen. It displayed a missing person's report. The poster featured a picture of a young girl named Mya.

"Her father reported her missing about four days ago," the technician said.

"Who is her father?" Sue asked.

"Dr. Henry Howard," the technician replied. "He's the

head of the diagnostics lab department at OSU. He's been calling every day to check on the progress."

"What about the child's mother?" Olivia asked.

"Candy Howard," the technician answered. "She lives on the West Side. She hasn't reached out, though. Only the father has been in contact."

Danny turned toward the woods while Sue stayed in the van. Olivia followed behind him.

"Okay, Gregory," he began, gesturing with his hands, "the next step is Bentley's. He's gotta take the girl to the morgue and do the autopsy. Once he's cleared her, he can release the body to the father, but the father has to identify her first."

Olivia knew she needed to be the one to talk to the father. It was something she felt she had to do.

Deep in thought, she was interrupted by Bentley's voice. "Let me get her back and do the autopsy. It will be tomorrow morning before I can release the body."

Olivia didn't realize they'd walked all the way back to the crime scene. Danny looked at her. "We're done here. Now we wait on the medical reports. Once Bentley clears the body, we have to notify the family. Do you feel okay about talking to one of the parents while I talk to the other?"

"Yes. I'll talk to the father." She nodded with confidence as she crossed her arms.

27

That night, Olivia held Amelia a little tighter, her heart swelling with gratitude and a twinge of sorrow. She couldn't fathom what she would do if someone ever harmed Amelia. The thought sent a shiver through her, and her mind drifted to the heartache she had caused her own family when she disappeared to Cleveland. Matt and Robin must have thought she was dead or had been murdered. The guilt settled heavily on her chest, and tears began to spill from her eyes.

As she rocked Amelia in the nursery, the baby's soft breaths were a soothing rhythm. Tears streamed down Olivia's face until she felt a small, gentle hand on her cheek. She looked down to see Amelia's sweet, curious face gazing up at her. Their eyes met as Amelia's tiny hand brushed away her tears.

Olivia smiled softly. "Mommy's okay," she whispered.

When Amelia finally drifted off to sleep, Olivia placed her gently in the crib and tiptoed into the living room. She sat cross-legged in the center of the room, her hands resting palms-up on her knees. After a day like this, she yearned for meditation and prayer.

Closing her eyes, she inhaled deeply, but instead of finding balance, her thoughts spiraled into doubt. The insecurities that haunted her flooded her mind. Anxiety gripped her as she anticipated the conversation with Mya's father. But then, unexpectedly, a wave of comfort washed over her.

Her thoughts shifted, filled with sorrow for the victims she had encountered. She knew all too well that bad things often happened to those who didn't deserve it; she herself was proof of that. The grief weighed on her, but it also sharpened her focus.

Another turn of her mind brought Danny's face into view. Despite their short time working together, there was undeniable chemistry between them. This realization made her cautious. She hoped they could become close friends, but her apprehension about forming deep connections lingered. She had distanced herself from others for so long that the idea of emotional intimacy felt foreign and daunting.

Her reality came crashing back as her thoughts scattered. She recognized how she had cut herself off from true human connection, pouring all her energy into Amelia, meditation, and her ongoing recovery. The word "fear" echoed in her mind. She was afraid, afraid of getting close to anyone, afraid of the cravings that still occasionally clawed at her. She didn't want anyone to see that part of her: the caged animal still fighting to be tame.

She felt unworthy of someone like Danny. He was a kind soul, gentle in spirit, and while she didn't know him well, she could already sense his goodness. Self-doubt constricted her like a vice. Could she do her job effectively? She felt like she was fumbling, but she knew she had to learn quickly.

After a half hour of grappling with her thoughts, she finally found solace in prayer. She gave thanks to her Creator for her second chance, for Amelia, for her job, for Sarah, and for countless other blessings. Slowly, peace settled over her, easing the tension in her body. When she finally rose, she felt ready to rest. For the first time that day, she believed she might find sleep.

28

Things remained quiet for the rest of the weekend. By Monday, Danny stood against the doorframe of Olivia's office. She sat behind her desk, stirring the coffee in her mug as he strolled across the room and sat down on her couch. He held a file in his hand.

He wore a pair of khaki cargo pants and an army green polo shirt. Olivia quickly realized that Danny didn't dress up. He always had the same look. Whether it was a scoop-neck shirt or one with a collar, the shirts he wore were always mesh material or breathable cotton. His pants were always cargo style. He always wore treaded boots. Thinking of his consistency, she smiled, still stirring the coffee in her cup.

She leaned over her desk. "Is that the M.E.'s report?" she asked.

"Yeah. Bentley said he thought we'd had enough drama for the weekend, so he came by this morning and dropped it off," Danny answered.

"That was nice of him."

"He's cool like that," he agreed.

Olivia leaned back and pushed away from her desk. She walked to the sofa and sat down beside Danny, who leafed through the file in his grasp.

"Okay, so the tattoo on the inner thigh was postmortem. It was made with typical, run-of-the-mill tattoo ink, so that's not going to help us." He paused as he scanned the documents. "Bentley found evidence of sexual assault again, but no DNA. No fibers. No stray hairs. No trace. Nothin'. This guy is really smart and really careful."

Danny scooted closer to Olivia. He pointed to a photograph. "Look at her neck. What do you see?"

She briefly looked at Danny and then back at the photograph. The smell of his cologne quickly took her by surprise, and for a moment, she lost her concentration. She made eye contact with him once again, then focused on the picture. She studied it carefully. She tried to forget everything Mya told her. "Um, well," Olivia began, "I see marks on her neck that indicate strangulation. I mean, there's bruising where the rope…" she trailed off.

"And notice the pattern," he added, leaning closer still. He traced the pattern on the photograph.

"It looks like handprints, just like last time," Olivia said, taking the photo from him. She studied it carefully and replayed Mya's words in her mind. "Strangulation is very personal," she added.

"Take a look at this one," Danny said as he pulled another photograph out. It was of Mya's side.

"Bruising," Olivia said quietly as she observed the darkened skin.

"And this one," he said, showing her yet another photo of Mya's right side.

Olivia suddenly realized what she was seeing. She met Danny's gaze. "The killer straddled her while he choked her. These are bruises from pressure being applied during the act."

"See, you're already getting the hang of this!" he said as he nudged her with his elbow.

She gave a half-smile. She was grateful that she was starting to catch on, but the circumstances were grim. Still, she was understanding things more and feeling more confident in her job. However, the sinking feeling in the pit of her stomach couldn't be disregarded. Her ability to learn meant terrible things were happening.

Sue popped her head into the office. "I talked to Dr. Harris." Sue shook her head as she corrected herself. "I keep calling her that. It's Dr. Harris-Bennette. Anyway, I overnighted the reports and crime scene photos to her. I faxed the M.E.'s report. It usually takes her a week or so to get back to us on things."

"Thanks, Sue," Danny said with a wave and a nod. She pursed her lips, turned, and walked back to her office.

"So we notify the family today, right?" Olivia asked.

"Yep. Since the father filed the missing person's report, he needs to identify the body."

The anticipation felt terrible. Olivia sighed.

"Hey, Gregory," he said, seeing a twinge of distress in her eyes. "You don't have to do this alone. I can go with you if you want."

"No," she replied. "I said I would do it, and I will. I'll leave Nigel here. I'll talk to Seth in the K-9 unit to make sure they have room for him today."

Danny stood as Olivia followed his lead. "Really, I can go with ya if ya want."

The chivalry in his tone was clear, but Olivia gracefully declined his help. "No. I need to do this on my own. All part of the job, right?"

He put the file down on the desk and folded his arms. "Listen, we're partners. That means we lean on each other. We're there for each other. So, if you don't feel comfortable doin' somethin', that's where I come in. Same goes for me. If I feel like I'm doin' somethin' that I'm not okay with, then I look to you."

"I understand that," she agreed with a nod. "I just feel like I need to do this. Don't ask me why. It's just something I know."

He nodded again and gave her an approving smile. "See, that's what I'm talkin' about. Instinct. You got intuition," he said, pointing a finger at her. "That's important as a detective. I can see why Wallace moved you up so fast. Instinct can't be taught. It's somethin' you just have. You got to be able to look inside yourself doin' this job and find what feels right. You're off to a good start."

"I hope so. I feel like I'm wandering around in a fog right now," she reluctantly admitted.

"Those instincts… they're there. I can see it. You got a handle on that. That's a good thing." Placing a hand on her shoulder, his lips curved into a closed smile. "You'll be fine. I can tell."

29

Olivia parked her car in the garage adjoining the OSU Medical Center. She made her way to the main entrance and stepped into the busy hospital atrium. The sound of the PA announcements caught her attention first, followed by the low roar of voices. The voices gave way to wanderers, spirits she knew were stuck for whatever reason. It was as if they were all screaming at her. They knew who she was and what she could do.

Living, breathing human beings sat in various areas waiting for procedures. Doctors and nurses passed by her. The atmosphere was pure chaos, and the racket was overpowering.

For a moment, she thought she might need to step out. However, Madrich appeared. He extended his wings and wrapped them around her. The commotion from the nomadic souls stopped. Then she watched as the ghosts vanished. Madrich smiled at her and then faded away. She grinned and thought, "So that's how you do it."

Although he wasn't visible, she felt his wings wrapping tightly around her as she walked toward a large circular counter, her heels clicking against the stone flooring as she went. She observed the attendants answering phones and helping other visitors. Leaning against the counter, a tall, slender woman stood. She wore a red tailored suit. Her black coal hair was pulled back in a neat ponytail. The woman's skin reminded Olivia of freshly fallen snow.

Olivia wore white straight-leg slacks with a modern, curvy fit that sat just below her belly button, complementing her long legs. Her fitted black-and-white striped button-down featured a Y-neck, French cuffs, and a pointed collar that highlighted her long neck. Black pointed-toe leather pumps completed the look. With her hair in a messy bun and silver hoops tying the ensemble together, her gun and badge sat neatly on her belt.

Olivia smiled at the woman as she approached. "Can you tell me where I can find Dr. Henry Howard?"

The woman smiled back and said, "I'm Dr. O'Dell. I'm the Chief of Medicine. I can walk you up if you'd like."

Olivia nodded. "That would be great."

They made their way through the crowded area and then onto the elevator. "Is everything alright?" Dr. O'Dell asked.

Olivia fixed her eyes on the illuminated numbers above the elevator door. "I really need to talk to him first, ma'am. He will probably need to come with me, though," she replied.

"Oh God, what has he done now? Are you arresting him?" she asked frantically.

"Oh, no," Olivia answered, shaking her head. "He's not in trouble."

Putting her hand to her throat, Dr. O'Dell exhaled with relief. "Oh thank God. I thought he might have killed someone else."

Olivia's eyebrows narrowed and her head tilted. Her voice naturally higher, she said, "Excuse me?"

"Oh no, I didn't mean it like that. Dr. Howard is a little different," O'Dell emphasized. "He marches to his own drum sometimes. I can see you're a cop, so I assumed the worst. Anytime we have cops here, they are usually coming to see him."

"Why is that?"

"It's a long story. To make it short, he is a bit of a trailblazer."

"I don't understand."

"Well, he is the Lab Supervisor for the entire hospital and one of the most gifted research scientists I've ever seen. Sometimes he offers suggestions for treatments. Those treatments can be a little unnerving. But the doctors believe in his work and have seen what his research can do. Many people just see him as a simple scientist, but he is much more than that," O'Dell explained.

She paused and looked at the numbers, too. Then she continued. "Anyway, because he's a scientist, he backs up his suggestions with research, but when the doctors try to put his methods to the test on patients, sometimes it doesn't quite work out, and then the doctor who gave the treatment gets sued. I can't count how many doctors I've lost because sometimes his suggestions don't pan out. So there I am trying to replace the physician, deal with Dr. Howard, and balance a pending lawsuit all at the same time."

Olivia nodded. She wasn't sure if Dr. Howard was good at his job or a mad scientist using human beings as experimental lab rats. His ability to be compassionate immediately came into question. Olivia didn't understand science, though. She knew from hearing her father talk that sometimes it was necessary to lose lives for the greater good. She tried to take what Dr. O'Dell said with a grain of salt.

Following Dr. O'Dell off the elevator, they proceeded down a long hallway and reached a set of glass windows. The white letters on the door read "Laboratory Science & Research Center." Dr. O'Dell pushed open the glass door and allowed Olivia to go in first. Behind a desk sat an attractive man with graying brown hair, his face long and symmetrical. He was a little scruffier than Olivia anticipated.

In her mind, she compared doctors to her father. Matt had always been well dressed, even with his goatee, now a full beard, and his perpetually messy hair. He wore suits and ties to work. In contrast, Henry's light blue graphic T-shirt under a black sports jacket caught her off guard.

Henry glanced up from his computer screen. "Damn it. I was looking at porn again," he bit out. "Can't you come back in about an hour?" he joked dryly.

Even though Olivia was shocked by his sarcasm, her face remained unchanged.

"Howard," Dr. O'Dell began, then paused, realizing she hadn't even asked for a name.

"I'm Detective Gregory with the Franklin County Sheriff's Office," Olivia said.

His countenance changed, his eyes filling with urgency. He took off the silver glasses he wore and placed them on the desk. "Is this about my daughter?" he asked in a smooth tone.

Dr. O'Dell smiled. "I'll leave you two to talk," she said as she turned and left the room.

Olivia took in the room briefly. Diplomas and plaques lined the walls, interspersed with band posters, some familiar, others not. A stereo system sat in the corner near the windows, while a large wooden file cabinet stood on the opposite side. On top of the cabinet, framed photographs were displayed, mostly of Mya.

Despite Henry's disheveled appearance, his desk was impeccably organized. Pens sat neatly in a container at the corner, while medical journals were stacked alongside files and papers.

As he stood, his full height and lean build became evident, slim but not frail. He wore light-colored jeans, his casual attire catching her off guard as she once again found herself thinking of her father.

She nodded and answered his question. "Yes sir. I am here about your daughter."

He stepped out from behind the desk and gestured toward an adjoining room. He grabbed the door handle and stepped aside to allow Olivia to enter first.

A long table sat in the middle of the room with rolling chairs placed perfectly under the tabletop. A sink and cabinets lined the back wall. A small refrigerator sat next to the cabinets with a microwave and coffee maker on top of it. The windows overlooking Columbus provided plenty of natural light for the plants that sat sparsely around the room. A whiteboard stood in front of the windows, and a light blue sofa sat in the corner.

Olivia watched Henry come into the room.

"May I?" she asked, her hand on the back of one of the empty chairs.

He nodded as he took a seat, too.

Olivia smiled as best she could. "Dr. Howard, I need you to come with me. I was called to a crime scene over the weekend, and we believe we found your daughter, Mya."

His face dropped, and things became uncomfortably quiet. Finally, he spoke and said, "She's at County?"

"Yes sir," Olivia answered. "I'm so very sorry to ask this of you, but we need you to identify her, and then the medical examiner can release her to you."

His eyes filled with tears. "Bentley handling it?"

"Yes," she answered softly.

"Good," he said as he cleared his throat.

"How do you know Bentley?" she asked.

"I handle the county's lab work," he answered.

She nodded.

Olivia expected him to break down, but instead, his expression hardened.

"Where's your car, Detective? I want to get this process moving."

30

The drive to the morgue was awkwardly quiet. Olivia figured Henry needed time to process things. Nonetheless, he surprised her with his lack of emotion.

They reached their destination. Once parked in the garage, they stepped onto the elevator and made their way to the basement. In the reception area, behind an old wooden desk, Bentley's secretary sat busily typing. Olivia cleared her throat and made eye contact with her.

They signed in and then continued down a darkened hallway to a bench. The atmosphere was cold and unfeeling, gray and devoid of life. It seemed appropriate for such a place.

Sitting down, Olivia waited patiently, staring at the cinderblock walls. Finally, the silence broke with the sound of Henry's voice.

"Does her mother know?" he asked, leaning the back of his head against the hard wall and closing his eyes.

"Not yet. We needed you to identify her first. Then my partner will notify her mother," she answered.

He opened his eyes. Olivia continued to observe him in her peripheral vision.

Bentley walked through the swinging double doors. He smiled. "Henry," he began, moving closer as both Olivia and Henry stood. Henry's hand stretched out, and Bentley met it with a strong handshake.

"I am so sorry to see you under these circumstances," Bentley said empathetically.

Henry nodded. "I was glad to hear you were handling things."

"Are you ready?" Bentley asked as they finished shaking hands.

"No," Henry said, lowering his head and pinching the bridge of his nose.

Olivia stood. She still was not sure what to say.

"Will you come with me?" Henry asked as he turned to her.

"Of course," she answered compassionately.

They proceeded down the hall toward a set of metal doors. Bentley opened them, allowing Henry to enter first, followed by Olivia. As they stepped inside, Olivia's eyes were immediately drawn to the metal table at the center of the room. A sheet covered a body, pulled down just below the neck, revealing Mya's pale, young face.

Henry stopped as if his feet were cemented to the floor. Olivia looked up at him and reached for his arm.

"Can I get you some water? Do you want me to call someone to be here with you?" she asked.

He shook his head. "No, no," he trailed off.

As if her words had released him, he walked to the table. Bentley stood on the opposite side.

Olivia watched Henry closely. He stood directly beside the metal table and looked down. His eyes filled with tears as he gently touched Mya's cold cheek with the back of his hand.

"It's her," he said.

"Mya Ann Howard?" Bentley asked for clarification, glancing down at the chart.

"Yes," Henry answered, his voice quivering.

"I know this is a terrible time," Bentley said, "but I need you to fill out some paperwork so I can release her for burial."

"I understand," Henry nodded, his voice unsteady.

His gaze shifted toward Olivia. "Where did you find her, Detective?" he asked.

"In a very remote part of the county, but I can explain everything later, sir," she answered. "I will leave you alone so you can complete the paperwork."

She turned and walked out of the room.

Olivia sat on the hard bench in the hallway, unable to imagine the depth of Henry's grief. She did not want to know that kind of loss.

Then Mya materialized in front of her.

162

He'll never even let on that he cares, Mya said, light radiating softly from her skin. *My dad has been through a lot. I didn't know everything until I crossed over. I treated him so badly. I should have been better.*

Some things we don't fully understand until we cross over, Olivia thought. *Parents are supposed to protect us from their past, from their mistakes. That is exactly what your father did.*

I've been assigned to him. I'm a spirit guide now. I don't know why. It hurts to be with him, but they say I have to do it, Mya continued.

The buzzing phone in Olivia's pocket startled her. She pulled it out and looked at the screen.

Danny: Everything going alright there?

She typed back.

Olivia: This sucks.

A few seconds passed.

Danny: I know. BTW, we have court in about 1.5 hrs. I have to testify. Could be good for you to observe.

Olivia: I will be back as soon as I'm done here.

Danny: Okay.

Nearly fifteen minutes later, the double doors swung open and Henry stepped out. As he walked down the hallway toward her, Olivia searched his face for any sign of grief but found none.

She stood as he approached. "Dr. Howard, if there's anything I can do"

"I need to know what happened to her. I need to know why this happened," he interrupted, his voice sharp.

"Now isn't the time for this," she responded gently but firmly.

"When is a good time, Detective?" he snapped.

Olivia raised her hands slightly in a calming gesture. "Take my advice. Work through grief first. When you're ready, we'll talk."

"I am ready right now, damn it!" he shouted, his arm shooting upward as he pointed back toward the room. "My daughter is lying on a slab. Is there ever going to be a better time to talk about this?"

Footsteps echoed down the hall as Bentley approached. He reached Henry and placed a steady hand on his shoulder, silently urging him to lower his arm.

"Listen to Detective Gregory," Bentley said evenly. "Give yourself some time. This isn't her fault, and yelling at her won't change anything."

Henry exhaled sharply. "I just have to know."

Olivia's expression hardened. "She was found hanging from a noose in a tree on a farmer's property, Dr. Howard. She was raped. She was strangled," she said, her voice clipped. "We believe she may be the second victim of a serial killer. We are still working on that. Does that answer your questions?"

Henry's eyes filled with tears, but he forced them back. After a long moment, he nodded respectfully.

"Yes, it does. Thank you," he said, his voice quieter but firm. "I'd rather have someone shoot straight with me, Detective. Don't sugarcoat things. Just tell me the truth, no matter how brutal it is."

31

As they drove back to the hospital, Olivia felt the weight of pity for Henry.

"I'm very sorry for your loss, Dr. Howard," she said as she concentrated on traffic. "And I didn't mean to spit it all out to you like that. It was very unprofessional of me, and I apologize."

"Like I said, I'd rather you shoot straight. There is something to be said for brutal honesty."

"I want justice for your daughter," Olivia remarked.

"I want more than justice. I want someone to bleed. All my life, I've had everything taken from me. I'm not exaggerating. My entire life has been one loss after another. And now her. Just when you thought lightning couldn't strike twice."

Olivia felt the venom in his voice. She worried that he might do something extreme.

"Please let us do our jobs. Vigilante justice won't help. It won't bring her back. Doing your own investigation won't help either. It will just complicate things."

"You know," he continued, "I don't know why I'm surprised about this, really. She's the only thing that mattered to me." He paused and turned his head to look out the passenger-side window. "I hadn't seen her since she was a toddler. Her mother took her, and we divorced."

"We don't have to do this now," Olivia said.

"No, we might as well get this part over with. I know you're going to question me and line me up in the suspect pool, so I'd just as soon get this done now," he bit out.

Instead of responding, Olivia simply listened.

"I finally started having contact with her again four years ago," Henry started. "I felt like I was looking into a mirror when I saw her. People say genetics is only partially responsible for the way we turn out. That's bullshit, Detective. Genes have almost everything to do with who we become. When she walked or tilted her head, I saw so much of myself. Of course, I also saw her mother, but really, she was more me."

He brushed a tear from his cheek and continued. "Candy and I both sucked as parents. We had no business having her. We were kids ourselves."

"How did you meet her mom?" Olivia asked, hoping for a lead.

"It was not your normal means of introduction, believe me, but we made the best of it. I don't really like to talk about that part of my life." He paused. "The point is that I was kept from Mya up until four years ago. I had no idea where she and Candy were. I threw myself into my own life, into my own goals. I had been functioning as if they were both dead, and now, well, Mya is dead."

He exhaled heavily. "Do you have children, Detective?" he asked, his voice trembling with emotion as he glanced over.

"A daughter."

"Have you ever been separated from her?"

"Yes, I have."

"Were you able to see her? Were you able to see her change and watch her grow?"

"I was able to see her, but I had very limited contact."

"The fact is, Detective, I wasn't a good father. I didn't know how to be one. No one had ever shown me. When she came back into my life, I should have done better. Instead, I took her to a monster truck rally with thousands of sweaty, perverted men. Obviously, one of them had his eye on her, and now she's gone. I didn't do what fathers are supposed to do. I didn't protect her."

"This wasn't your fault, Dr. Howard." From the corner of her eye, Olivia watched as he shrugged.

"Nothing I can do about it now." He reached into his pocket, pulled out a pill bottle, dumped a few tablets into his palm, and tossed them into his mouth.

32

They arrived back at the hospital. As he moved his right hand to the door handle, Olivia impulsively grabbed his left arm. She did not even understand why she did it. Their eyes met briefly, and then his head turned away from her.

"Don't blame yourself, Dr. Howard. I promise I will be in touch. When you're in a better state of mind, I'll talk to you again, but until then, give yourself time to grieve."

He did not say anything. Instead, he pulled the door handle, leaving her with her thoughts and with more questions than answers.

As she drove back across town, she thought about their interaction. He was so cold, but under all of that, she felt he was tortured. She wanted to know why.

She pulled into the parking garage at the station and shut off the engine. After stepping out, she headed toward the elevators and noticed a very handsome gentleman walking toward her. He wore a gray suit with a white button-up shirt and a burgundy tie. As they got closer to each other, Olivia realized that it was Danny.

She smiled as he twirled around, modeling his snazzy ensemble. "Take a good look. You won't see me like this very often," he joked.

"Is this for court?"

"Yes, ma'am. I know you typically dress upscale all the

time. Me, on the other hand, don't do this unless I have to testify. Give me cargo pants any day."

"You clean up nice," she said with a smile.

He grinned and took his aviator sunglasses from his pocket. "You ready to roll, Detective?" he asked.

"Absolutely," she answered.

They walked back to the SUV. "How did the father take it?" Danny asked.

"It was odd," she replied.

"Everyone handles loss differently. He's probably just processing it."

"I know."

"You hold up okay?" he asked as he stopped beside the back of the vehicle.

"I did okay. He made me mad at one point, so I'm sure Wallace will get some sort of complaint."

"Ahh, don't sweat it. If we don't get complaints from time to time, then we're doin' our jobs."

33

Henry stood at the graveside, looking down at the settling pile of dirt. Only two weeks had gone by since he buried his daughter. He visited the grave each day, hoping it was a nightmare he might awaken from, but it wasn't a dream. The truth was that his little girl had been taken from him. He tortured himself with all the might-have-beens and what-ifs.

Heartbroken, he didn't see much of a way out of this. He kept coming to the same conclusion about coping with Mya's loss. Nothing seemed to temper the sorrow. Nothing calmed the raging grief. All of the things he didn't say to her and all of the things he didn't do haunted him continually, every moment of every hour of every day.

Jim sat in the car waiting. It hurt him to see Henry struggling through yet another tragic loss. He knew everything about the abuse and the misfortunes Henry had endured, but this topped it all. He wondered if he would finally break. In fact, that's what he feared. He worried about what he might do.

After walking back to the car, Henry got inside, slamming the door angrily.

"You've got to talk to someone," Jim suggested.

Henry looked over at him, a hardened expression on his face. Jim had always been so considerate. He had always been the voice of reason for Henry, but this time it wasn't working.

"To hell with that," Henry said. "I don't need to talk to anyone. I need to talk to my kid. That's who I need to talk to. I've never needed to talk to anyone in my entire life. I'm sure as hell not going to start now."

"You can't deal with this alone. The loss of a child is too much, Henry."

"Hopefully you'll never have to know what it's like, Jim." Henry turned his attention back to the front windshield. "Just take me back to my apartment."

Jim was an attractive middle-aged man with dark brown hair, parted to the side. He had been blessed with a youthful face. His heart seemed to be made of pure gold, and his personality certainly complemented his appearance.

In his personal life, he usually found that he was easily taken advantage of. That's why he was single. After so many failed marriages, he decided to take a break from women. In fact, he'd given himself a three-year break.

Henry remained silent in the car, his mind racing. Even though he didn't want to admit it, the carefully crafted armor he wore was breaking down under the pressure of Mya's loss. He didn't think that, after all he had lived through, it would even be possible for him to feel such extreme pain again. But all the things he'd endured paled in comparison to this. He had never imagined having to bury his only child. After all, that's not how it was supposed to be.

His soul filled with anger, frustration, betrayal, and fear.

Still, he couldn't let any of that out. He had to stay strong and conceal all the ache. He didn't know how else to survive. He had done things the same way for so long that he had no idea how to change or how to let someone in.

Jim was different, though. He could tell Jim anything. They were like brothers. However, even with his faith in their friendship, deep down, Henry knew he needed more than the help Jim could offer. He had no idea where to even start.

Jim felt the tension in the air. He knew a foreboding existed. He was spiritual to a fault. Jim's discernment allowed him to feel strong emotion, and he knew Henry was sinking into something he might not emerge from. However, until Henry admitted it, Jim knew he couldn't do anything else. He simply had to watch as his best friend self-destructed.

He pulled up in front of the apartment. "You sure you don't want me to come in for a bit?" Jim asked.

"Are you kidding? I have company coming later. It's date night," he lied. "I'm not letting you cramp my style," he concluded as he pushed the door open.

"If you need to talk," Jim started.

"I won't," Henry said as he kicked the door shut.

He walked into the apartment and sat down on the couch. He looked around the room. Everything had its place. He'd lived in the apartment for years. It was on the ground floor in an upscale neighborhood. He kept to himself, too. In fact, he didn't even know his neighbors.

In the living room near the picture window stood a black baby grand piano on a shiny cherry wood laminate floor. An acoustic guitar sat beside it. A large flat screen hung on the wall in front of the long leather couch. End tables sat on each side of the couch with a matching coffee table on top of a red oriental rug directly in front of the sofa. Bookshelves lined the walls, all of them filled with medical journals and Henry's music collection. A matching leather recliner sat amid the arrangement.

Restless from his thoughts, Henry stood and walked down the short hallway into a kitchen filled with stainless steel appliances. They were of little use to him because he rarely cooked.

Off the kitchen was the only bedroom and bathroom. In his room, tidy and well-kept, his king-sized bed also served little purpose. Being alone rendered some comforts completely unnecessary.

The wine-colored walls throughout the room were accented by long beige window sheers on the two windows, along with darkening shades. Because his mind rarely stopped, he was constantly restless. He spent most of his days off sleeping during daytime hours.

The bathroom had a very cold feel to it with white tile floors, a white bathtub, and a stand-up shower. He was rarely able to take baths because he could barely get out once he got in. The pedestal sink matched the chilly tone of the room.

He made his way into the bathroom and stood at the

sink, his hands gripping both sides of the cold porcelain. He looked at his reflection in the mirror. "How has it come to this?" he muttered. "Haven't I suffered enough? What the fuck more do you want from me?"

He didn't believe in God. He couldn't afford to. What kind of God would allow him to endure such agony growing up and then do this to him now? He didn't need God anyway. The only person he had ever been able to rely on was himself. He knew that was still the way the balance fell.

He continued looking into the glass and focused on his own pale blue eyes, his unhealed soul staring back at him. He wondered what sort of hope there was now. He was growing older. He knew kids were not really a possibility for him, especially since he didn't have the strength to even open up to another human being, let alone make a new life for himself. If he connected with someone, he knew the door would open to more loss and more disappointment.

He sighed and opened the cabinet, pulling out an extra bottle of benzodiazepines. "I don't want to be here anymore," he whispered, the tears finally surfacing in his eyes.

He closed the door and glanced back up at himself, still unsure of his decision. "My baby girl is gone," he whispered. "I have screwed up everything I have ever touched," he continued. "And what has it all been for? My suffering. Has it even meant anything? How much more can I pay?"

He looked back down at the bottle in his hand and popped the lid. It fell into the sink, clanging against the surface. He poured the entire contents into his palm. He quickly realized the cocktail was incomplete. So, he picked up the bottle and poured the pills back in. Putting the lid securely on it, he stuffed it into his front pocket.

He walked into his bedroom and sat down on the side of the bed. He pulled the nightstand drawer open and prepared the heroin. After carefully ensuring its perfection, he tied the rubber tourniquet around his arm and made a fist. He penetrated the skin with the needle and closed his eyes as he pushed the plunger slowly, letting the liquid enter his body. Then, to finalize his last transaction on this earth, he stood and walked to the kitchen. He found the bottle of whiskey and, with his teeth, unscrewed the lid.

Swiftly, he chugged the liquid, the burn rushing down his throat and into his stomach. Some of it streamed down the side of his face. He put the glass bottle onto the countertop and then turned his attention back to the pill bottle. He pulled it from his pocket, popped the lid again, and tossed the contents into his mouth. As the pills hit the back of his throat, he grabbed the whiskey bottle and washed them down. Then, he waited.

He slid down to the floor, his back against the cabinets. He sat on the cold kitchen floor. As he began drifting, he saw something extraordinarily terrifying. A row of black hooded figures stood before him. He couldn't explain it. His scientific mind told him it was his brain beginning to detach from the hopelessness of reality.

Then he saw her, his daughter sitting in front of him, her legs crossed with tears in her eyes. Her appearance was exactly how he remembered, pink cheeks and full of life. The glow around her took him by surprise, though.

Daddy, don't do this, Mya said softly.

"Mya?" he asked, his eyes struggling to stay open.

Daddy, this isn't your fault. Me dying is not your fault. Don't do this. You can help people, she said softly.

The drowsiness began pulling at him. "Who are they?" he asked as his eyes floated toward the figures behind her.

They are going to take you away if you don't make a different choice, Mya explained.

"I've already made my choice," Henry said as his eyes met hers.

There's still time. Please, call Jim.

"How are you here?" he asked as his hand rose to touch her face. Her skin felt solid under his fingers. "You're here," he whispered. "How is that even possible?"

I can't stay long. You need help.

"I don't want to leave you," he said as the sobs finally surfaced.

Her eyes were glued to his. *Listen to me. I will never, ever leave you. Ever. You don't understand right now, but someone will help you understand. For now, I need you to hold on. You can't die, Dad.*

His eyes began rolling around like marbles. He believed

Mya. He didn't comprehend anything, but he believed her.

On all fours, he crawled toward the hallway as the dark hooded beings waited patiently.

You have to step back, Mya called out with authority. *He's not yours yet! He has to make his choice.*

A sinister voice echoed. He already has.

Henry collapsed on the ground, rolling onto his back. The light from the window was even brighter than usual.

Mya's face appeared over him. *Dad, listen to me. You have to do things differently. They told me everything about you. They told me about you and about Mom.* Suddenly, her face filled with deep sadness. *I am so sorry that you had to go through all of those things. I know they beat you and hurt you, and they hurt Mom. I know you tried to protect her. You tried to save her. You took her away from it.*

"How did you…" he trailed off.

I didn't know what you went through. I'm so sorry, Mya said as her tears fell onto his face.

"Don't cry, sweet girl," he slurred as he reached for her cheek.

It's not your time. You have to stay.

"Everything I've ever loved has been taken from me. I'm dying. I've made my choice," he whispered.

No! I won't let you do this to yourself! There's still time!

She stood and then disappeared.

Henry's life flashed before him as his eyes grew heavier. All of the wrongs that had been done to him and all that had been taken from him. All the losses he'd suffered.

In his mind's eye, he saw Candy leaving with Mya so long ago. He remembered seeing Mya again for the first time. All he wanted to do was take her into his arms and tell her how much he'd missed her.

The pain came flooding into his heart, and he sobbed uncontrollably. Even so, he had no desire to alter the course. He didn't want to suffer anymore. He was done with life.

Then one of the black hooded figures knelt beside him, looking down at him.

You're almost finished. All of the good you could have done, happiness you could have had. It's almost over. You're going to be ours soon. You've been given chance after chance, but you always waste it. Always. You're just like all of the others. You've sealed your fate.

"Happiness?" he asked.

Of course. You didn't think there was happiness out there for you, but there was. Your daughter is right. We can see things, too. You had more chances coming to make right all that was wrong, but here you are dying on your kitchen floor, waiting for us to take you.

"I don't understand."

Most of you don't until it's too late. Until you draw your last breath. It's then that you realize all the things you could have done. All the lives you could have touched or, in your case, all of the lives you have already touched. That's what makes the reaping so sweet for us.

Henry searched for a face, but darkness stared back at him.

You all are such foolish little creatures anyway. So prone to your selfishness and disbelief. It's only at the end that you see, the demon said with a laugh.

"I don't want to go with you. I want to be with my daughter," he said as the light dimmed a little.

Oh no. She's on the other side. You'll never see her again.

Henry's tears ran like rivers. All the years of injury and decay came flooding out with each cry. "I just don't want to hurt anymore," he whispered.

Poor Henry. You're going to experience the worst pain you've ever felt once we tear you apart. Then we'll put you back together. You'll roam the earth doing exactly what we do. You'll take souls that have lost their way. Souls who've been given chance after chance, and you'll devour them, just to spit them back out again.

Then he heard a voice echoing as if he were in a tunnel. "Henry!"

He felt the dark figure's hand clasp over his mouth. *Oh no, Henry. No, no, no. No words. You're ours.*

He began pounding his hand on the wooden floor. In an instant, Mya appeared again.

He's made his choice, devil. Now get away from him.

The demon stood, Mya looking small in comparison.

You think we're done here?

Validus appeared. *I know you're done here.*

Instantly, the demons disappeared, as did Mya and Validus.

"Henry," he heard again, followed by footfalls coming toward him.

Through his tears, he could hardly make out Jim's features.

"Hang on, buddy," he said. "Help is coming."

Henry grabbed Jim's arm with all the strength he could muster. "How did you know?"

"I just knew."

"Don't let me die," he whispered.

"Hang in there, Henry," Jim said.

In the distance, Henry heard the sirens, and as they grew closer, he realized the terror of death was much worse than the reality of living. He wasn't sure how he would overcome all that lay ahead of him, but he had to try.

34

Henry's eyes opened. His ears registered the sounds of hospital equipment. He felt the presence of someone else in the room.

Jim stood and walked to the bed. "How are you feeling?"

"Like someone shoved a red-hot poker down my throat," Henry replied.

"They had to pump your stomach," he added. "Narcan counter acted the heroin." Jim exhaled. "Henry, you have to get some help. You won't be able to get off the drugs by yourself."

"I don't want to go into inpatient. I need to work."

"I don't think O'Dell is going to give you a choice. I've been talking to her the entire time you've been out."

"How long *have* I been out?" Henry asked as he looked down at the IV in his hand and the track marks on his arms.

"Two days."

Henry sighed. "I'm not doing inpatient. I can't do my job if I'm locked up in some facility."

"I'll leave that for you to discuss with O'Dell."

Henry had more questions. The unresolved grimace on his face gave it away. "Jim, I have to ask you something," he began, "and I know you're going to think I'm crazy, but…"

"I already know where you're going with this. The answer's 'yes.' I believe in divine intervention. I believe in miracles, absolutely." Jim finished for him.

"How did you?"

"Henry, we've talked about this hundreds of times," he said as he pulled up a chair. "I have to believe that there is something more to this life than our everyday experiences. Otherwise, what kind of doctor would I be? I treat patients with cancer, most of them dying. I've watched patients pass on and I've watched as their souls leave them."

"But how do you see that?"

"I don't believe everyone can see it. You never have."

Henry thought about some of the patients who'd died under his care, and Jim was right. He'd never seen anything happen.

"You must be looking for it, Henry. I can't explain to you why I came back to your apartment. It was like my car drove back there on its own. I knew something terrible had happened. I felt a voice inside my head tell me to go back to check on you. I listened to that voice. I trusted it. If I hadn't listened, you'd be dead," Jim explained.

Henry told Jim everything that had happened. He talked about the beings in his kitchen and seeing Mya. He inspected Jim's reaction. Henry expected to see judgement in Jim's expression.

Jim smiled. "Have you ever thought that the reason why you have had to live through so much horror is because there is a massive purpose for your life? That there's some greater calling?"

"Not really."

"Maybe now that you've seen behind the curtain, you can start figuring out what you're supposed to do. You can be who you're supposed to be. Henry, you're a gifted scientist. You save lives. That's why O'Dell has kept you on despite all of the trouble you've caused."

Henry smiled halfheartedly. "How do I figure out who I am?"

"I don't know. I think that's something you'll have to do on your own. I had to do my own soul searching. It's never too late though. It sounds like Mya will always be a part of you. That should give you some direction and some security."

He sighed. "It does. I just," he hesitated for a heartbeat. "She was my little girl," he said as his voice trembled. "You know?"

"I do. You forget I have a son her age and I have daughters. I don't blame you for trying to end your life. I can't say that I wouldn't have done the same thing."

"I don't know if I *want* to know who I am, Jim. I don't like myself very much."

"You can change who you are, but you're going to have

to get help. You have to get clean," he advised.

The heavy wooden hospital door opened, and Michelle O'Dell walked in. She stood in a finely tailored navy-blue suit with matching heels, her dark hair resting on her shoulders.

"Do you ever wear jeans and a t-shirt?" Henry asked attempting humor.

She walked in and pursed her lips. "It's good to see you're feeling better."

"I'm alive," he shrugged.

"We need to talk about recovery, Henry. You can't come back until you're cleared through rehab," she announced.

"I'm not doing an inpatient program. I have to work," he protested. "I'm not doing it. You find someone who can help me, but I'm not staying locked up like an animal."

"Henry, you've been shooting up heroin and you can't be trusted to use your anxiety meds appropriately. You can't fight this alone," she said.

"There has to be something out there so that I don't have to be caged up."

"As your administrator, I have to demand you go into inpatient rehab. You stay upstairs in detox. You get counseling. You go to group meetings. If you are working a plan, I don't have to fire you. I don't *want* to fire you." She sighed. "Just get better, okay?" Then she hesitated.

"What?" he asked.

"You're going to have to undergo a psychological assessment also."

"I'm not crazy," he argued.

"No one is saying that you are, although this situation indicates otherwise. You tried to kill yourself. I can't let that slide."

His head fell back onto the pillow. "You're right. I will do whatever you need me to do. I just want to get back to work. I want to keep my job."

"Good," she nodded. She walked to him and put her hand on top of his. "It's going to be alright, Henry. I promise you."

35

Nearly a month passed, a month of early mornings, late nights, and learning when to listen instead of speak. June ushered in warmth. It had always been Olivia's favorite time of year. It wasn't scorching hot yet, but the chill of spring was over.

Olivia still waded through her new responsibilities as a detective. She was shadowing Danny closely, desperately trying to learn. Every day felt like a quiet test. She focused on absorbing procedure, watching how decisions were made, and reminding herself that patience mattered more than proving anything too quickly.

Olivia stood in the break room at the precinct, pouring coffee into her cup. She yawned and sighed. It wasn't like her to need caffeine so late in the day, but sleep was scarce in the Gregory household right now. Amelia was up and down during the night with an ear infection. Balancing work and motherhood felt heavier lately, but she refused to let either one slip.

"Hey girl," Sue said as she walked in.

Olivia turned her head. Smiling brightly, she replied, "Hi, Sue."

"Hey, if you're not doing anything tonight, I'd love for you and Amelia to come to my son's ballgame," Sue said warmly. "You've been pulling a lot of long days lately. It'd be good to get out for a bit."

"I appreciate the invitation. Amelia wasn't feeling very well last night, but if she's feeling better when I get home, I think a ballgame sounds great."

"No ballgame for us," Danny interrupted as he entered the break room.

"What do you mean?" Sue asked, folding her arms.

"Stakeout," he answered as he grabbed the pot of coffee and poured some into his thermos. "I owe Ben in Narcotics a favor. He and his wife are celebrating their anniversary, so I told him I'd do the stakeout for him."

Olivia nodded. "I'll have to call my sitter."

"I'm sorry, Olivia," Danny said with sincerity in his tone. "I'll always try to give you some notice, but Ben asked me pretty last minute."

"Oh no, I understand," she nodded. "Part of the job."

"We need Nigel on this one, too. That's what Ben said. If we get the drop on these creeps, we need him to do a sweep of the premises. See if there's any drugs hidden from view," Danny concluded as he left the room.

Sue shrugged. "Welcome to Major Crimes. Maybe next time, huh, sweets?"

"It sounds like a plan," Olivia said as she smiled.

Walking back to her office, Olivia set her coffee cup on

the desk and turned her attention to paperwork. She picked up her phone and sent a quick text to Sarah. As expected, Sarah was happy to help. She agreed to keep Amelia overnight. Relief settled in, brief but steady, and Olivia refocused on getting through the rest of the day.

At the end of the workday, Olivia wrapped up loose ends and changed into one of the two extra outfits she kept in her closet at work. She put on a pair of black cargo pants, black treaded boots, and a black polo. She swept her hair up and put her gun belt around her waist. The uniform grounded her, a reminder that preparation mattered more than comfort.

The case they were working on for Ben was one they had been involved with for a while. So, it made sense that they were point on the stakeout. She strategized as she thought about the details of the case, running through protocols and contingencies the way she had been taught.

Danny popped his head into Olivia's office. She was bent over, putting a file into her drawer. Instead of making himself known, he stood speechless. The first thing that hit him was not desire, but awareness. He shouldn't be thinking about her this way. He felt the blood pump faster through his body as he watched her. The reaction unsettled him immediately. She was beautiful, and he couldn't help but notice. Just as quickly, the consequences followed. Partners did not blur lines. Careers were ruined that way. Trust was broken. He shut the thought down.

Nigel's whines blew Danny's cover. Olivia turned her head, still bent over. He cleared his throat. "Um, you about ready? I figured we could go grab somethin' to eat first.

Could be a long night."

Standing up straight, she kicked the file drawer shut and turned. "Sounds good to me."

"Did you get your daughter squared away?" he asked with concern.

"Yes, I did. My sitter is a lifesaver."

"I'm really sorry I couldn't give you more notice," he said, scratching the back of his head. "I had no idea we were doin' this today. I thought we were going to wait until Ben could be there."

"It's okay. I understand," she replied with a shrug.

They locked glances and stared at one another for what seemed to be an eternity. Something unspoken hovered between them, quickly and deliberately ignored. "I uh... I... I'll meet ya in the garage. I can drive, but we need your SUV," Danny added.

She grabbed the keys from her pocket and tossed them to him. As he walked away, he settled down a little, but the awareness lingered. He did not like it. He knew romantic involvement with a partner could cause significant problems. The Chief would separate them. They wouldn't be allowed to work together. That was the last thing Danny wanted.

36

Danny and Olivia headed downtown. He pulled into a diner in Grandview. Olivia grabbed Nigel and led him into the restaurant following behind Danny. They found a seat, and Nigel lay on the floor under her chair, well behaved as always.

The waitress took their order and then disappeared behind the swinging metal doors. Olivia propped her elbows onto the table, a cup of coffee in her grip. She yawned.

"You're tired, Livy," Danny said.

"Livy? That's new."

"Yeah," he shrugged and smiled. "You look like a 'Livy' to me. If you don't like it, I won't—"

"Oh no. It's fine. Everyone usually calls me Olly."

"Na. You're a Livy."

She beamed as she let the hot cup warm her hands. The A/C blasted in the small establishment, so the heat from the ceramic mug was a welcome sensation. She then realized she hadn't responded to Danny's statement. She rectified that quickly. "And yes, I am tired. Amelia has an ear infection."

"Oh, now I really feel bad."

"Why?"

"You need to be home taking care of her. This job,

Olivia, it'll steal from you, even when you don't know it."

"She'll be fine. I know this case we've been helping Ben with is really important. We need to do it together." She sipped her coffee. "What did it steal from you, Danny?" she asked curiously.

"Oh wow. Where do I start?" he asked. "Well, I was a New York cop," he began.

"I knew you were from New York. I could tell by your accent and the tattoo," she said with a shy smile. "Why did you leave there?"

"I was nineteen and I thought I was freakin' invincible, ya know? I thought nothin' could get to me. I had been an officer for about a year. I went straight to the academy after high school.

"My folks lived in Brooklyn. My dad and mom struggled to make ends meet as it was. I knew they couldn't afford to send me to college. My sister Margie was the brilliant one. She got scholarships. Me? I was average," he said with a shrug. "I didn't want to go to the military, though. My mom would've lost her mind. So, I thought being a cop was more my style. Well, that didn't help her either, especially since I was a New York cop," he said as he pursed his lips.

Olivia nodded. "Moms worry. That's what we do. It's in the job description."

"You're right. I know you're right. Ma always says to me, 'No matter how old you are, you're still gonna be my baby.'"

After taking another sip of coffee, Olivia lowered the cup back onto the table. "So how'd you end up here?"

"9/11. That's what did it for me."

"Were you there? In the buildings?"

"No. I got called back on shift. I saw the entire thing happening from the street. My partner and I, uh, we stayed and helped with clean up. Our friends, our brothers and sisters in uniform," he stopped for a moment, obviously choked up.

"Danny, I'm sorry. You don't have to."

"No, no. I was in therapy for a pretty long time, so I've gotten pretty good at this," he said with a smile. Then he nodded and said, "We lost so many officers that day. The first responders, they were all gone. All of them were on site when the first tower came down, but everybody knows that, right? But they were family to us." His eyes brimmed with tears. "Things were never the same after that, not for me."

He paused, took a drink of water, and then continued. "I met Wallace and Rick at Ground Zero. We hit it off right away. When it was all over and Wallace was elected sheriff here, he called me up and offered me a job. I'd quit working already and was pretty much living off my folks again. I couldn't really function. Subways scared me. Loud sounds scared me. I was a mess."

"PTSD," she said softly.

"Yeah, that's what the shrink said. There are still some things that set me off, but for the most part I'm okay now. My parents moved here after that whole thing, too. They knew it would be too hard for me to come back to visit them, so they followed me here."

"That's great. What do your parents do that they could just pick up and leave?"

"They are businesspeople," he smiled. He leaned over as if to tell her a profound secret. She leaned in, too. "They own this diner."

Olivia grinned. "That's wonderful."

"Of course, they're not here right now. Pop usually leaves around three in the afternoon. Ma usually comes in for the breakfast rush, does the books, and then goes home. They're okay now. Got a good life for themselves, ya know? It was like a blessing in disguise, I guess."

"I've never met anyone who personally experienced 9/11."

He smiled. "Now ya have."

She sipped her coffee again.

"So what about you?" he asked curiously. "Why are you here? What made you wanna be a cop? You're smart. You could've been anything else."

Fear gripped her as she wondered how honest she should be. Very guarded about her past, she speculated he might look at her differently if he knew the entire truth. What scared her most was losing his respect. Clearing her throat, she put her cup on the table gently. "I, uh. I. God, I don't really talk about this..."

"I didn't mean to," he said as he sat back in his chair. "I don't wanna pry or anything."

"No," she said as she felt the fortitude fill her. "You're my partner, right? Partners share things. They trust each other."

Danny nodded with conviction. "That's right."

"Danny, I don't know how to say this."

"Just say it. Nothin' you could tell me would make me think less of you."

His statement settled on her, and she smiled. He was so incredibly sweet. So, with a deep breath in, she exhaled heavily. "I was a heroin addict." She looked up at him trying hard to read his expression. He didn't seem surprised, shocked, or disgusted. In fact, his eyes softened and filled with kindness.

"I want you to listen to me," he started as he leaned across the table, the seriousness in his eyes almost startling. "Salyers has a big mouth. He also doesn't know his ass from a hole in the ground, so we all take what he says with a grain of salt. If you don't wanna talk about this, you don't have to."

"I want you to hear this from me," she protested, "instead of rumors."

He nodded and thinly smiled.

Olivia confessed how she had run away to Cleveland right after high school. She explained that she ended up with the wrong crowd and that she did anything to score, including sex work. She talked about her pregnancy and how she didn't even know who Amelia's father was. Then she told him about her overdose and losing time with her daughter, but that becoming a K-9 handler put her back on track.

"Wow," he said, nodding knowingly. "You're a brave lady. Not many addicts can share a story like that." He glanced upward before meeting her eyes again. "Do you ever struggle, working in Narcotics? With cravings or anything?"

"No. I feel like I'm helping. It doesn't bother me."

"I want you to know that I appreciate this… you tellin' me. Salyers painted a very different picture."

Olivia sighed, a sad countenance coloring her face. "I hate that, but I can't say I'm surprised. He called me a drug addict whore before he was put on leave. I didn't think that would hurt me, because during that part of my life, that's exactly what I was, so in a sense, he was right. I'm ashamed of who I was, but I've learned to accept it and try to heal. What Salyers said did hurt me, though."

"Wallace has him on desk duty now. He's not out in the field anymore at all. Wallace cleared your name. You need to know that, too. He met with the detective division before you started. He made it pretty clear that you were a respected officer."

She smiled. Hearing that made her happier than she could even express.

"He thinks the world of you, Livy," Danny continued. "He wouldn't have promoted you if he didn't think you were worthy and capable of doing this job. Trust me."

Pausing to take a drink, he quickly continued. "And I don't see you any differently than I did five minutes ago. What you did... recovering, getting things back together for yourself and your daughter. That's rare. So, you don't have a thing to hang your head about. You understand me?"

She nodded agreeably. The relief swept over her threatening to make her emotional. Still, she held it together. She couldn't believe she'd met someone who could truly accept what she'd done. She carried doubt with her, thinking that no man would ever be able to understand her past. Now, here she sat with a man who had not only accepted her but praised her for her strength and determination.

37

Danny and Olivia sat in the car as darkness settled on the streets. The illumination from the streetlights became brighter as the sun completely set and the moon rose into the night sky.

Danny glanced over at Olivia, who appeared deep in thought. She was obviously studying the surroundings. He was pleased by this. She was learning to be mindful of the world around her.

"We're looking for Donte tonight, right?" she asked.

"Yep. When we see him, we get out and knock on the door. All we want to do is question him," Danny clarified. "Need him to invite us into the house. I couldn't get a warrant."

"Even with Wayne's confession?"

"Couldn't get anything from the prosecutor," Danny replied. "Donte is the loose end, and he's been avoiding us. I think he'll talk if we can just get to him."

They spotted Donte walking on the sidewalk and into the house, shutting the door behind him. Danny and Olivia got out of the SUV, calmly walking onto the porch. Danny knocked on the door.

"Donte Jacobs, Franklin County SO. We just wanna talk, man," Danny called.

Suddenly, they heard a back door slam.

"He's running," Olivia said. Instinctively, she leapt over the banister and hit the ground running. Behind her, she heard Nigel barking in the car and Danny on his radio calling for backup.

Going as fast as her feet would carry her, she had Donte in her line of sight, even though he was erratic, zigzagging toward the alley.

She called out, "Police, stop running!" She knew she was required to identify herself in the pursuit, so she called out three more times. She heard footfalls behind her. She knew it was Danny, but she was faster.

She turned a corner and unexpectedly felt a jolt to her throat. Disoriented, she realized she'd been clotheslined and now lay flat on the pavement. She struggled to collect herself, but Donte grabbed her and threw her onto her stomach. She felt his knee in her back and zip ties tighten around her wrists. He lifted her up and put a blade to her throat.

Amelia's face came to her mind first. Next were her parents and siblings. Then she wondered why on earth he had zip ties on him. Praying he didn't do something rash was her priority nonetheless.

Danny rounded the corner and stopped. A quick assessment of the situation caused him to pull his gun from his holster. He slowly stepped closer. "You don't wanna do this, Donte. We just wanna talk to you, that's all," Danny said.

"Ain't nothin' to talk about. I ain't going to jail," Donte bit out as he held tightly to Olivia.

"You're not going to jail. We just need to talk. Don't do something stupid," Danny said in a calm, even tone.

The knife pushed further into Olivia's neck, and she felt the warmth of blood falling down her chest.

"Listen to me, we just wanna talk to you, but you got my partner in a pretty bad position there. Why don't you let her go? We don't need this to be messy," Danny pleaded.

"If I talk to you, I'm a dead man," Donte retorted.

"We can protect you."

"You can't protect me!" he shouted.

"Don't do anything stupid, man."

The silence seemed to stop the hands of time as Olivia stood helplessly. The sound of Donte's voice shattered the quiet as he asked, "How much she mean to you, bro? You look nervous," the knife digging a little further into her skin.

"Listen to me," Danny continued. "I will shoot you. I will not hesitate. I can't let you kill my partner, Donte."

"I said, 'I ain't goin' to jail, and you can kill me, or they can kill me. Don't make much difference.'"

"We can work this out. But right now, you're holding an officer hostage. That's pretty serious."

"If you so sure we just gonna talk, then put your gun

200

down and we'll talk," Donte said.

"I can't do that," Danny said, shaking his head slightly.

"Whatchu gonna do 'bout this, Knight? Huh? It's my life or hers."

The twitch of Donte's hand on the knife's handle clearly indicated his intent. He was going to slit Olivia's throat and then be taken out by gunfire. Danny knew this was the plan too, and he took aim at Donte's shoulder. He didn't want to kill him. He just wanted Olivia safe. Still, he feared that shooting him would cause the knife to slip and Olivia would pay the price.

"We can calmly talk, Donte. I know you're afraid for your life and your family's life. This isn't what you want. Let us help you."

"They gonna kill my daughter, bro. If I talk, she's dead."

The sirens in the distance quickly closed in. The lights from the cruisers lit up the alley. Other officers suddenly arrived behind Danny. There were four behind Donte, and those officers were who Danny was counting on. Still, he gave them the signal to stand down for now.

"Donte, you know me. My word is good. We can protect you and your family. You just have to put the knife down and let my partner go."

"I was a heroin addict," Olivia said quietly. "It's not worth dying for, Donte. I'm not worth dying for. Trust us. We can help you get out of this."

Donte looked at Olivia, shocked by her confession.

"I was a prostitute. I did anything for a high. I lost my little girl for a while. I know what you're fighting. Don't fight it alone," she whispered. "Let us help you."

Tears streamed down his face. "This ain't the life I want."

"Then choose another path," Olivia said softly. "Choose something else."

Donte's grip loosened on the knife, and it fell to the ground. "I just wanna keep my little girl safe," he confessed. "They gonna kill my kid."

"Put your hands up, Donte," Danny demanded.

Instead, Donte fell to his knees, his hands raised high. The backup officers came up behind him and cuffed him.

Olivia stood still, frozen with shock, her eyes wide with fear. Danny put his gun back in his holster and rushed to her. Walking behind her, he pulled a knife from his boot and sliced the zip tie from her wrists. She put her hands to her throat, trying to assess the damage from the blade.

Danny stood in front of her, lifted his hands, and cupped her face in his palms. He studied her expression. It was easy to see she was terrified, but she'd kept her wits. "You okay? How bad is it?"

"Not too bad," she whispered, still holding tightly to her throat.

"Let me see, Livy," he said as he moved her hands away slowly. He examined the wound. "I need a medic," he shouted. Then he focused on her again. "It's not too bad. You'll probably need a few stitches."

Olivia felt stiff, but her brain worked perfectly. She knew her life was spared once again. She also knew that she owed Danny a life debt. "Thank you," she whispered, tears brimming in her eyes.

"You talked him down," he said. "You sure you're okay?"

She nodded, her lower lip quivering a little, the tears now streaming down her face. She hated feeling so vulnerable and victimized. It made her look weak again. The optics were bad. She looked like she couldn't handle the job. It made her angry.

"Come here," he said, pulling her into an embrace. She trembled in his arms. "It's goin' to be okay. I got ya."

As he held her shuddering body close to his, a connection formed instantaneously between them. Born of dramatic circumstances, Danny's protective nature swept over him, and he now knew nothing would be the same. The urge to protect her went beyond his duty. He knew he had to keep her safe at all costs. It felt like a spiritual calling. He knew in that moment, without a doubt, he'd die for her.

He couldn't explain it. He'd had partners before, female ones even, but somehow Olivia was different. He couldn't describe it and didn't even want to. It was just something he knew. Undoubtedly, the game changed.

38

Danny sat at Olivia's kitchen table, watching Amelia eat the chopped-up hot dog, applesauce, and green beans. In the couple of weeks that had passed since the near-death incident in the streets of downtown Columbus, things transformed. After work, they spent time together either at Olivia's house, Danny's apartment, or simply talking on the phone or texting. They already had a solid work-related partnership that easily opened the door for friendship, but until the night with Donte, neither of them dared to walk through it.

Olivia shared everything about her life with Danny. However, she didn't talk about her spiritual abilities. Still feeling very uncomfortable sharing that, she censored any spiritually related conversations.

As she stood at the sink washing the dinner dishes, she looked up at the clock on the wall. She had to be at the church by 6:30 for group. Sarah planned to come back to babysit Amelia.

"You want me to watch Amelia for you tonight?" Danny volunteered.

She turned around and smiled. "You don't have to do that."

"I don't mind. I'd save your friend from driving all the way back over here, and you've got to pay her, right?"

"Really, Danny, you don't need to stay here. Aren't you going to Sue's son's game?" she asked.

"I can stay here. Or better yet, I can take Amelia to the game with me. Nigel can come, too. I just need the car seat."

Olivia walked to the table and sat down, a dish towel still in her hand. "Danny, you don't owe me anything. You did your job. You know that, right?"

"Partners can be friends, too," Danny remarked.

"I'm fine with friendship, but you don't have to do this. I'm okay. I'm fine," she said convincingly. "Listen to me," she started as she put her hand flat on the table. "You don't have to be here all the time."

"So, I'm suffocating you?"

"No, no," she answered, shaking her head. "I'm just saying, you're a good-looking, young guy. I'm sure you have plenty of other places you could be besides here. I have really enjoyed your company, and I know Amelia has, but I don't want you to lock yourself in. Do you understand what I'm saying?"

He dropped his head. "I see what you're saying. You think you're cramping my style. You're not. If I had a date, I wouldn't be here. If my folks needed me at the diner, I'd be there."

"I'm a single mom. I work a full-time job. I'm a recovering drug addict. I have to balance and structure every single part of my life and Amelia's. I don't think you know

205

what you're getting into here, Danny."

He looked Olivia squarely in the eye. "I know exactly what I'm getting into here. I want to be friends with you. You deserve someone who'll take care of things."

"I don't want you to be my friend out of obligation or pity. If we're going to be friends, I want it to be because we have common interests." She paused and dropped her head a little. "I'm not good enough for you," she said sadly.

"Stop it," he said. "I'm proud to be your friend."

She smiled.

"Now, let me take your daughter to the ballgame while you go to group."

Olivia smiled, tears welling in her eyes. She nodded. "Okay."

39

Olivia sat in her car at the church. She was early, so to pass the time she played a game on her phone, but her thoughts drifted to Danny. His kindheartedness was something she wasn't used to. Even though he'd told her not to feel guilty, she did. She hoped he didn't expect anything romantic from her. She didn't even think she was capable of that anymore.

Then her thoughts led her to Mya and the murders. Nothing significant had been established in the medical report. She hadn't heard from Dr. Howard, and when she contacted the hospital, all they would say was that he was exercising a leave of absence. Olivia had also gone to his apartment to try to speak to him, but no one ever answered the door.

She looked down at her wristwatch and saw that it was nearing 6:30, which meant she needed to go into the church. Others were already getting out of their cars, heading inside. They filed into the foyer and then down a flight of stairs to a meeting room. Ellen, the group leader, stood at a table where coffee and tea were being served.

Olivia took her usual seat in the back row. She pulled her phone out of her purse to pick up where she left off with the game she'd been playing, but someone caught her eye. A tall man made his way in with six seats between them. Other than the fact that he was new to the group, she paid him no mind and returned her attention to her game.

In her peripheral vision, nonetheless, she noticed his gestures, and she felt the nervous tension in the air. Knowing how uncomfortable it was to be a first-time attendee, she turned her head to greet the stranger. She thought maybe she could break the ice or ease his anxiety with some light conversation. She was shocked to see that Dr. Howard was the newcomer.

Shock colored her expression, and her mouth gaped open. She quickly recovered. "Dr. Howard," she said.

He turned his face toward her. With a slight smile, he pointed at her. "Detective Gregory."

She nodded and stood, moving to him with only one chair separating them. With a smile, she said, "What are you doing here?"

"I could ask you the same thing. An upstanding officer like you here among the addicts of the underworld," he answered curtly.

She shrugged. "I guess we all have our vices."

He nodded. "What happened to your neck?" he asked, pointing to it.

She touched the bandage she still wore to cover the healing cut. "Occupational hazard," she answered.

He nodded.

"I've been trying to find you," she continued.

"I've been locked up in rehab. I tried to kill myself. I

swallowed a handful of pills, chased it with whiskey, and shot up a shitload of heroin," he said in a blasé tone, followed by a quick, thin grin. "As part of my probation at work, I now have to come to these meetings."

Olivia didn't quite know how to react to his admission of attempted suicide, although she understood it. Finally, she formed words. "Oh, the meetings aren't that bad. They do help."

He shifted in his seat, turned, and rested his arm on the vacant chair back. "Why in God's name are you here?" he asked curiously. "Are you doing undercover work?"

"No. I wish it was that honorable," she answered with a sigh. She pursed her lips and continued. "I was a pretty hardcore heroin user myself. Remember when you asked me if I'd ever been separated from my child?"

"Yes."

"I used while I was pregnant, and my dad and stepmom took my daughter while I got clean."

"Wow." Astonishment colored his expression. "I would have never guessed," he said, his voice trailing off.

She still smiled in spite of her brief confession.

He paused, silently looking at her, examining her closely. The attention felt less like admiration and more like assessment, and it unsettled her. Admiring the curve of her nose, he took note of her conspicuous innocence along with the shape of her mouth. He noticed the kindness in her eyes.

Her beauty hadn't escaped him despite the circumstances under which they met.

She wore a pair of white shorts with cuffs resting at mid-thigh. Her skin, tanned by the sun, looked youthfully supple. Her navy-blue V-neck cotton tee was conservative, and Olivia's perfectly pedicured feet sat comfortably in a pair of white flip-flops.

She felt his stares and turned to him, still beaming.

"Are you always this cheerful?" he asked sarcastically.

"Why be bummed about things? We're all here for the same reasons, aren't we? Life is too short to be sad all of the time." Then she realized how pompous that sounded, especially with the recent passing of his only daughter. She dropped her head in shame and covered her face with her hand. Composing herself again, she said, "I'm sorry. I didn't mean to sound so flippant."

He threw up his hand, offering reprieve, and grinned. "It's okay. I need a good lesson in positivity."

"I am truly sorry for your loss, Dr. Howard."

He looked away and gazed straight ahead at an imaginary focal point on the wall. Olivia saw the tears brimming in his eyes as he nodded, unable to make the words come out of his mouth.

Without hesitation, Olivia gently placed her hand on his as it rested on the back of the seat. "Everything will be okay," she murmured. "It just takes time."

He nodded, still unable to speak.

40

During the meeting, Henry and a few other newcomers introduced themselves. However, Olivia found herself distracted, observing Henry as if studying a rare bird.

Her gaze lingered on his face, drifting upward. She was still struck by how confidently he wore two days' worth of stubble and had to admit he was quite attractive. A slight smirk played on her lips as she considered his appearance.

The lines on his face were faint, and she couldn't quite see his eyes as he remained focused on the group leader. But she wanted to. She wondered what she might discover in them. Realizing she hadn't truly looked into his eyes when they first met, she fought the sudden urge to turn him toward her.

His attire was just as casual as the first time she had seen him—a black graphic T-shirt, dark-wash jeans, and white athletic sneakers. The faint scent of his aftershave reached her, warm and inviting.

Once the meeting ended, Olivia watched as Henry stood up. She did the same and then approached him.

"Dr. Howard," she began, following behind him, "I need to schedule a time to speak with you. We're still working to solve the crime involving your daughter."

Without breaking his stride, he responded, "I'll be back at work tomorrow at the hospital. You can meet me there.

I'm at your disposal, Detective." As he spoke, he turned slightly and gave a polite bow.

Then he turned back around, and Olivia watched as he crossed the parking lot to a motorcycle. He climbed on, slammed down on the starter, and sped off.

41

Olivia arrived home around 8 p.m. and noticed both Sarah's and Danny's cars in the driveway. Entering through the back door, she was greeted by the sound of laughter coming from the living room.

After saying hello to an excited Nigel, she hung her purse on a kitchen chair and headed toward the living area.

Sarah was seated in the rocker-recliner, while Danny lay flat on his back on the floor, lifting Amelia into the air as if she were flying. Her delighted giggles filled the room. "Hey," Olivia said, trying not to cause too much disturbance.

Sarah turned her face toward Olivia, a welcoming smile across her lips. "Hey there," she began. "I came by to give Amelia her bath. You texted me that Danny was taking her to a game, but I wanted to try to get her cleaned up before you got home."

Olivia cherished Sarah's protective instincts. She assumed that Sarah might be concerned about Danny's character since she hadn't met him.

"You didn't have to do that," Olivia said sweetly. "But I really appreciate it."

"It's no trouble at all," she replied with a dismissive gesture.

Amelia jumped from Danny's arms and ran to Olivia. "Mama," she said in a high-pitched voice. Olivia scooped her up and hugged her.

"Hey, monkey," Olivia said softly. "Did you have fun with Danny?"

Amelia nodded confidently and squirmed to be released. Her feet hit the floor, and she ran back to her spot on the floor. She stacked blocks and played with Nigel while Sarah stood to leave.

"I need to go," Sarah said. "Paul's going to wonder where I am." She walked to Olivia and kissed her cheek. "See ya tomorrow."

"Thanks again," Olivia said as Sarah walked to the kitchen and out the back door.

Danny made it to his feet and then stood with his hands on his hips. "Your daughter loved the game. She played with the other kids there. I think she really had fun."

"Thanks for taking her. Hopefully, I can go next time," Olivia said.

"I think there's another game Friday night if you wanna come."

"That sounds tempting," she said, then quickly changed the subject. "Hey, you'll never believe who I ran into at group." She walked to the sofa and sat down.

Danny walked to the couch as well and sat down on the opposite end. "Who?"

"Dr. Howard. He tried to kill himself after Mya died. He

was a heroin addict. I told you I was having a hard time finding him, right? That's why he's not been around. He's been in rehab. I told him I'd meet with him tomorrow to see if he can give us any new leads."

"You want me to come?" Danny asked.

"No. I got this."

"I can come if you need me to," he insisted.

"I'm sure I can handle it," she protested.

Danny rose to his feet and grinned. "Well, I'm going to head out."

Olivia stood politely. "Thanks so much for everything. I'm glad she had a good time at the game."

Amelia jumped up and ran to Olivia, who scooped her into her arms and balanced her on her hip.

Danny moved closer, but focused on Amelia. Gently putting the tip of his finger to her nose, he smiled. "See ya later, Amelia."

Her little hand went up, and she waved bye-bye, smiling sweetly.

"That's right. Bye-bye," he said as he waved back at her.

Beaming, Olivia felt a sense of peace when Danny was around. She felt safe. "I'll see you tomorrow," she said.

"Yep," Danny replied as he waved one last time and made his way through the kitchen and out the door.

After a shower and tucking Amelia in for the night, Olivia lay in bed, staring at the ceiling. Eventually, her eyes drifted shut.

She found herself standing in a cemetery, the air warm around her. A deep, overwhelming grief settled in her chest, her eyes filling with tears as hopelessness consumed her.

Then she felt the warmth of a hand in hers. Looking down, she tightened her grip before slowly raising her gaze, eager to see the face of the one offering her comfort.

Suddenly, she jolted awake, sitting up in bed with a gasp. The room was dark, the house silent. Her heart pounding, she wondered what it all meant.

42

Olivia sat in her office at her desk, drinking her morning cup of coffee. Nigel lay contentedly in his crate. She read over Mya's autopsy report once more, hoping to find something she might have missed. However, nothing jumped out at her.

She heard Sue approaching and looked up to see her standing in the doorway. "Missed you at the game last night," she said.

"I heard my daughter hit it off with the other kids."

Nodding happily, Sue answered, "She is so sweet."

Danny walked in next and sat on the couch. "Hey, what time are you going to see Dr. Howard today?"

"In just a little bit. Why?"

"I just wondered. Thought we could have lunch at the diner."

"I can't, Danny. I need to get over to the hospital. I'm not sure how long I'll be."

He nodded. "I can wait on you," he said. He paused for a heartbeat. "And you still don't want me to come?"

"I got it," Olivia said, raising her hand to stop him.

"Good grief, Danny, you act like you don't think she knows what she's doing," Sue interrupted.

He looked up at Sue, who peered down at him. "Will you lay off? I'm just making sure she's okay."

"Really, I'm fine," Olivia insisted.

"You know what I don't understand yet?" Danny said, in an effort to change the subject. "How our guy is targeting his victims. Granted, we've only got two bodies, but I wonder how he's choosing the girls. It's not like they look alike. They are also different ages. I just don't get it."

"I don't think we'll know more unless he kills again. To me, that's the saddest part. Someone else will have to die before we find more answers," Olivia concluded.

43

Olivia drove her SUV to the hospital and parked in the garage. She made her way to the elevator and into the lobby. She caught another elevator to Dr. Howard's department.

The doors opened, and she walked down the familiar hallway. Pushing through the glass doors, she could already hear Henry's voice. His tone sounded brash and irritated.

She entered his main office and turned to see what he was doing. He sat at the head of the table in the adjoining room. Around the table were several individuals. She assumed it was a departmental meeting.

Olivia stood and waited patiently. She didn't want to disturb the gathering, so she stood with her arms folded, watching the interaction.

As Howard talked, a woman at the table leaned forward and said, "Howard, there's someone here to see you." The woman nodded toward the main office.

Olivia waved awkwardly. He nodded her way. "Class dismissed," he concluded. "And please remember to go over the policy book. You'll need to familiarize yourself with the new processes."

Everyone sitting at the table stood and left through a second set of doors in the conference room. Henry made his way to his office, where Olivia waited. He opened the door and then walked to his desk, flopping down into his chair.

"I'm sorry," she began. "I didn't mean to interrupt, but…" She trailed off.

"You're not interrupting. I always have time to talk to beautiful, young women. It makes the other boys jealous," he said smartly. He took his glasses off and put them on the desk. Placing his elbows on the arms of his chair, he brought his hands to his face and rubbed his eyes.

"Not sleeping well?" she asked.

He dropped his hands and leaned back. "No. Not so much, Detective."

Olivia sat down on the edge of an empty chair in front of the desk. Attentively, she gazed at him. "It will get better. It's just going to take time. You're battling two major issues at once. You're grieving, and you're trying to stay clean. You should really lean on your sponsor."

"I'm going to let you in on a little secret about me, Detective," he began with a sarcastic tone. "I'm not really all that great at leaning on anyone. I never have been. I've never had that choice. When I can't sleep, I play the piano or my guitar. That's how I cope now without the drugs. That doesn't make the neighbors very happy," he snickered.

"I understand that you feel like you need to do this alone, but with both of these stressors, you need to be able to seek help through your sponsor. That's why we have them."

He leaned back, clasping his hands behind his head and propping his feet up on the desk, smoothly changing the subject. "So, how can I help you, Detective?"

"Well, I was hoping you could help me get to know Mya. Tell me a little about her habits and her friends. Things she enjoyed and things she didn't. How she did in school," she replied.

"As far as her daily habits, I'm not the one you should really be talking to. Her mother would be able to answer that. Candy would also be able to tell you about Mya's friends. As far as what she enjoyed, she liked her phone. She liked reading, too. Things she didn't like? Well, that'd be me. I'm pretty sure that she resented me for not being there during the majority of her childhood. She never told me that, but I could hear it in her voice when she talked to me. I know she put the blame on me."

"I'm sorry," Olivia said, dropping her gaze. "I hate bringing all of this to the surface."

"It's way above the surface, Detective. All I did in rehab was talk about this shit. I feel like I'm pretty well rehearsed by now."

Olivia sighed, her heart feeling heavy for him. "And school? How did she do in school?" she said, looking up at him again.

His eyebrows raised, and his face filled with pride. "She did really well in school. That part was my responsibility. Her mother left the conferences and stuff up to me. She always said that because I was a doctor, Mya's teachers would automatically respect me. She was right about that. All of her teachers were polite and seemed to like Mya, but she earned it. She was very smart. Brilliant, even."

"Did she mention any problems at school?" Olivia continued. "Bullying? That sort of thing? Perhaps drug problems of her own?"

Henry shook his head. "No. She kept to herself. She did her work, turned it in, got her grades, and that was it. Like I said, she spent a lot of her free time on her phone. She wasn't using drugs either. I would have seen the signs."

Olivia looked up and met Henry's gaze. His eyes were a stunning crystal blue, the most beautiful she had ever seen. Then a memory struck her. The dream. Those were the same eyes she had seen in her dream.

She stood suddenly. Turning away from him, she tried to gain her composure. Her head flooded with questions about her own life and her own destiny. However, for the moment, she needed to focus. She turned back and continued standing. "What's your background, Dr. Howard? Your parents? Your associations?"

"I didn't have a very kind upbringing, Detective. Probably very unlike yours. I was in the foster care system. I was emancipated. I married Mya's mom, and that was that. We were two kids, bound by circumstances out of our control and totally on our own. As far as current friends, I have Jim. He is my closest friend. We are more like brothers."

"Do you associate with any of the foster children from your past?"

"Well, I contacted Miller when I found out about the death of his daughter. I wanted him to know that if he needed anything, to let me know. When he found out about Mya, he came to see me in rehab.

"There's also Kyle. He emails every now and again, but we don't talk on a regular basis. He was always sort of an odd bird, but who could blame any of us that lived in that foster home for being a little insane?"

"What foster home?"

"We lived in a pretty harsh environment." He shifted in his seat, the discomfort almost tangible in the room now. He shook his head. "I'm sorry, but I can't talk about it. If I thought it might help in Mya's case, I would spill my guts, but I just don't see how dredging up my past is going to help find answers."

He stood and walked to Olivia. Their eyes locked again. She just couldn't shake the dream from her mind.

"You don't want to know about my past, Detective," he said softly, looking down at her. "It's very ugly, and I have tried my damnedest to shield my little girl from it. But she was taken from me twice. I know that I am who I am today because of the lack of mercy that was shown to me growing up."

The emotional pain coming from Henry was overwhelming. Being an empath certainly had its drawbacks. "I am so sorry, Dr. Howard."

"And it's Henry," he said, his face softening.

With a nod, she pursed her lips. "Olivia, not Detective."

He smiled.

"I do want to understand your past, Henry," she continued. "Perhaps there is something there that could help, but I understand that it's painful and you're not ready. When you are, please reach out to me. I want to bring your daughter's killer to justice, and I will take any information that might help."

He nodded. "I am still trying to talk about my childhood in therapy. I really don't see how any of it could help, but I trust your instincts. So, when I'm able to, I will tell you about it."

Her feet felt immobilized as she and Henry stared at each other. "You have interesting eyes, Henry, but so much sorrow in them," she observed, almost whispering.

The door opened, startling both of them. Jim walked in. "Are you ready to go to lunch?" he asked.

Olivia turned and faced him. She must have seemed startled.

"I'm sorry. I didn't know you were with someone, Henry," Jim apologized.

"Oh no, I was just leaving," she said.

"I'm Jim Lindley," he said, with his hand outstretched.

Henry spoke up. "This is Detective Olivia Gregory. She's here about Mya."

They shook hands genially.

"I can come back when…" Jim started.

"No, it's fine. We've covered enough today," Olivia said. She broke away from Jim and turned back to Henry. "We'll talk soon. I'm sure I'll have more questions as we get deeper into the investigation."

"My door is always open. I will help however I can," Henry assured her.

She nodded and shook his hand, her gaze drawn once more to his beautiful eyes. Her heart ached at the pain and regret reflected in them. Yet beneath the deep ocean of sorrow, she glimpsed hints of light, maybe even hope. With a calm smile, she released his hand and walked away.

****

Henry waited until he heard the elevator doors open and close. Jim shot him a wary glance.

"What?" Henry asked.

"She," Jim began, pausing slightly, "is stunning."

"I can't disagree with you there," Henry said as he walked toward the door.

"How old do you think she is?"

"I don't even want to think about it," Henry concluded as he made his way past Jim and into the hallway.

44

Olivia made it back to the station in time to have lunch with Danny. They drove into the city and pulled into the back lot of his parents' diner. They got out, Olivia following him through the back door. They walked into the hustle and bustle of the kitchen.

Danny spotted his father at the grill. "Hey, Pop!" he called.

The man turned, revealing a tall, broad-shouldered frame. Deep lines etched into his face spoke of years of hard work and worry. His graying hair was receding, and a full beard framed his square jaw. But what stood out most were his eyes. They were the same color as Danny's.

He waved kindly. "Danny! Whatcha doin' here? I thought you were workin'," he called in a very thick New York accent.

"I am, but it's lunchtime. I wanted you to meet my partner," he answered.

The man cleaned his hands with a towel and walked to them with a hand outstretched. "Olivia Gregory, this is my dad, Cecil Knight," Danny said.

They shook hands. "A pleasure to meet you, sir," Olivia said respectfully.

"Oh no, the pleasure's mine," he said. "Danny can't stop talkin' about you."

"Where's Ma?" Danny asked.

"She's back in the office," he answered.

Danny rested his hand on the small of Olivia's back, guiding her toward a nearby room. As they approached, the rhythmic clicking of an adding machine caught her attention.

"Ma," Danny said as he walked into the office, leaned down, and kissed her cheek.

"Danny. What are you doing here? Aren't you working today?" she said, her Irish accent unmistakable.

"I'm workin'. I wanted to bring Livy by to meet you."

Olivia stepped into the office as the woman got up from behind the desk. She was short, with reddish-brown hair cut into a bob. Her complexion was fair, and her eyes were a rare greenish blue.

Olivia held out her hand.

"Ma, this is Olivia Gregory, my partner. Olivia, this is Sharon Knight," he said.

"Very nice to meet you," Olivia remarked.

"Likewise," Sharon replied. "Hey, are ya stayin' for lunch, dear? Cecil just made a meatloaf. It's going to go pretty fast, I would expect."

Danny nodded. "We're pretty hungry. Is it okay if we eat in the break room?"

"Yes, yes. I will get Sylvie to bring your food to you."

Olivia waved as they walked out of the office and into another part of the diner.

They sat down at a large table and waited. "So how'd it go with the doctor?" Danny asked curiously.

"It was fine. I can't seem to make any headway, though. He told me a little about his childhood and a little about Mya. From what I'm gathering, Dr. Howard had a terrible time growing up. He wouldn't reveal a lot. To be honest, he didn't offer much help."

"He's hiding something."

"I don't think so," she disagreed. "I think he is just so traumatized by whatever happened to him that he can't talk about it."

"You think he's still using? He could have connections that cost his daughter her life?"

"I thought of that, but what would that have to do with the first victim?"

"I guess you're right," Danny concluded.

As they sat eating the delicious meatloaf, their phones sprang to life. Olivia looked down to see Dispatch's number. She looked up at Danny, who said, "Sue." He held up his phone to show her his LCD screen.

Olivia's heart sank. She knew someone else was dead.

45

Olivia and Danny arrived at an abandoned building just off Interstate 270. As they stood in front of the structure, they both glanced at each other. The building was partially burned, and smoke still rolled from the brick. It was obviously arson.

Danny folded his arms. He spotted the fire marshal in the midst of the chaos and waved. "What the hell are we doing here, Brad?" Danny bellowed. "This is obviously arson."

"There's a body inside," Brad replied. "I've already called Bentley. The person didn't die because of the fire. This is a body dump. She wasn't even burned. Come take a look at this," he said as he led them through the rubble.

They walked through the still steaming bricks and metal. The portion of the building they were led to wasn't damaged.

Olivia looked up. A girl with a slip noose around her neck hung from a steel rafter. She was sooty but not burned. Completely naked, the girl's eyes were wide open. Olivia estimated her to be around seventeen or eighteen years old.

"Another victim," Danny said quietly.

Olivia glanced around but didn't see the spirit of the girl anywhere. She hoped that she would be close by.

She walked closer to the body. A tic tac toe board was

tattooed on her inner thigh. An X appeared in the right corner, and an O appeared in the bottom left corner.

"Look," Olivia said as she pointed to it.

"That's it. I'm calling Dr. Harris. This can't wait," Danny insisted as he briskly walked out of the building.

Olivia stayed behind for a few minutes. She looked on the floor for any evidence left behind. She hoped there might be ladder impressions or even boot prints. Then she continued scanning the scene. She still didn't understand why the girl's spirit hadn't come forward. It troubled her.

She was startled when she heard the voice of the deputy. "Forensics is on their way. I need to tie off the scene, Detective."

"Of course," she said with a nod. She walked back outside, where she heard Danny talking on the phone. His voice was firm, with an assertive hint in his tone.

"I think it's going to get worse, absolutely. We can meet you at the station. Yes. We will both be there, and then we'll bring you back to the scene. Yes, bring him along. We need as many eyes on this as possible. Thanks a lot. Bye."

Danny hung up. "That was Lauren Harris-Bennette. She and Nick are coming."

"Her husband? I thought he worked for the FBI. This isn't federal yet, is it?" Olivia remarked.

"Nope, but his expertise in violent crime will be helpful. He worked on the Phantom case with her and countless others."

"So what do we do now?" she asked.

"We wait. Forensics can go ahead and process the scene. They can mark and gather any physical evidence, but Harris doesn't typically want the body moved if she's been called out," he explained.

Olivia nodded and then walked back inside. She continued scanning the area for the spirit of the girl, but she didn't see her. Impatiently, she exited the building again and carefully scanned the crowd that had gathered in the street. An uneasy feeling swept over her. Her level of concentration didn't go unnoticed.

"You seem edgy. What's wrong?" Danny asked.

"Oh no, I'm fine," Olivia replied. "You taught me to be mindful of my surroundings, right? We've got a crowd of people gathering over there, and I wonder if our murderer is among them. Some killers like to stay at the scene. They take pride in their handiwork and all the excitement they've caused," she explained.

Danny pursed his lips and then put his hands in his pockets. "If you ever think you're not cut out for this, think again. You have instincts, Livy. What you just said, that's something profilers say."

"To be honest," she started as she leaned against the SUV, "I would love to be a profiler. I just can't afford to go back to school right now."

"What would you need to do to become one? What would you need to study?"

"Any psychology degree would suffice, but typically it's forensic psychology that most employers want to see. Since I'm already a cop, I don't think I'd have to have a double major in criminology, but it certainly wouldn't hurt."

"Sounds to me like you need to go for it. You figure stuff out pretty quick."

"I just can't," she said, shaking her head. "Not with Amelia being so small. I don't have time to go back right now."

"Someday you'll have time," he said encouragingly.

Their eyes met as his smile intensified. She felt her cheeks warm with confidence as she filled with pride. Then she looked down into the back of the vehicle. Nigel lay quietly, panting.

"I don't think I could leave him either," she said, nodding at the dog.

"You wouldn't have to. If you went back to school, you could retire Nigel. No big deal. He actually gets a little bit of a payout, too."

"The timing just isn't right." Olivia paused for a moment and dropped her head. "I also wonder if I'm actually smart enough to go back to school," she said with a shrug.

Danny's gaze deepened as he, too, leaned against the car. "Let me tell ya somethin'. You're plenty smart." He took a deep breath and exhaled. He shook his head disapprovingly. "You always do that. You need to stop it."

"Stop what?" she asked, looking back up at him.

"You always sell yourself short. You're clever. You never have to take notes. You always remember everything."

She grinned. "Someday, I'll figure out what I want to be when I grow up," she laughed.

46

Danny and Olivia went back to the station and started on the mountain of paperwork. By 3:00 p.m., they were still waiting on Dr. Harris-Bennette. Olivia sat in Danny's office with her laptop, typing in the report information as he helped her through some of the dictation. Because they hadn't yet toured the scene intensively, it was hard to be precise.

Sue knocked on the door frame. "She's here," she said.

Both Olivia and Danny stood and made their way to the reception area. Olivia was very excited to meet Dr. Harris and her husband. She had read Dr. Harris-Bennette's autobiography about the Phantom serial murders. She had also read her case studies and all of her fictional novels.

The Phantom had terrorized college campuses. He had captured his victims, set them loose in the woods, and then retrieved them. He had buried his victims alive. In the book, Dr. Harris-Bennette recounted her own experience as a victim. She had given all of the credit to her husband, Nick, her team, and the K-9s that had been dispatched to the scene.

Olivia and Danny stepped into the lobby, where Wallace stood chatting with Lauren and Nick. Lauren's pregnancy was unmistakable, her belly rounding beneath a black maternity shirt paired with jeans and sturdy, treaded boots. Her hair was much shorter than the photo on the back of her novel, now styled into a sleek wedged bob. Ash-brown highlights framed her fair complexion, and as she tucked her hair behind her ears, her striking blue eyes became even more prominent.

Nick, dressed in dark jeans and a gray graphic tee, also wore boots. His dark hair, similar in length to Danny's, was styled into sharp spikes, giving him a polished, put-together look.

"Ah, there they are," Wallace began as he motioned for Danny and Olivia to hurry up. "Dr. Lauren, Nick, this is Daniel Knight and Olivia Gregory, the two detectives working the case. Sue has been providing support."

Olivia held out her hand as Lauren shook it. "Pleasure to meet you. I love your work."

With a confident nod, she said, "Thank you. Please, call me Lauren."

"Or Doc, if you want to get under her skin," Nick interjected as he smirked at her.

Lauren flashed a grin his way.

"And Agent Bennette," Olivia continued as she shook his hand.

"It's just Nick," he instructed with a smile.

"And you know me," Danny said as he smiled.

"Yeah, Danny, it's always good to see you," Nick said, shaking his hand.

"Lauren," Danny nodded.

"Daniel," she nodded back. "Always happy to help,"

Lauren said. "So, how soon can we leave for the third crime scene?"

"We can leave right now if you want," he answered.

Olivia interjected. "Let me put Nigel in the kennels downstairs."

"You are a K-9 handler?" Lauren asked.

"Yes. I am."

"You have my deepest respect. I commend you, Detective Gregory. As you know from reading my work, I admire K-9 work. I think that dogs are angelic. Can I meet your dog?"

"Absolutely. I'll go get him. I'll be right back," she said as she walked to the elevator.

Danny stayed behind and explained the latest scene. He waited for Lauren's opinion.

"I have read all of the information you've sent me," she started. "I have already been to the two other scenes. That is why we're so tardy. I wanted to stop at each of them. I wasn't expecting we'd be going to an inner-city building for this one, I must admit. It just goes to show you... Well, perhaps we should just go to the scene before I say much more."

"She doesn't like to give her opinion until she knows she'll be right," Nick snickered.

"I'm just saying that I need to see everything first."

"Joking, Doc. I'm joking again," Nick clarified.

"Oh. Well, ha-ha," she replied plainly.

Olivia walked down the hallway with Nigel on his lead. Lauren spotted the two of them immediately and walked toward them. She knelt out of respect and held out her hand.

"May I?" Lauren asked, looking up at Olivia.

"Yes," she answered. "Nigel, sitz," Olivia commanded. Nigel sat, and then Olivia said, "Nigel, platz." He lowered his body down obediently.

Lauren gave him several pats and then looked deeply into Nigel's eyes. It amazed Olivia that he was connecting with Lauren. Her energy felt peaceful, and Nigel obviously recognized that, too.

47

After dropping Nigel off at the kennels, Olivia met everyone in the parking garage beside Nick's black Suburban. They drove to the crime scene where Bentley waited. Forensics was still processing the scene. Although the building was still smoldering a little, the fire marshal had cleared the structure.

Olivia and Lauren walked into the building first, followed closely by Danny. Nick stayed outside and spoke to members of the forensic team.

Finally, Olivia saw the spirit of the girl. The poor thing was crouched in the corner, cowering in fear. She wore a pair of blue pants, sneakers, a matching monogrammed blue polo shirt, and a ball cap.

Olivia scanned the area for Emma. She wasn't there. This was very odd.

Olivia locked eyes with the young girl. *I'm here to help you, but there are some things I have to do first. Don't be afraid.*

Lauren's expression changed. She quickly turned her head and looked at Olivia, puzzled and amazed.

Where am I? What happened to me? the girl asked.

Olivia communicated again, but this time the message was jumbled with another voice.

I can't hear both of you, the girl said.

Olivia turned to Lauren. She too stared at the corner where the girl stood. Their mouths dropped open as the realization became clear to them.

She briskly walked to Lauren. "You can see her," Olivia said quietly.

Lauren's eyes turned to her in disbelief. "I can, yes. Can you?"

"Yes. I can hear your voice when you talk to her, too," Olivia explained.

"This is amazing," Lauren whispered. "We'll talk later. Gather your information from the scene. Let me handle the girl."

"But I have to cross her over," Olivia said.

"Not yet. I need to understand what happened here. I will tell Nick to keep the others distracted."

Olivia walked to the body hanging from the rafter, then turned her attention back to Lauren. She watched Lauren speak to Nick before walking toward the corner. Olivia heard Lauren's voice, but her mouth didn't move.

What's your name? Lauren asked.

The girl answered sheepishly, *Kristen. Where am I?*

Lauren walked to the adjoining wall and stood still. She appeared to be in deep concentration, her hand pressed against the wall to steady herself.

Olivia pulled herself away from the intriguing situation and focused on Bentley and the forensic team.

"What do we have?" she asked.

"Preliminarily," Bentley said, "she looks to be in her late teens. Jerome is already running facial recognition. The tattoo on her inner thigh tells me we've got our third victim."

She jolted at the sound of Danny's voice near her ear.

"What do you see, Livy?"

He stood so close that his body nearly pressed against her back as he spoke again, his voice low. "Tell me what you see."

His proximity threw her off balance for a moment, but she steadied herself. "I see our third victim, just like Bentley said. Same killer."

"What else?"

"This is a body plant. The primary crime scene is someplace else. That's been consistent across the victim pool."

"Good." He paused. "I'm gonna talk to Jerome and see if there was a missing person's report."

Olivia nodded.

Nick walked toward her as she stood watching the body being taken down. "You and Lauren have a lot in common," he said softly, his arms folded.

Olivia wasn't sure what to say.

She saw Lauren motion to her and walked over. The girl was still standing in the corner. Lauren faced Olivia. "Her name is Kristen Swaggart. She's seventeen and was taken from her job four nights ago."

"She told you that?" Olivia asked.

"She walked me through the crime. Well, at least what she can remember. I can see pieces of what happened," Lauren said. "I think your ability allows you to see what's left after it's all over."

Olivia looked past Lauren and met the victim's gaze. "Kristen, have you been to the In-Between?" she asked quietly.

I have been there for a while. With a little girl.

"What's the In-Between?" Lauren asked.

"It's the place where people go when they die. It happens before they move into the light," Olivia explained. She turned her focus back to Kristen. "You have to go back there. The little girl you met will help you find your way through the light. Have you shared everything you need to with Lauren?"

Yes. I really want to go home, Kristen pleaded. *My parents. My sisters.*

Olivia's heart hurt for her. "You can't go home right

now. You have to cross on, sweetie."

Kristen's eyes filled with tears. *But why can't I just go home?*

Emma appeared.

"Who is that?" Lauren asked.

"She's a guide," Olivia said, then turned her attention to Emma. "Help her. I'll talk to Lauren and find out what I can. Kristen, you're allowed to come back and talk to me when you're ready. You can see your family anytime you wish once you've crossed over. They may not be able to see or hear you, but they'll sense your presence sometimes."

One of my sisters is a medium. That's what she's always said. That's why I want to go to her.

"You can," Olivia said softly, "but only after you cross over. Don't be afraid."

Emma and Kristen disappeared in a mist.

"We need to talk privately at some point," Lauren said as her cool blue eyes met Olivia's.

"Agreed," Olivia replied.

Danny interrupted. "Kristen Swaggart was reported missing four nights ago. She worked at a local fast-food place and didn't come home from work. Her parents, Terry and Shanda, reported it. We'll talk to the parents once they've identified her." He looked at Lauren. "Ready to give us a profile?"

"I think we should speak with the parents first," Lauren said. "I have a feeling they'll offer information that may be helpful."

"But the body…" Danny began.

"We've already positively identified Kristen based on facial recognition, correct?"

Danny nodded.

"Then we can speak with the parents and have them identify the body afterward," Lauren said firmly.

47

Lauren and Olivia drove across town to the home of Terry and Shanda Swaggart while Nick and Danny stayed behind at the crime scene. When they approached the door and knocked, it was answered by a young woman strikingly similar in appearance to Kristen.

"Can I help you?" she asked.

"I'm Detective Gregory with the Franklin County Sheriff. This is Dr. Lauren Harris-Bennette. She is a consultant from the FBI. Is Terry or Shanda here?"

"Oh my God, you found Kristen?" the girl blurted out. "And she's dead. I can feel it."

"Please, we need to speak to your parents."

"They're here. Come in, please," she said, stepping aside.

Olivia and Lauren stood in the large foyer. The young woman led them to a living area and invited them to have a seat. She left the room and returned with a petite woman and a tall man. The young lady who answered the door introduced herself as Kristen's older sister, Michelle, and then introduced her parents.

Once everyone was seated, Olivia began. "Mr. and Mrs. Swaggart, we were called to a crime scene today. A warehouse was set on fire. We believe we found your daughter's body inside that structure. We need you to identify her."

The reaction was typical. Both parents broke down into tears, sobbing and wailing in each other's arms. Michelle stood and walked out of the room crying.

"We are so sorry for your loss," Lauren said quietly.

"The medical examiner must assess her, and then she can be released," Olivia interjected. "You'll have to come downtown. I know this is a very difficult time, but a crime has been committed, and we think that Kristen is the third victim in a very serious serial murder case."

Kristen's parents seemed flabbergasted.

"What?" Terry asked.

"We believe she was targeted for some reason," Olivia continued. "Do you know of anyone who would want to harm her? Was she having problems at school? At work?"

"No," Terry replied. "She had the regular petty problems of high school, but nothing that we felt alarmed by."

"She had friends, but she was selective," Shanda interjected. "She attended Columbus City Schools. We couldn't afford to send her to a private school. She was a very good judge of character, though."

"What about a boyfriend? Anyone that she'd been talking about lately?" Lauren asked.

They both shook their heads.

"No. She's been seeing Ashley. That's her boyfriend," Shanda said. "They've been dating for about six months now, but we know him and his parents. We all attend the same church. Ashley is a very respectable young man."

"Same age? Older? Younger?" Lauren asked.

"He is nineteen," Shanda replied. "He's a freshman at Indiana University. He seemed to sincerely care about Kristen."

Terry sighed. "He's in college full time. We'll have to call him."

"What about either of you?" Lauren asked. "Has anyone threatened you in any way? Any money issues? Marital discord?"

Terry spoke up first. "I'm an accountant for the cable company. I have a very boring job. No one would want to hurt me. I get along with all of my coworkers."

"I'm a nurse for Riverside," Shanda said. "We live very normal, low-profile lives."

"What are your backgrounds?" Olivia persisted. "Do you have extended family that you associate with that might be able to shed some light on this?"

Shanda's features changed. A hardness appeared that wasn't there before. Still, she remained quiet. Both Olivia and Lauren noticed the energy shift.

"I'm from a Catholic family," Terry continued. "There are nine of us altogether. We are all pretty close. We all have good jobs. Some have stayed around here while others have moved away. My parents are elderly. My siblings lead uneventful lives."

"And you, Mrs. Swaggart?" Olivia asked.

"I grew up in foster care," Shanda admitted.

"Can you tell us about that?" Lauren asked.

"I was in three foster homes growing up. The last one worked out, and they adopted me. The two before that were terrible. I was sexually abused in the first one, which is why I was moved to the second placement. The second set of foster parents just didn't want me. Then I was put with Tyron and Mindy Wetzell. They were older and had been doing foster care for a long time. They took me right in. That's how I met Terry. They were Catholic. Our families attended the same church."

"Do you stay in contact with any of the previous foster parents or any of your foster siblings?" Lauren asked.

"No," she answered. "The first couple died in a car accident a few years back. The foster brother who raped me did some time, but I lost track of what happened to him. My other foster brothers and sisters sort of fell off the grid. The second couple I stayed with moved out west somewhere. What does this have to do with anything?"

"Maybe nothing," Olivia explained. "But we just want to make sure we cover all of the bases. We want to bring your daughter's killer to justice. Any information we can gather to help us with that, we'll take it."

"Had Kristen said anything to you about being followed?" Lauren asked. "Noticing anyone coming into her job or bothering her?"

Terry and Shanda looked at one another blankly.

"No," Shanda answered.

Lauren and Olivia stood. They had reached yet another dead end.

Michelle walked back into the room.

"Well, thank you so much for talking to us," Lauren said. "Again, we are so very sorry."

"If you think of anything else," Olivia said as she took a card from her back pocket and handed it to Shanda, "please call me."

Michelle walked them to the foyer. "Kristen was a good person," she said. "She'll come to me when she is ready."

"You're the medium?" Lauren asked.

"Yes. My parents don't know it, though. The church doesn't exactly agree with my abilities, and Mom and Dad are devout."

"I know this is a strange request," Olivia said, "but if you happen to hear from Kristen, will you give us a call?"

"You're believers?"

They both nodded.

"I will contact you both, of course," Michelle said.

"Thank you," Lauren replied.

They walked off the porch and made their way to the car.

"We have a pattern emerging here," Lauren said.

"I see it, too."

Lauren lifted the car door handle. "You're going to need to gather your major crimes and street patrolmen. I will give the profile at eight a.m. tomorrow."

"I'll radio Danny and let him know."

"Are you hungry?" Lauren asked.

"Yes, but I really need to get home. My daughter—" Olivia started.

"Why don't we swing by the station, grab your car, leave the Suburban, and then go to your house and order a pizza? My treat. We have a lot to discuss. I'll have Nick pick me up later."

Nodding and smiling, Olivia replied, "Sounds good. I will call Steve and ask him to keep Nigel in the kennel overnight."

48

Once Olivia and Lauren devoured the pizza, they played with Amelia for a little while. At 7 p.m., it was Amelia's bath time, so Olivia excused herself to perform her motherly duties. By 8:15 p.m., Amelia was tucked into her crib for the night.

Olivia returned to the living room where Lauren stood admiring the pictures sitting on the mantel. She held one in her hand. "Your family means everything to you," she said.

With a nod, she replied, "Yes. I owe them more than I could ever repay." She sat down on the couch, observing Lauren as she placed the framed photograph back on the mantel.

Lauren took a seat in the rocker-recliner. "As you've figured out by now," she started, "I have a very specific gift. I can see the victims after they die. They show me things, but only in pieces. It's my job to put those pieces together. I have to try and put what they show me out of my mind to formulate a profile, though. That isn't easy. I rely on my education and training to compile the characteristics of the type of killer or offender police should be looking for. Nick is the only living person that knows about my abilities. My grandmother knew, but she passed last winter. My mother and father knew, but they died when I was quite young."

"Go on," Olivia said with a nod.

"My job as a profiler and as an empath is to seek out

clues. I want to offer peace to the victims. But as I'm sure you know, being an empath is draining."

"It is absolutely draining," she agreed.

"The gift you have is obviously very different than mine, but yet quite similar. I am fairly certain, however, that your gift limits you in that you cannot see the crimes or even pieces of the crime. Your purpose is to get the souls safely to the other side. Given the differences, we complement one another, Olivia. I believe we can work together to solve this case."

With a sigh, Olivia looked down at her hands. "I never thought I'd meet anyone who could do what I do. Someone who could see the dead and talk to them. I had a ghost hunting team growing up, but it was pretty superficial. I grew up in a home with spirits. That was my first experience with doing what I do."

"I've been able to do this since I was a child, too," Lauren added. "Most often, we are born with these gifts."

"Will you stay and help us?" Olivia asked with a hint of desperation in her voice.

"I will stay to give the profile, and I will help as much as I can from afar, but I have to go back home tomorrow. I'm due anytime. My doctor tends to get quite angry when I leave the local area. However, I've explained time and time again that I am in great demand and that sometimes I have to leave. It's like talking to a wall sometimes," Lauren said with an eye roll.

Olivia snickered. "Doctors think they know everything. My dad is one, so trust me. I know what you mean."

"Still," Lauren continued, "I think you are very capable of handling this. You are smart and observant, and you have your gift working in your favor."

"But the victims," Olivia said, her eyes filled with anxiety, "they don't tell me anything. When I speak to them, they don't remember anything. I need your help in all of this."

"And you have it. I truly think you can do this, though. You are a vessel used to cross them to the light. My gift focuses on what's left undone in their lives."

The energy in the room grew intense. Lauren went on. "I'll admit, Olivia, I feel very connected to you. Our meeting was certainly not a coincidence. If while I'm off with the baby, you discover more bodies, please send me the information. You are also welcome to come to my home to discuss the case. Perhaps it's possible that just being with one another, we can summon the victims and perhaps learn things from them. Is it true that once they cross, they can still come back?"

"I believe they can come and go as they please, if they go through the light first. At least, that's what I've seen happen."

"If that's so, then we can use that to our advantage. We can communicate with them still. When I've had the baby and am recovered, I'll work this case with you."

Olivia smiled. "Thank you so much. And I completely understand your absence. Being a mom should come first. Life also looks much different from the perspective of a mother. You'll see what I mean."

Lauren pursed her lips. "To be perfectly honest, I'm afraid. I'm not very good at connecting with people. I did with you because of what we share, but in general, I am terrible at it."

"You'll be a great mom," she said reassuringly.

"I don't think I quite knew how to be human until I met Nick."

"He seems wonderful," Olivia agreed.

"He saved me in every way possible. That man is a gift to me."

Olivia's heart sank a little. She couldn't hide the disappointment on her face.

"You've not found that," Lauren assumed.

Shaking her head, she replied, "No."

Olivia felt comfortable enough with Lauren to explain about her past. She spoke of her abuse growing up. She also talked about her parents and her siblings. She explained the darkness she'd lived through and how it nearly consumed her. She also revealed her experience with death. "The instant connection with you gives me confidence that there are still people out there that can accept me," Olivia added.

"Daniel accepts you."

"He is a good partner and a good friend."

"Does he know what you can do?"

"No. I can't tell him. It's too soon," she said wearily. "He would probably pink slip me." She tried to smile, but she wasn't kidding.

"You'd be surprised at what a man can accept when he cares about you. Nick surprised me."

"But you're in love."

"We weren't always," Lauren explained. "I hated him when I first met him. He was annoying and brash and pompous. He didn't like me very much either, but once we let the walls crumble, everything changed. I can see you still have very high walls built up, Olivia."

"They keep me safe, I guess." She shrugged. "And they keep Amelia safe."

"Someday, you'll have to lower those walls, you know. Take it from someone who knows firsthand."

"I'm not sure I know how to," Olivia admitted as tears stung her eyes.

"You will when the right person comes along. You have to be brave enough to let someone behind those walls. Then you have to be even braver to let them take each brick in the wall down to see exactly who you are."

A tear made its way down Olivia's cheek. "I don't know if I can ever do that, Lauren."

With a serene smile, Lauren concluded. "I believe that you can and that you will. I think you'll do great things, and I think you'll find someone to share those things with you. In fact, I think you already have."

49

The next morning, as Olivia sat at her desk, she reflected on her conversation with Lauren. Their discussion about the case and spirituality had given her much to consider. She, too, recognized a pattern in the crimes, and for the first time, she felt she had gained real insight.

The fact that both Miller and Henry had been in foster care did not seem like a coincidence. Olivia also knew she and Danny had a difficult task ahead. They needed to revisit Miller and his wife to gather detailed information about their childhoods, as well as Henry's.

Glancing at the clock on the wall, Olivia noted the time, seven forty a.m. In twenty minutes, Lauren would present her profile. Olivia was eager to see if they were on the same page.

Danny walked in and sank onto the sofa, a perplexed frown on his face. Olivia narrowed her gaze.

"What's wrong?" she asked.

He lifted his hand and mimed drawing a timeline in the air. "How did we go from bodies hanging in trees in the woods to bodies hanging in burned buildings?" he asked rhetorically.

"I have my suspicions," she said.

Danny leaned forward. "What are they? Educate me."

"Two offenders," she answered as she stood, grabbing her pen and notepad before heading for the door.

Danny immediately got up and followed.

Officers gathered in the large training room, their attention drawn to the front where a projector rested on a table. A slide displaying crime scene photos was projected onto the screen, while photographs of the victims were pinned to a whiteboard.

Lauren stood at her laptop, making final preparations for the presentation. Nearby, Nick chatted with Wallace.

Danny settled into an empty seat in the back row, but Olivia chose to stand.

Lauren glanced at her watch, clicked a button on her laptop, and began.

"Good morning, ladies and gentlemen. I'm Dr. Lauren Harris-Bennette, a profiler contracted with the Ohio State Police and a consultant for the FBI. Over the past few days, I have analyzed the two previous crime scenes, reviewed case notes, and, as of yesterday, visited the third crime scene. Detective Gregory and I also spoke with the parents of the most recent victim. Based on my assessment, I believe you are dealing with a serial team."

Danny shot Olivia a glance. "Point for you," he whispered.

Lauren continued. "Due to the changes in modus operandi, we are likely looking at two offenders: one younger male in his late twenties to early thirties and an older male, probably in his early to late fifties. They may be related or could have met through a shared trauma that bonded them. Regardless, they are connected by something significant.

"Victimology suggests that the offenders, or unsubs, specifically target white females between the ages of twelve and seventeen. This pattern strongly indicates that the perpetrators themselves are white, as offenders typically choose victims within their own racial demographic.

"The method of disposal reveals a complete lack of remorse. The hangings are not just executions; they are power plays. These killers want the world to see what they are capable of. It is a deliberate display of dominance and authority.

"However, it is important to note that these unsubs are not arsonists. While there is a clear fascination with fire on the part of at least one, possibly both, setting fires is not their signature. The purpose of the fires is not the thrill of watching something burn, as seen in serial arsonists. Instead, the fires are a means of drawing attention to the crime.

"The real signature here is the tic-tac-toe pattern tattooed onto the victims." She clicked to a slide showing close-up images of each victim's leg. "This serves a dual purpose. First, it sends a message to law enforcement: the killers see this as a game. Second, it is a form of branding. It is a way for them to claim ownership of their victims. This also feeds into their desire for notoriety. Once the media catches wind of the pattern, they will be given a name, which will only escalate their need for dominance. As a result, the cooling-off period between murders will likely shorten, and the body count will rise at an accelerated rate.

"Geographically, the offenders are likely stable. This suggests they both hold jobs and function normally within society. They would not stand out in a crowd. No obvious physical disabilities, deformities, or distinguishing features. Their behavior is predatory, meaning they likely stalk their victims over time. This level of planning indicates they are organized killers. In a team dynamic, roles are often divided. One offender may be the primary stalker while the other handles logistics. They complement each other's strengths to achieve their shared goal.

"The shift in MO, the move from bodies displayed in trees to bodies displayed in burned buildings, is also about attention. While hanging the victims in trees was already a blatant display, setting fires in urban areas ensures quicker media coverage.

"The sexual assaults noted in the medical examiner's reports for the first two victims will likely be confirmed in the third. These acts are not about desire but about control, which is common in crimes like these. Based on the victimology and offender profile, the older male is likely using the younger one as a surrogate to fulfill his sexual conquests, meaning it is probably the younger offender committing the assaults. Given the ages of the victims, the older offender may be a preferential pedophile. There is also a possibility he has a history of incarceration for similar offenses. Keep this in mind when narrowing your suspect pool.

"The key to finding this team lies in understanding their motivation. A pattern is emerging. Each victim comes from a family where at least one parent was in the foster care system at some point in their life. I strongly recommend investigating the past placements of the victims' parents. Detectives Gregory and Detective Knight, you need to return to the parents of the first two victims and gather as much information as possible about their foster care history."

Olivia and Danny nodded.

Lauren continued. "Be aware, however, that this research will take time. Many adults who have experienced trauma, particularly in the foster system, are reluctant to discuss their pasts. Additionally, if you identify a common foster care provider, you will likely need a court order to access records, as most adoption and foster care files are sealed and confidential. I recommend consulting with a judge as soon as possible.

"Examine the family histories carefully. There is a significant pattern hidden in the victims' backgrounds. I believe that understanding the parental connections will help you narrow the suspect pool. Stay focused on evidence-based research and interviews. There is a deeper psychological and emotional source driving these crimes. This is not random violence. These killers have a mission, which means they are working toward a specific goal within a specific timeframe.

"Finally, consider the most common motivators for crimes like these: anger and revenge. These offenders may believe they are righting a past wrong. Like most serial killers, they are hedonistic, fixated on power and control. In team dynamics, there is usually a dominant and a submissive offender. If you can identify the weaker of the two, that will be your way in. Exploiting the submissive's vulnerabilities could break the case open."

Lauren nodded and clicked off the projector, signaling the end of her presentation.

"Thank you for your attention, ladies and gentlemen. Good luck."

50

Henry found himself in a dark tunnel, but a faint light shone from the other side. As he moved toward it, the silhouette of a person stood at the tunnel's end. With each step, the figure became clearer. It was Mya. Her warm smile melted his heart.

"Hi, Daddy," she said, extending her hand. "Come with me for a while."

He took her hand, and suddenly the tunnel opened into a breathtaking field filled with wildflowers and towering trees. A serene lake shimmered in the distance. A gentle breeze carried the overwhelming fragrance of blossoms.

"Where are we?" he asked, mesmerized.

"This is my heaven," she replied.

"What do you mean?"

"Everyone is given a heaven when they pass, a place they love. I've always loved nature, so this is mine," she explained with a smile.

Henry's expression darkened with regret. "I didn't know that," he admitted, his voice tinged with shame. "I didn't know you loved nature."

"It's okay. I never told you," she said reassuringly. "Growing up in the city made me long for the countryside.

Here, if I want horses, they appear. If I want dogs, they appear. Anything my heart desires, I have. The only thing I can't do is interfere with life on Earth."

"Can you explain?" Henry asked.

"When you were dying, I couldn't stop it. I wanted to, but I wasn't allowed. That's one of the rules here. The only thing I could do was be with you and give you hope. The final choice had to be yours."

Henry exhaled heavily, shaking his head. "I don't understand any of this."

"You're not meant to, at least not yet. You can only comprehend part of it right now. Everything becomes clear once you fully cross over. But because I'm your spirit guide, I have access to you. I can bring you here with me whenever I want. That's all you need to know for now."

She led him to the lake's edge and sat down.

"This place is unbelievable, Mya," he said, taking in the peaceful surroundings.

"It's all mine."

Henry turned to her, admiration in his eyes. "I'm so proud of you."

She smiled. "I'm proud of you too, Dad. But all the pain you've endured has hardened you. You've shut yourself off from the world, closed your heart and mind to life's possibilities, both spiritually and emotionally. It's time to let people back in."

He cast his gaze over the still, blue water. "I don't know if I can," he admitted.

"Don't be afraid." She squeezed his hand gently. "You've convinced yourself that you can't open up, but that's not true. Let your counselor help you. You need to reconnect with who you are inside. I can help you a little, but there's someone else who can guide you even further."

"Who?"

"Detective Gregory," she said without hesitation. "She has a profound gift, Dad. You don't realize how spiritually connected she is. She can help you understand."

Henry shook his head. "She'll think I'm crazy," he muttered.

Mya smiled knowingly. "You'd be surprised. She's been through more in the spiritual realm than you can imagine."

His brows furrowed. "Are you serious?"

She nodded. "It's not my place to tell you everything. She can help you find the answers. But she's going to need your help, too."

Henry hesitated, considering her words, but his mind remained clouded with confusion. "Mya, can you see the future? The past? Do you know who killed you?"

She lowered her gaze. "I can see glimpses of the future, but it's not set in stone. Every choice you make changes the outcome. As for my past, no, I don't know who killed me.

Those memories were taken from me when I crossed over. And honestly, I don't want to remember. As much as I wanted to help Detective Gregory, I couldn't."

Henry's eyes widened. "She can see you?"

Mya bit her lip. "I've said too much. I'm still new at this, and I can't say anything else right now. You need to get some rest."

They stood together, his hand still clasping hers. He reached out, brushing his fingers through her hair, his eyes welling with tears. "Will I see you again?"

"I'm always with you."

"But will I see you?"

She hesitated. "That's up to the Creator. But please, Dad, don't cry. Even when you think I'm far away, I'm right here."

In an instant, Henry's eyes snapped open. He found himself lying on the couch in the dimly lit room, the television screen casting a faint glow. He sat up, his feet touching the floor, and ran his fingers through his hair, his head dropping into his hands.

A dream… or a vision? He wasn't sure.

Lifting his head, his eyes settled on a framed photograph of Mya on the bookshelf. He stared at it for a long moment, then exhaled deeply.

He knew, without a doubt, that he needed to talk to

Olivia. Even if it was hard to believe she would understand. He had to try.

For the first time in a long time, he felt hope.

51

Olivia typed in notes on her laptop. Nigel rested in his crate beside her desk. The sun streamed through the large window, warming the room. She and Danny planned to meet in an hour. Now that they had been given a profile, they needed to get a game plan together.

She heard someone knock on the door facing and looked up to see Henry standing there. "I would have called," he began hesitantly.

"Oh no, come in," she said as she stood up and walked to him. "Have a seat." She gestured toward the sofa. "I planned to reach out to you. Can I get you some coffee? Water?"

"No thanks," he said, sitting down.

She felt Henry's eyes on her as she stood. It wasn't an uncomfortable feeling, though. She sat down on the opposite end of the sofa.

"I wanted to know if you'd made any progress on Mya's case," he asked. "I know it's been a very short time since we spoke, but I am curious."

She pursed her lips. "Well, another victim was found. A profiler came in, and we have a little more to work with now, so I think we're making some progress," she said in an optimistic tone. "I need to ask you some things, though. Personal things that I have a feeling you won't want to discuss. I really need to understand what happened to you growing up. I need more information about your placements in foster care."

His eyes dropped. "I wasn't expecting this."

"I'm sorry, but that's why I was going to contact you. We plan to talk to Candy also."

Henry took a deep breath, his eyes filled with apprehension as he looked at Olivia. Seeing his unease made her heart sink. She hated asking him to revisit a subject that brought him so much pain.

He closed his eyes, and when he opened them again, tears welled up. "I had been in foster care since I was a small child," he began. "My mom died of a drug overdose, and there was no one left to take care of me. I messed up a lot of my placements, sometimes on purpose. But deep down, all I really wanted was a home. A family. I ran away a lot, and eventually, the state had enough. They placed me in another foster home.

"Everyone in the community thought my new foster parents were wonderful. My caseworker told me they had been fostering kids for years and that they had helped a lot of them. The family lived on a farm. We all had chores to do. I learned to pull my weight."

"Who lived there with you?" Olivia asked.

"Miller, Candy, and Kyle. Holly and Mike Henson were good to us at first. I liked being in their home. I got an allowance for my chores. I finally liked my life."

Henry recounted his experience with Candy's assault, detailing every painful memory. He described Holly's reaction and revealed everything about his life with the Hensons. He told Olivia how he had been shackled and punished, how he had been beaten until he bled.

"Candy and I depended on each other after that," he continued. "It was a turning point for us. We began a sexual relationship, but it was much more than that. We needed each other. I loved her."

Henry continued, recounting Candy's pregnancy and the moment he confronted Mike. He shared his plans to marry Candy and escape from the foster home, hoping for a better future together.

"So you confronted Mike?" Olivia asked.

Henry nodded. "It was after supper one night. He was in the barn, tossing hay from the loft down into the stalls. I climbed up the ladder, looked him straight in the eye, and told him point blank that Candy was pregnant. I remember the way the color drained from his face.

"I didn't hold back. I told him he was an idiot for not using a condom or making sure Candy was on birth control. And then I dropped the bomb. I told him I'd been with her too, so there was a chance the baby was mine. That's when he lost it.

"The next thing I knew, I was on the barn floor, staring up at him. He stood over me and said he was leaving me there to die."

Tears filled Olivia's eyes as she listened.

"I have no idea how long I was out before I felt Candy's hand on my face. She said she'd called for help. I was rushed into emergency surgery. When I woke up, a nurse told me that Holly and Mike claimed they had no idea what had happened to me, that they didn't understand how I could have fallen. That's when I snapped. I spilled everything.

"I spent months in the hospital, undergoing surgery after surgery to repair the damage. While I was still there, I was officially emancipated. Candy and I got married right there in the hospital chapel."

Olivia, now leaning forward on the edge of the couch, reached out and gently placed her hand over Henry's. "I am so, so sorry."

He exhaled deeply. "Well, there you have it. My life story."

"Where are Holly and Mike now?" she asked.

"In prison, I'm sure," he replied. "I haven't heard from them since the trial."

"You sued them?"

"You bet I did."

"And you still keep in touch with Miller and Kyle? That's what you told me before."

"We're not best friends or anything. Like I said, when Miller's daughter was killed, I reached out to him. When

Mya died, he did the same for me. Kyle checks in every now and then. He sent me an email when Mya passed."

Olivia managed a small smile. "Thank you for telling me."

Henry lowered his head, nodding. "I actually did better than I thought I would."

"You did great."

His voice grew unsteady. "I didn't kill my daughter, Olivia. You need to know that. I had nothing to do with it. I just want her to have peace." Tears slipped down his face.

Olivia's expression softened even more, and she held his hand firmly. "She is at peace. And I will give her justice."

"There's so much more I need to say to you," he admitted, hesitating. "But I'm afraid you'll think I'm crazy."

"How about this?" she suggested. "After group next week, we'll grab a coffee and talk. Maybe by then, you'll have the courage to say whatever's on your mind."

A glimmer of appreciation shone in his eyes, and he smiled kindly. "I want you to understand. I'm out of my league with some of the things that have been happening to me lately."

"It might feel that way now," she said, "but I know from experience that sometimes all you need is someone to listen."

He nodded, grateful. As she released his hand, he

sighed. "I want to help with the investigation however I can. I know I'm just a lab geek, but I can help. I'm a medical doctor first, though. I'll assist Bentley directly if needed."

"I don't think we'll need anyone else on the case. We have plenty of help. It's just up to Danny and me to follow up now."

He stood. "Thanks for listening."

She rose as well. "I'm glad you told me. And I'll let you know if there are any new developments."

He nodded. "Thank you."

As he turned toward the door, he added, "I'll see you at group."

"Okay, Henry," she said, watching as he left.

52

As Olivia sat at the kitchen table in the Swaggart household, she lifted the cup of coffee to her lips.

"Is there news?" Shanda asked.

"Well, we're working on some leads right now," Olivia replied. "Shanda, it may mean nothing, but I wanted to follow up about something you said. You explained you grew up in foster care. Can you tell me about your experiences there?"

Shanda's facial expression changed, and the tension in the room intensified. "Is this really necessary?"

"I just need to know what foster homes you were placed in. I need names."

With a deep breath, she steeled herself. "The first one was Shawn and Celia Gingric. The second was Tom and Nancy Pollock. I already told you about my adoptive parents."

"How did you end up in foster care?"

"My dad died. My mom left me with my sister. My sister wasn't old enough to take care of me. The State intervened."

"When did you enter care?"

"I was four years old."

Olivia sighed. The Hensons weren't involved. She worried she would reach another dead end. "Shanda, did you have a particular caseworker that helped you?"

"Not a consistent one. It felt like I got a new one each year."

Olivia stood, preparing to leave. "I appreciate your time."

"Sorry I wasn't more help. I hate discussing my childhood. I'm just glad it's behind me."

"I understand. Again, thank you for your candor," Olivia concluded.

53

After a quiet weekend, Danny resolved to speak with Henry Howard himself. He waited in the hospital atrium, an unshakable distrust gnawing at him. He could not explain it. He had never met the man, but something felt off. Olivia's report detailed Henry's traumatic childhood, yet Danny remained unconvinced of his innocence. A past steeped in violence only made him more inclined to consider Henry a suspect.

When the elevator doors slid open, Henry stepped out. Danny approached him.

"Dr. Howard," he said.

"Yes?" Henry offered his hand.

They shook.

"Detective Daniel Knight. Do you have a minute?"

Henry's brow lifted. "Where's Detective Gregory?"

"She's tied up with other matters. Is there somewhere we can talk?"

Henry hesitated, then nodded. "There's a consultation room down the hall."

Inside, Henry took a seat while Danny remained standing.

"I know Detective Gregory spoke to you about your

past," Danny began. "I have a question. Do you have any contact with the Hensons?"

Henry's expression darkened. "Are you joking? I already told her. I haven't seen or spoken to them since the trial."

Danny's face remained unreadable. "Do I look like I'm joking?"

Henry let out a sharp breath. "You think I had something to do with this?"

"I'm not sure. Detective Gregory doesn't think you're involved. Me? I'm not convinced."

Henry leaned forward, his eyes cold. "Detective Knight, are you forgetting that my daughter was murdered?"

"No. I'm not forgetting," Danny said evenly. "Sociopaths don't have a conscience. They justify everything. They lie without missing a beat. Maybe you decided to target people from the foster system. Maybe you didn't do it alone."

Henry scoffed. "Listen to what you're saying. I tried to kill myself after my daughter was murdered. I was in rehab. Would a sociopath do that?"

Danny's gaze stayed locked on him. "And ironically, no one died while you were there."

"If Detective Gregory believes I'm innocent, why don't you?"

"Because I've been doing this longer than she has. She thinks you're a nice guy. I can tell from the way she writes about you in her notes. The way she talks about you." Danny crossed his arms. "You've got her fooled. You don't fool me."

Henry smirked. "I think you're intimidated."

Danny's jaw tensed. "By what?"

Henry stood, stepping closer. "You care about her. You see me as a threat."

Danny did not flinch. "I just want the truth. And I don't want her getting hurt."

"I won't hurt her. I'm not a murderer. And if your theory is right, she isn't even a target. She wasn't raised in foster care."

"Would you take a polygraph? A voice stress test?" Danny asked.

Henry's expression hardened. "If you had evidence, you'd have already arrested me. Unless you have a warrant, I'm not taking any tests. I didn't do this, Detective. But I'll do whatever I can to help you find who did."

Danny's stare remained unwavering.

"In fact," Henry continued, "I've already offered my services to Bentley. I can rush labs. Consult on crime scenes. I have a trained eye."

Danny's fists clenched at his sides.

"My daughter was collateral damage in all of this. I want the truth as much as you do. But I'm not your guy."

Danny exhaled slowly. "I think you know more than you're letting on."

Henry glanced at the door. "I have work to do. And maybe you have some things to work out yourself. Sounds like you need a heart-to-heart with your partner."

With that, Henry brushed past him and left the room.

54

Tuesday was uneventful. Olivia and Danny used the quiet day to catch up on paperwork. The eve of a holiday always seemed to clear out the precinct, leaving a skeleton crew to hold things down.

On Wednesday, Olivia called her dad and stepmother to wish them a happy Independence Day. She also spoke with Hope and David, with Amelia happily jabbering in the background. As always, they invited her home for the weekend. As always, she didn't give a definite answer.

By Thursday evening, Olivia stood in front of the mirror, scrutinizing her reflection. Sarah sat on the bed, playing with Amelia, while Nigel lay on the floor, watching them both.

Danny was working a narcotics case, so he couldn't watch Amelia, not that Olivia had asked. She didn't want him to know she was meeting Henry.

"You are way too stressed about this," Sarah said bluntly.

Olivia frowned at herself. "It's just a group meeting, for God's sake. What is wrong with me?" she muttered.

She wore denim capris, a snug white V-neck tee, and white flip-flops, casual, simple. So why did she feel like she was going on a date?

Sarah smirked. "You like this guy."

Olivia scoffed. "It's not like that."

"Then why are you acting like it is?" Sarah teased. Then her expression turned thoughtful. "Let me ask you something, why not Danny?"

Olivia sighed. "Danny's my partner. My friend. I don't see him that way."

"Why not? He's good-looking. He's great with Amelia. He cares about you."

"I care about him, too. But we work together. That complicates things."

Sarah shrugged. "Only if you let it."

"He's a great man, but if something went wrong, it would be awful."

Sarah studied her. "I guess you're right. I just see the way he looks at you. The way he is with Amelia."

Olivia hesitated. "You think he sees me like that? Romantically?"

Sarah nodded. "I think it's very possible. Whatever happened in that alley when he saved your life, it changed things for him. Can't you feel it?"

Olivia exhaled. "I know that's when we really became friends."

"I think it's more than that," Sarah said gently. "And I think you're nervous about Henry because you like him. Just make sure you like him for the right reasons."

Olivia scowled. "What do you mean?"

"I mean, don't settle because you think you don't deserve more." Sarah's voice softened. "We've talked about this before. I know you've talked about it with Danny, too. It's written all over you, Olly."

Olivia didn't reply. The silence said enough.

Sarah sighed. "Look, I'm not here to tell you what to do. Whoever you choose, I'll support you. But remember, you've been in recovery for a while. You haven't gone out once. Henry's a recovering addict, too. Just be careful. I don't want you being influenced by someone who's still struggling."

"I know you're worried." Olivia glanced at Amelia. She thought about how nurturing and caring he was with her. "Danny is a good man."

"And you deserve a good man."

"Henry seems nice, too," Olivia added.

"Only time will tell."

Olivia let out a breath and picked Amelia up. She nestled against her and rested her head over Olivia's heart. "Oh, little one," Olivia murmured. "You make me a better person."

Sarah smiled. "You're going to be late."

"I know," Olivia said softly. "I need to get going."

55

Armed with as much confidence as she could muster, Olivia arrived at her group meeting. She pulled into a parking space and saw the motorcycle already parked. She exhaled heavily, the anxiety welling within her.

She walked into the meeting room. Henry had his usual seat in the back. Timidly, she walked to the back row and sat down, one seat separating them.

"Hey," he said as he turned, looking at her.

"Hey," she replied quietly with a shy wave.

His weight shifted toward her, and he put his arm on the back of the empty seat. "We still on for coffee?"

"Absolutely," she said with a confident nod.

"Do you want to take the bike? I brought an extra helmet just in case."

"Sure."

The apprehension nearly choked her. Henry, on the other hand, seemed completely relaxed. He wore a pair of khakis and a white cotton T-shirt with a blue Oxford over it, and a pair of black Converse lace-ups on his feet. The stubble on his face looked more endearing now for some reason. At least he did not seem dressed for a date.

As group continued, Henry shifted uncomfortably in his

chair. The visit from Danny did not rattle him so much. What did make him jumpy was being ushered into the world of the paranormal, which was a world he did not understand.

Until his brush with death, he had not been exposed to such things. Now he was forced to embrace something new, a belief system he knew nothing of. Still, he was stepping out on the ledge of faith, believing what his daughter told him. If Olivia held the key to understanding all he had been exposed to, then he wanted the door opened. He was tired of being held back by doubt.

Tonight, he wanted to know more about Olivia as a person. Most of all, he wondered how a former heroin addict could become such a dedicated cop. He feared that she might shut down on him, but he hoped she would not, especially since he had opened up to her.

The meeting ended, and the anticipation built between them as they stood.

"Ready?" he asked.

She nodded, unable to speak.

He stepped out of the row and then let her step out. He followed behind her.

As she stood beside the motorcycle, she realized there was no place for her purse. Seeing the concern on her face, Henry suggested she lock it in her trunk. "Coffee's on me, so you won't need any cash anyway," he assured her.

Olivia put her car keys in her pocket and then shut the

trunk lid. She still held her phone in her hand.

"I can put your stuff in the compartment under the seat," he suggested.

"Sure," she replied.

Once that was done, he turned his attention to her and put the helmet on her head. He bent down a little to make sure it was fastened. Olivia had not realized how tall he was.

"Feel tight enough?" Henry asked, looking down through the tinted plastic visor.

"Feels like it," she replied.

He turned and grabbed his helmet and put it on. He then turned back to Olivia to help her get on the bike. She climbed on like a pro. He threw his leg over the seat and kicked the stand up. With the motor running now, he leaned back so she could hear him. "Hold on tight, and don't lean unless I tell you to."

She secured her arms around him, locking her hands together. She felt his abdominal muscles under the material of his shirt. The heat coursed through her as she realized how he felt against her. His back muscles were well defined, too.

The sensation of her against his back caused his blood to run a little hotter as well. The desire felt foreign. Being near her made him calmer, yet he felt like a caged animal. He wanted more. He felt her energy and the aura surrounding her. It was something he did not know how to explain.

It only took fifteen minutes to get to the coffee shop.

After the helmets were secured, they walked in and ordered. They found a vacant table and sat down.

Carefully, they studied each other's facial expressions. Olivia broke the silence first. "Don't be afraid," she said softly. "What did you want to talk to me about?"

He took a deep breath and exhaled. "Can we talk about some other things first? How old are you? Where are you from? Why are you in group? How did you become a cop?"

Her bright smile nearly stopped his heart.

"One question at a time, Henry."

"Okay. Where are you from?" he asked as he took a sip of his coffee.

"I'm from western Ohio. I grew up in Butler County."

"I know it is completely unacceptable to talk about a woman's age, but exactly how old are you?"

"I'm twenty-two years old."

Henry started choking on the coffee.

"Oh my God. Are you okay?" she asked.

"I'm sixteen years older than you."

"Really?" she asked, surprise coloring her face.

He nodded. "I'm old enough to be your dad."

Bravely, she spoke. "But does age really matter at this point in the game?"

Surprised by her acceptance, he smiled. "I suppose it doesn't."

"I'm legal, and to be honest, I think numerical age means nothing in the scheme of things. I am an old soul. I've known that since I was a kid."

"An old soul, huh? What exactly does that mean?"

"It depends on who you are. It means different things to different people."

Henry smiled. "You're avoiding the question."

"No, I just don't know how to explain it to you," she said as she stirred the coffee in the mug.

"Doesn't having an old soul have some sort of spiritual meaning?"

"It can."

"What makes you tick, Detective?" Henry asked, leaning slightly forward. "I need some answers, and I know this is going to sound crazy, but I was told to seek you out for those answers. I experienced something when I tried to kill myself. I didn't think anything like that was possible. I saw things that I will never forget, but I don't understand any of it."

"What did you see, Henry?"

He hesitated.

"It's okay. Tell me what you saw."

"I saw a bunch of people or things. I don't know, really. They had hoods on. I never saw their faces, but I knew they were there to take my soul. I didn't even know I had a soul. I didn't believe anyone had a soul."

"What else?"

"I saw Mya. She said something about being a guide for me. I've seen her in a dream since. I asked questions. She told me that you were the one with the answers, so here I am talking to you about this fairytale, and you probably think I need to be committed again."

Olivia sighed and looked down at the caramel swirling in the cup. "I don't think you're crazy." She was relieved that he needed spiritual guidance. She could handle that.

"Well, I'm beginning to think I am completely nuts."

"You're not. I promise. You've been introduced to a realm that we coexist with. That world is closed to many, but for those who have opened their minds to it, there are endless possibilities and a higher plane of knowledge."

"Wow, you are good at this," he said as his eyes met hers.

"I've been exploring this since I was a child," she started. She explained her past and how she believed that sexual abuse had opened her to a spiritual world. She confessed that when she started using drugs, her gift went dormant.

She paused. "The fact is, Henry, I'm damaged."

"Who the hell isn't?" he asked. "We all have our vices. Isn't that what you said? And look at me. You want to talk about damaged? I don't think you could get any more damaged than me."

She went on to tell him about her experiences as a prostitute. She shared her darkness with him. She talked about Amelia. She explained how she became a cop.

Henry shared many things with her, too. They opened up parts of themselves that had not seen the light of day in a very, very long time. They found a common ground.

"I've built up this insurmountable wall to protect myself from everything," Henry admitted.

Olivia remembered the conversation with Lauren and the analogy she had offered. "A good friend once told me that you can't live your life like that. You must have a human connection with someone."

"I guess what I'm trying to say by telling you all of my secrets," Henry continued, "is that I'm just as damaged. You won't hear any judgments coming from this direction," he said, pointing to his own chest.

"Thanks," she said, dropping her head.

"I guess I want to understand all of the things that are happening to me, especially the things that involve Mya. I don't completely understand the things she's shared with me," he admitted.

Olivia met his gaze. "I can help you with that. I helped

Mya cross over. When you came to me the other day, I could, with confidence, tell you Mya was safe and at peace. I was there when she found it, but you knew that too."

Henry leaned in further. "Are there dead people in here right now?" he joked.

"It's not that simple either," she answered.

"What do you mean?"

"Each person has spirit guides. You told me that Mya was assigned to you, right?"

He nodded.

"I have guides assigned to me, too."

"How do you know that?" Henry asked, fascinated.

She told Henry about her guides. She explained what each of them could do, the roles they played in her personal journey.

"That's incredible," he said. "I know this is way out of left field, but did Mya tell you who hurt her?"

"No," Olivia replied. "I wish she could have, but she didn't. Most of the time, memories are taken when someone dies. Only an empath can tap into traumatic events."

"What's an empath?"

"It's someone with a very special talent. They can either see or feel things that the dead person felt or experienced. It can come in pieces, or it can come in dreams, or in whatever way that person's gift works."

"This sounds like science fiction."

"It's very real. More real than you or me. You've experienced things. You know I'm not lying."

"Those hooded people scared me, and nothing scares me. They said that they tear people's souls apart."

"I don't know much about the darker world because I spend most of my time communing with the light."

"Communing? How do you do that?"

"Meditation. It's sort of like prayer. You quiet yourself and concentrate. You can pray. You can give thanks. The most important part is that you allow yourself to be open to the spirit world and communicate with your guides."

"So, if I meditate, I can communicate with Mya?"

"Possibly. Each person's journey and experiences are different. You have to seek out what makes sense to you."

He shook his head. "Wow. I just don't get any of this."

"It takes time."

He smiled. "Do you know how truly incredible you are? You're not damaged at all."

"Oh, but I am," she disagreed. "I haven't been in a real relationship ever. It scares me to death. I have Danny, my partner at work, and my babysitter, Sarah, and a new friend, Lauren."

"I've met Danny. He is something else."

She scowled. "When did you meet him?"

"He came to the hospital. He accused me of knowing something about the murders, then he wanted me to take a polygraph. He's quite a catch, that guy."

"He's just doing his job," Olivia defended.

"Maybe, but he is very protective of you."

"He saved my life. I would be dead if it weren't for him. Ever since then, we've been close."

"I see."

The silence fell for only a few moments. Olivia spoke up again. "Both of us have deep scars. Some may never heal. Others may heal over time. It sounds to me like we're more alike than we are different."

He nodded in agreement. "Sounds like it." He took a moment to sip his coffee. "It feels nice talking about this with you. I feel like I don't have to hide who I really am."

She smiled. "I agree. It's nice to feel like I can help."

"I appreciate it. I'm really lost."

"It'll get easier," she encouraged.

"Do you still battle the cravings? For the heroin?"

"Sometimes, but it's gotten easier with time. What about you?"

"I want it all the fucking time," he answered, his eyes glazing over a bit.

As his words settled, Olivia felt emotions that were alien to her. Knowing that she could help Henry was a bonus, but her interest in him strengthened. However, fear and hesitation still gripped her. Knowing that they were both recovering made her apprehensive. She did not want to be hurt either.

56

As they drove back to the church, Olivia held tightly to Henry. She was fearful. The quick connection petrified her. As her heartbeat sped, she felt her body temperature rise, her breasts pressing against his back.

They arrived in the parking lot, the sky dark and the stars shining. Henry cut the bike's engine and hopped off. He removed his helmet and hung it on one of the handlebars. Offering his hand to assist Olivia, she took it graciously and swung her leg over the seat, stepping onto the pavement. He carefully unfastened the strap under her chin and pulled the helmet from her head. She shook her hair out and then put it back up in a ponytail as he fastened the helmet to the back of the bike.

Opening the seat lid, he grabbed her belongings and handed them to her.

She looked up at him, his face serious. "Thank you for opening up to me, Henry. That's a very hard thing to do for people like you and me."

He sighed and nodded. "It's not easy at all. I want to learn more, though. I want to understand the things you've told me about."

"That's all it takes is desire," she said. She stood still. The awkward silence was deafening.

Henry leaned in. Quietly, he asked, "If I asked you to

dinner, would you tell me I'm too old for you?"

She looked deeply into his eyes. "No," she answered softly and seriously.

"If I asked you to dinner, would you tell me that you couldn't because I'm an addict?"

"No," she answered, still looking up at him.

"If I asked you to dinner, would you tell me that you can't because you're working on my daughter's case?"

She shook her head slightly. "No."

"Would you say yes?"

She smiled. "I would say yes."

"So, will you let me take you to dinner?" he asked.

"Yes," she replied with a smirk.

Her inhibitions and apprehensions suddenly fell away as she pushed up onto her toes slightly, her lips meeting his in a sweet kiss. She felt his arms as they wrapped around her. She pulled away slightly and stared at him for what felt like an eternity.

"So, what are we waiting for?" she asked before she even realized the words came out.

He was taken by surprise. "Tonight?"

"Yes," she beamed. "I can stop and pick up Chinese."

"Your place or mine?" he asked.

"Mine is fine," she answered. "I can text you my address."

They exchanged numbers. Then Olivia sent her address to his phone. After that, she winked and walked to her car.

57

As she drove home, she phoned Sarah, who agreed to keep Amelia for the night. Then she stopped for Chinese. After she placed the order, she walked into the women's bathroom. She checked herself in the mirror. She couldn't believe she'd been so bold. She prayed she wouldn't regret the decision. She felt the draw to Henry. She wanted him. There was no doubt about that.

Once she grabbed the food, she made her way home. She pulled into the driveway and turned off the car engine. She took a deep breath and closed her eyes for a moment.

Suddenly, she heard the motorcycle engine pull in behind her. She looked into the rearview mirror and saw Henry getting off the bike. She pulled the door handle and got out. She walked around the car and grabbed the bags of food.

She walked to the back door and unlocked it. She felt Henry behind her. They walked in, and then Henry shut the door behind them. Olivia put the bags on the kitchen table and then walked to the kitchen cabinet.

"What do you want to drink? I have water and milk and juice," she said.

"Water is fine."

She grabbed two bottles of water from the fridge and walked to the table where Henry was already seated.

As they enjoyed the meal, they talked about various different topics. Henry's job. Olivia's scholastic interests. Olivia's family. Her childhood. Henry's musical abilities.

Each story, each path in the conversation, laid the foundation between them. It allowed them to form an emotional attachment. The bricks in the walls they'd put up began to crack and crumble.

Olivia glanced up at the clock on the wall and saw it was slightly after midnight. That caused Henry to look down at his watch. "It's getting late," he said. "And we both have to work tomorrow."

She nodded as the disappointment washed over her. She felt his hand on hers.

"You are an intriguing young woman, Olivia," he said softly.

"Thank you. I really enjoyed this evening."

He nodded.

Their eyes locked, and Henry leaned in. Olivia met him halfway. The touch of his lips on hers made her blood run a little hotter. The gentleness of the kiss evolved into something more passionate. She was completely drawn in, the temptation to give in to her desires clouding her judgment. Her willpower disappeared.

They stood, Olivia's hands gripping his button-up shirt. The thrill was too much, so she hoped the tight grasp she had on his shirt might hold her feet to the ground.

She felt his hands on her waist as she pressed against him. He traced the hem of her T-shirt. A slight hesitation existed, but was soon dashed as Olivia unfastened his leather belt.

Their eyes quickly met. "Are you sure?" he asked thoughtfully.

"Yes," she answered breathily.

The passion ignited as Olivia stripped the belt from the loops, throwing it to the floor. The warmth of his breath on her cheek and then her neck felt foreign, but she welcomed the sensations. She closed her eyes.

Hands steady, she unbuttoned his khakis and unzipped them. She traced a design on the fabric of his boxer briefs and then slipped her hand down the front of them. She stroked him gently. He moaned quietly as he kissed her neck.

He pulled her shirt from her body, then kissed her shoulder. He traced designs on her back. He loosened the hooks of her bra, and the band released, the straps falling off her shoulders. The white cotton bra fell to the tile floor.

Olivia focused on undressing him. She pulled off his blue oxford and then his cotton shirt, both of them falling into a pile on the floor. Her soft lips brushed against the skin on his chest, her fingertips barely touching his stomach.

She caressed his back and felt the scars beneath her touch. Abruptly, she stopped and looked up at him. Her eyes filled with sadness, but he smiled down at her. "It's okay," he whispered as he tenderly kissed her forehead. "It's in the past."

He loosened her hair tie, and the golden strands fell down her back. He touched her locks. They were smooth as silk.

She dropped to her knees and untied his shoes. He slipped out of them. Then she pulled his pants to the floor.

He helped her to her feet, and their lips met once again. He broke the embrace once more and pulled a kitchen chair toward the middle of the room. He sat down and looked up at her, beckoning to her.

She stood in front of him. He unbuttoned her capri pants and loosened them. Along with her panties, he inched them off her hips. They dropped to the floor, and she kicked them aside.

He held out his hand, and she took it. She eased onto him, his hands firmly on her waist. As she felt him mold to her, she exhaled deeply and closed her eyes with satisfaction. He too let out a pleasurable sigh.

Holding tightly to the chair back, she found the spokes of the chair and placed her feet on them. It was just the leverage she needed. She leaned down and kissed him as she moved slowly. His grip tightened around her waist as their lips met briefly.

As they became lost in one another's bodies, in one another's gaze, Henry's lips brushed against her breasts, teasing her nipples. He moved his hands to her bottom and moved her faster.

The passion between them peaked as she climaxed, the tension falling away and her moans filling the room. He groaned as he orgasmed, too, his breaths heavy with each pulsation.

As they calmed, he rested his head against her breasts. Then he looked up at her, an appreciation in his eyes that Olivia couldn't quite describe. She smiled down at him.

"Why don't you go lie down in my bed," she suggested.

"I think that's a good idea," he agreed.

She got off Henry and stood naked before him. He also rose to his feet. She took him by the hand and led him through the living room and into the bedroom.

"I need to freshen up," she said. "Make yourself comfortable."

She walked out of the room and back into the kitchen. She picked the clothing up off the floor. She put Henry's shirt on and fastened a few of the buttons.

Once she finished in the bathroom, she walked into the bedroom to see Henry resting on his side, facing the door. His smile was rugged and sexy, and she blushed as she walked to the bed. She slipped under the covers.

"You look pretty hot in my shirt," he remarked.

With a grin, she lay facing him. "I hope you don't mind."

"Not at all," he said with a grin.

She leaned in and kissed his lips gently. Rolling over onto his back, he opened his arm to her, inviting her to lay her head on his chest. She gladly accepted, tucking herself close to him, quickly falling asleep.

58

The alarm on the nightstand sprang to life at 7 a.m. Olivia rolled over reluctantly to shut it off. With a heavy sigh, she turned back over. She quickly realized she was alone.

Kicking the covers off, she swung her feet around, putting them on the floor and sitting up. She dropped her head into her hands as the distinct feeling of disaster crept into her mind.

Then she heard a loud crash in the kitchen. With Henry gone, the loud noise put her on high alert. She grabbed her gun from the nightstand and stood. She readied the firearm as she crept out of the room. Rounding the corners, she heard Henry's voice. He was on the phone. She stood still and listened.

"I will be there in about an hour. I know I'm late. I know we had a managerial meeting. I promise, I'll be there as soon as I can," he grumbled.

Dropping the gun to her side, relief swept over her. He didn't leave. He hadn't run away.

She walked into the kitchen and saw him standing in the middle of the room wearing his khakis. He talked on his phone for a few more moments and then hung up. He placed it on the table and walked to the refrigerator, still unaware of Olivia's presence. Then he turned, holding the gallon of milk. He appeared to turn into a statue. "Do you have a gun?"

he asked.

Olivia looked down at the hand at her side. "Yes."

"Why?"

"Because I thought you were gone, and then I heard someone in the kitchen. I was afraid someone had broken in," she answered.

He smiled. "Well, I'm an unarmed man, unless you want to count the gun I carry in my pants," he joked.

The dirty humor made her laugh. "Do you want me to make breakfast for you?" she asked.

"No. I'm okay. I just wanted something to drink. I can grab something on the way to the hospital."

"I need to get dressed," she said, walking out of the kitchen and back to her bedroom.

Henry followed and sat on the bed. Olivia stood in front of the closet and unbuttoned the shirt she'd borrowed from Henry. She held it out to him. "Were you waiting on this?" she asked.

"Nope," he began as he pursed his lips. "I was waiting on that," he said with a smirk. He stared at her as she stood in her panties.

She grinned and turned her attention to her wardrobe, searching for something to wear. She felt the warmth of his clothed body against her back. He moved her hair from her neck and caressed her ear with his lips.

"I would love to stay here all day," she said, turning and putting her arms around his neck, "but I have to go to work, and it sounds like you have to go, too."

Henry kissed her lips softly. "I know. Responsibility sucks," he said as he started out of the room. "I'll call you later."

59

After getting Nigel from the kennels, Olivia made her way up to her office. Once she put Nigel in his crate, she headed to the break room for a cup of coffee. After such an active night, she needed some extra fuel.

As she stood watching the coffee brew, her mind drifted to the previous night's activities. Her thoughts raced. She still had so many questions for Henry. Then she realized she was analyzing things too much. She needed to enjoy the experience, not dissect it.

Olivia walked back to her office, coffee in hand, and sat down at her desk. She pulled up the precinct's computer database to dictate notes. A red asterisk appeared beside the file named "Tic-Tac-Toe." That indicated that a new note had been added to the case file. So, she navigated to the icon, double-clicked, and opened the file. Danny had added a note late Wednesday night.

She remembered Henry mentioning the interview with Danny. The anger swelled inside her as she read Danny's summary. Danny outlined his suspicions about Henry. One of those bullet points alluded to the belief that Henry murdered his own daughter.

As she kept reading, Danny's assumptions made absolutely no sense. The biggest disappointment, however, was that Danny didn't even bother to discuss his theory with her. They were partners, as he had pointed out many times before. They strategized. They consulted each other. Her trust in him was suddenly shaken.

She pushed away from the desk and stomped out. Her heels clicking against the hard flooring, she reached Danny's office in the corner of the room. His door was closed, so she pushed it open without knocking. He was talking on the phone and held his finger up for her to wait. She shut the door behind her and stood, arms folded, glaring down at him. He finished his conversation and then smiled.

"What's up?" he asked.

"Can you tell me why the hell you would think Henry has something to do with his own daughter's murder? Better yet, why didn't you tell me you were going to go talk to him? I would have gone with you," she said contemptuously.

"I didn't think I had to clear it with you," he answered arrogantly.

"We're partners. We talk about approaches and game planning, right?"

"Olivia, it's not a big deal. So, I interviewed the guy. So what?"

"Not a big deal? Seriously? We move together," she shouted as she pointed at him. With her hands firmly on her hips, she went on. "And how could you accuse Henry of killing his daughter? The other victims? You've read my assessments. You've double-checked my notes. Do you think I can't do my job? Are my assessments faulty? Don't you trust me, Danny?"

He stood up, walked to the front of his desk, and then leaned against it. He looked at her, his eyes serious, his mouth slightly open. He dropped his head and shook it. "Did you sleep with him? When?"

Olivia was flabbergasted. Almost speechless, she quickly recovered. "That is absolutely none of your business."

"Oh, it is very much my business, especially when it involves a victim's father," he disagreed.

"Just because you saved my life doesn't give you the right to run it!" Olivia argued. "What I do in my personal life isn't any of your concern."

"If it is a conflict of interest, that's gonna be a huge problem, Livy," he reiterated. Their eyes locked. "Like you said, we're partners. We look out for each other. I'm only lookin' out for you."

"You're right. We are supposed to be looking out for each other, not setting each other up to fail."

"Seems like you're setting yourself up to fail," he said calmly.

Olivia's face flushed red with anger. She felt her blood pressure spike slightly, so she took a deep breath in an attempt to compose herself. "I'm still struggling to figure out why you would interview Henry again. Why would you ask the man to take a polygraph or a voice stress test? Danny, he didn't do this. The evidence says he didn't have anything to do with this. He not only has an alibi, but he doesn't have a motive to kill any of the victims, especially his own child."

Danny shrugged and put his hands in his pockets. "Maybe he didn't do it. Maybe he has nothing to do with this, but I think he knows somethin'. Maybe he knows who's involved."

She shook her head. She felt as if she were talking to a solid brick wall. "If you don't think I can do this job, then you need to say that. I've interviewed him more than once. I'm telling you... he is not involved."

"This is exactly why a conflict exists now. You're so personally invested that you can't be objective."

"He was cleared, Daniel!" she exclaimed. "And I'm not too involved," she protested.

"You are," he replied as he shook his head.

"He is not a suspect!"

"So that's why you slept with him?"

"I told you that's none of your business!" she said as the indignation became almost too much to contain.

"Livy, I can see it in your face. I've done this job for a long time. Long enough to know when someone's heart is getting in the way."

"My heart has nothing to do with this. Do you know how much that man has been through?"

"Who hasn't had bad shit happen to them?" he asked as

his anger became visible. His cool exterior was beginning to crumble as his thoughts cluttered his reasoning. 9/11. Personal tragedies. He had had his fair share of heartache, too.

"Have you ever been abused?" Olivia bit out. "Have you ever had every shred of dignity stripped from you? Have you ever been in such a dark place that you never thought you'd find your way out? This man has experienced the most horrifying abuse I've ever heard of. You were raised by good people, Danny. You can't possibly relate."

"So, you slept with him out of pity?"

Olivia's eyes filled with fury as she dropped her head and pinched the bridge of her nose. She wanted to slap Danny but refrained, of course. Sadness and hurt took the place of anger as she fought back tears. "You can go to hell, Danny," she said as she raised her head and made eye contact again.

She turned and pulled the door open, only to slam it behind her. The glass rattled as it shut, and she walked down the hallway quickly, knowing she needed to get to her office where she could weep in private.

60

Danny stood immobilized. His heart felt like it was breaking. The secret he carried burdened him. He too had a conflict of interest, and it was clouding his judgment. His mission to protect Olivia was becoming more than he'd bargained for.

He'd grown close to Olivia, but something greater than friendship sprang up inside him. Unmistakably, and much to his shock, he was falling in love with her. He couldn't believe that something so intense could happen so fast. Never had he felt this way about anyone. He was so connected and invested.

It hurt him to know that Henry was now intimately involved with Olivia. Somehow, he'd broken down her walls. Danny prayed he didn't yet have her heart.

Danny felt sick about their disagreement. The last thing he wanted to do was hurt her.

He loved Olivia, but he loved Amelia, too. He'd kept quiet, though. She couldn't possibly know how he felt. Danny knew he had no one else to blame but himself. Trying to keep their work relationship healthy and develop a solid friendship had been his priority. Everything was backfiring.

Walking back to his chair, Danny sat down hard, putting his hands to his face. He heard a knock on the door. He hoped it would be Olivia, but Sue popped her head in. His countenance fell.

"Everything okay?" she asked as she slipped in, quietly closing the door behind her. She sat down on the chair in front of his desk. "I heard you and Olivia yelling."

"I'm an idiot," he said quietly as he turned his head, looking out the window.

"What happened?"

"She's pretty pissed at me."

"Why?" Sue persisted.

"She's sleeping with Henry."

"One of the victim's fathers?" Sue asked.

"Yes."

Sue paused for a moment, but then continued. "Why's that a problem, Danny? He's been cleared as a suspect, right?"

"I guess it shouldn't be a problem, but I'm tellin' you, something isn't right. He's involved somehow," he protested. "I can feel it."

"You have to prove it, and so far, you can't. The evidence doesn't point to him, and neither does Dr. Harris's profile."

"I didn't have a choice but to clear him, Sue. Like you said, the evidence doesn't implicate him."

Sue stared at Danny. "Hey, look at me," she said softly.

He turned to her. "What?"

Sue's mouth dropped. "Oh my God," she said. "You're in love with her."

He shrugged. There was no point trying to hide it from her. She knew him better than he knew himself sometimes.

"And so quickly, too," she added.

"That's the part I don't understand."

"Take it from me, love chooses you. I never anticipated falling in love with Rick the way I did. We dated, what, maybe two months and got married. Sometimes, you just know." She folded her arms and looked at Danny disapprovingly. "Why haven't you told her?"

"I can't. I didn't think she was ready. I didn't wanna kill the friendship," he replied.

"And now she's tangled up with the doctor." She pressed her lips together, eyeing him knowingly. "You should have told her how you felt. What did you say to upset her so much today?"

"I checked out the doctor again. I went to the hospital to talk to him. I didn't tell her I was going."

"You did what?"

"When she read my notes, she got mad at me."

"I don't really blame her. You're partners."

"She stormed in here to defend him, and the moment she

did, I knew. The way she acted, it was obvious she'd slept with him. So I called her out on it. She didn't even deny it. Instead, she started going on about how rough his childhood was, making excuses for him." He hesitated, the weight of his own words sinking in. His stomach twisted. "And then I accused her of sleeping with him out of pity."

Sue shook her head. "Danny."

"It was a knee-jerk reaction. She was in tears when she left."

"I'm surprised she didn't punch you in the mouth. I would have," Sue admitted as she shrugged.

"I think she would have if she'd have stuck around."

With a heavy sigh, Sue pursed her lips. "She's connected with him because of his past and their recovery. That is their common denominator. Her instinct is to help people. She's good at saving people who need saving. They might have been through similar situations. Your only choice is to respect her choice or change her mind."

"I have never been good at this shit," he admitted as he stood and began to pace.

"Then you'll just have to accept what is," Sue concluded.

61

The day passed quietly and quickly for Olivia. She'd requested to leave at 2 p.m. After the harsh exchange with Danny, she decided to take Amelia to Pikeview Manor to visit her family. Going home early would allow time for her to pack.

As she drove, the conversation with Danny replayed in her mind, each word adding to the pain. His attack on her character left her shaken, chipping away at the trust she had in him. His lack of respect for her choices ignited a deep anger, making it hard to think clearly. She wondered if they could ever move past this, or if it had already done irreparable damage.

It was almost 3 p.m. when Olivia pulled into her driveway at home. After packing everything into the car and putting Nigel in the back seat, she made her way to Sarah's house to pick Amelia up.

As Olivia stepped out of the car, her cell phone buzzed with a text message. She looked down to see Danny's name on the LCD screen. She pulled up the message: *I'm sorry. Please call me so we can talk.*

With no desire to even reply, she shut her phone off, put it back in her pocket, and walked inside Sarah's house. Sarah sat on the floor playing with Amelia. Olivia waved. Amelia jumped to her feet and ran to her. Taking her into her arms, Olivia kissed Amelia's cheek. "Wanna go see Granny and Papaw?" she asked.

"Yeah!" Amelia said, clapping.

After putting her back down, Olivia began gathering up Amelia's belongings. "Thanks for keeping her," she said to Sarah, who was now standing.

"I take it things went well with Henry?" Sarah said as she started putting some of Amelia's things in a duffle bag.

Olivia smiled. "Things went well."

"Is he going with you to see your folks?" Sarah asked.

"No. I want to be alone," she answered.

"Does Danny know you're leaving the county?"

"I don't really care what Danny knows," she snapped, still gathering up Amelia's things.

"Mmm. He must not have taken it well."

Olivia shook her head. "We argued today over a case. And no, he didn't take things well about Henry."

Sarah stopped. "You know all I want is for you to be happy, doll," Sarah started. "Like I said before, no matter who it is that comes along or who you choose, the world be damned. You've been alone for far too long. You're strong and you're worthy of being happy, Olivia. Don't ever forget that."

"Thanks. I think it's too soon to say where anything between Henry and I might be heading. It was just one night. I haven't heard from him today."

"Do you think Amelia will like him? She sure did bond quickly with Danny," Sarah inquired.

"I hope so," Olivia said with a sigh. "I don't want to introduce them just yet. It's just too soon."

62

With everything finally packed, Olivia, Amelia, and Nigel set off on the two-hour drive to Pikeview Manor. As they turned onto the familiar lane, a wave of bittersweet memories washed over Olivia. This was where she had grown up, a place of both refuge and loss.

Her dad and stepmom had taken her in when she needed protection from her stepfather's harm. Her childhood had revolved around school, Matt, Robin, her half-siblings, and the unique spiritual gift that set her apart. She had friends, of course, but beneath it all, she constantly battled the deep emptiness left by the scars of sexual abuse.

Pikeview had also been where she experienced her first paranormal events. Those profound events required her to grow up quickly. She had provided support and communication between her father, stepmother, and the other side.

The house itself was just as beautiful as ever. The historical home, now peaceful and free of the evil that had once haunted it, was stunning and still well maintained. The woods behind the home made its splendor even more breathtaking. Nonetheless, Olivia still had reservations about visiting. She hoped the memories would not be too agonizing.

Pulling up to the entrance, she took a deep breath. She parked the vehicle and turned the key, the engine coming to a stop. Putting her hands on the seatbelt latch, she stopped and saw her phone sitting in the passenger seat. Reaching over, she turned it back on. When it booted up, she saw she had missed four text messages and there were two voicemails.

The text messages were from Danny and read:

I know I hurt you. I'm so sorry. Just call me, please. Olivia, quit being stubborn and call me. Okay, now I'm worried. Please call. I won't push you, but please call me when you're ready.

She listened to the voicemail. Of course, one was from Danny. "Livy, this is Danny. Listen, I've sent you text messages. I can't leave things like this. I just need ya to call me, please."

The next voicemail was from Henry. "Hey Olivia. Sorry it's taken me so long to call. Busy day. Just give me a call when you get the chance."

The tap on the glass of the back door made Olivia jump slightly. Then she heard her dad's familiar voice. "There's Pap's girl."

Olivia looked over her shoulder and saw Amelia kicking gleefully as she reached up. The back door opened and Matt unfastened the car seat. As Amelia continued giggling and smiling, Matt scooped her up and out of the car, shutting the door behind him.

Keys now in her hand, Olivia opened her door and got out. She lifted the latch on the back passenger side door so Nigel could hop out. He ran to Matt, wagging his tail and barking.

Walking to the trunk, Olivia unlocked it and started pulling luggage out. She felt Matt's hand on her shoulder and turned. Embracing him with Amelia still in his arms, he said, "Hey angel."

"Hi, daddy," she said, kissing his cheek.

Stepping back, she smiled up at her father.

"Rough week?" he said.

"Very."

"You want to talk about it?"

"Na. I do have a question for you, though. Do you know a scientist by the name of Henry Howard?" They were both pretty prominent in the medical community, so she assumed Matt might know him.

"The Henry Howard that runs the entire diagnostics lab at OSU?" he asked.

"Yes," Olivia said as she took one last piece of luggage from the trunk.

"I've read his work. It's fascinating. He is a legend. He's very gifted. I've attended some of his lectures, too. Why do you ask?"

"Well, we've sort of gotten to know each other."

"What do you mean by that?"

321

"We went out on a date last night."

"A date?" His face hardened a little. "Isn't he a little old for you?"

"I knew you'd say that," she said, shutting the SUV hatch.

"Dating," he said with a distinct lack of enthusiasm.

"Okay, can we just drop it? It was one date."

Matt sighed. "Dating."

"Daddy," she scolded.

"Just wait. You'll see. The moment the word 'dating' is linked to your daughter, you'll feel a pit in your stomach. Just wait until it happens to you." With a knowing smile, he added, "Robin's inside cooking. I'll send David and Hope out to help with the bags and Amelia's things."

Just as Matt reached for the screen door handle, it swung open. Hope burst outside, throwing herself into Olivia's arms, nearly knocking her off her feet.

Hope had always kept in touch with Olivia, especially when she was in rehab. Emails, greeting cards, letters, phone calls. Hope had always kept the lines of communication open between the two of them.

Hope was a beautiful young girl with long, dark brown hair and deep brown eyes. She favored Matt's appearance. With the most beautiful skin and a beamingly positive personality, Hope was extremely bright and did very well in school. In fact, she was in several gifted classes. She spoke Spanish and German fluently. She was also very well received by her peers. Additionally, Hope was very musically inclined. Her voice sounded like an angel's, and she had been playing the piano since the age of three.

Hope pulled away, still holding tightly to Olivia's hands. She seemed to be in a trance. "Hope, are you okay?" Olivia asked.

Her eyes refocused. She smiled half-heartedly. "Sure. I'm fine."

Olivia was skeptical but brushed off the situation.

The door to the house opened again, and David stepped outside. Tall for his age, he had ash-brown hair, just like Robin's before she started coloring it, and light brown eyes that mirrored hers as well. He was lean and undeniably handsome.

Though he was not as close to Olivia as Hope was, he deeply respected his older sister for the darkness she had overcome. Over time, he had also formed a strong bond with Amelia, shaped by the time she had spent in Matt and Robin's care.

Somewhat shyer than Hope, David was soft-spoken, but he could be assertive when pushed. Things did not come as easily to him academically either. He had to take time to study, whereas Hope could look at something once and remember anything about it. Her photographic memory often angered him because he had to work much harder to do just as well. His social skills were comparable to Hope's

323

though. He had close friends and was well liked by his classmates.

A talented athlete, he loved basketball and cross country. He ran daily. Official practices for the fall cross country team would start at the beginning of August. For now, however, he was busy going to the public pool with his friends and playing online games, with Robin and Matt's approval, of course.

With a shy wave, he smiled. "Hi, Olly," he said. "Dad sent me out to help," he concluded as he grabbed a piece of luggage.

"Thanks," Olivia said sweetly.

They walked in, David and Hope ahead of Olivia. Robin stood at the island in the middle of the kitchen cutting up vegetables. She looked up and beamed. Wiping her hands off with a towel, she walked to Olivia and embraced her. "Welcome home," she whispered.

Olivia pulled away gently and smiled. "The house looks beautiful as always."

The interior of the home was spectacular. All of the remodeling and updating Matt and Robin had done when they first purchased the home had held up well. The home still smelled of spice, and the primitive décor was something Olivia always loved.

"Am I still in the basement?" Olivia asked.

The basement still housed the laundry room and gaming

area, but part of it had changed over the years. What was once a play area had been converted into a bedroom for Olivia when Hope was born. She had not minded moving to the lower level as she got older. It gave her privacy and space away from her much younger siblings. Upstairs, the room that had once been a study had been given to David.

"Yes. It's all ready for you," Robin answered.

Amelia's laughter echoed throughout the house as she and Nigel sat on the floor in the living room playing. After delivering luggage to the basement, David came back up and played with Amelia, too.

"I'm going to take the rest of our things downstairs," Olivia said. "Can you keep an eye on Amelia?" she asked as she looked at David.

"Sure," he answered.

Olivia stood in her room looking around. It had been updated with new light-colored carpet. A wedding ring quilt with varying shades of pink covered the bed. Cherry wood nightstands and a desk matched the bed's wooden frame. There were not many of Olivia's personal belongings left in the room. After all, it had been a very long time since she had slept there.

63

After dinner, Olivia, Robin, and Hope cleaned up the dishes. Matt and David took Amelia and Nigel outside on the east porch. As Olivia stood at the sink rinsing off dishes, Hope brought more plates and glasses in while Robin packed leftovers into the refrigerator.

The east door opened. Matt called in, "There's someone coming up the lane."

They all looked at each other, confusion on their faces. "We're not expecting anyone else," Robin said.

"I'll go see who it is," Olivia said, heading toward the coat rack. She grabbed her gun and tucked it into the back of her pants before stepping outside.

When she opened the west entrance, she saw Danny driving up. Her eyes widened with surprise, her mind filling with questions.

He put the vehicle in park and shut off the engine. He had barely opened the door when Olivia's sharp voice cut through the air. "What the hell are you doing here? How did you find me?" she demanded, crossing her arms.

Danny sighed. "When you turned on your phone, Sue pinged it off the nearest tower," he admitted.

Olivia's eyes narrowed. "So you guys are spying on me now?"

"No," he said, shaking his head. "She knows we had a fight. She just wanted to help."

"I'll be sure to thank her when I get back," Olivia said, her voice dripping with sarcasm.

"Don't be mad at her," Danny pleaded, stepping closer. "I asked her to do it. I couldn't let the weekend pass without talking to you. I want to fix this."

"You made it pretty clear where we stand," Olivia bit out.

"I was stupid," Danny admitted. "I should've asked you to come with me to interview Henry."

"No, you should have told me your theory so I could tell you how dumb it was."

He nodded. "You're right. I should've talked to you first. I just... I didn't know you were sleeping with him. Not until today. It caught me off guard."

Olivia's eyes flashed. "Why do you care who I sleep with, Danny? And why should it matter?"

"Because you're my best friend, Livy. I don't want to see you get hurt, that's all. And I want you to keep a clear head. This guy is a hell of a lot older than you. I don't want him taking advantage of you."

"Taking advantage?" she scoffed. "I don't have money, Danny. I have nothing to offer him besides sex, and if I'm consenting, then there's no harm, no foul."

"Sex isn't all," he countered. "You have yourself to offer him. And I don't think you realize what a great person you are. You deserve someone who sees that."

Olivia exhaled sharply. "You can't keep protecting me like I'm going to break."

"It's my job to protect you. You can't ask me to stop doing my job."

Her voice softened. "Why? Why is my life so important to you?"

Danny held her gaze. "Isn't mine important to you?"

Her arms dropped, hands sliding into her pockets. She looked down, tracing a circle in the gravel with her toe. "Yes. Of course it is. We're partners."

"Exactly," he said. "That's why I get crazy sometimes. I just want you to be safe. It's your life, you're right. Live it however you want. Just… be careful, okay?"

She nodded.

"But no more secrets," Olivia added. "You need to ask me before you pull something like that again."

Danny stepped closer, locking eyes with her. "It'll never happen again. I promise."

"Okay."

"We good?" he asked, his gaze unwavering.

She held his stare for a moment, then nodded. "We're

328

good."

"Okay," he said as he smiled.

"So, Danny, what's your plan now? Are you going to drive all the way back to Columbus?" Olivia asked.

He folded his arms and dropped his head. "I hadn't thought it out that far. All I cared about was getting here to talk to you."

Amused by his lack of planning, she grinned. "Are you hungry?"

"Starvin'."

She smirked. "Of course you are," she joked. "We have leftovers. Come on in. You can stay here. The couch in the game room is a sofa sleeper. Did you bring clothes?" she asked as she headed toward the back door.

"Other than the overnight bag I keep in the car, no."

"You can borrow some of my dad's stuff. You look a little crazy in cargo pants and hiking boots, especially for a leisurely weekend," she said with a laugh.

"I guess I do," he agreed as he glanced down at himself.

64

Olivia and Danny walked into the kitchen. Hope was loading dishes into the dishwasher as Robin continued putting leftovers in the fridge.

"I'd leave some of that out," Olivia said.

Robin spun around. "Alright," she replied.

"Everyone, this is my partner, Danny Knight. Danny, this is Robin, my stepmom, and my little sister Hope."

Robin walked to him with her hand outstretched. "Danny, so nice to meet you," she said cordially.

"Pleasure to meet ya," Danny said as he smiled and nodded. "And Hope, Olivia talks about you a lot."

The young girl smiled but didn't offer her hand. "Nice to meet you, Danny."

Matt walked in with Amelia in his arms, Nigel following. When she saw Danny, she squirmed out of Matt's arms and ran to him. Danny threw out his hands and picked her up. "Monkey girl," he said endearingly as she threw her arms around his neck. He tickled her sides as her laughter filled the room.

"Dad," Olivia began, "this is Danny Knight. We work together."

Matt walked to him with a hand outstretched. "So

you're the man I need to thank for saving my little girl's life."

"It was a life worth saving, sir," he answered with a nod.

"Just call me Matt."

"Yes sir," he said, then quickly corrected himself. "I mean Matt."

"Do you have to go back tonight?" Robin asked. "Is there a case that you both need to work on? Is that why you came to get her?"

They both smiled bashfully. "Um, no," Danny answered as he glanced at Olivia. "I… uh… I was a stupid idiot today, and she deserved an apology in person, so here I am."

Matt's face brightened. "A true gentleman always admits when he's wrong. That's something you don't see every day. I think my son, David, should hear that."

Everyone smiled.

As if David knew the subject had shifted his way, he entered the room from outside. His face filled with confusion as he noticed the new face among them.

"Speaking of the devil," Matt began, "this is David. David, this is Danny, Olivia's partner at work."

David walked to him and shook his hand.

Amelia still clung to him, her head resting on his shoulder. Everyone stood for a moment in awe at how attached she was to Danny. Olivia wasn't as mesmerized as the others since she was around it all the time.

"We just had baked chicken, green beans, and cornbread. You just tell me how much you want on your plate," Robin said, walking to the fridge.

"Oh, I can get it," Danny said.

"Oh no you won't. Olivia, take this man to the dining room, and I'll get a plate ready," Robin insisted.

Olivia walked to the dining room, Danny following. They sat at the long table, Amelia still in his arms.

"Amelia, why don't you go with Pap? Go play with Nigel, sweetie, and then we will get your bath," Olivia suggested.

"I go," she said as she slipped out of Danny's arms and toddled toward the kitchen, yelling, "Pap!"

Danny looked around. "This house is somethin'. Really beautiful."

"They restored it and put it on the historical registry," Olivia said.

He dropped his head and put his hands on the tabletop. "I hope I'm not intruding. For you to take off like that today, you really must've wanted to get away."

"I did," she admitted. "I needed to think."

"I hope I didn't…" he trailed off.

"No. I needed to think about where I want things to go with Henry. I needed to figure out whether I wanted to continue working with you after the stunt you pulled. I needed to be by myself."

"And I've crashed your weekend," he said guiltily. "I know I really pissed you off."

"Well, the problem between us is fixed now, so I don't need to think about that anymore."

"Why do you need to think about the thing with Henry? What's there to think about?" he inquired.

"I don't know if I'm ready for any kind of relationship."

"Is that what he is saying he wants?"

She shrugged. "I don't think so, but we haven't really talked about it. All of this just kind of happened."

"So then why are you stressing about it?" he said, with a twinge of confusion in his tone.

"I just thought that since we—"

"Yeah, yeah, go on," he interrupted.

"That we need some kind of status, I guess. I don't know," Olivia replied. "Danny, I've never been in a real relationship before, at least not one that was normal and healthy."

"Is there any relationship that's normal?" he asked. He pursed his lips and then grinned. "The first thing you need to do is just relax and quit analyzing things. Let it move where it's supposed to, if it is supposed to move any place at all. Sometimes a one nighter is exactly that. Nothin' more."

"That just makes me feel like a whore, especially with my past."

"Maybe you want a relationship. That way you don't have to feel like that anymore. Most people, at one time in their life, have had a one night stand. Sometimes they go places, and sometimes they don't. It doesn't make you a bad person. Sometimes it's just friends with benefits for a while, and things fizzle. Sometimes it's just the one night and that's all."

"How many one night stands have you had?" she asked curiously.

"We're not talking about me," he smiled. "We're talking about you."

"You're avoiding the question. I want to know," she pressed.

He clammed up, but she persisted. "Oh come on. Tell me."

Hope walked in with a plate of food, saving Danny from the interrogation.

"Oh, thank God," he said with relief.

Olivia's mouth dropped open even though she kept a slight smile. "Don't think that food is going to save you from this conversation."

"It is for now," he said with a smirk.

"I'll go get you something to drink. What do you want?"

"Soda's fine."

Olivia stood and walked to the kitchen, where Hope lingered near the island. The air crackled with tension, though Olivia couldn't understand why.

"Olly," Hope began, "there's a man, another man."

Olivia walked to her and turned her slightly. "Hope, what are you talking about?"

"The other man is a good man, but he is going to lead you someplace you didn't plan on going," she said.

With a troubled grimace, Olivia looked intensely into Hope's eyes. "What are you doing? What are you even talking about?"

"When I touch you, I can see things," Hope answered.

Olivia narrowed her gaze. She couldn't believe what she was hearing. "So you can touch people and see things? That's your gift?"

She nodded. "I've been able to do it since I was small, but I didn't tell anyone until a few months ago."

"Do Mom and Dad know?" Olivia asked.

"I told Mom first. She told Daddy."

"Hope, what do you see?"

"I only see flashes," she explained. "The other man... I saw him in pain. I don't know why he was hurting. I heard you crying. Then I saw tombstones."

Olivia was astonished and amazed. With her mouth gaping open, she couldn't quite find the words. Then she recovered and composed herself. "I think you see Henry. He's a friend of mine. He did go through a lot of pain when he was growing up. That's probably what you see."

"I don't see the past. I see what's coming. He's going to get hurt again," she said in almost a whisper.

"I don't know what it means," Olivia said.

"I don't either. All I know is that I can do it," Hope continued. "It comes and goes. I can't explain it either. I'm still trying to figure this out. Mom's trying to help me, but sometimes we both get confused."

"Does David know what you can do?"

"He does, but he doesn't believe in anything. He's been a jerk about it," she remarked. "He thinks he's in a house full of freaks most of the time. He even calls me a freak."

Olivia took Hope's hands into hers, looking deeply into her unsure eyes. "You're not a freak. You're touched. That's all. It's your gift."

"Like right now," she said as tears filled her eyes, "I can see you standing over a casket. You're crying. I don't know why or who is dead." The tears streamed down her cheeks. "And I can feel your grief before it's even happened. What

336

does all of this mean?"

Olivia kissed her forehead and then knelt before Hope. Gently brushing away the tears, she wanted to reassure her. "Sweetheart, I don't know what it means, but I do know that you have been given a beautiful talent. In time, I know you'll learn to use it, and you'll understand it. Just stick close to Mom. Let her help you."

With a nod, Hope embraced Olivia.

Danny walked in with his empty plate in his hand. "Oh, I'm sorry, I didn't mean to interrupt."

Olivia turned to him and stood. With a smile, she replied, "You didn't. It's just a girl thing."

Olivia walked to him and took the plate. She opened the dishwasher and put it in with the other dirty dishes. She grabbed the soda from the fridge. "Dad is outside with Amelia, if you want to go out while we clean up."

"Sure," Danny answered as he walked to the screen door and opened it.

Matt stood on the porch, leaning against the wooden pillar as he gazed out at the field. Memories flooded his mind. Things he thought he had forgotten came rushing back. Olivia's visit had stirred emotions he had buried long ago, including the first time he had seen the ghostly woman in the fog and explored the cemetery on the property. More shadows from his past clouded his thoughts.

Nearby, Amelia played with her toys on the porch while Nigel lay protectively beside her. The warm night air carried the soft rustling of leaves, blending with the rhythmic croaking of frogs. It was a peaceful contrast to the storm of memories swirling in Matt's mind.

Turning around, Matt saw Danny approaching. He offered a small smile. "Did you get sent away?"

"Yeah, afraid I did," Danny said, lowering himself onto the porch swing.

Matt sat in the rocking chair. "How was the drive?"

"Uneventful," Danny replied, taking a sip of his soda. He glanced around. "You have a beautiful home. I've seen pictures Olivia's shared, but being here is completely different."

"Thanks. We're proud of it. Took a lot of blood, sweat, and tears."

Danny nodded. "I'd love to build something like this

one day. Be out in the country. I've always lived in the city."

"I wanted the same thing," Matt said. "That's what brought me here. Where are you from?"

"Brooklyn. Born and raised."

Matt smirked. "I figured from the accent."

"I get that a lot."

"And now you're in Columbus?"

"Yeah. That's what happens when 9/11 takes over your life."

Matt's expression grew solemn. "Were you a first responder?"

Danny nodded. "Yeah. I did cleanup at Ground Zero."

"I volunteered at some of the hospitals in the area," Matt said. "Felt like I was there forever."

"That day changed everything."

"It really did."

Danny exhaled, then shrugged. "But I've got good friends in Columbus, and my family moved with me, so it's all good."

Matt leaned forward slightly. "I can't thank you enough for saving Olivia's life. We almost lost her once. Spent months thinking she was dead. Then watching her go through rehab was like losing her all over again. The withdrawals were brutal. I was the only one allowed to see her, just because I'm a doctor. Even with the Suboxone, she suffered. It was hell knowing I couldn't take the pain away. Then Nigel came along, and once she was strong enough, he gave her purpose. I swear, that dog's an angel. He saved her life and inspired her to help others. I'm so proud of who she is."

"You should be," Danny said. "She's brave. I respect her a lot, and so do the other officers and detectives. She's been open about her experiences. That's helped us understand addiction and what we're up against when dealing with people."

Matt studied Danny for a moment. The expression on his face was all too familiar. It was the same one Matt had when he thought about Robin.

"You love her."

Danny looked up, surprised.

"It's alright," Matt said. "Your secret's safe."

Danny sighed, lowering his head. "Is it that obvious?"

"Only to someone who's been there."

"I care about her. A lot," Danny admitted. "I feel like I can't breathe when she's mad at me. It doesn't happen often, but today, when we argued, I knew I had to fix it. I couldn't stand knowing she was upset."

"She has no idea, does she?"

"I hope not."

Matt frowned slightly. "Why not?"

Danny hesitated, then sighed. "I don't think she's ready for something like that."

Matt nodded. "It's good that you're thinking about her feelings and the impact it might have on her. That's love, son."

Danny lowered his gaze briefly. "I'll know when the time's right. If this guy she's with doesn't beat me to it first."

"Dr. Howard?" Matt asked. "She told me they went on a date last night."

"Yeah. She's known him for a couple of months from a case, but I didn't think she'd actually be interested in him, you know?"

Matt nodded. "He's older. Wiser. But be careful about waiting too long. At the end of the day, the choice is Olivia's, but if she doesn't know you're an option, you're shutting yourself down before you even try. Just think about that."

Danny nodded. "Yeah, I know." He gave a quick breath. "I can't believe I just told you all of this."

Matt chuckled. "Sometimes it's easier to talk to someone you don't know well."

"But you're her dad."

"Exactly. Who better to tell you what makes her tick? I

raised her, remember?"

Danny smiled. "I guess you're right."

Matt leaned back. "I never had to compete for Robin. We just fell in love almost instantly. I met her in the emergency room. She was dirty, sweaty, and stunk to high heaven. Twisted her ankle playing softball. But I couldn't take my eyes off her. She had this energy, something I couldn't explain. I just knew my life would never be the same."

Danny smiled. "Yeah. I know what you mean."

Matt nodded. "Things will work out, Danny. Just be patient with Olivia. She's independent and terrified of love. Everything she's been through, addiction, survival, rebuilding herself, it's shaped her into who she is. But don't let that stop you. Push through like a soldier. She'll respect you for it. Just like tonight. You took a chance and came here, and look what happened. She forgave you easily."

Danny chuckled. "Yeah. All it took was an apology. Most of the women I've been involved with hold a grudge and put you through hell forever."

Matt smirked. "The fact that Olivia forgave you right away should tell you something. She values your friendship. That's your way in."

The screen door creaked open, and Robin stepped onto the porch. "You boys sure have been chatting it up out here."

Matt and Danny exchanged smiles.

"I just set an apple pie on the counter. You'd better grab a slice before the women in the house eat it all."

With a playful smirk, she turned and disappeared back inside.

Danny scooped Amelia into his arms, making her giggle. Matt watched for a moment before speaking. "That right there is another reason I know you're a good man," he remarked. "Amelia absolutely adores you. She trusts you."

Danny smiled. "She's an amazing little girl."

Matt nodded. "Olivia sees how much you care about her daughter. That doesn't go unnoticed by a parent. I know that feeling well. When Robin met Olivia, they clicked right away. Same with you and Amelia." Matt stood and patted Danny's shoulder. "You're a good guy, Danny. I wish you all the best."

Danny met his gaze and nodded. "Thanks. That means a lot."

66

The sleeping arrangements were set: Danny took the pull-out sofa bed in the basement. Matt slept on the couch in the living room, and Amelia stayed upstairs with Robin. When Amelia had lived there before, her crib had been in their bedroom.

Lying on her side, Olivia stared at the wall, unable to sleep. Her mind drifted to Henry. Then, suddenly, she was no longer in bed. She was standing outside a warehouse. She looked up at the unfamiliar structure, confusion washing over her.

A wave of panic surged through her. Spinning around, she saw dozens of police cruisers lined up in the vacant lot, their flashing lights cutting through the darkness.

Then Amelia's cries pierced the silence.

Heart pounding, Olivia turned back toward the warehouse. The sound of her daughter's cries fueled her desperation, and she rushed toward the building.

"Amelia!" she shouted, her voice raw with fear. She screamed her name over and over, frustration mounting as the cries echoed from nowhere.

Suddenly, a sense of comfort washed over her. Then Danny appeared. Relief was short-lived, though, as he turned away and sprinted toward the warehouse.

"Danny!" she screamed. "Amelia!"

Her voice broke with desperation.

A firm shake jolted her.

She couldn't stop screaming.

The shaking intensified.

Olivia's eyes flew open. She gasped for air, her heart racing as she sat up in bed.

Danny sat beside her, concern etched across his face.

Tears blurred her vision as she struggled to catch her breath. "Oh my God," she gasped. "Danny."

Instinctively, she threw her arms around his neck, still trembling. He wrapped his arms around her, holding her close as she sobbed.

"Where's Amelia?" she asked, pulling away, panic flashing in her eyes.

"She's upstairs with your mom," he reassured her gently.

The basement door creaked open, and Matt's voice carried down the stairs. "Everything okay?"

"Daddy," Olivia called, still breathless. "Please check on Amelia."

"Okay."

Running her fingers through her hair, Olivia tried to steady her shaking hands. "That was a terrible nightmare."

Danny placed his hands on her shoulders, his gaze steady. "Tell me about it."

"I couldn't get to her," Olivia whispered, her voice unsteady. "She was somewhere, and I couldn't reach her. You tried to help. I felt like my heart was being ripped out of my chest."

The basement door opened again. "She's fine," Matt called down. "Asleep in the bed."

Olivia exhaled in relief. "Okay, Dad."

"You need anything, Olly?"

"No. I'm fine. It was just a nightmare."

The door shut, leaving Olivia and Danny alone again.

"It was just a dream, Livy. We're all fine," Danny assured her.

Her lip quivered. "My little girl. I'll always be afraid something will take her away after everything I've done. I don't deserve to be her mom."

Danny pulled her back into his arms. "You're a good mom," he said firmly.

She clung to him, still feeling the weight of guilt pressing down on her chest. Slowly, her sobs quieted.

Danny brushed away her tears and smiled softly. "You're a good mom," he repeated. "I won't let anything happen to either of you. You understand me?"

Olivia hesitated, then asked, "Can you stay with me? Just for a while?"

Danny nodded, then stood and walked to the other side of the bed. Pulling the blanket up, he slipped under the sheets. Olivia turned onto her side, molding into him as he wrapped his arms around her. She felt safe, yet the emotions still lingered, and she began crying again.

"It's okay. I'm right here," Danny murmured, stroking her hair.

"I'll always be paying for what I've done," Olivia whispered. "The nightmares remind me she's only with me temporarily."

"I don't believe that," Danny said. "I think this Tic-Tac-Toe case is getting to you. But I won't let anything happen to either of you. You know that, right?"

She nodded against his chest, still sniffling.

"Try to get some sleep, Livy. I'm not going anywhere."

As she lay in his arms, a deep certainty settled within her. Their connection was unlike anything she'd ever experienced. It was as if he had been sent to her, to protect, to guide, to stand beside her. Sometimes, she wondered if he was more than just a man. Maybe he was something greater. A guardian. Maybe that's why Amelia adored him. His protectiveness wasn't driven by jealousy or disapproval. It came from something deeper. Loyalty. Purpose.

Danny pressed a gentle kiss to her forehead, and it felt

natural, as if it had always belonged there.

Olivia looked up at him. "Thank you."

"For what?"

"For finding me," she said softly.

He smiled and kissed her forehead again, but that simple gesture wasn't enough for her. She propped herself onto her elbow and leaned down. Gazing into his eyes, she caressed his face with her hand and then bent down, kissing his lips tenderly as she felt his hand contour to her cheek.

Her leg draped over him, and she felt him hard against her inner thigh. She pressed her leg against it. His hand moved to her bare leg as he traced invisible shapes on her skin. Moving his hands to her bottom, he teased the waistband of her panties. Then he pulled her on top of him.

She straddled him and kept kissing him, her hair cascading around them. She felt his hands under her shirt, warm against her skin. She moved on him rhythmically, the clothing still a barrier between them. He leaned up and kissed her neck as she nuzzled his forehead.

In one swift motion, she was on her back, Danny kneeling between her legs. She sat up, kissing his stomach and putting her hand up the leg of his shorts. His breaths grew heavier as she slowly brought him to full arousal.

He pulled her shirt from her body and threw it to the floor. The pause becoming unbearable, she pulled his shorts from his hips as he wiggled out of them. Once they were off, he pulled her underwear from her body and pushed her thighs apart.

She gripped his forearms and pulled him gently to her. He pushed into her. Their breaths hitched as they formed to one another. The movements were slow and deliberate.

He leaned down and kissed her ear, his breath warm against her skin.

She smiled and turned to him. He propped himself on his elbow, still moving steadily. Their lips met again as she wrapped her legs tightly around him.

They rolled, Danny now on his back. She sat up on him, feeling him deep inside of her. She rested her hands on his upper thighs. He reached up and cupped her breasts.

He closed his eyes as she moved faster, nearing the edge. She placed her hands firmly on his chest as she felt the heat rise through her body. She tightened around him as she reached orgasm. She struggled to stay quiet, biting her lip as she rocked on him, taking every ounce of pleasure that she could.

She felt his muscles tense under her touch, and she knew he was close. She moved faster, bringing him to climax, his hands tightly gripping her hips. His mouth was open, and he tightly gripped the sheets, trying to stay quiet, too.

The afterglow embraced them as Danny's chest rose and fell rapidly. Olivia smiled down at Danny, a hint of deviousness in her gaze. She was surprised by their unexpected encounter.

67

While Olivia cleaned up in the bathroom, Danny had time to think. He wondered how he would manage to keep things light now that he'd had a taste of her. He enjoyed making love to her and felt even more connected to her. He knew that he was helplessly in love with her, and having a physical experience with her was an extension of those powerful feelings.

Olivia walked back into the room wearing her nightshirt and underwear again. He still lay naked, not moving from his spot on the bed. He was at a full erection again after reminiscing about sex with her.

"Didn't I do the job?" she asked, glancing down at him.

"Oh, no. You did. That's just me."

"You can go again?"

"I can go more than again," he said with a smile.

"Are you serious?" she asked as she stood and pulled her shirt off, exposing herself to him again.

He looked at her admiringly. "Oh yeah. Again... and again... and again," he said as he reached for her.

"Well, then," she said as she crawled onto the bed, "what are we waiting for?"

68

By 4 a.m., they'd finally gone through their energy reserves. At 11 a.m., Danny glanced over at the alarm clock on the bedside table. He put his feet on the floor and sat on the side of the bed, his head in his hands. He wondered what would happen now. A line had certainly been crossed.

He felt her hand on his back. He smiled over his shoulder. "Morning," he said sweetly.

"Morning," she replied.

"You still tired?" he asked. "If you are, I can come get you in an hour or so."

"No, I'm good," she replied with a stretch.

"Yes, you certainly are," he agreed as he turned his body toward her and leaned onto his elbow. He kissed her lips softly and then pulled away. He stood and put his shorts on. With his hands on his hips, he looked down at her. "You okay with this?"

Her face was contorted as she sought clarification. "With what happened between us?"

"Yeah."

"Are you okay with it?" she asked, evading the question.

"I'm fine. I just want to make sure you are."

"I thought it was great," she admitted.

"Well, I just know you're trying to figure this thing out with Henry. Now I've..." he trailed off.

"I'll figure it out," Olivia replied. "No matter what, we're still friends. We always will be, Danny. I don't want you to treat me differently just because we've slept together."

"I won't. I would never..." He paused. "You're just really hot. I mean that," he said, folding his arms.

She smiled, the cover falling slightly off of her right breast. "You're too sweet."

"I could stand here and look at you all day. Hell, I could stay in here with you all day, getting wrapped up in you."

"You are pretty incredible, too, not just sexually though. You're just so open with me," she said with a beaming smile.

He sat back down on the side of the bed and leaned over. He balanced his weight on his hands. "I... Livy..."

She rose up on her elbow and put her finger to his lips. "Shhh... let's not talk, okay? Let's just be. Whatever comes, we'll deal with it. Let's take your advice and not overthink any of this."

He kissed her finger and nodded. "Okay."

69

Olivia and Danny spent the entire day on the trails behind Pikeview with Amelia and Nigel. They packed a picnic lunch and lounged on a blanket beside the creek, enjoying the peacefulness of the outdoors. When their adventure came to an end, they made their way back to the house for dinner with the family.

Both Danny and Olivia needed the break. The Tic-Tac-Toe case had put an immense strain on their mental states, and they craved time to recharge. But no matter how much they tried to focus on relaxation, they could not ignore the reality that the sexual relationship that had developed between them was bound to complicate things later.

On Sunday morning, as Olivia lay in Danny's arms, she felt the weight of reality creeping back in. The warmth and comfort of the moment were fleeting, and sadness settled over them.

As he traced circles on her back, Olivia longed to stay curled up next to him.

"What time are we leaving?" he whispered.

"After lunch," she murmured, eyes still closed.

"I had a great time with you and your family," he said. "They're good people. It's easy to see how you turned out so great."

She smiled, her eyes remaining shut as she felt his lips

brush against her nose in a soft kiss.

"Thanks for being here with me," she whispered. "You made coming here easier."

"Why was it hard for you to come home?"

"It's a long story," she sighed. "And we need to get dressed and go upstairs. It's almost 9. I can smell the bacon cooking, and they're making a big breakfast for us."

Danny exhaled heavily. "I don't want to leave," he admitted. "I don't want to go home and act like this never happened."

"I don't plan on acting like that," she said, propping herself up on her elbow to look down at him.

He studied her for a moment, his expression serious. "I just know you need to sort things out with Henry first, so I'm going to give you the space to do that."

"But, I"

"Livy," he interrupted gently, "right now, you're caught up in this because I'm here, right in front of you. But when we go back, Henry is going to take my place. I know that."

"Danny"

"I'm not saying I don't want things to stay the way they've been this weekend," he said, his voice steady. "But I know you're confused, and it wouldn't be fair for me to make it harder on you. Figure out what you need to with Henry. No matter what, I'll be here. I'm your best friend, and that's never gonna change."

He loved her. That love was the very reason he was willing to step back and let her choose. He had made himself an option. It was up to her now. He would continue to be present, to show her what they could be, but the decision had to be hers.

Danny didn't want to be a consolation prize or someone she chose out of convenience. He wanted her to love him the way he loved her. And right now, he knew she didn't.

70

After breakfast, Matt stood outside, watching Olivia and Danny walk through the field together. On the porch, Amelia and Nigel played, their laughter carrying through the crisp morning air.

Matt felt Robin's arms wrap around him from behind.

"What are you doing?" she asked softly.

Still staring at Olivia and Danny in the distance, he smiled. "He loves her so much."

Robin moved to his side, keeping one arm around his waist. "I know," she agreed.

Matt draped his arm over her shoulder. "Do you think she'll realize she loves him, too?"

"I think she will," Robin said. "She's just scared. But when you find the one who takes away the fear, you get over it."

Matt sighed. "I hope so. I think he'd die for her. You can just feel it."

Robin looked up at him, hesitation in her expression. "Matt, do you know something I don't?"

He glanced down at her, his face unreadable. Then, shaking his head, he said, "No. I just know he'd take a bullet for her. He's her partner. And she'd do the same for him."

Robin studied him for a moment before saying, "Hope told me she sees them together, but she doesn't know where or when."

Matt nodded. "Then you can take it to the bank. If Hope sees it, it'll happen. It's just a matter of time."

71

When Olivia and Danny returned to their everyday lives, Olivia tried to let things unfold naturally, resisting the urge to overanalyze everything. Her weekly routine was well established. Tuesday and Thursday evenings were for her group meetings, followed by time with Henry.

Friday nights were reserved for her standing date with Amelia and Nigel, usually spent at home with pizza delivery, and Danny often joined them. Saturdays meant the card game at Sarah and Paul's, which is where she first introduced Amelia to Henry. Though Amelia was kind to him, the connection wasn't the same as it was with Danny. Henry remained guarded around Amelia, which concerned Olivia, though she understood why, given his past.

Sundays were spent at Sue and Rick's, where the adults caught up while the kids played. Danny stopped by most weekends, sometimes to watch a ball game, other times just to enjoy the weather. Olivia didn't care what they did. What mattered was being with her friends and her daughter. For the first time in a long while, she felt joy.

When it came to intimacy, Henry was the only one she focused on. Their relationship remained casual. They went to dinner after group, spent the night together, then went their separate ways the next morning. They kept in touch by phone and text, but there was no discussion of commitment. Henry maintained his distance, and Olivia didn't mind. She wasn't ready for anything more. He satisfied her physically and was good company.

Still, she wasn't naive enough to compare what she had with Henry to the passion she'd experienced with Danny. That single weekend at Pikeview with Danny had been more intense. And yet, Olivia hesitated. She worried about how a deeper relationship with Danny might affect their ability to work together. More than that, she doubted she was good enough for him. She carried the weight of her past, convinced that Danny deserved someone whole, not someone as damaged as she was.

So they kept their promise and moved forward as friends, strengthening their platonic bond. But sometimes, Olivia caught herself reminiscing about his touch, his lips, the way he made her feel. She wondered if he thought about it too. She cared for him more than she had ever thought possible, but holding back felt necessary.

Her spirituality also kept her tethered to Henry. She was teaching him to meditate, guiding him toward a deeper understanding of his own mysticism. Their shared journey in self-discovery made her feel important, like she was truly helping him. In her mind, Henry was the only one who could fully understand the emptiness she sometimes felt. Their shared struggles with addiction reinforced that belief.

For Danny, keeping things strictly friendly was a constant battle. He knew Olivia wasn't ready for more, and pushing her would only drive her away. So, to keep her close, he accepted her boundaries. He wanted to talk to her about their feelings, but the timing was never right. Instead, he leaned into their friendship and work relationship, the foundation that held them together.

Danny often sought counsel from Rick and Sue. What he didn't know was that Olivia confided in Sue as well. Olivia had shared everything, her weekend with Danny, her fears about a relationship with him. Sue remained neutral, offering no advice, aware of both perspectives. She and Rick supported them both, neither Olivia nor Danny realizing they were turning to the same people for guidance.

Olivia also spoke with Sarah about Danny and Henry. Sarah, more outspoken than Sue, prioritized Olivia's happiness but saw clearly who cared for her most. She liked Henry well enough, but Danny was the one she favored, and Amelia's natural openness to him was proof enough. Still, Sarah knew Olivia lacked the confidence to fully pursue Danny, so she supported her in whatever way she could.

The web of relationships was intricate, constantly shifting. But through it all, Olivia found herself surrounded by true friends and companions, people she cherished and respected. For the first time in her life, she had exactly what she had always longed for.

72

Olivia stood in the rubble of the freshly burnt building, looking up at the fourth victim, naked and exposed, hanging from a concrete rafter. Another tic-tac-toe board was tattooed on her thigh, with an X in the upper right corner, an O in the lower left corner, and another X in the upper left corner.

Lauren walked up behind Olivia. Her dedication to the case was admirable. It took her away from maternity leave and her four-week-old son, but Nick was happy to have some time with his new baby boy.

"Do you see her?" Olivia whispered, referring to the victim.

"Yes. I'll handle it. Stay right here," Lauren replied.

Olivia watched as Lauren walked to the spirit of the girl. She wore a confused scowl. She stood in a pair of jeans, a T-shirt, and flip-flops, with her hair in a ponytail. Although she wasn't able to hear the conversation, Olivia saw the girl's mouth moving.

Danny walked up to Olivia and folded his arms. "The forensic team is running facial recognition right now. I'm guessing that they'll find another missing person's report," he said.

Olivia nodded. "You're probably right. This girl looks very young," she said, looking back up at the body.

"This'll be on the news tonight. The media is crawling all over the place outside. If it is recognition these bastards want, they've got it," Danny bit out.

Busily, the forensic team worked the scene, collecting evidence. Then Olivia saw Bentley and Henry come into the building. She noted Danny's facial expression. He was not pleased.

Henry walked toward them. "Bentley," Danny said with a nod. "And Dr. Howard, why are you here?"

"He's consulting for me," Bentley answered. "He's a doctor, and I need a second set of eyes. He's offered his expertise. He can also rush labs for us."

Olivia's eyes met Henry's, and then her attention turned back to the body. Dropping her head and walking toward Lauren, she hoped that Danny wouldn't be confrontational.

Lauren turned toward Olivia. "Her name is Penelope Zeila. She was taken from the dog park about four days ago. She's ten. She was blindfolded the entire time, but she heard two distinct voices. She was strangled, just like the others. Raped, just like the others."

Olivia focused on the girl. *Hello, Penelope,* she communicated through telepathy. *I'm Olivia.*

I'm scared, Penelope answered meekly.

I know. There's nothing to be afraid of, she assured her.

Emma appeared, her smiling face filled with serenity. *I'm here to help you, young one,* she said in a melodic voice.

I don't want to go, Penelope cried.

You can let go of all of the things you've come to know here, Olivia encouraged. *Emma is here to help you find your way to the light, but you must let go. It will be all right.*

My mom is alone, she continued. *My dad died when I was small. She has no one else.* Her cries intensified, and she fell to the ground, crossing her legs and putting her face in her hands. Emma walked closer and put her arm around the poor, frightened girl.

Your mom will be strong, Emma said.

Penelope, do you see the light? Olivia asked.

Looking up, she stood. *It's beautiful,* she said softly. Tears ran down her face as she grinned. *My dad. Oh my God, my dad.* Her eyes met Olivia's. *I can see him. He's waving at me.*

All you have to do is walk to him, Olivia encouraged.

Emma and Penelope vanished before Lauren and Olivia's eyes. They looked at each other.

"Your gift never ceases to amaze me," Lauren said.

"I feel the same way about yours."

"I fear I've not gathered as much information as I'd like. The younger victims tend to be able to communicate less."

They walked back to the others. The body now lay on the plastic tarp. Henry and Bentley knelt over her. Henry collected evidence under Penelope's nails as Bentley examined the marks on her neck. A forensic technician put the rope in an evidence bag.

Danny stood quietly, watching, his arms folded and his jaw set.

Bentley tested her liver temperature, puncturing the skin with the thermometer. He looked at the digital reading. "She's been dead about eight hours. Obviously, she's been strangled, just like the others. Killed somewhere else and brought here. MO is consistent, at least."

He spread her legs apart slightly. "Bruising on the inner thigh and vaginal tissue indicates sexual assault. Pretty rough, too. There are lacerations, from what I can tell."

"There were no bruises on the others, right? You assessed sexual assault based on internal damage, correct?" Olivia asked.

He nodded. "That's correct. The perp was especially rough with this one."

A forensic technician walked up to the group. "She was reported missing four days ago. Her name is Penelope Zeila, age ten. She's from the Dublin area. She went missing at the dog park. The mother was right there with her. According to the report, her mom turned her back to speak to another mother, and the child was taken. No one saw anything."

"So they've had her for the last four days?" Danny asked.

"Seems that way," the technician replied.

"That's no different than the other victims. So why the extensive bruising and the cuts to the vaginal area?" Henry said.

Bentley stood. "We'll know more when we get her on the table. It would be nice if we could get some trace off of the body."

"This is the youngest victim yet," Olivia said in a troubled tone.

"It confirms what I thought, and it confirms my profile," Lauren added. "One of the unsubs is a pedophile. Perhaps even both."

"We need to go get the mother," Danny said as he looked at Olivia.

She nodded and followed him out of the building. A very large crowd had gathered, complete with members of the media. Television station vans lined the street. Reporters stood on the sidelines, giving reports to viewers.

Henry walked out behind them. She heard Henry's voice as he said, "Kyle, what are you doing here?"

She eavesdropped on the conversation as she followed closely behind.

"I was taking my lunch and saw the crowd. I walked over when I saw all the news crews," Kyle answered. "What the hell happened?"

"Body," Henry answered.

Standing beside him now, Olivia smiled. "We can't really say anything more. It's an ongoing investigation."

"Kyle, this is Olivia Gregory," Henry started. "She's a detective and a close friend of mine."

"Hello," Olivia said with a nod.

"Pleased to meet you."

Kyle flashed a polite smile and then turned his attention back to the building. He sighed. "I hate stuff like this. It's so sad. Was there a fire?"

"Like I said, we can't really talk about it," Olivia answered.

Kyle nodded as he put his hands in his pockets. "I understand. I guess I can watch the news tonight and find out, huh?"

"Probably," Henry said, glancing around at the news vans.

Changing the subject quickly, Kyle continued. "So, how are you doing, Henry? Getting along okay? I wondered if you were doing better with things."

"I'm doing better. I meant to reply to your email. I've just been swamped with work and now helping with this…"

"Well, if you need anything, just get ahold of me," he suggested.

"I will, Kyle. Thanks," Henry concluded as he turned to see the gurney being wheeled out to Bentley's van. "I'd better go. I can't miss my ride."

"Sure, sure. Hey, it was good seeing you, Henry," he said, still smiling, "and great to meet you, Olivia," he concluded with a casual wave.

"Very nice to meet you, too," she finished as she and Henry walked away.

"Where does he work?" Olivia asked.

"I'm not sure," Henry answered. "Why?"

"Well, he said he was down here eating lunch, so he must work nearby," she replied.

"Probably. God knows lunchtime traffic on the interstate is crazy. I'd assume he must work within walking distance."

"He seems very nice," she added.

"He got it worse than the rest of us, like I told you."

Sadness filled Olivia's eyes as she shook her head.

She heard Danny calling to her. "We need to go."

Henry bent down and kissed Olivia's forehead. The public display of affection pleasantly surprised her. "I'll talk to you later," he concluded.

"Okay," she said as she walked to the SUV.

73

The drive to Dublin took longer than expected, but at last, Danny and Olivia arrived at Jayne Zeila's apartment. They knocked and waited. After a moment, a woman's voice called out, and the door opened.

A young woman stood before them, her expression marked by worry and exhaustion. She was petite, with curly black hair and deep brown eyes. Her waitress uniform, streaked with grease and food stains, hinted at a long day's work.

"Jayne Zeila?" Danny asked.

"Yes?" she replied.

"Ma'am, we're here about your daughter, Penelope," he continued.

"Oh God, come in," she said, stepping aside.

They walked in and stood in the middle of the living room.

"Is she okay? Did you find her?" Jayne asked.

"Come sit down, Ms. Zeila," Danny said.

Her face contorted as reality settled in her mind. She fell to her knees, sobbing uncontrollably. Olivia stepped in and knelt with her, embracing her and trying to offer comfort. The emotions poured from the young mother as Olivia glanced up at Danny. He stood helplessly, and then he knelt.

Things finally calmed after a few moments. They helped her to her feet, and she shuffled to the kitchen, sitting down at the tiny table. She peered out the window, dazed and still obviously in shock.

Olivia followed her in and sat down across from her. She reached out and touched her hand. "Is there anyone we can call for you?"

She nodded. "My sister, Joyce."

Fifteen minutes later, Joyce opened the door and walked into the living room. She rushed to the kitchen and took her sister into an embrace. They sobbed, the grief weighing heavily on them.

Olivia hated the next part, but she knew it had to be done. "Ma'am, we're very sorry, but we need you to identify her. Then we can talk to you about what happened," she explained in a hushed tone as she gently touched her arm.

They departed and met at the morgue. Waiting in the dank hallway was Henry, who escorted Jayne and Joyce to the swinging doors and then disappeared.

The wailing from the room was heartbreaking, and Olivia suddenly felt sick with emotion. Tears filled her eyes as she sat down in a vacant chair. She felt her hands trembling a little. She didn't understand what was happening. She was usually composed.

Danny sat down beside her. He put his hand gently on

top of hers. "We're gonna get these guys," he said, trying to reassure her.

"I sincerely hope so," she bit out.

The door flung open again, and Henry entered the hallway. He motioned for Danny and Olivia to follow him. They made their way down the dimly lit hallway and into a conference room.

"She seems to be settling down a bit," Henry began.

Olivia and Danny waited with bated breath. Both could easily see there was more to say.

"Bentley found evidence of severe vaginal trauma," Henry replied, his voice solemn and controlled. "He said her uterus was even damaged. The trauma is much worse than he initially thought."

"What exactly does that mean?" Danny whispered.

"Well, the way it was explained to me, the thrusting was so violent during the sex act that her uterus became tilted and damaged."

"So this was happening while the girl was still alive?" Olivia asked as bile rose into her throat.

Henry nodded with pursed lips and then went on. "Bentley said that there are lacerations on the vaginal walls, and her cervix is destroyed. The injuries were inflicted perimortem because of intercourse. There are also indications of sexual torture. He said that the bruising is worse than anything he's ever seen. He said even with traditional rape victims, he's never seen anything this brutal. This poor girl was repeatedly raped and tortured while still alive. Then they mutilated her genitals."

"Find any trace on the body?" Danny asked.

"Afraid not," Henry answered.

"Anger," Olivia said softly, her eyes staring blankly across the conference room.

"What?" Danny asked.

"The killers are escalating. They're angrier. Why? Why so much rage now?"

"Bentley says that everything else is consistent with the other victims, so there's that," Henry added.

Danny and Olivia nodded at Henry.

"We need to interview her," Olivia said as she walked to the door and turned the knob. She pulled the door open and walked down the hallway where Joyce and Jayne sat. They both held bottles of water and tissues in their hands.

Instead of leading them to an interview room, Olivia pulled up a chair and sat in front of them. Danny and Henry stood close by.

"Ms. Zeila," Olivia began softly, "I am so sorry for your loss."

Jayne only nodded.

"I cannot imagine the pain you are in. We want to find

the people responsible for her death. Can you help us do that?" she asked compassionately.

Jayne nodded again. "I want her to be at peace," she replied.

Olivia's expression became determined. "I'd like to put together a timeline and try to understand what the last few hours of her life looked like. Your daughter was taken from the dog park, yes?"

"Yes, she was."

"Did you see anyone suspicious while you were there? Any vehicles that looked out of place?"

"No," she said as she shook her head. "She walked dogs to save money for a computer she wanted. Our friends all have pets, and they all work during the day. So she started a little business walking their dogs for the summer. I went with her every day to walk the dogs. I was very protective of Penelope."

"Can you tell me what you remember about that day? Anything might help."

She nodded in agreement. Tears streamed down her cheeks as she dropped her gaze for a moment. She dabbed the dampness from her face and began.

"We got there at about 4 p.m. Um, I got off work at 2 that day. I worked the early shift, so Joyce stayed with Penelope. They walked the dogs for our neighbors during the day. Nothing unusual there. We went to the park and planned

372

to stay for about an hour. I saw a friend of ours there, so I talked to her for a few moments. When I turned around, I didn't see Penelope. The dogs were tied to a bench. My friend and I looked everywhere for her. She literally vanished."

"And you didn't see anyone there that you hadn't seen before?" Olivia asked.

"No. I didn't really pay attention, to be honest." Choking up, she put her face in her hands. Pulling herself together once more, she looked up at Olivia. "I don't remember."

"It's okay. I know this is devastating. But I'd like to try something to see if it helps. The brain has a funny way of cataloging things without your conscious awareness. So we're going to see if we might be able to tap into that. Is that all right?"

Jayne nodded.

"I want you to close your eyes," she instructed. She gently put her hand on Jayne's knee. "I want you to think about that day. Think about the smells in the park. Think about what you heard. Put yourself back there in your mind. You're talking to your friend. What do you see around you?"

Jayne took a deep breath. "We were talking about school getting ready to start. She is a teacher."

"Good. That's good. What else?"

"I can hear all of the dogs barking. I hear kids laughing.

I turned around to check on Penny. She is running with one of the dogs and waves at me." She choked up. "I shouldn't have turned back around."

"It's okay, Jayne. Keep going. You're doing great. So you turn back to your friend."

"Yes," she replied as she cleared her throat. "She is telling me what she's done over the summer. I can see someone out of the corner of my eye. He's wearing a pair of gray sweats and a blue hoodie. I kept thinking about how strange that was because it was so hot outside."

"That's good, Jayne. Follow him with your eyes. Where did he go?"

"He is so out of place. He is waving at someone behind me."

"Can you see his face?"

Jayne scowled with concentration. "No. I can't. He's wearing sunglasses and a red ball cap with the hood over it. So strange."

"How tall do you think he is?"

"Maybe six feet or so. He's thin."

"What color is his skin? Hair color? Age?"

"He's white. He has a really nice smile. I can't see the color of his hair. He looks like he's in his thirties, maybe."

"Do you see anyone else with him?"

"I can't see who he is waving at, but there's no one else with him."

"Can you tell me what happened next?"

"I turn back around. I am still talking to my friend. When we finished, I started scanning for Penny. There are a lot of people at the park right now. She's not where she was before. The dogs are just tied to a bench, which isn't something she would do unless one got loose or unless someone asked for help. I fully intend to scold her for that. She can't do that to the dogs. I'm scanning her friends. She isn't talking to them. I walked to them and asked if they've talked to her, if they've seen her. They haven't. I keep looking for her, but I don't see her. I can't find her. I walked to the bench with the dogs. I'm looking in the parking lot. She isn't there. I looked in the bathrooms. She's just gone," she concluded as her head fell into her hands once more.

"Jayne, it's okay. You did so good," Olivia praised.

Jayne composed herself again, Joyce's arm tightly around her shoulders.

"This might sound very odd," Olivia continued, "but were you ever in the foster care system as a child?"

"No, why?"

Danny spoke up. "We think that somehow the murderers are targeting former foster kids."

"I wasn't in the system, but my husband was. He died two years ago of a heart attack," Jayne replied.

"What was his name?" Olivia asked.

"Jared. He ended up in juvenile detention when he was seventeen. He told me he had been in lots of different foster homes growing up. He stole a car and ended up serving time."

"Did he ever tell you the names of any of the foster families?" Olivia probed.

"No."

"What agency placed him in foster care?"

"The county agency, of course."

A conclusive nod from Danny told Jayne that the interview was over. Olivia stood and pulled a card from her pocket, handing it to her. "If either of you think of anything, please call."

74

Danny and Olivia made their way outside. He gently touched her arm to grab her attention. She faced him.

"Where did you learn to do that?" he asked. "What was that?"

"It's called a cognitive interview," she answered. "I've been doing a lot of research with interviewing techniques. It seemed like it might work with this case because it calls to mind events in the subconscious. Our brains catch way more than we do, so there is information locked in there. Through a guided process, someone can explore those memories and possibly see things that they didn't before."

"That was amazing," Danny said. "I've never seen that done before."

Olivia smiled. "Well, we have some information we didn't before. We know he is tall, generally built, an approximate age. We also know he's white." She paused for a heartbeat and went on. "We are going to have to inquire at the county agency, Danny. I want the files of the parents whose children are dead. There's a connection, and we're going to figure out what it is. It's going to be in those files."

"We'll have to get a court order, Livy," Danny said. "We can't just walk in and ask for files like that."

"We're going without one first," she said as she walked to the parking garage, Danny trailing behind.

"Livy, stop," he said, grabbing her arm and turning her back around.

Her expression desperate, she shook her head. She wasn't about to be told she couldn't do this. "This girl was a baby, Danny. She was ten. She was raped, mutilated, and hanged like a piece of meat. This is the youngest victim we have. She was targeted because of her dad. I have no doubt. Someone is trying to make former foster kids pay. Haven't they paid enough? They were in foster care! Orphaned!"

The anger swelled in Olivia as she thought about all of the victims. The thirst for justice would only be quenched when they found the lunatics who were killing innocence in the county.

"You've got to calm down," Danny implored. "You're not thinking straight. We gotta get a court order for any files."

She pointed at Danny, her hand trembling as the adrenaline rushed through her body. "We have to solve this. No matter what we have to do, we have to stop this!"

"Come here," he said as he pulled her close. He just wanted to hold her. She was visibly upset, and his heart **sank**. "We'll get'em."

75

As Olivia sat at her desk writing up the report from the interview with Jayne, Danny walked in and plopped onto the sofa. He crossed his leg, his foot bouncing uncontrollably. He wore an anxious expression.

Glancing up from the computer, Olivia waited.

"Guess what?" he asked, still not getting her full attention.

"What?" she asked as she continued typing.

"I checked on the Hensons. The woman died in prison. She committed suicide. But the guy, Mike, was released about six years ago. He skipped out, and they think he left the country. Parole never caught up with him, and there have been no records of him since his release. He's either in Canada or Mexico. That'd be my guess."

Olivia stopped typing. "You think he's involved?"

"Maybe. He abused kids, right? Raped Mya's mom? Maybe he's killing these girls. Maybe he targeted Mya especially, afraid she was his illegitimate daughter. Or maybe he thought she belonged to Henry, and he wanted to hurt Candy and Henry for defying him when they were kids."

"Those are a lot of maybes, Danny. Why would he come back here and risk being caught? That's pretty unlikely, don't you think?"

He shrugged. "It's possible. The problem is that he has no living relatives. Who else would help him commit these crimes?" He folded his arms, a look of dissatisfaction on his face. "I guess the theory is pretty thin."

Olivia stopped what she was doing and leaned forward, planting her forearms on the desk and folding them over one another. "What we need to do is go to CPS and get records. I'm going with or without a court order. I'm taking Nigel as an intimidation tactic."

"I'm telling you, Livy, you're gonna need a warrant. They won't hand over anything without one," Danny argued.

"I don't care. I want them to know we mean business. Someone has access to those records, and it's someone on the inside. How else would these victims be targeted so specifically?"

"I'll go with you, but don't get pissed when I tell you that I told you so."

Olivia focused on typing again, the keys clacking as Danny remained seated on the couch in her office.

"Dad's birthday is Friday," Danny said with a hint of shyness. "We're throwing a surprise party for him. Ma's shutting down the diner, and they're having a DJ. I thought maybe you'd like to come. You can bring Amelia, too. It'll be kid-friendly. My sister and brother-in-law are flying in with their kids."

Olivia stopped typing and looked at Danny. Smiling warmly, she took in his eager expression. "Of course, I'll go."

Danny stood, grinning. "I'll pick you guys up at seven."

"I can just meet you there if you'd like."

He turned toward the door, already heading out. "I'll pick you up at seven."

76

After her group meeting that night, Olivia stayed with Henry at his apartment. Amelia slept over at Sarah's house, while Nigel spent the night in the kennels.

As Olivia lay on the couch, listening to Henry play the piano, she closed her eyes. "I love listening to you play," she said.

"I know. That's why I do it," he admitted, teasing the keys.

He finished the song, then stood and walked to the couch. Olivia sat up slightly as he took a seat. She rested her head in his lap while he ran his fingers through her soft hair.

She gazed up at him. When she put her hand to his cheek, he tilted his head, kissed her palm, and smiled down at her. "Do you have plans Friday?" he asked.

"Yes, I do. Why?"

"I wanted to fix dinner for you. Thought maybe you and Amelia could come over."

"Can I take a rain check?"

"Of course you can."

"What were you planning on cooking?"

"Just wanted to try out a chicken recipe Jim gave me."

"I'll be your guinea pig," she laughed.

"Well, I appreciate that," he said. "You know, I am a master cook."

"Really?" she answered.

"Never would've guessed, huh?"

"I think you can do just about anything you put your mind to, Henry," she said, taking his hand in hers. "I am so proud of you. And I'm proud that you're helping us with the case. It must be hard for you."

"Nah," he said, shaking his head. "Makes me feel like I'm helping Mya in some strange way."

"You are."

"You've taught me so much, Olivia." He touched her face. "What are you thinking about?" he asked.

She shook her head slightly. "Things. Did you see the news report tonight? I watched it on my phone before group. They've given these monsters a trademark: The Tic-Tac-Toe Killer. The profile hasn't been released to the press, so the reporters assume it's one man."

"I saw the report."

"They got what they wanted. The press is all over this."

"Maybe it'll calm down now that they've gotten some attention."

"Nope. It'll get worse. The attention just adds fuel to the

fire."

Henry traced her face with the tip of his finger. "You should go back to school and become a profiler. It's so natural for you."

"Danny and I have talked about that. I can't afford it right now. I need to focus on Amelia and keeping myself together."

"You've been clean for a while now. Is that what you're worried about? Relapsing?" he asked.

"I am always afraid of relapsing."

"Me too," he confessed.

"Sometimes I feel like I'm on the edge of it, and then I find the strength to pull myself back. I think about what that would do to you, to Amelia, to my career, all the people who depend on me to stay sober. The pain doesn't stop, though. I still have nightmares and flashbacks. The heroin numbed all of that." Olivia looked up into his eyes. "You can't relapse. You've come too far."

"I haven't. I don't plan on using again. I'm just saying it's hard sometimes not to."

"I agree. It is hard."

Henry gently lifted Olivia's head off his lap as he stood. He didn't let go right away, his fingers brushing against her cheek before he reached for her hand. She hesitated only for a second before taking it, letting him lead her to the bedroom.

There were no whispered declarations, no grand gestures, just the quiet understanding of two people who had found solace in each other's presence. When he pulled her close, her body responded instinctively, arms circling his neck as his mouth met hers. The kiss was deep but unhurried, not urgent, not desperate, just necessary.

Their hands moved with familiarity, tracing over skin they knew well. Clothes slipped away, revealing old scars and the silent reminders of everything they had survived.

They moved together in the dim light, neither rushing nor lingering, finding something in each other that neither could name. When it was over, Olivia rested against Henry's chest, his fingers absently stroking her back. The comfort they felt in one another wasn't something that required communication. The moment was all that mattered.

Neither of them moved. Eventually, exhaustion took over, and they drifted off, together, but still alone in their own ways.

77

When Olivia arrived at work, the next morning, she set her things down on the sofa before heading to the break room for her morning coffee. As she approached, she heard Danny talking to Sue.

Walking in, her eyes immediately went to Danny's attire: black cargo pants, black lace-up treaded boots, a black polo shirt, his Kevlar vest, and a shoulder holster.

"Late night?" he asked, already knowing the answer.

She smirked and then yawned.

"Well, you better pull it together because we got a fresh one," he added.

"Already?" she asked, eyes widening. "I guess that explains why you look like you're switching jobs and joining SWAT."

"You need to get changed."

She glanced down at herself. She always kept spare clothes at Henry's, and today she'd grabbed light gray slacks, white open-toed heels, a white cami, and a short-sleeved white cardigan. "Where's the body?" she asked.

"The woods again. But they've switched it up, hung a girl in the trees."

Olivia shook her head, disgusted. "I'll go get changed."

She turned and walked to her office, stooping down to pull spare clothing from her bottom file cabinet drawer. After shutting the door, she locked it, pulled the blinds, and swapped her outfit for khaki cargo pants, white socks, and a powder-pink polo shirt. She twisted her hair up just as a knock sounded at the door.

Walking over, she unlocked and opened it. Danny stepped inside, waiting as she sat on the sofa to lace up her leather hiking boots. She couldn't believe the killer had chosen another victim so quickly.

78

The drive to a rural part of Franklin County was quiet. Olivia was preoccupied, and Danny could easily see it.

"You okay?" he asked.

"I'm fine. Just thinking. I really wanted to go piss some people off at CPS today."

"You'll get your chance, tiger. Nick and the baby are in town, by the way. They drove in to see Lauren. They wanna get together for dinner later, if you're up for it."

"That sounds good. We can do it at my house."

"Lauren should be at the scene when we get there. You can let her know we're game tonight."

They turned onto a secluded dirt road, rolling up to a gaggle of police vehicles parked haphazardly along the roadside. Once parked, Olivia stepped out, heading to the back to check on Nigel. Danny surveyed the scene, a field crawling with investigators and technicians. Some scribbled in notepads, others snapped photos, and a few worked on handheld computers.

"Do you realize we found Penelope yesterday?" Danny said, glancing at Olivia. "Less than twenty-four hours ago. Do you know what that means? It means both victims were taken and kept together."

"That's not necessarily true," Lauren interjected,

approaching them. "It's possible they were housed at separate locations, or even the same property, just in different rooms."

"I just can't believe we're finding another victim this fast," Danny muttered.

"Escalation usually indicates desperation," Lauren added.

"Have you already been in?" Danny asked, motioning toward the woods.

"No. I wanted to wait for you two."

A forensics team member met them, leading them through. As they neared the scene, Olivia's attention caught on a female apparition standing at the edge of the clearing, a girl in black cotton gym shorts, a sports bra, and a messy bun.

I'm Olivia. What's your name?

The girl's mouth didn't move, but her voice echoed in Olivia's mind.

Violet.

Have you spoken to Lauren yet?

Yes. There's a little girl here, too.

That's Emma, Olivia answered.

Danny suddenly grabbed Olivia's arm. "Are you okay? You seem like you're somewhere else."

She nodded quickly. "Oh, I'm fine. Just thinking."

As they stepped under the dense canopy of trees, dew clung to the grass and leaves, droplets falling onto Olivia's bare arms with each gust of wind. The air carried the first hints of fall, though it was only early August.

The crime scene was controlled chaos. Investigators rushed to collect soil samples and evidence. Olivia's eyes trailed up the marked-off area until she saw the body hanging from a thick tree limb.

It was Violet. Naked, her long blonde hair veiled her face.

Lauren, Olivia, and Danny stood by as Bentley positioned himself beneath the body, carefully guiding investigators as they lowered her onto a plastic tarp.

"Think you'll find anything this time?" Danny asked, referring to trace evidence.

"Probably not." Bentley pointed to the girl's wrists. "See the ligature marks? She was bound. No defensive wounds, so I doubt we'll get any skin cells under her nails. Same as the last victims."

Olivia's gaze fell to Violet's thigh. The killer's signature was there. A tic-tac-toe board, this time with an additional O in the lower right corner. "At least four more victims left," she murmured, looking back at the tree.

Then a sudden presence washed over her. Violet was standing among them.

Lauren stiffened beside her, eyes widening in shock. Violet sobbed, her cries piercing through them like a blade.

Moving swiftly, Olivia and Lauren guided her away from the scene. Emma appeared, trailing behind them.

I'm sorry, Emma said softly. *I turned around, and she came back from the In-Between.*

I've never had that happen, Olivia replied. *She was so close she scared both of us.*

Without warning, Lauren stumbled, leaning against a tree. Her breathing turned shallow, and she brought a trembling hand to her throat.

"Lauren?" Olivia gripped her arm. "Are you okay?"

Lauren's eyes snapped open, dark with something unreadable. "Violet was alive when they hung her." Her voice was hollow. "The others were already dead."

Silence stretched between them before she added, "They took her two days after Penelope. They were here just before dawn."

Footsteps approached. Danny. His hands on his hips, his expression grim.

"What is it?" Olivia asked, folding her arms.

"Bentley says liver temp suggests she died this morning." He exhaled sharply. "She's only been out here a few hours. If we're going to find fresh evidence, it's now."

"Tire tracks? Anything?" Lauren asked.

"Boot prints?" Olivia added.

Danny shook his head. "Nothing."

Lauren exchanged a knowing look with Olivia. "They walked her out here. They marched her to her own death."

Olivia's stomach twisted. "Why the sudden change?" she whispered.

Lauren's expression darkened. "The thrill of control. They're evolving."

Without another word, she turned and hurried back to Bentley. Olivia and Danny followed.

"Check her legs for abrasions," Lauren instructed. "She must have fallen. They probably blindfolded her. Look for fibers."

"What if one of them carried her?" Olivia suggested.

"Then we might find hair or epithelial cells on her," Lauren replied, hopeful.

Bentley nodded. "I'll get her to the morgue, wash her off, and document anything I find."

A sudden shout rang through the trees. "Here! I need plaster!"

Danny, Lauren, and Olivia sprinted toward the voice. A forensic tech stood in the middle of the woods, hand raised. "I've got a boot print. Only one so far. I need plaster and a marker."

Investigators rushed in, working quickly. More prints were found, but then they abruptly vanished. It was like someone had disappeared into thin air.

Danny spoke up. "You and Lauren go talk to the family. I'll go with Bentley to the morgue and document preliminary findings."

"Can you take Nigel back with you?" Olivia asked. "I'll ride with Lauren."

"Yeah. I'll meet you back at the precinct." Danny turned, already refocusing on the body.

79

Lauren and Olivia traveled to a small suburb and arrived at the home of Quincy Davis and Iris McDonald. A petite woman with long blonde hair and a youthful appearance answered the door. As soon as she spotted the badge on Olivia's gun belt, she clapped a hand over her mouth, let out a strangled sob, and collapsed to the floor.

A gray-haired man with a heavier build rushed to her side. His green eyes met Olivia's, then dropped onto the badge. Tears welled up instantly and spilled down his cheeks as he clung to the woman.

"No, no, no, no!" he shouted. "She's not dead. Please tell me she isn't dead!"

Lauren knelt beside them. "Mr. Davis?"

He nodded weakly.

"Let's go inside," she said gently. "We can talk there."

Quincy lifted the woman from the floor and guided her inside. Olivia followed, closing the door behind them. Lauren was already standing in the spacious living room.

"I'm so sorry," Olivia said, her tone softer now. "But we need you to identify her. Is there someone we can call to drive you downtown?"

Quincy sniffed and shook his head. "My brother is already here," he said hoarsely. "He's upstairs."

Lauren sat in a chair across from the couch, where the couple held each other, still sobbing. She leaned forward, resting on the edge of her seat.

"Which one of you was in foster care?" she asked.

Iris stilled, her sobs trailing off as her expression shifted to one of unease. "I was," she admitted.

Lauren met her eyes. "You're Iris McDonald?"

"Yes."

"Are you Violet's biological mother?"

Iris hesitated, then glanced at Quincy before answering. "Yes," she murmured. "We never got married."

Lauren turned to Quincy. "And you're Violet's biological father?"

He nodded. "My parents were foster parents. That's how I met Iris. My family didn't approve of our relationship back then, but my parents are gone now, and my siblings have come around."

"We'll give you some time to collect yourselves," Olivia interjected. "We can meet you downtown in about an hour. I'm sure we'll have more questions then."

80

Lauren drove in silence for a moment, scanning the streets for the on-ramp to the interstate.

"Take me to CPS," Olivia said firmly.

"I was just about to suggest that," Lauren agreed.

To shift the conversation to something lighter, Olivia brought up a different subject. "So, Nick and the baby are here?"

"Yes. I insisted they come. I couldn't stand being away from Jason for more than a day."

Olivia smiled. "Jason. I forgot, you named him after your dad."

Lauren nodded. "I got your card and the gift. Jason loves the blanket. I think it's his favorite."

"Why don't you three come to my house for dinner? Danny mentioned you wanted to get together."

"That sounds wonderful. It would be nice to just relax for an evening. I know Nick has a great deal of respect for Daniel, and for you."

"I have no idea what I even have in my kitchen for dinner," Olivia admitted.

"Don't worry about that. Nick is an excellent cook."

Olivia laughed softly, but Lauren studied her for a moment. "Something's different about you, Olivia."

"What do you mean?"

"I don't know. I can just feel it. Something's going on or… something's happened."

Olivia shook her head, genuinely puzzled. "I have no idea what you're talking about."

Lauren exhaled. "Maybe I'm wrong. But… something just feels different."

81

They pulled into the parking lot of CPS and stepped out of the car. As they approached the entrance, they found the reception desk just inside. A woman sat behind it, typing on a computer, while a deputy stood in the far corner of the room.

Noticing Olivia's gun, the deputy took a step forward. Before he could say anything, she grabbed her badge from her belt and placed it on the counter.

"I'm Detective Olivia Gregory with FCSO, and this is Dr. Lauren Harris-Bennette, a consultant for the FBI and the Ohio State Police," she stated firmly. "We need to review some files on former foster children. We're investigating a series of murders that may be connected to your agency."

The receptionist barely looked up. "Ma'am, you'll need a warrant. Those files are confidential, and we can't release them without one."

"So you're fine with obstructing an ongoing investigation?" Lauren asked, her tone sharp.

"I'm sorry, but it's the law. I can't make an exception."

Olivia exhaled slowly, keeping her frustration in check. "Anything else we need when we come back with the court order?"

"I'll need a list of the individuals whose files you want pulled."

"When we get the order, we expect the files to be ready that same day," Olivia said, her voice edged with warning. "I'll provide a list, but one way or another, we're walking out of here with what we need."

The woman merely shrugged and returned her attention to her computer.

Angered by the blatant indifference, Olivia snapped, "Hey, thanks for your help." Without waiting for a response, she turned on her heel and strode out of the building, Lauren close behind.

As they reached the car, Lauren smirked. "You've gotten assertive. Much more dominant in your approach."

"I'm tired of playing games," Olivia muttered. "I want answers."

Lauren nodded, a note of admiration in her voice. "I have to say, I'm impressed with your transformation. That must be what's different about you. Your timid nature is gone. Olivia, you're becoming a real detective."

Olivia glanced at her, a small smile playing at the corners of her lips. "I hope so."

"Oh, trust me," Lauren said confidently. "I know so."

82

Danny stood beside Bentley as he examined Violet's body. To avoid contamination, both wore latex gloves and sterile gowns. Danny observed as Bentley carefully sprayed down Violet's hair and body, watching the catch tray intently, hoping to spot any trace evidence. Then, he saw it.

"Wait! Stop!" Danny said. "Give me the tweezers."

Without hesitation, Bentley handed them over.

"Pass me a dish," he added.

Bentley complied again.

Danny carefully picked up a dark hair, about three inches long. He held it up to the light. "That doesn't look blonde to me. Does it to you?"

Bentley's lips curled into a hopeful smile. "No, it certainly doesn't."

"Can you put a rush on the DNA?"

"I most certainly can."

After finishing the cleaning process, Bentley spread Violet's legs apart to examine for signs of sexual assault. "No bruising on the inner thighs," Bentley noted. "There are some lacerations in the vaginal cavity. Some bruising. It doesn't appear she was raped as violently, though."

Olivia's voice cut through the conversation. "The unsub

who assaulted her is likely the younger of the team. My guess is the older one is more violent in his assaults. The younger unsub is probably still unsure of himself."

Bentley glanced at her, impressed. "Very good."

Danny grinned, feeling proud of her. "I keep telling you, you need to be a profiler."

Olivia simply smiled.

"I agree," Bentley added.

"Are the parents on their way?" Danny asked.

"Yes. We also stopped at CPS. We'll need to see the judge."

"Told ya," Danny said with a smirk.

"I know you told me," Olivia admitted.

"We'll go see Judge Kramer tomorrow. He'll give us an order," Danny assured her. "Which parent was in foster care?"

"The mother."

"So we have Miller Stevenson, Henry, Shanda Swaggart, Jared Zeila, and now this kid's mom."

"Iris McDonald," Olivia clarified.

"Alright, so we need to specify to the judge that we need any and all records on those individuals," Danny said.

As he spoke, he noticed Olivia's expression shift. Her

gaze drifted to the corner of the room, her eyes distant, as if she were focused on something unseen. Danny frowned. He had no idea she was communicating with the dead, working to cross Violet over.

He waved a hand in front of her face, and she blinked back to reality.

"You okay?" he asked, studying her.

She nodded quickly. "Oh, yeah, I'm fine." Then, shaking off whatever had distracted her, she added, "I'll go interview the family." With that, she turned to leave.

Just before she pushed through the doors, Danny called out, "I'm heading back to the precinct to start writing up the report. You sure you're good?"

"Yes. Lauren's in her car. I'll catch a ride back with her."

"We still on for dinner tonight?"

"Yep."

"Alright, I'll see ya later."

"Okay," Olivia said, flashing a smile before stepping out.

83

That evening, Olivia received a phone call from Lauren. Baby Jason had been fussy all day, and with both her and Nick exhausted, they asked to postpone dinner.

Olivia quickly texted Danny to let him know about the change of plans.

Disappointment settled over her. She had been looking forward to spending time with her friends. The connection she shared with Lauren was reassuring, and she had been eager to meet the baby.

They rescheduled for Saturday night.

84

Olivia stood among a crowd of people. Their voices were muffled, blending into an indistinct hum. Panic gripped her as thoughts raced through her mind. She didn't know why, but she felt certain Henry was in danger.

Then, a gunshot rang out.

She screamed, frantically trying to push through the crowd, but something held her back. No matter how hard she fought, she couldn't break free.

Her screams carried into reality as she jolted upright in bed. The room was dark. She was alone.

Breathing heavily, she wondered what the dreams meant. Deep down, she felt they were warnings, but of what, she didn't know. Were they mere manifestations of her own fears, or something more? A premonition?

She wanted to believe it was nothing. But in her heart, she knew better.

85

Thursday morning, Danny and Olivia sat outside the judge's chambers as the prosecuting attorney made his case for a warrant.

Anxiously, Olivia tapped her foot against the marble floor, unaware she was even doing it.

Danny stole a glance at her. Her hair rested over one shoulder, exposing her striking features. She wore white linen slacks, paired with leather crossover sandals. A navy cami highlighted her slender neck, and her matching white linen jacket complemented her tanned skin. A natural flush colored her cheeks.

His mind drifted back to their weekend together, the feel of her skin beneath his fingertips, the warmth of her body against his. He could still see the passion in her blue eyes as she gazed up at him, the memory making his pulse quicken.

But it wasn't just her beauty that captivated him. It was her strength, her unwavering determination. That's what made her truly irresistible. He admired her will, her ability to stay true to herself. And he knew, without a doubt, his connection to her could never be severed. She wasn't just someone he wanted. She was someone he needed.

But she wasn't his. Not entirely. He shared her with another man. He'd promised to give her space, but the more time passed, the harder it became.

Danny exhaled, forcing himself back to the present. He smirked as he watched her foot tapping nervously.

"You okay there, Livy?"

She stopped, returning his smile. "Yeah, I'm fine."

Her eyes met his. "What?" she asked, intrigued by his expression.

"Nothing. Just looking at ya. Thinking." His New York accent thickened slightly, his nerves rattling inside him.

She tilted her head. "Thinking about what?"

Before he could answer, the judge's office door opened.

Both of them stood as prosecutor Sylvis Thomas emerged, a document in hand.

"Here's your court order," he said, handing it over.

Danny took it with a relieved smile. Maybe, just maybe, these files held the key to solving the brutal murders.

"Thanks, Sye," he said, gripping the paper tightly.

86

After a quiet drive, they arrived at CPS. Without hesitation, Danny pushed open the doors, Olivia trailing closely behind.

"Give me the order," Olivia said, cutting in front of him.

Danny handed it over without a word. She strode straight to the receptionist's desk, confidence radiating from her. He noticed the sharp smirk tugging at her lips and the assertive way she carried herself.

"Hi," Olivia greeted, her tone smooth and agreeable. The receptionist barely glanced up. "Remember me?" she continued, sliding the court order onto the desk. "I brought you something today. We'll take all of the files on the listed individuals."

The receptionist's expression darkened. She stood abruptly. "I'll have to get the supervisor," she snapped, turning sharply on her heel.

"You go right ahead," Olivia replied, leaning casually on the counter.

Danny smirked. "You're pissed," he murmured.

"Yes, I am," she confirmed.

He nodded, matching her posture against the tall reception counter. "I like it."

Her smile nearly knocked the wind out of him.

Moments later, the receptionist returned, her face set in irritation. "You'll have to come back in a few hours."

Olivia's expression hardened. "Oh no," she barked. "That order says the files are to be provided immediately. You do know what 'immediately' means, right?"

The receptionist glared.

"It means promptly. Straight away." Olivia tilted her head slightly, her gaze narrowing. "Now."

"I'm sorry," the woman began, "but."

"We want to see the supervisor," Danny cut in, his tone firm.

"I can't."

"You either go get the supervisor, or we'll have you charged with obstruction. I'll cuff you right here in front of God and everybody."

A security officer approached. "Is there a problem here?"

"Yeah," Danny said smoothly. "We've got a court order for some files. So, if you could just head back to your post, I think we're getting everything squared away."

The officer hesitated, then gave a curt nod and returned to his desk. The receptionist's mouth fell open in disbelief. She had expected backup. Instead, she shot them a venomous glare, shoved her chair away, and stomped off.

Olivia turned to Danny. His blue eyes were calm, his stance unyielding. "You're pissed too," she observed.

"Yep," he said with a confident nod. "I'm not playing games."

A man emerged from a hallway, his movements deliberate. He was tall, his skin warm brown, his deep brown eyes alert. His jet-black hair was neatly styled, and his white oxford shirt and tan slacks made him look professional but approachable.

Olivia's stomach tightened with recognition.

"Olivia?"

"Kyle?"

"We met the other day," he said, shaking her hand. "What can I help you with?"

"Well," she said, her voice dripping with saccharine sweetness, "we have a court order to retrieve some files."

Kyle took the paper, scanning it. "I'll need time to gather them. They're likely in the archive across town. We don't have space to store everything here."

Danny folded his arms. "We can save you the trouble. Just tell us where the archive is, and we'll serve the warrant there."

Kyle hesitated. "I'm not sure I can."

"You don't have a choice, Kyle," Olivia interjected. "If the files aren't here, we have to go get them. If you refuse to tell us where, that's obstruction." She leveled her gaze at him. "I don't want to arrest you."

Kyle let out a soft chuckle. "Well, I certainly don't want to be arrested." His tone was light, but his eyes held something unreadable. "I'm not trying to be difficult, but we have to notify the records keeper. There are thousands of paper files. It takes time."

"The fact is," Danny said, "we don't have a lot of time." He paused. "What's your last name?"

"Kyle Armstrong," he answered, extending his hand.

Danny shook it but didn't let his guard drop. "Mr. Armstrong, we need those files. Tell us where to go."

Kyle exhaled and glanced at Olivia. "Let me write down the address. I think you'll be disappointed when you get there, but if you insist."

"Disappointed or not, we have to go," Olivia said.

The receptionist handed him a post-it, and he jotted down the address. Handing it to Olivia, he added, "I'll call ahead and let them know you're coming. They'll cooperate."

"Appreciated," Olivia said.

Kyle hesitated. "This about the murders? The Tic-Tac-Toe Killer?"

Danny raised a hand, shutting him down. "We can't

discuss ongoing investigations."

Kyle nodded knowingly. "I understand." Then he turned to Olivia with a warm smile. "We should get together sometime. Henry, you, and me. My wife would love to meet you both. She works here too. Maybe dinner one evening?"

"That would be nice," Olivia replied with a small smile.

"I'll get in touch with Henry."

"Sounds good."

As they reached the door, Kyle called after them, "Good luck."

Walking toward the SUV, Danny glanced sideways at Olivia. "Who is that?"

"He grew up in the same foster home as Henry," she said, shaking her head. "It bothers me that he works here. He has access to all the files connected to our victims' families." Her voice dropped. "Henry told me Kyle had issues growing up, more than the others. The abuse only made it worse. Maybe he's worked through it, but…" She trailed off. "It's too much of a coincidence that both he and his wife work here."

"That is a little."

"Disturbing?" she finished for him.

Danny nodded. "He could be good for it."

"I'm going to get close."

Danny stopped in his tracks. "You're going to do what?"

She turned, her expression resolute. "I have a way in. He knows Henry. He seems comfortable with me, too. Maybe if we get to know him, I can find answers. Maybe he has nothing to do with this. Maybe his wife does. Maybe they're our team. Who the hell knows? But I have access. I need to use that."

Danny's jaw tightened. "I don't like this."

"It's the only way I can size him up." She spun on her heel and walked to the SUV. "I'm not telling Henry. I don't want to risk him slipping up."

Danny caught up with her, stepping in front before she could grab the door handle. He gripped her arms gently but firmly.

"Listen to me," he said, his voice low and serious. "Be careful. If he's involved, he's dangerous."

"I'll be fine."

"Think about the consequences. Keep yourself safe."

Her expression softened. "I'll be careful. I promise."

87

As they drove to the address they'd been given, Olivia kept her eyes on the road, but her mind was elsewhere. She needed to strategize. They had uncovered something profound, she was sure of it, but now they needed solid evidence. Something concrete. Deep down, she didn't want to be right. She felt compassion for the abuse Kyle and Henry had endured as children. She wanted to believe it was just a coincidence that Kyle worked at CPS. But she couldn't ignore the fact that his position gave him full and open access to the files they needed.

Her thoughts raced as she stole a glance at Danny. She trusted him with her life, truly. They had opened up to each other in ways she never had with anyone else. He had made it clear from the start that his priority was protecting her. No one had ever done that before. Henry had been open with her, she knew that, but it was different with Danny. He made her feel safe. He filled a part of her soul that had longed for someone courageous and steadfast, someone who would always have her back.

Still, she wondered if Danny could accept all of who she was, her beliefs included. She was tempted to tell him, but she hesitated, reminding herself of their agreement. No more secrets.

They pulled into the parking lot, found a spot, and Olivia turned off the engine. She sat still for a moment. Danny shifted, about to open his door, but stopped when he noticed she hadn't moved.

"What's wrong?" he asked.

She looked down at her trembling hands. "Danny, we've never talked about faith. Our backgrounds. What we believe in."

He frowned slightly. "I'm not following."

"I've told you everything about myself. My past. My darkest moments. My most unbearable secrets." She turned toward him. "You know what I've done and who I am now. But you don't know what I can do."

Confused, he shook his head. "What are you talking about?"

She shifted in her seat, turning to face him fully. Taking a deep breath, she said, "You have to promise not to judge me or think I'm crazy."

Danny's expression softened. "Olivia, I would never think you're crazy. And I don't judge. That's not who I am. Like you said, you've told me everything."

She hesitated, then said, "When we go to these crime scenes, I have a job to do."

"We both do," he interjected.

"No, mine goes beyond this world." She took another breath. "I told you I overdosed on heroin."

"And?" he prompted.

"I had a near-death experience." She paused, watching for his reaction, but he didn't flinch. No judgment. No disbelief. "I saw things. Experienced things most people wouldn't believe. But even before that, I had abilities. I don't know how to say this exactly." She exhaled slowly. "I guess you'd call me a medium. I help earthbound spirits cross over. Every time we see these girls, the victims, my job is to send them safely to the other side. To the light. That's just what I do. I assure them that it's okay to go, and they go."

Danny's eyes flickered with understanding. "Is that why you were staring at the wall at the morgue? You kind of checked out on me."

She nodded. "I've been able to do this since I was a child. I know it sounds insane." She swallowed hard before continuing. "When my stepdad, when he molested me, it was like something in my brain woke up that hadn't been awake before. After that, I started seeing spirits everywhere. At first, it was overwhelming. My stepmom helped me understand it, but as I got older, I just wanted it to go away. I was tired of it." She paused for a heartbeat.

She struggled to keep her composure but went on. "The heroin helped me escape. From everything. The pain. The visions." She hesitated again. "I don't know what you believe, or if you even believe in God, but I do. And I feel like He gave me this ability for a reason, to help people."

Danny was quiet for a moment, then asked, "Do they, the spirits, tell you what happened to them? Who hurt them?"

Lauren's face flashed through Olivia's mind. She shook her head. "No. Other people have that gift, but not me. I'm just here to help them cross. That's all I can do."

Danny studied her, saying nothing.

"You think I'm nuts," she muttered, turning to stare out the window.

"I don't," he said firmly. "My mom sees things before they happen. I never understood it, but she does. She checks out sometimes, like you, and then she tells my dad what's coming. And she's always right. It's usually nothing huge, just things about our family. But she knew 9/11 was going to happen. And she knew what happened with Donte before I even told her."

Olivia's eyes widened. "Seriously?"

He nodded. "When I told them I had a new partner, she told me to watch out for you. Said your life was in danger. I've learned to listen to her. I don't question it anymore." He smirked. "And my sister, Margie? She can see people's pasts."

"Like past lives?"

"I think so. She's always had these nightmares about being trapped in a burning barn. She'd wake up screaming, saying she could smell smoke and see flames. Eventually, she started giving names and dates. My mom looked into it. Turns out, there was a fire in that exact location, just like Margie described. A little girl died in it."

416

A wave of relief swept over Olivia.

"Why have we never talked about this before?" Danny asked.

"I was afraid you'd think I was crazy."

He scoffed. "Olivia, I grew up with this stuff. I don't just believe in it. I've seen it." He took her hand in his. "I have no doubt that you're gifted. You understand people in a way most of us never could. Honestly? Your talent is wasted in this job. You're meant for somethin' bigger." He squeezed her hand. "I respect you, Livy. I always will."

She smiled. "Thank you. I just knew it was time to tell you. If I'm risking my life for this case, I want you to know everything. Just in case you ever have to tell Amelia about me."

His jaw tensed. "Don't say that."

"It's true." She softened. "Amelia adores you. If something happens to me, she'll look to you for answers."

"What about Henry? Doesn't she like him?"

"She does, but it's different with you."

Danny grinned. "Probably because I'm just a big kid."

Laughing, she nodded. "That might be it."

She let out a deep sigh, feeling lighter, as if a weight had been lifted.

Danny glanced at the building ahead. "We ready to do

this?"

Olivia met his eyes. The understanding she saw there gave her peace.

"Let's do this," she said, releasing his hand and opening the car door.

88

As they walked into the building, Olivia observed Danny. His confidence never came across as arrogance. Today, he wore a pair of army-green cargo pants, a tan polo shirt, and, of course, his treaded boots. It was hard not to admire his physical build. The sun cast beams over his short, messy brown hair, and his aviator sunglasses made him look rugged and mysterious. His squared jawline told her he was on a mission.

A memory of their time together at Pikeview flashed through her mind. She remembered how perfectly sculpted he was—his defined abdominal muscles, his cut biceps. The way he watched her as he made love to her, his blue eyes roping her in. The way his body fit with hers so perfectly. A shiver ran down her spine, and warmth crept into her cheeks. She was blushing.

Snapping herself out of it, Olivia refocused on their surroundings. The building was old, its architecture dated. Danny grabbed the door handle, stepping aside to let her walk through. The foyer opened into another reception area, where the polished marble floors caused an echo as she approached the desk. A Hispanic woman greeted them with a slight accent.

Once again, both Danny and Olivia explained the court order. Once again, a supervisor was consulted. This time, the cooperation was better. They were escorted to a conference room on the third floor while the supervisor and another worker searched the archives for the requested files.

Half an hour later, the supervisor returned, accompanied by a tall young woman whose badge identified her as Amy Ison.

"I'm so sorry," she began, "but we don't have those files in the archive."

Danny leaned back in his wooden chair. "Are you serious?"

"Where else could they be?" Olivia asked.

"They've likely been checked out by a worker or supervisor, but I'm not seeing anything in the logbook."

"Why would someone check out files that old?" Olivia pressed.

"Sometimes the agency gets requests from biological family members. If they can provide proof of relation, we can copy certain documents from the file and either mail them or prepare them for pickup. For example, if an adoptee is searching for their biological parent, they might request a birth certificate or something of that nature."

"Can you tell us if any requests have been made for the files listed in the court order?" Danny asked.

"I already checked. No formal requests have been made for those files. I also cross-checked with the logbook— nothing there either. The only explanation I can think of is a procedural error or a staffing issue. We have some temps working here who don't always follow protocol. It's very possible something was overlooked."

Suspicion prickled through both Danny and Olivia.

"I'm truly sorry," Amy continued. "Someone must have checked the files out and failed to log it. That's the only explanation I have."

"Can I see the logbook?" Olivia asked, already standing.

Amy handed over the large, thick book. Olivia flipped to the last entry, shaking her head. "Who is Tina Stone? She's the last person to check out any files, and that was two days ago. And you're telling me there's no digital record?"

"Ma'am, we do track everything in the computer as well. I cross-checked all possible sources. The system shows the files should still be in the archive, but physically, they aren't there. I promise you, we have a double-check system. A worker has to sign the logbook and also log into the database, which tracks the date and time of the check-out. They also have to note the specific files they took. When they return them, they go through the same process. In the hard copy log, they write the return date." She sighed. "We have safeguards in place to prevent this exact situation, but human error still happens. Sometimes people forget to log out a file. Sometimes they take it for a quick review, get interrupted, and walk off with it without signing it out properly. There are plenty of plausible explanations for why this happened."

"I don't buy it," Olivia said firmly. "I refuse to believe it's just a coincidence that these particular files are missing."

Amy exhaled. "I don't know what to tell you. The hard copies are gone."

Danny stood realizing they'd hit another brick wall. "Thank you for your time."

89

As they drove back to the precinct, Danny fumed. His grip tightened on the steering wheel, knuckles turning white. "You're right, Livy. It's Kyle. He's taken the files."

"We don't have proof of that," Olivia reminded him, her voice calm but laced with frustration. "What's worse is we don't know what other files he has, if any. He could have taken dozens. He could be covering years of tracks."

Danny exhaled sharply, shaking his head. "You know what this means, right? We're going to have to have enough probable cause to get a warrant to search his office and his home for those files. Right now, we don't have that."

"We will," she said firmly, her mind already turning over possible angles.

Danny shot her a sideways glance. "What are you thinking?"

She smirked, a determined gleam in her eyes. "Let me work on that."

For the first time since leaving the agency, Danny felt a sliver of hope. Whatever Olivia was planning, he knew one thing for sure. She wouldn't stop until they had exactly what they needed.

90

Friday morning, Danny sat in his office, typing up the dictation. Armed with coffee, he focused intently, detailing their findings, the missing files, and his growing suspicions. The door opened, and Rick walked in.

"Hey, man. How's it going?" Rick asked.

"Thank God it's Friday," Danny muttered, barely looking up.

"You're telling me. So, Sue said you made some progress in the case yesterday?"

"Yeah, we've got some solid leads." Danny sighed, rubbing his face before turning in his chair to face Rick. "But I gotta tell you, I don't know how much longer I can be patient."

"With the case?"

"No." Danny shook his head. "With Livy. She's talking about going undercover, putting herself right in harm's way. It makes me fucking nervous."

"Is it a solid plan?"

Danny hesitated. "Yeah, honestly, it is. But that doesn't mean I have to like it."

Rick studied him for a moment before asking, "Have you told her how in love with her you are?"

Danny let out a short laugh. "No way. I'm giving her space. I want her to fall for me on her own, not because she feels pushed into it."

Rick shook his head. "You're crazy. You need to get this ball rolling, or you're going to lose her."

"What do you mean?"

Rick hesitated, lowering his voice. "Look, I haven't told you this before, but she talks to Sue. She talks to me a little, but mostly Sue. And, Danny, she's not thinking about a future with you. She's focused on Henry."

Danny's stomach tightened. "She's getting serious about him?"

"She hasn't said that, but I can see it heading that way. If you don't step up, you will lose her. She thinks you're fine with the way things are."

"I'm not okay with any of it!" Danny snapped, shaking his head. "I'm tryin' to be the good guy here."

Rick smirked. "Maybe it's time you stopped playing so nice."

Danny looked down at his desk, thinking.

"You mean to tell me you haven't slept with her since you visited her at her parents' place?" Rick asked.

"No. When we hang out, we talk, watch TV, play with Amelia. You see us on Sundays, we're best friends. We don't kiss. We don't hold hands. Nothin'."

"Doesn't mean you're not sleeping together."

Danny gave him a hard look. "She's still involved with Henry. She's been really focused on tryin' to be faithful to that."

Rick leaned forward. "Then maybe it's time you give her a real choice."

Danny exhaled. "I don't want to give her an ultimatum."

"Then don't," Rick said. "Just make it clear you're very available for an upgrade."

Danny narrowed his eyes. "That's Sue talking. That sounds exactly like something she'd say."

Rick grinned and shrugged. "Sounded good coming from her, too."

91

That evening, Olivia sat on Amelia's floor, dressing her for Cecil's party. Nigel lay nearby, quietly watching the interaction. Amelia's outfit consisted of pink cotton shorts with a matching short-sleeved top. Her little tennis shoes and white socks completed the look.

"We're going to a party for Danny," Olivia said, turning Amelia around and settling her into her lap. She combed through her curly, blondish-brown hair.

"Danny!" Amelia clapped excitedly.

"I know, you love Danny," Olivia said with a smile, parting Amelia's hair into pigtails.

"Wuv Danny," Amelia murmured, playing with her fingers.

A knock at the back door made Nigel stir. He trotted out of the room, barking, before Olivia heard Danny's voice.

"Where are my pretty girls?" he called.

"We're in Amelia's room," Olivia answered, smiling at the compliment.

She listened as Nigel bounced around, his playful huffs letting her know Danny was entertaining him. Moments later, Danny appeared in the doorway, leaning against the frame. Dressed in light-wash jeans, leather flip-flops, and a black graphic t-shirt, he looked effortlessly handsome.

"Danny!" Amelia squealed, scrambling to her feet and running toward him.

Lifting her with ease, he balanced her on his forearm as she threw her little arms around his neck. "Monkey girl," he teased.

"I not!" she protested. "Not munkie."

"Uh-huh," he joked, grinning as he tickled her sides. She cackled with joy.

Olivia stood. She had chosen flared denim capris, yellow plaid flip-flops, and a fitted yellow scoop-neck tee. As usual, she had her hair pulled up.

Danny's eyes swept over her. "You look good."

"Thank you," she replied.

92

At the diner, Danny pulled around to the back, where dozens of cars were parked. He carried Amelia while Olivia grabbed the backpack she always packed with Amelia's essentials. As they stepped inside, the room fell silent. Then, realizing it was just Danny, the crowd erupted into greetings.

Danny took a moment to introduce Olivia and Amelia. Olivia met Margie and Aaron, Danny's sister and brother-in-law, along with an extended family of cousins, aunts, and uncles who had flown in from New York and beyond. Everyone was warm and welcoming.

A loud chime rang as the front diner door opened. The lights dimmed, and the crowd fell silent. Olivia listened intently.

"If you'd take this damn blindfold off, I could see where I'm goin'," Cecil grumbled.

Sharon's amused voice followed. "Oh, be quiet and trust me."

The door swung open, and as Sharon yanked off the blindfold, the crowd sprang to life.

"Surprise!" they shouted in unison.

Cecil's eyes welled with emotion as a grin spread across his face. He took his time greeting every single guest before the festivities began. Food was served, followed by cake, and then the dancing started. Everything from '50s classics to modern hits played.

At first, Olivia stayed back, chatting with Margie and keeping an eye on Amelia. But her feet didn't stay idle for long. Danny approached her, holding out a hand as a slow song filled the diner.

"Come dance with me," he said, his tone leaving little room for refusal.

Margie gave Olivia a reassuring nod. "I'll watch Amelia."

Taking his hand, Olivia let Danny guide her to the dance floor, where couples swayed in time with the music. He pulled her close, his arm wrapping around her waist, his other hand clasping hers against his chest.

As they moved together, she studied his face, noticing the tension in his expression. "What's bothering you?" she asked softly.

Danny dropped his head slightly, smirking. "Nothin' really. There's just something I want to talk to you about later."

Her brows furrowed. "Are you okay?"

"Oh yeah, I'm fine." He pursed his lips. "Actually, why don't I go ahead and take you two home? It's almost 10. Amelia's probably getting tired, and I need to talk to you."

Her forehead creased with concern. "Are you sure everything's alright?"

"I'm good." He gave her hand a reassuring squeeze as he changed his mind. "It's nothing bad, I promise. Just let me hold you and dance with you. We'll talk later."

She hesitated but eventually nodded. "Okay."

He pulled her closer, pressing her against his chest.

The scent of her perfume wrapped around him, intoxicating his senses. As nervous as he was, he knew Rick was right. Waiting wasn't getting him anywhere. It was time to take a risk.

93

During the drive back to her house, Olivia and Danny were quiet. Amelia fell asleep in her car seat. When they pulled into the driveway, Danny turned off the engine and opened the door. He stepped out and shut the car door quietly, trying not to wake Amelia. He hurried to the back and opened the door. Olivia watched as Danny unlocked the car seat and pulled her up into his arms.

"I can take her," Olivia whispered, reaching for her.

"It's alright. I've got her," Danny insisted.

They walked into the house. Danny continued into the living room and then turned into the hallway leading to the bedrooms. Olivia hung the backpack on one of the kitchen chairs and then followed them.

Standing in the doorway of Amelia's room, she watched as Danny gently placed Amelia into her crib. Taking her shoes off her little feet, he then covered her with a light blanket. He put his fingers to his lips and then gently placed them on Amelia's cheek. "Sweet dreams, Monkey Girl," he whispered.

The scene brought tears to Olivia's eyes. Henry had never done anything like that with Amelia. The bond between Danny and Amelia was tremendously strong. He treated her like his own child, and Amelia loved him like he was her father. It was a fact Olivia couldn't ignore.

Danny turned, shocked to see her standing in the doorway.

Smiling at him, she whispered, "That was sweet."

"She's sweet," he said quietly.

"What did you want to talk about?" she whispered again.

"Let's go in the living room," he suggested.

They sat down on the couch. Olivia's heart thudded in her chest, the anxiety building.

"I don't know how to start this," Danny said quietly.

"What's wrong? You're killing me with this."

"I am just going to come right out and say this." He took a deep breath and blew it out. "I wish you belonged to me. I think about how perfectly you fit in my arms. You would never believe how often I dream of being a permanent part of your life. All I wanna do is make you happy. You're in my heart now. I've looked for you my entire life. You're an impossible reality for me. I'm suffering here, Livy. Suffering. I've kept my feelings a secret, but I can't anymore." He paused, trying to gauge her reaction, but her face was blank. "You can't tell me that you don't think about that weekend. Can you sit here and tell me you don't care about me?"

Her mouth dropped open as he moved closer to her, sitting on the edge of the couch now, taking her hands into his. He kept going but trembled with nerves. "I know I shouldn't be putting you in this position. I've struggled with this. I've given you space like I promised I would. I've let you try and figure stuff out with Henry."

"Danny," she said, trailing off.

"I don't want to push you, and I don't want to pressure you," he said. "That's why I've let things go, but I can't anymore."

She knew she'd been holding herself back from him. She was incredibly insecure. She'd explained that to him in various ways. She carried guilt from her addiction and all the things she'd done to support the addiction. That reality kept her chained like a prisoner. She'd convinced herself that Danny didn't deserve the agony of looking at her, knowing what she had been. She didn't have to feel ashamed with Henry. He had lived through terrible things, their trauma bond keeping them tethered together.

She knew from therapy that a trauma bond was a horrible foundation for any relationship. Now she felt confused. Did she really want Henry, or was he just safe? Then the insecurities spoke loudly in her ear. "Danny, you don't deserve someone like me."

"What do you mean?"

"Look at me, Danny. My very first sexual experience was with my stepdad. I was a junkie, a prostitute. I lost my kid because I almost died overdosing on drugs. You're a good man. I'm not good enough for someone like you."

Indignation rose inside of him. "I don't care about all of

that. I love you for who you are now. All of that stuff comes with you, but it's not who you are now. It doesn't need to define you."

"You love me?" she asked, staring up into his eyes. Those were not the words she expected to hear.

He paused and smiled. He put one hand on top of hers and answered, "I love you. I would do anything for you, Olivia. I know that I have a gift, too."

Confusion colored her expression. "What do you mean?"

"You are my gift. You and me, we were put together for a reason. When you had that knife to your throat, somethin' happened to me. I know that I was born to protect you. That's my calling. I'm meant to be by your side to keep you safe and to keep Amelia safe. Don't ask me how I know it, but I know it's true."

"Danny, what if I relapse?"

"I can handle it. Will Henry be able to handle it, or will he relapse, too? I can be strong for you. I'm going to support you, not enable you." He paused. "I still wonder if you're just with Henry out of pity or fear, or if you think you can save him. You just admitted you don't think you're good enough for me, and I don't get that. You don't think I've got problems?"

The words settled on her ears like hot coals, burning her from the inside out. "I admit it, I felt sorry for him. It's more than that now, though. And what problems do you have,

Danny? You've never been an addict or sold yourself to feed your habit. I have slept with so many men I've literally lost count. Sometimes I didn't even remember doing it. I don't even know who my daughter's father is. I'm a used-up whore."

"Don't say that. Don't you dare say that about yourself," he protested. "First of all, I feel like I'm Amelia's father. I love her like she's mine. She sees me as her dad. The way she attached to me..." He trailed off and then rebounded quickly. "Has she done that with Henry?"

A deafening silence fell.

"And I've struggled with a lot of stuff," Danny continued. "No, I've never been an addict. I don't know what that's like. I have lived through one of the most traumatic events in America, though. I know what it's like to lose yourself. I pulled mangled bodies out of what was left of the World Trade Center. Friends. Brothers. People I'd known my entire life. You're not normal after that, Livy. I'm damaged from it. I thought I was gonna lose my goddamn mind." He shook his head as the memories nearly took his voice. He composed himself and kept going. "You think that you're too damaged. You think finding someone who's just as damaged compensates for everything? It doesn't."

She stood abruptly. "It doesn't even matter. I can't believe we're even having this conversation. I'll just hurt you. Do you really want that?"

Standing and walking to her, he cupped her face in his hands, looking deeply into her teary blue eyes. "I want you.

That means everything that comes with you, good or bad." He paused for a heartbeat as their glances remained locked. "The fact is that I want you to choose me. I'm not saying I'm better for you or that I love you more than he does," he continued. "I'm not saying he's not a good guy. I don't know him. I can only tell you that I know me, and I know that I love you and I accept you, all of you."

Tears ran down her cheeks, and with her emotions jumbled, confusion clouded her vision as he stood motionless in front of her. His hands rested on her shoulders now.

"I do think about that weekend. I think about you and me," she admitted. "I'm afraid."

He pulled her to him. "Don't be afraid, Livy. Not of me."

He kissed her forehead and then her eyebrow. His lips brushed against her cheek and then found her mouth. She leaned into him as he wrapped his arms tighter around her, frozen in the intense moment. His familiar kiss lowered her resistance, and she welcomed his touch.

He pulled her up onto him and lifted her, her legs wrapping tightly around him. She tucked her face between his neck and collarbone, the heat of her breath fueling his arousal. He carried her through the hallway and into her bedroom. He closed the door with his foot and carried her to the bed. Placing her on the mattress, he knelt in front of her. Looking up longingly into her eyes, he brought her hands to his lips and kissed them softly.

Without another word, he leaned up and kissed her. She cupped his face in her hands as their lips danced with one another. He reached up, pulled the band from her hair, and wove his fingers through it. Pulling gently, she looked up at the ceiling as he leaned in and kissed her neck. Her eyes closed as the desire rose inside of her.

He stopped and stood to his feet. He pulled his shirt from his body as she watched. He kicked his flip-flops off, unbuttoned his jeans, unzipped them, and then stepped out of them, his underwear falling to the ground with them.

She looked up at him, welcoming him, and stood to her feet. He pulled her shirt from her body and then unbuttoned and unzipped her pants. He pulled her jeans and underwear off, and she stepped out of them. He turned her around, her back facing him, and unfastened her bra. He kissed her back, licking and biting at her skin, his hands reaching around her to cup her breasts.

The soft moans carried through the air as he squeezed her nipples between his fingers. She wanted his mouth. She turned around and kissed him deeply.

"Lay down," he said between kisses.

She did as she was told and looked up at him as he stood beside the bed. She held out her hand, and he took it. He hovered over her, bearing his weight on his hands as he pushed into her. The sensation was like heaven to both of them.

She admired his body as he moved, his muscles tensing and then relaxing. As he kissed her forehead, she leaned up on her elbows, putting her lips to his chest.

She relaxed again, lying flat. He shifted his weight to one elbow and then touched her warm cheek with his free hand. Intensely, he looked into her eyes. "I do love you," he whispered.

He rolled onto the mattress and led her to sink onto him. He grabbed the wooden headboard tightly as she began moving. Her hands rested firmly on his chest as she sped.

"Come, Livy... I know you want to," he whispered.

Her movements quickened with anticipation, her mouth slightly open and her eyes closed.

"Look at me," he said. "Look at me, Livy."

She opened her eyes and lost herself, the blood rushing through her as her heart sped. Her teeth clenched together as she felt the ecstasy rise from deep within her. She moaned with delight as she climaxed.

He released with her, pressing his head hard against the pillow, his muscles tensing and beads of sweat peppering his body. Still moving on him to ensure he finished, the sensations sent electricity through his body, each pulse losing strength, but the pleasure still lingering.

With exhaustion, she collapsed onto his chest, heaving as she tried to calm her breathing. He pushed her hair away from her face as she rested her head. Turning her face toward his, Danny kissed her lips. "You are," he said in between kisses, "incredible. Absolutely incredible, and I love you so much."

Silence.

He pursed his lips. "You don't have to say anything. I know you're not ready, Livy. I still love you just the same."

"I'm sorry," she whispered as she closed her eyes, her head still resting on his chest.

"Don't be. I know you love me. You just don't know how to say it yet."

"You mean so much to me," she admitted. "I don't know what I'd do without you."

"See. That's enough for me."

She rolled over onto her back as he turned on his side.

"I'm going to lie here until you fall asleep," he continued, "but I'm gonna move to the couch."

Her head turned quickly toward him. "Why?"

"I don't want Amelia to wake up and find us in here together. Not a good example to set."

"Wow, Danny. You are old-fashioned."

"No. I just know what kind of example I'd want to set if she were my daughter. I don't want her thinking that it's okay."

Quiet for a moment, she smiled. "You are truly a father to her."

"Like I told you, I think of her as being mine. I know she isn't, but I'm the closest thing she's got to a dad. I hope it doesn't bother you."

"No," Olivia said with a reassuring smile. "She needs a good male role model. You are wonderful with her."

Drowsiness slowly took over, and the last thing Olivia saw before closing her eyes was Danny looking at her. The last thing she felt was his fingers caressing her arm. The last thing she heard before falling asleep was, "I love you."

94

When Olivia woke, she was covered with her blankets. She turned onto her back and looked at the clock. It was a little after four in the morning. A soft voice drifted from Amelia's room.

She sat up, rubbing her eyes. Grabbing Danny's t-shirt from the floor, she slipped it over her head and stood. Quietly, she walked out of her room and across the hall to the nursery.

Inside, Danny sat in the glider, Amelia lying comfortably in his arms. He spoke to her softly as her eyes fluttered closed.

Olivia didn't want to disturb them. If Amelia knew she was awake, she'd never go back to sleep. She stayed in the shadows, watching.

She stood in the dim light and thought about their conversation earlier. Denying herself and denying Danny was only depriving her of the happiness she deserved. In her meditations and prayers, she had learned that she was worthy of something wonderful. Yet, accepting that truth was a challenge all its own. She wondered if Danny was the blessing she had been promised, the missing piece she had been searching for.

She watched as Danny gently stroked Amelia's hair. He whispered to her, telling her what a blessing she was and how perfect she was. Then he said, "You saved your mama's life."

Tears welled in Olivia's eyes as she listened.

"If it weren't for you, where would she be? You and Nigel are angels sent straight from heaven. And your mom is my angel. She doesn't know it but she gave me a purpose. A reason to breathe. She thinks I saved her, but she has no idea she saved me first. She took away the nightmares and gave me hope. You both give me hope. I don't think I was alive until I met you two girls."

Olivia clasped a hand over her mouth to stifle a sob, but the tears kept coming. Saved him? From what? She had never doubted that Danny cared for her, but now she no longer doubted that he loved her.

Torn between Danny and Henry, she didn't know what to do. Henry had never let her see him fully, not the way Danny had. He always kept her at a safe distance. Then again, she had done the same to him. Did Henry even love her?

A choice would have to be made, but not now. She could simply stand there, absorbing the moment. The warmth of Danny with Amelia. The love in his voice. The peace in the air.

A strange, comforting glow settled over her, a presence she could feel but not see. Validus was near.

For the first time since leaving Pikeview, since running from the shelter of her father and stepmother, Olivia felt truly loved. The realization nearly brought her to her knees.

Turning away, she tiptoed back into her room and gently closed the door behind her. She pressed her forehead against the cool surface and wept silently. She didn't have all the answers. She didn't know what the right choice was. But she did know one thing. She was thankful for the man in the other room, rocking her daughter back to sleep.

Living in the moment while still being responsible for the future was a lesson she was still learning. But she was determined to master it.

95

Olivia's eyes opened to the sun peeking in from behind the blinds in her room. The smell of breakfast filled the air, and Amelia's laughter drifted through the house. Glancing at the clock, she couldn't believe she had slept until after nine.

She got out of bed and grabbed a pair of black yoga pants, slipping them on while still wearing Danny's graphic t-shirt. Walking out of her room and into the living room, she spotted Nigel lying in the kitchen beside the table, waiting patiently for Amelia to share her food. Though obedient, nothing in the world could stop him from begging or expecting a free handout, especially when Amelia was involved.

Danny's voice changed slightly, drawing her attention.

"Detective Knight," he said.

Olivia walked into the kitchen and saw him with his cell phone pressed to his ear. He stood over the stove, frying bacon. On the griddle, pancakes sizzled, and in another skillet, scrambled eggs cooked.

He wore a white muscle shirt and a pair of gray sweatpants. Olivia figured he must have had them in his car. He glanced up, gave her a quick wave, and mouthed, "Bentley."

She nodded and walked over to Amelia, leaning down

to kiss her little forehead. "Are you eating your breakfast, sweetie?"

Amelia grinned. "I eat." Kicking her legs happily, she picked up a piece of bacon and took a bite.

After a dozen "uh-huhs," Danny hung up and set his phone on the table.

Walking back to the stove, he turned slightly and said, "Morning, beautiful. I hope you're hungry. Figured I'd make us breakfast."

She smiled and sat down in a vacant chair at the table and yawned. "Was that Bentley?"

"Yep."

"Please tell me we don't have another body."

"We don't have another body."

"Thank God."

"And we don't have DNA from the hair. Initially, Bentley didn't think it was the victim's, but it turns out it was."

"Oh, that stinks."

"The good news is that we now have casts of the boot print from the woods. We have the information from your interview. There's progress."

96

After breakfast and a relaxing day of watching movies and playing, Lauren and Nick came over with Jason. Danny stood on the concrete pad, grilling sirloin steaks, while Nick sat in a lawn chair watching.

"So, Danny, when are you going to come work for me in Dayton?" Nick asked.

"You ask me that every time we talk."

"You belong in the FBI. You'd be great."

"You know I can't leave my folks. They moved here because of me."

"Dayton isn't that far away," Nick retorted. "You'd be out in the field most of the time. I'd be working right there with you."

"I just can't. The timing isn't right."

Nick folded his arms. "It's not just your parents. You don't want to leave Olivia either. You feel responsible for her."

"She's my partner."

"She's more than that. Anyone can see it. You hover over her like I hovered over Doc when we first started working together. I was always on her heels. I probably drove her crazy. But I wanted her to be safe. Then when she was taken, nothing was ever the same for me after that. She changed too, of course. She focused more on her teaching and mental health work. Truth be told, I think she was afraid."

"I can understand why. She would've died without you and her team."

Nick agreed with a confident nod. "She knows that. That's why she took so much time off from profiling. But I will say she's found a connection with Olivia. It's hard for her to get close to people, and she took to Olivia right away."

"I noticed that, too."

"Doc is always pretty guarded, but with Olivia, it was like she had known her forever. She even told me that."

"Livy has a lot of respect for Lauren," Danny agreed.

"The respect is definitely mutual. But let's get back to the subject at hand. The FBI job. I understand your reservations, Danny. Still, I think if Olivia knew about the opportunity, she'd tell you to take it."

Danny sighed. "Don't tell her. Please. I don't want"

Nick stood and placed a hand on Danny's back. "The job in Major Crimes is yours if you want it. You belong in the FBI. I can offer you a good pay raise and full government benefits."

Danny sighed. "I'll keep thinking about it, but I just can't leave right now."

97

As Olivia stood at the counter making coleslaw, Amelia sat on the kitchen floor, playing with colorful toys alongside Nigel. Lauren paced the room, gently rocking Jason in her arms.

Olivia glanced over her shoulder. "Lauren, he's just beautiful."

Lauren's voice softened. "I've never known anything so perfect in my life. I never thought I could love something this much."

"I understand exactly what you mean," Olivia agreed, then shifted gears. "So, we still don't have any DNA?"

"Not yet," Lauren said, "but I heard you conducted a cognitive interview and gathered some useful information."

"I did, yeah."

"Very impressive. I also heard that you and Danny made progress with CPS."

"I think we have a really strong lead."

Olivia filled Lauren in on Kyle's connection to Henry, his presence at the crime scene, the court order situation, and the missing files. She emphasized how Henry could be the key to cracking the case.

Lauren's expression darkened. "What exactly are you

planning, Olivia?"

"I can get access to the house. If Henry distracts Kyle and his wife, I can snoop around."

Lauren's voice grew sharp. "Do you realize how much danger you're putting yourself in if Kyle is one of the unsubs?"

"I'll be fine. I'm careful. I won't do anything reckless."

Lauren hesitated before pressing on. "I wish you'd involve Daniel instead of Henry."

Olivia's expression shifted.

"What I mean," Lauren clarified, "is that Daniel is trained. He knows how to handle an intense situation and get you out if things go sideways. Henry isn't. He's a doctor, a consultant, not someone equipped to save your life. I don't like this plan."

"I think it's our best shot," Olivia said firmly. "I don't know what else to do. This is my way in."

"Nothing you find will be admissible, especially if you are digging. It has to be in plain sight or obtained with a warrant. You must have probable cause. You know that," Lauren scolded.

"I promise, I know what I'm doing. Ever hear the saying, 'keep your friends close and your enemies closer'? That's exactly what I plan to do."

98

After an enjoyable evening, Lauren, Nick, and Jason returned to their hotel. With Amelia bathed and tucked in bed, Olivia walked into the living room and joined Danny on the couch.

He opened his arms, welcoming her against his chest. She snuggled in close as he wrapped his arm around her.

"So, what now?" she asked, listening to the steady rhythm of his heartbeat.

"What do you mean?"

"Us. What now? I still have so much to figure out. I need to decide what's best for Amelia and me. I'm still so confused and scared."

He stroked her soft hair. "I wish you'd just give in and realize I'm not going anywhere. I love you. That's not changin'. Do what you need to do to work through all of this. I know you care about Henry, but I also know you care about me, too. The choice is yours, Livy. I can't make it for you. But at least you know where I stand now. This thing between us isn't just physical. You've got all of me. Until you can give us a chance, I'll try to be as patient as I can."

"I feel terrible not being able to give you everything. I just don't know what I have left to give."

"You have more to give than you realize. And one day, you'll see it." He sighed and shrugged. "Sure, I'd like you to come to a decision sooner rather than later, but I know you'll get there. And when you do, it'll be me, because I'm the one who loves you."

"It might take more time than you think. Don't give up on me, okay?"

He kissed the top of her head. "Are you kidding? Never."

99

August ended without any more Tic-Tac-Toe victims. As expected, Danny and Olivia couldn't secure a warrant for Kyle's home or office without probable cause. The trail had gone cold once again. However, that didn't deter Olivia. She was determined, and she knew Kyle was involved somehow.

She also found herself questioning Henry's explanations. Though she had been his strongest advocate from the beginning, she began to wonder if he had been lying to her all along. Maybe he was closer to Kyle than he let on. Olivia worried that he might be a sociopath and had, as Danny suspected, sacrificed Mya. Her research into the criminal mind, along with multiple discussions with Lauren, had deepened her understanding of sociopathic behavior. Given Henry's past abuse, it was very possible he fit that profile.

Still, she couldn't shake the possibility that Henry might not even realize his connection to the situation. Confusion reigned, and for now, she proceeded with caution.

She also knew Henry was her only way to gain access to Kyle's home and personal life. She needed him, but she wasn't sure whether she should share her true intent with him or keep it to herself.

Despite her doubts and questions, Olivia kept up her regular routine. Tuesday and Thursday evenings, as well as some Saturdays, still belonged to Henry. Though she continued helping him with his spirituality, her focus remained on their physical relationship. Olivia was still deeply attracted to Henry. Yet, no commitments had been made between them, and discussions about feelings were carefully avoided.

As for Danny, she continued spending her Friday evenings and Sunday afternoons with him. Every moment alone together made it harder to tear themselves away from each other. She nurtured their physical bond as well. The chemistry between them was undeniable, and their intimacy was intense. But their connection wasn't just physical.

Olivia was drawn to Danny for the unconditional love he offered, the fatherly role he played in Amelia's life, and the fun they had together. Working side by side during the week only made her struggle more. She needed both men. She was completely torn between them, and there was nothing she could do about it.

To her knowledge, Henry didn't know she was sleeping with Danny, though she wondered if he would even care. Danny, on the other hand, knew she was still intimate with Henry and did his best to accept it.

100

Olivia rested peacefully in Henry's embrace after a passionate romp. Feeling him against her back, his warmth gave her temporary resolve. His breaths were steady, and she felt his lips on her ear.

"What are you doing Saturday afternoon?" he asked.

"I don't have anything planned," she answered, her eyes still closed.

"Do you remember Kyle?"

Her eyes quickly opened. "Yes," she answered.

"He called me just the other day. He invited you and me over for dinner Saturday."

She wondered if this was divine intervention. It was too ironic that Kyle reached out to Henry, given the situation. "I'm sure I can talk to Sarah and see if she can keep Amelia."

"We talked for about an hour," Henry continued. "He told me that a few weeks ago, you saw him at work. I had no idea he worked for CPS."

"Did he say anything else?"

"He just said he felt bad because you needed help and he couldn't help you. Something about a court order."

Olivia turned over and faced Henry. As she contemplated whether or not to tell him her plans, she felt the struggle within her. "I didn't realize he worked at CPS either until he came walking out."

"He seems to be better. He's not the kid I grew up with. He is happy. He told me about his wife and that they had a son last year. He's really turned his life around."

"Do you think he really has?" Olivia asked.

With a slight shrug, Henry answered, "He talked to me like he has."

"Henry, do you think it's possible to endure that type of severe abuse and still turn out whole?"

"I don't know. I didn't. I became a drug addict. I don't really like people in general. I just tolerate them. So, really, I don't know how to answer that."

"But you're not vindictive. You're not malicious, right?"

His eyes met hers, and in them, she saw confusion reflecting back at her. "Olivia, do you have something you want to say to me?"

"No, I just worry about you. I can't imagine going through all that you did. And from what you told me, Kyle suffered more than any of you."

"There's more to this. I can see it in your face."

She sighed. "Henry, I can't tell you. I can't tell you anything right now. The only thing I can say is that I don't trust Kyle. In my gut, something just doesn't feel right."

"Well, first of all, I know you well enough by now to say that you have pretty accurate intuition. If you don't feel comfortable going to dinner"

"No, I have to go."

His hand reached up, his fingers brushing her cheek before he tucked her hair behind her ear. "You don't have to go at all. I wish you could tell me what you're thinking."

"I can't. But I'll go to dinner at his house. He's your friend, right?"

"Well, I wouldn't say we're friends. I just thought it might be nice to visit with him. I mean, we do share some type of twisted bond, I guess."

"I'll go."

"Are you sure you're okay with this?"

"I'm fine. I'll be fine."

101

As Olivia sat at the kitchen table, enjoying her usual Friday night pizza with Amelia and Danny, she thought about the upcoming plans involving Kyle. She did not even know if she wanted to tell Danny at all. However, she remembered their promise.

Amelia squealed with delight as she kicked her feet. Danny was trying to tickle her little toes as they ate supper. His smile and their interaction nearly made Olivia's heart melt. Nigel panted and whined because he wanted to be part of playtime. The smell of the food tantalized him too. His tail wagged as Amelia and Danny continued their fun.

Covered in pizza, Amelia finally stopped eating. Danny wiped his hands with a napkin and smiled. "Come on, Monkey Girl. You're a mess. We'll let Mommy clean up the table. What do ya say?"

Amelia hopped down and stood beside Olivia, a very serious grimace upon her little face. She pointed at Olivia, her eyebrows narrowed, and said, "Mommy, you clean."

Olivia finished chewing a bite of pizza and threw her hands up as if she were being held up by a robber. "Yes, Majesty. I will clean."

Amelia nodded seriously, and then Danny took her hand, leading her into the bathroom.

Staying behind and following orders, Olivia cleaned up

the dishes and tidied the kitchen. She lit a scented candle on the table. Standing and watching the flame burn, she suddenly felt unsettled. In her ear, she heard Validus say, "Stay strong. You must stay strong."

It was unusual for her to hear him outside of meditation.

Then a sudden wave of sickness hit her. Her head felt light, and her stomach cramped. She quickly pulled out a chair and sat down, her elbows on the table and her head in her hands. She regulated her breathing.

Nigel ran out of the room and then paced back and forth between the kitchen and the bathroom, whimpering.

Danny walked in, Amelia veering off toward the living room, where she planned to watch some cartoons. He stood behind Olivia and then sat down in the empty chair.

"Are you okay? What's wrong?"

"I don't know. I just felt sick all of a sudden."

"I can get you some water. Do you want me to help you to bed?"

Shaking her head, she replied softly, "No."

Danny reached over and put the back of his hand to her forehead. "You don't feel like you have a fever."

"Danny, I'm going to Kyle's with Henry tomorrow night," she blurted out.

He pulled away and sat back in his chair. "Why?"

"You know why."

"You need to wear a wire."

"He's not going to confess during dinner. Get real," she argued.

"I don't want you going over there without some kind of protection."

"Henry will be there."

He rolled his eyes. "What's he gonna do?"

"Danny," she scolded. "I haven't even told him what I'm doing."

"And what are you doing exactly?"

"I'm going to do a sweep of the house, if I can. See if I can find the sweats and hoodie or the files or anything that might help us."

"You're serious about this. Olivia, think about this. Think about the profile. If this is one of our guys, do you actually think he will be stupid enough to keep incriminating evidence at his house?"

"You know as well as I do, people can be pretty stupid."

"I don't think you're going to find anything. And if it isn't in plain sight, it isn't admissible."

"It's worth a shot. What else do we have? This case is going to go cold if we don't do something."

"Just don't get killed in the process. If you get caught snooping, you will become a target. Think about Amelia. What if she becomes a target?"

"Don't think that way. I'll be careful. I'd never do anything to put her in danger."

102

Lauren and Olivia stood at the edge of the woods, watching the forensic team work their magic. Melissa Sorinson, the sixth victim of the Tic-Tac-Toe Killers, stood in front of them, an eleven-year-old brunette wearing a pair of faded jeans and a white T-shirt. She looked confused and lost.

Lauren closed her eyes and focused for several seconds. The ghost said nothing. When she opened them again, she looked over at Olivia.

"A mall. She was taken from the mall," Lauren started. "She was in the toy aisle. A man approached her, but I couldn't see any defining features. He asked for her help. He told her he needed help finding his grandson. He said that he lost him in the parking lot. She hesitated, but the man showed her a picture. The photograph convinced her that he was telling the truth. When he got her into the parking lot, he hit her in the head." She paused. "He blindfolded her, and I smell pine trees."

"Pine trees?"

"Yes, pine. I don't hear anything distinctive, but I smell pine trees."

"We're standing in a pine forest, Lauren."

"No. That's not it. The things I sense are coming from the victim."

"Maybe she was alive when they brought her out here."

Olivia and Lauren looked at the growing crowd of reporters.

"You go," Olivia said. "I'm going to help Melissa find her way to the light."

Lauren walked away, leaving Olivia with the apparition and the duty of crossing the child over.

Melissa, I'm Olivia, she said gently.

I know who you are. They all told me to wait for you.

Who told you that?

Them, she answered as she pointed behind her.

Olivia's mouth dropped as she saw all of the victims standing in the distance.

They said you would be coming to help me.

Smiling softly, she replied, *I hope I can help you, as well as all of them.*

I always knew I would die young, Melissa murmured, lowering her head.

Why?

It's just something I've always known. I wasn't meant to be here. My aunt and uncle took me in when my mom died. I knew I wouldn't live a long time. I'm okay with that. I miss my mom. I want to be with her again.

Do you see her in the light?

Yes, she sighed. *She's been there for a while, waiting. Emma said that my mom would guide me in, but I had to wait for you first in case I could help you.*

Knowing that Melissa had already found peace made Olivia's responsibility easier, bringing a slight smile to her face. Then she turned to see Danny standing beside her. His expression told her that he knew something was happening. She relayed the girl's name as well as some of the information Lauren had shared.

"She's still here?" he asked in amazement.

"Yes. She is right in front of us."

Olivia turned back to Melissa.

I'm going now, Melissa said softly. *I want my mom.*

We'll find the answers, Olivia promised.

I know you will, Melissa replied.

As she disappeared, the birds perched in the trees suddenly took flight, causing a ruckus.

"She's gone?" Danny asked.

"Yes."

She saw complete acceptance in his eyes.

"Well," he said, turning and leading her further into the woods, "we've got more boot prints. Preliminarily, they match the other prints. And there's more."

Olivia stopped. "What do you mean?"

"This girl was severely beaten. Bentley and Henry say there's evidence of blunt force trauma to the back of her head. She's covered in bruises. They've already got her on the tarp."

"Why the change in MO?" Olivia wondered aloud.

"Because the other killer is stepping up," Lauren interjected as she came in behind them. "The more dominant murderer is starting to assert himself. I think you'll find severe trauma due to rape and mutilation when you complete an internal exam," she added as Henry stood.

"So far, we have another tic-tac-toe board with an 'O' in the middle left column. Have either of you figured out the significance of this branding?" Henry asked.

"Only that it's a signature," Olivia answered.

"I think the killers are simply playing a game. They're keeping score," Lauren added.

"Smile for the cameras," Bentley muttered as he stood. He looked toward the road, where television vans had gathered.

"The media is playing right into their hands," Olivia commented.

A forensic technician walked up to Danny and handed him a printout. The report indicated that Melissa's aunt and uncle had reported her missing four days ago.

Henry read over Danny's shoulder. "So where do you go from here?" he asked, frustration lacing his tone.

"We keep working the case," Danny replied.

"Do you think this is winding down?" Henry asked.

"Oh no, on the contrary," Lauren interjected. "This serial team will likely start killing more frequently and with more brutality. Their evolution is far from complete."

"So, what are you all going to do about it?" Henry asked.

Lauren's voice was steady. "Desperation leads to mistakes, and evolution doesn't always precipitate success. Transition of any kind can cause significant stress, making a perpetrator more prone to errors. This may be exactly what we need to break this case."

"At what cost?" Henry asked, crossing his arms.

"Dr. Howard, I never feel satisfaction when victims are found," Lauren clarified. "But each time we examine the circumstances, we gain a deeper understanding of the perpetrators. Knowledge is power in this situation."

"And that's how you justify the fact that these girls are dying? That my daughter died?" Henry's voice was raw.

"Henry," Olivia rebuked. "This isn't Lauren's fault."

He shook his head. "But look at her. She's standing here

telling me that my daughter was sacrificed so we could get to know the bastards that killed her."

"That isn't what she's saying at all," Olivia defended.

"Henry," Bentley began cautiously, "I think you need to take a break. Go to the van. I can have the techs help me with the body."

"Fine," Henry muttered, storming out of the forest.

"He's too close to this case," Danny said.

"I thought he would be okay," Bentley admitted. "He's a scientist. I thought he'd be able to stay objective."

"This is personal for him," Lauren said. "There's no way he can be objective. I'm surprised at you, Bentley. He shouldn't have been allowed to volunteer in the first place."

"Lauren," Bentley started, "he's brilliant, and his connection to the OSU lab was well worth the risk. Or so I thought."

"He's too close," Danny agreed. "Get him off this case."

103

After a couple of hours, Melissa's aunt and uncle, Anita and Chad Merritt, arrived at the precinct. Seated in the conference room, Olivia brought them some water. Anita was still crying hysterically, even though she had already identified the body. Chad did his best to comfort her, but he wasn't holding together well either.

Behind the observation mirror, Danny and Lauren watched. As Olivia began the interview, they listened, but Lauren's mind drifted elsewhere. She studied Danny's body language—his arms folded, his posture defensive. She had noticed he often stood like that. She wasn't sure if it was a law enforcement habit or simply his personality, but Nick stood that way, too.

"You're very protective of her," Lauren observed.

Danny turned slightly toward her but kept his eyes on the interview. "I am."

"You love her very much."

He didn't respond.

"She loves you too, Daniel."

"I just want her to be happy," he said quietly.

"I also know that you're sacrificing what you truly want for her sake."

"What do you mean?"

"Nick offered you a job with the FBI. But you won't leave her behind."

"I can't. She's my partner."

"She can find another partner."

"I don't want to leave."

"Tell her about the job, Daniel."

"The timing isn't right. I want to solve this case first. Then, I'll tell her. Eventually," he replied.

"She should further her education."

He agreed. "I wish I could afford to give her that. She'd be a great profiler."

"She has a brilliant mind," Lauren agreed. "It would be such a shame to see her waste it."

"I know."

"She's still learning her own strengths," Lauren concluded. "Give her time. It will fall into place."

At that moment, Olivia stood and walked out of the conference room. She opened the door to the observation room.

"So, what'd you find out?" Danny asked.

"Were you two even listening?" Olivia asked, eyeing them suspiciously.

"We were talking. What'd you find out?"

"Melissa's mom died when she was very young. Anita and Chad aren't the connection here—Melissa's mom is. She was in foster care from age four to eighteen. Get this," Olivia continued, "she lived with Mike and Holly Henson from age six to eleven. Mike raped her repeatedly. Anita told me Melissa's mom was involved in the lawsuit and criminal trial against them, too. What I don't understand is how Kyle could have linked Melissa to Kathy, Melissa's mom. Kathy went through a private agency to give Anita and Chad adoptive rights to Melissa."

"Only someone who knew about the adoption would have been able to target Melissa," Lauren said.

"So, Kyle is our link? I just didn't think he'd have access to private adoptions."

"There's some access somewhere. He's smart, he could figure it out," Danny assumed.

Olivia's phone buzzed with a text from Bentley. Attached was an email report. She opened it and read quickly. Bentley had found evidence of severe vaginal trauma. The uterus was displaced. There were no fibers on the body and no trace evidence linking Kyle, or anyone else, to the murder.

104

After such a defeating day, Olivia rested on the couch at home, unable to shake the feeling that nothing about it was finished. Earlier, she had noticed a missed call from Henry and chosen not to return it. With Amelia and Nigel asleep, she was startled by a knock at the back door. She stood, instinctively grabbing her gun from its holster.

Nigel woke and cautiously walked into the living room. His posture shifted, head lowered protectively, as he moved in front of Olivia.

As she neared the back door, she saw Henry standing outside. Exhaling, she placed her gun on the kitchen table and opened the door. Nigel, realizing the visitor posed no threat, quietly left the room.

"Henry," she started, concern in her voice, "are you okay?"

"I'm sorry for coming so late."

"It's okay," she said, stepping aside. "Come in."

Henry sat at the kitchen table, and Olivia took the seat across from him.

"I need to talk to you," he said, his voice tense. "I know you're holding something back about the investigation."

"What do you mean?"

"I know you're not telling me everything."

"Henry," she said.

"Please." His voice wavered with frustration. "I lost my only daughter in this mess. I need to know if you have something. And I know you do."

She swallowed hard. "I could never forget that you lost Mya."

But her hesitation gave her away.

"You're wondering how I know," he said, studying her. "How I can tell that you've made some progress. I've gotten better at reading people since you've been teaching me things. You only have yourself to blame for that."

She exhaled, giving in. "I think it's Kyle. I think he's involved."

"I've wondered the same thing," Henry admitted. "Something doesn't feel right. I saw Kyle at the monster truck rally the night Mya was taken."

"What?" Olivia's stomach tightened. "Why didn't you tell me?"

"I didn't think it mattered. He said he was there with a couple of friends. We ran into each other at the concession stand. Mya was with me."

"Did he seem suspicious?"

"Not at all. No red flags."

"Now I know he's involved," Olivia bit out.

"So go arrest him."

"I can't, Henry. We don't have probable cause. There's no evidence placing him at the crime scenes, nothing linking him to the abductions or the murders. We tried to get CPS records, but he's a department supervisor. He sent us to archives. The files were gone."

"I thought we were going to go to his place for a meal. Can't you do something while you're there?"

"I've given that a lot of thought. If I don't have a warrant, nothing I find can be used in court. It isn't worth the risk," she explained.

"So even though he was at the truck rally, that doesn't matter?"

"It might have helped if you'd told me earlier. But unless we can prove he took Mya, no, it doesn't matter. Danny reviewed surveillance footage from that night. He found nothing. No sign of Kyle, or he would have mentioned it to me."

"Damn it!" Henry shouted, standing abruptly.

"Please, Henry, Amelia's asleep," Olivia reminded him gently.

He exhaled sharply, shaking his head. "I'm sorry."

Olivia stood and pulled him into an embrace. "We are trying to get him." She pulled back slightly, her hands resting on his face reassuringly. "I won't quit. You know I won't give up. So don't you give up either, okay?"

He nodded, his grip tightening as he pulled her close again.

105

Amy at CPS had become an ally, the only person Olivia could truly rely on. She wasn't about to use Henry to get to Kyle, but now that he knew about her suspicions, Henry could be more vigilant and report any new activity to her.

Amy assured Olivia that if she noticed anything unusual, she would contact her immediately. She also informed her that none of the missing files had been checked back in. Since the agency had been served with the warrant, the staff had been keeping a close watch on all records, monitoring the check-in and check-out process. She reassured Olivia that CPS would do everything in its power to assist the sheriff's office.

As the weeks passed, September arrived. One morning, Olivia stood in her bathroom, feeling woozy and unsteady on her feet. Gripping the sink for support, she squeezed her eyes shut, willing herself to push through. If she didn't get moving, she'd be late for work.

But the dizziness intensified, overtaking her completely. Before she could stop it, she dropped to her knees in front of the toilet, vomiting violently.

In her experience, throwing up was the worst feeling in the world. She had done it more times than she cared to remember while going through rehab. The withdrawal had been eased by Suboxone, but not enough to prevent some of the worst physical symptoms.

After several mornings of starting her day hunched over the toilet, she knew something wasn't right. In fact, she had been through this before.

Now she stood in the bathroom, staring down at a pregnancy test. Her heart pounded as sweat beaded on her forehead, her hands trembling slightly. Sarah sat on the edge of the bathtub, watching her anxiously.

"I thought you were on birth control," Sarah said.

"I am," Olivia muttered.

"Maybe it's just a stomach bug."

"But wouldn't I be sick all day if that were the case?" Olivia countered, though she already knew the answer.

Sarah shrugged. "I don't know. Ask Henry."

"Oh my God," Olivia whispered. "I have no idea who the father is. That's what happens when you're not faithful to one man."

Sarah's expression softened. "If you're pregnant, you're going to have to tell Henry everything."

Olivia pressed a hand to her forehead, exhaling shakily.

A faint plus sign appeared in the results window. Her breath caught in her throat. She dropped her head as tears slipped down her cheeks. "I think I'm going to throw up again," she admitted.

Sarah immediately stood, gripping Olivia's shoulders.

476

"Look at me," she urged. "You are a wonderful mother."

"I am a very single mother, Sarah. I can't have another child."

"The sign is really faint. Maybe it's a false positive."

"I doubt that."

"Go see your gyno."

Olivia let out a frustrated sigh. "I can't believe this. I was on birth control," she said, her voice rising. "What the hell am I going to do?"

"You're going to go to the doctor," Sarah said firmly. "And you're not going to tell a soul until you get the results back. We'll deal with whatever comes next when we know for sure. I'll go with you."

Overwhelmed, Olivia pulled Sarah into a hug. "Thank you, Sarah."

"That's what friends are for. To panic with you and, obviously, to encourage you to lie."

Despite their tears, they both let out a watery laugh.

106

The week passed quickly. Olivia, Sarah, and Sue had been invited to spend the weekend at Lauren's house. After the stressful week she'd endured, especially with the anxiety over the pregnancy test, Olivia desperately needed a break. Matt and Robin had arrived Thursday night to take care of Amelia.

As Sarah and Olivia sat in Dr. Sendrick's office, Olivia gazed out the large window. The parking lot of the medical arts building was filled to capacity.

Dr. Sendrick came highly recommended by both Sarah and Sue, and her reputation preceded her. Still, Olivia wasn't thrilled about ending her week waiting for test results.

The doorknob turned, and the doctor entered, offering a calm smile. "The urine screen is negative," she said.

Olivia pressed a hand to her heart and closed her eyes, exhaling in relief. "Thank God."

"But," Dr. Sendrick continued, "I'd like to run a blood panel to be certain. You already had a positive urine reading before today, so let's confirm, shall we?"

"Yes, I want to be sure," Olivia agreed.

"One of my staff will call you Monday afternoon with the results."

"So why am I so sick?"

"Stress is a heavy thing, Ms. Gregory. Is there anything going on at work that might trigger such a significant stress response?"

"You could certainly say that."

"I'm inclined to believe that your body is trying to tell you to slow down and take care of yourself."

"Well, I've got a weekend away planned," she said.

"That's good medicine," the doctor said with a grin.

107

Olivia's mini-vacation officially began. Once everyone settled into their sleeping arrangements, Lauren decided pizza would be the perfect way to kick off the weekend. Nick stayed at Lauren's brother's house with the baby.

The women gathered on the living room floor around a large coffee table, each holding a drink except for Olivia. She didn't drink, both because of her past struggles with addiction and because she wasn't completely certain she wasn't pregnant.

"Are you sure you don't want some wine?" Lauren offered again.

"No, I'm fine."

"Oh, come on," Sue said. "Have a drink!"

"No, thanks."

Lauren interjected, "Individuals in recovery don't drink."

Olivia nodded. "She's right. That's why I don't. I'd rather not open Pandora's Box and replace one addiction with another."

"There's more to it. I can see it in your eyes," Sue pressed.

Sarah glanced at Olivia.

"What am I missing?" Lauren asked, dabbing her mouth with a napkin.

"This cannot leave the room," Olivia said, looking between the three of them.

"Of course," Lauren agreed.

Sue nodded.

"I was at the doctor today," Olivia confessed. "I took a pregnancy test."

Sue's face lit up, and she clapped her hands. "That's awesome!" she squealed.

"No," Lauren shook her head. "No, it's not. Look at her face. This wasn't planned."

Nodding, Olivia sighed. "The urine test was negative, but they took blood to confirm."

"I get it," Sue said, taking a sip of beer. "It's because you don't know who the dad is, right?"

"It's not just that," Olivia admitted. "I can't have another child, not like this. I want to be married, or at least in a committed relationship, before I have more kids. I can't imagine raising two children on my own. I can't believe I'm even in this situation right now."

"I know for certain you wouldn't have to raise another child alone," Sue said.

"How do you know that?"

"I think what Sue is trying to say," Lauren explained, "is that we all know Daniel is in love with you. Even if it weren't his child, he'd step up."

"And you don't think Henry would?" Olivia asked, looking at them.

"No," Lauren said bluntly. "From what I've seen, Henry isn't the chivalrous type. He's always been a loner."

"Not always," Olivia corrected.

"Well, for most of his life," Lauren continued. "I know he's been a great comfort to you in recovery, and I know you've been an anchor for him. But I don't think he's right for you. I don't think he can commit."

"Commit?" Sarah scoffed. "Hell, she's the one who can't commit. I don't know how she keeps up with Henry and Danny. I never could do that sort of thing."

A flicker of hurt crossed Olivia's face.

"I'm not criticizing you," Sarah clarified. "We'll support you no matter what. I'm just saying…"

"I was indecisive too," Sue added. "I juggled men for a long time." She smirked. "Kept things interesting. I was never lonely. But for me, it was just sex. Hell, that's how Rick and I started out. Eventually, I grew out of it." She set her beer bottle down with a sigh. "But I do agree with Lauren. I don't think Henry is capable of taking this, whatever you two have, to the next level."

"I can't either," Olivia said defensively. "I'm not ready

482

for that."

"Are you using protection?" Lauren asked abruptly.

"I… I…" Olivia stammered.

"I can answer that," Sarah interjected, raising a hand. "No."

"And if you're not using protection, are you on birth control?" Lauren continued.

"I am. That's why none of this makes sense."

Shaking her head, Lauren pressed on. "Birth control isn't foolproof. The only way to avoid pregnancy without abstinence is to use both birth control and a condom."

"Which we all know Olivia is incapable of," Sarah interrupted with a smirk.

"Thank you, Dr. Harris, for that wonderful analysis," Olivia quipped. "And what the hell, Sarah? You're supposed to be supporting me."

They all laughed.

"It's true, though," Olivia admitted with a sigh. "I can't resist either of them. They're both incredible in their own way."

"Who's better in bed?" Lauren asked.

Olivia froze.

"Seriously. Who?" Sarah prodded.

"They're both different," Olivia said, clearly embarrassed.

"But who satisfies you the most?" Lauren pressed.

Olivia's cheeks flushed.

Sue grinned. "It's Danny. I knew it!"

"He is pretty hot," Olivia admitted.

"More than hot," Sarah added. "Have you seen him mow the lawn? Shirtless? Built like a god. I could have an orgasm just watching him."

They all burst into laughter.

"So, how good are we talking?" Sue pushed.

"Ladies, please," Olivia said, still smiling.

"I bet he has a strong back," Sarah teased.

"It's not just the sex," Olivia admitted. "It's the way he moves, the way he talks. He has a beautiful spirit. His soul just glows. He's so funny and selfless without even thinking about it."

Lauren set down her half-eaten slice of pizza. "Olivia, listen to yourself. Who do you want? What do you want?"

"I don't know," Olivia whispered, her eyes brimming with tears.

"My grandmother used to say," Lauren continued, "that you know you're with the right person when you can't imagine living without them, when they're the air you breathe. My parents had that kind of love. I think that's why, in the grand scheme of things, they left this world together. I encourage you to think about it. Which of these men, Henry or Daniel, could you live without? Who helps you breathe?"

Sarah and Sue nodded in agreement.

"You don't have to decide today," Sue reassured. "But Danny won't wait forever. If nothing changes, he'll probably take the job in Dayton."

Olivia's eyes widened. "What job in Dayton?"

Sue's mouth fell open. "Oh, God. He didn't tell you?"

Lauren sighed. "Nick offered him a position at the FBI field office in Dayton. Major Crimes. It would be a huge opportunity, but he told us he wouldn't take it because of you."

Olivia stared at them, stunned. "A job in Dayton?" She paused for a heartbeat, the thought of him leaving swirling around in her mind. She couldn't catch her breath, and that's when she knew. "I love him," she admitted, "but I don't know if I love him enough."

Lauren met her gaze. "Then ask yourself one thing. Who can you not breathe without? Because from where I'm sitting, the answer is pretty clear."

108

After Sunday brunch, Olivia and Sarah drove back to Columbus, the weekend coming to a pleasant close. Spending time with Matt and Robin had been the perfect way to wrap things up.

Once everyone left, Olivia sat on the living room floor playing with Amelia. Nigel lay beside them, his soft snores filling the quiet space. A knock at the back door was quickly followed by Danny's familiar voice. Olivia wasn't surprised. It was Sunday, his usual time with her. Sue must have told him she was home.

Standing, Olivia made her way to the door and opened it with a smile. Seeing Danny again sent a rush of warmth through her. Before either of them could say a word, Amelia's tiny feet pattered across the floor, her delighted squeal ringing through the house.

"Danny!" she cried.

"Monkey Girl!" he exclaimed, scooping her up with ease.

As Amelia chattered excitedly, Danny listened, nodding along as he carried her back into the living room. Nigel greeted him with a wagging tail, his panting enthusiastic.

Olivia lingered in the kitchen doorway, watching the scene unfold. These moments always struck her, stirring something deep inside her. She thought about what Lauren had said, about whether she could breathe without Danny. The idea of him being out of her life left her feeling empty.

Shaking off the thought, she walked into the room and sat beside Danny and Amelia. He turned to her, his charming smile effortlessly drawing her in.

"I missed you Friday night," he said. "I almost didn't know what to do with myself."

"I missed you too," she admitted. "Though I'm sure you and Rick found something to do."

"Rick and I always find a way to have fun," he replied with a smirk.

Her expression sobered. "Danny, why didn't you tell me you were offered a job in Dayton?"

His smile faded. "Lauren told you."

"Actually, Sue let it slip."

He exhaled, looking away. "I don't want to take that job."

"Why not?"

He shrugged, still avoiding her eyes. "I just don't want it."

Olivia sighed, her frustration mounting. "We're not done talking about this. As soon as I get Amelia bathed and down for the night, we're finishing this conversation." With that, she pushed herself to her feet and strode into the bathroom.

Later, after giving Amelia a snack and rocking her to sleep, Danny joined Olivia in the bedroom. She sat on the bed, scrolling through university websites, lost in the dream of going back to school. But for now, there were other priorities, a daughter to raise and a murder to solve. Still, she allowed herself to wish.

Danny closed the bedroom door and turned on the baby monitor before sitting on the edge of the bed, peeling off his socks.

"So, why?" Olivia asked, not bothering to ease into the conversation.

He shifted, drawing one leg beneath him. "I'm not interested."

"I want to know why. Because if someone offered me a job with the FBI, I'd jump at the chance."

"The timing isn't right."

"What does that even mean, Danny? You're a brilliant detective. You'd make an incredible field agent."

"I can't go. My family is here."

"Dayton is barely an hour and a half away," she countered.

"My family left everything to come here with me. How fair would it be to leave them now?"

Olivia shook her head. "I know your parents. They would tell you to take this opportunity."

His voice softened. "I'm not leaving you."

She inhaled sharply, his words settling in. "Danny, I'm not worth giving up a chance like this."

His jaw tensed. "Are we really doing this again? The whole 'I'm not good enough' speech?" he asked, using air quotes.

"It's not that. I just…"

"I was offered this same position years ago. I turned it down then for different reasons. I'm turning it down now because I won't leave you, I won't leave my family, and I won't leave Amelia. This isn't just about you."

Her defenses wavered. "I'm sorry. I didn't realize…"

He stood and pulled off his shirt, crossing the room to the closet where he kept a few spare clothes. Olivia's gaze traced the lines of his back, the way his muscles moved beneath his skin. When he unzipped his jeans and stepped out of them, her breath hitched. The familiar rush of desire flooded through her.

Closing her laptop, she placed it on the floor just as he pulled on a pair of black cotton shorts and climbed into bed. He laced his fingers behind his head, watching her with quiet amusement.

She leaned over him, resting on her elbow. "I'm an idiot."

His brow lifted. "Why do you say that?"

"I assumed you were turning down the job just for me. That was selfish. I'm sorry." She hesitated. "Though I have to admit, I would miss you terribly. I honestly don't know how I'd survive without you."

His expression softened. "I know I can't survive without you." He exhaled, his voice quieter now. "Maybe I had different reasons for staying before, but Livy, I've told you. My job is to keep you safe. That's why I was born. I just know it."

"You don't have to worry about me."

"I don't have to," he agreed. "But I do. And I always will."

She held his gaze, her lips curving into a small smile.

"Come here," he murmured, reaching for her.

One kiss turned into another, the tension melting into something heated, something that neither of them wanted to resist. Time slipped away as they clung to each other, the outside world narrowing until there was only breath, warmth, and the steady rhythm of two bodies finding familiar ground.

When it was over, the room felt hushed, as though even the air had settled. Olivia rested her head against his chest, listening to his heartbeat slow beneath her ear. Their bodies were spent, heavy with exhaustion and closeness, the kind that lingered long after the moment itself had passed. For a while, neither of them spoke.

In the spirit of transparency, she knew she had to tell him about the test. "I took a pregnancy test," she confessed quietly. "I went to the doctor on Friday." She turned her face up to meet his gaze. "I thought I was pregnant."

His fingers traced through her hair. "You're not?"

"I won't know for sure until Monday. The urine test was negative. They sent out blood work to be certain."

Silence filled the space between them. It wasn't the reaction she had expected.

"I'd stand by you," he said finally. "No matter what."

She swallowed. "Even not knowing?"

His eyes drifted downward. "You know me better than that."

Relief washed over her. That was the reaction she had been hoping for. Still, she hesitated. "It wouldn't be up to you."

"You know me better than that. I'd never just walk away unless you told me to." He paused. "Does Henry know?"

"No. And I'm not going to tell him."

Danny studied her for a long moment. "So why tell me?"

She met his gaze, her voice barely above a whisper. "Because you're my best friend."

"I love you," he said quietly.

"Will love be enough?" she asked, her cheek resting against his bare stomach as she gazed up at him.

He sat up slightly, brushing his fingers over her hair. "I'm a patient guy. Until then, I'll be with you however you'll let me."

Olivia closed her eyes, her heart warring with her mind as Danny pulled her into his arms. Whatever the future held, for now, this was enough.

109

When Olivia woke up the next morning, a text awaited her. It was from Henry, requesting to meet for lunch. So, a little after 11:30, she waited for him in the hospital cafeteria.

He walked toward her, his head lowered as he approached. His attire never strayed far from the usual, jeans and a T-shirt. Today was no different, but she had always appreciated his simplicity.

She stood, dressed in brown career slacks, matching pumps, and a cream-colored button-up Oxford. Her hair lay neatly on her shoulders. Smiling as he approached, she waved slightly.

They sat down together. "Do you want me to get you something to eat?" she asked politely.

"Why didn't you tell me you thought you were pregnant?" His tone was sharp, almost accusatory.

Her stomach dropped. "Oh my God. They sent the labs here." She lowered her head in shame. "Henry, I…"

"You don't owe me anything," he cut in. "Not an explanation, not answers. I've never asked anything of you because you've never asked anything of me. That's how I want to keep it. I don't want a commitment. I care about you. I enjoy spending time with you. But I can't promise it will ever be more than that."

A flush of anger warmed her cheeks, though she

recognized his words echoed her own confusion about Danny. Still, they stung. "I understand," she said, swallowing hard.

"I don't want to risk hurting you or myself."

She nodded, looking down, her fingers fidgeting in her lap.

"So, you don't have to feel guilty if you're sleeping with other men," he added.

Her head snapped up, eyes narrowing.

"Like I said, you don't owe me an explanation."

"It's Danny," she admitted.

He sighed. "Do you love him?"

Lowering her gaze again, she whispered, "I don't know who I love."

"And you don't have to," he said matter-of-factly. "I don't believe true love really exists. Sure, we love our kids, but that's a different kind of love."

"There's no point in being cynical about it," she countered, the hurt creeping into her voice.

"I'm not cynical. I'm just not pretending. We need to stop lying to each other and be honest. I won't pretend to be something I'm not. Yes, I'm in recovery. Yes, I care about you. But I will never let myself hurt like I did with Candy. I won't grieve over anyone else."

494

She shrugged. "We never had anything permanent anyway, right?"

"You taught me to live in the moment. That's what I do. You gave me a schedule of when I could see you, and I accepted it. If I couldn't, I would have walked away."

His words cut deep. "Wow. I didn't know I was so expendable."

"Everyone is expendable," he replied.

Her eyes burned with unshed tears as she met his gaze. "Why are you acting like this?"

"This is who I am. Maybe you've just been too blind to see it."

She let out a bitter laugh. "So, I was too in love to notice? You really do think highly of yourself, don't you?"

"I'm not pretending anymore. If being brutally honest is what it takes to protect your heart, I'll do it. You can hate me for it, but I'm doing this for you."

"Who else are you sleeping with, Henry?" she asked.

"It doesn't matter. I'm not committed to this. What we had was good. It's been great for me. You've helped me heal. I've helped you with the investigation. I think you're an incredible woman, but I can't afford to think beyond that. We should have had this conversation a long time ago. I don't want you to think I misled you."

"You're right. We didn't talk about it. And you're right.

I'm not ready for a commitment." She hesitated.

"I should have warned you. I'm really a prick."

"You're sure acting like one now."

"This is who I am. Take it or leave it."

Her mouth gaped slightly as the shock settled in.

Seeing the hurt in her eyes, he reached for her hand, holding it gently. His voice softened. "Look at me. I've met Danny. He's a good guy. Better than me. If I had to pick someone for you, and it came down to me or him, I'd pick him."

Her throat tightened. "Why are you doing this? What are you afraid of?"

"I'm not afraid of anything. I just can't give something I don't have," he said taking back his hand.

His words echoed her own to Danny, and suddenly, she saw herself through Danny's eyes. She had been hurting him just as Henry was hurting her.

"Maybe we should stop this altogether," she blurted out.

He shrugged. "It's going nowhere. If that's okay with you, then I'm fine. If you wanted more, you should have told me that way I could have ended this charade."

Shaking her head, she lied. "Wow…"

A resolute glance, and then Henry dropped his gaze.

"We're both pretty broken," she said with a small, bitter laugh.

"That we are." He exhaled. "No matter what, Olivia, I'm still your friend. That's something I can give you unconditionally. I'm a shitty friend too, though. Just ask Jim. But friendship? That, I can do."

She looked at him for a long moment before nodding. "Well, thanks for being honest, Henry," she said sarcastically.

Her phone rang, startling her. She glanced at the screen. Danny.

Henry smirked slightly. "You better get that."

She answered. Another crime scene. Despite everything they'd just said, Henry decided to come with her. Bentley still hadn't removed him from the case, and as far as Olivia could tell, he had no intention of doing so. Henry's access to the lab made him too valuable.

110

They pulled up to the old brick building, where crime scene tape fluttered in the breeze and cop cars crowded the perimeter. The coroner's van and the forensic team's vehicle were parked nearby, and a swarm of reporters hovered like vultures.

An officer waved them through. Olivia spotted Nigel sitting beside Danny as she pulled the SUV up next to them. She stepped out, Henry following closely behind. Instantly, her eyes locked on the victim standing outside the warehouse, an apparition of a young girl radiating anger.

I'm Olivia, she projected telepathically.

I'm Claire, the apparition responded.

I'm here to help you, Claire.

I know who you are. Everyone in the in between knows you. I'll wait. I'm not going anywhere.

Claire's determination was striking. It was as if she remembered everything and was fueled by the need for justice. Fear did not touch her. She was driven.

Danny approached with Nigel, his gaze briefly flashing with disdain toward Henry, though he quickly masked it. "Henry," Danny greeted coolly.

"Danny," Henry replied with equal restraint.

"I thought you were off this case," Danny said.

"Not a chance," Henry responded, moving toward Bentley.

Danny shifted his attention to Olivia. "You okay?"

"I'm fine," she said, only then realizing how upset she must have looked.

The brief exchange between Danny and Henry struck a nerve, an unsettling reminder of how much she had hurt Danny and how hollow her connection with Henry truly was. A sense of being used and discarded weighed on her.

Snapping back to the present, she headed toward the building, dreading what awaited her inside.

Before she reached the entrance, a forensic team member approached and gestured for Danny to join. "The victim is Claire Roberts, seventeen. Reported missing two days ago after she did not come home from cheerleading practice."

Inside, Claire's body rested on a tarp as Bentley worked methodically, with Henry beside him, jotting notes and snapping photos. Bentley seemed to sense their arrival and began speaking. "Defensive wounds suggest she fought back. I'm betting there's skin under her fingernails. The tic tac toe mark is consistent with the others. This time, there's an X in the top middle square."

In the corner of the room, Claire's spirit appeared, wearing red cotton shorts, a white T shirt, and cheerleading shoes. Her ashen skin was untouched by the brutality she had endured in life.

Emma appeared beside her. *Claire,* Emma began gently, *you need to come with me.*

I'm not leaving, Claire said firmly.

You have to cross over, Olivia explained.

Where's the other woman? The one who understands what happens after death?

Lauren?

Yes. We all know about her. She's the one I need.

Lauren's too far away to respond right now.

I know you can help me cross, but she can help figure out what happened.

Do you remember anything? Olivia asked softly.

I got in my car. Someone hit me from behind. He must have been hiding in the back seat. My mom always told me to lock my doors. I forgot.

Do you remember where you woke up? Any smells or sounds?

I was on a bed. I remember being raped. Over and over.

Olivia swallowed hard, steadying herself. *Anything else?*

Music. Loud and nonstop. Everything smelled old, like

mildew and pine trees.

Claire, when you cross over, you can talk to Lauren. She can help. Olivia paused. *How did you manage to fight back?*

He zip tied my wrists. There was a spring poking through the mattress. I used it to cut through. When he came back, I fought. I scratched him. I think I got his hand, but he was too strong. He knocked me out again.

Anything else you can remember?

He had a black hoodie on, so I couldn't see his face. He had jeans on and black treaded boots, the kind you would wear at a factory. I don't remember much about the room. I punched him and punched him. The next thing I know, I woke up in this place with all of these little light beams. I want my life back, she said as the typical reaction settled on her.

I'm sorry this happened to you, but you did great. You left us a lot of things to work with, more than the others were able to. You did really well, Olivia praised.

Claire smiled. *I watch a lot of crime shows, so I sort of went off of things I learned from that. I hope it helps you guys catch him.*

Are you ready to go now?

She dropped her head and nodded a little. *I don't have a choice,* she answered as she shrugged.

Emma will lead you into the light. Listen to me, Olivia said. *You have really helped us more than you know. That should give you some comfort.*

It does. I just don't want to leave my family. I had a good life.

You can have another good life. Just talk to the others when you get there. It's possible to come back not only in spirit form, but for another life. This is only one journey for you.

You mean reincarnation?

Yes. Talk to your guides about it. If it's something you want to do, they can help you.

Claire's face brightened with hope. Olivia didn't know why she felt the need to tell Claire about her belief in reincarnation, but if it gave her some optimism, it was well worth it.

Claire and Emma disappeared. Then Danny stood beside her.

"What'd you find out?" he asked.

"A lot," she said as she began relaying the information she'd learned.

"So we might have some DNA evidence, just like Bentley said. And if she left marks on her attacker, we might be able to see it ourselves."

"I can go see Kyle."

"You're not going by yourself."

111

As they drove across town to CPS, Danny just stared at Olivia. He could tell something was very wrong. However, he wasn't sure how to get it out of her. So he used the best approach: bluntness.

"What is wrong with you? Did you find out that you're pregnant?"

She shot him a quick glance. "No. No, I'm not."

He sank a little inside. He knew Henry would never stand by her because he was too selfish. His hope had been that she would be pregnant, giving him a direct way in. Right now, he felt like he was standing on the outside. He hated sharing her. "So, what's wrong?" he pressed.

"I owe you an apology."

"For what?"

"I have been very unfair to you, Danny."

"I don't get it."

"I kept telling you that I didn't deserve you, and today I finally figured out why. I've been pushing you into the background, forcing you to wait on me to figure out what the hell I'm doing. That's not right."

"Here we go again," he muttered, frustration creeping into his voice.

"Let me finish before you get mad," she insisted. "I also figured out today that Henry isn't the man I thought he was."

"Big surprise there."

"I think there's good in him, but it's buried too deep. He found out about the pregnancy test and confronted me about you."

"Wow," he said, shifting in his seat. "And how did that go?"

"He didn't seem to care. He basically told me he isn't able to commit. He said many of the things I've said to you, and that's when I realized how truly undeserving I am of you. I've put you off. I've kept your life on hold. I've been chasing after someone who will never be mine, and I've been using you."

He dropped his head. "What are you saying?"

"I think we should cool things off for a while until I can get my head straight."

"Are you cooling things off with Henry?"

"We sort of left it unresolved in my mind, but yes. I'm going to seek out another group to go to on Tuesday and Thursday. I will still be his friend, but he made it very clear it would never go further than that."

"So, because he rejected you, I get rejected too?"

"No, that's not what this is."

"You're doing it again. You're pushing me away. I'm telling you, Livy, the reeling out and in is really making me motion sick."

"I know. I am so sorry."

"So now we're not hanging out?"

"We can hang out, but won't that be really hard for you?"

"I told you that I'd take you however I could get you. If that means I have to back off, then I can handle being friends. I'm not going to sit here and lie. The sex with you is incredible."

Her face flushed red.

"But that's not all we have. You know that," he continued.

"I do know that. You are my best friend. I tell you everything. There's nothing about me that you don't know. That's why I am being honest with you now. I am admitting to you that I'm hurt over what Henry said to me, but I'm glad he said it. It made me realize what an awful person I've been to you. If I can't commit to you, how is that going to work?"

"Working just fine right now," he said with a chuckle.

She smiled. "And the sex is absolutely incredible. You've shown me how to make love, not just fuck." She pursed her lips before continuing. "When I was molested, I got a pretty messed-up view of intimacy. Then, when I started using, that view became even more twisted. You've taught me how real it can be. It's more than physical. At least it is for me."

"What about with Henry?"

"Danny, are you a glutton for punishment? I'm not going to talk to you about sex with Henry. That's one thing I will not do."

"Stop the car and pull over," he insisted.

Confused, she did as he asked, shifting the car into park.

He turned to face her fully. "Does he make you feel safe? Like I do?"

Dropping her eyes, she shook her head. "No, Danny. He doesn't. You make me feel safe and loved and heard and seen." She choked back the emotions rising in her throat. "There was always something missing with him. I care about both of you. Out of the two of you, I know that you would risk your life for me."

"So if you know that, why are you still pushing me out?"

"I want to be fair to you. I want to be someone deserving of you. I need time to figure out what it is that I can give you. While I'm doing that, why should I use you?"

"I don't feel used. You said it yourself. I'm your best friend. You're my best friend. We're not using each other at all. So we have sex. Really good sex. What does that matter? It's no different than what we've been doing. But now that Henry's screwed with your head, you want to stop. Stop letting him control your decisions. Think for yourself. You are a smart woman."

"I'm trying to think for myself, and I'm trying to make a decision without the physical trumping the emotional," she argued.

"Why can't you just let things happen? Stop fighting this."

"I just need some time, Danny. That's all I'm asking."

"I have never crowded you," he said, his eyes locking onto hers. "I would never do that. I think you're telling me that you need space. I can give you that. I get it. But I'm not going to lie to you, Livy. I'm going to be lost. You're my compass. I was totally lost in my life until the night I watched Donte put that knife to your throat. Then I knew. I knew exactly why I was born. I knew why I was here. I knew why nothing else worked out. I'd been waiting for you."

She smiled, tears brimming in her eyes. "You're making this really hard."

"I love you with everything I am. If I could rope the sun for you, I'd do it. Our lives may have some bumps. Every relationship has challenges, but I will never hurt you. I will always protect you and Amelia. I love you both."

She put her hand to his cheek, then ran her fingers through his hair. Taking his hand, she smiled. "You are a wonderful, good man."

"I really wish you could see yourself through my eyes, Livy. I know every flaw, and guess what? I don't care. That's what love is. It's fully accepting the person, flaws and all."

She nodded. "You present a pretty convincing case."

"You know I'm right. You're just trying to protect yourself, but you don't have to with me."

He pulled her hand to his lips and kissed her knuckles. "Don't push me away. Let me show you what this can be like."

Her nose crinkled. "Can you just give me a little time? I just want to be sure."

His blue eyes met hers. "I can. I'll miss you, though. I'll stay away. I'll only see you at work. If space is what you want, I'm giving it to you."

She nodded.

He pulled her toward him, and Olivia leaned over the middle console. He stopped, cupping her jawline as his thumb brushed her cheek.

"Can I just steal one more kiss? Your lips always taste so damn good."

She pursed her lips.

"I never promised to make it easy," he admitted as he leaned in and kissed her softly.

112

Olivia pulled into an empty space and turned off the car. She got out, slamming the door behind her. "Let me handle this," she said firmly.

"No problem. Handle it," Danny replied, holding up his hands in surrender.

They walked through the doors and checked in with the receptionist, who thankfully seemed somewhat nicer this time. Olivia asked to see Kyle, and moments later, he arrived after being paged.

Smiling, he extended his hand toward Olivia. She shook it, immediately noticing the bandages, one across his face, another wrapped around his hand.

"Kyle," she began evenly, "we need you to come down to the station with us. We have a few questions."

"Of course. Anything I can do to help. Is this about the murders?"

Danny cut in, his voice brisk. "Let's just head to the precinct."

Kyle sat in the back seat of the SUV, separated by thick bulletproof glass. Nigel rode in the hatch, a cage between him and Kyle. Danny sat up front while Olivia drove.

Kyle sighed, shifting uncomfortably. "I feel like a criminal back here."

"Don't take it personally," Olivia replied, keeping her tone steady. "It's just how the vehicle's set up." She forced a small, reassuring smile to maintain the fragile rapport.

Kyle's eyes wandered. "Is that your daughter?" he asked, nodding toward the photo tucked into the visor.

Olivia didn't respond.

"Henry talks about her all the time."

Danny twisted in his seat, fixing Kyle with a sharp look. "So, what made you decide to become a child welfare worker?"

"My history, I guess," Kyle said, his voice softening. "I'm sure Henry's already told you about my past."

"Yes, he has," Olivia confirmed, catching his reflection in the rearview mirror.

"Well, why don't you enlighten me anyway?" Danny pressed.

Kyle hesitated, then let out a slow breath. "Imagine the worst possible environment to raise a child in. That's where I come from."

"That pushed you toward child protection work?" Danny asked, his tone skeptical.

"I wanted to help people, Detective Knight. I started out as an investigator and worked my way up. I figured if I could make the world even a little safer for kids, it would be worth it."

Olivia glanced back at him. "Kyle, why didn't you join the lawsuit against Mike and Holly?"

"I was scared," Kyle admitted quietly. "I was young. They told me if I said anything, they'd kill me."

Danny leaned back, arms crossed. "I guess that's understandable. Did you get any money from the settlement?"

Kyle nodded. "Yeah, I did."

"So you benefited from Howard speaking up?" Danny asked.

"We all did," Kyle said, his voice heavy with emotion. "He was brave enough to tell the truth. We all admired him for that."

When they arrived at the station, Bentley's report was waiting in Olivia's inbox. As Danny led Kyle to the interrogation room, Olivia grabbed the paperwork.

She was impressed the report had come through so quickly. It was only a preliminary, but it was something to work with. Skimming through it, she wasn't surprised to see the cause of death listed as strangulation. More telling, however, was the discovery of epithelial cells under Claire's fingernails, just as Bentley had predicted. The lab was already running the DNA through CODIS. The estimated time of death was between midnight and five a.m. The fire department's analysis of when the fire had been set was still pending.

Just as she started down the hall, her phone rang. It was Lauren. Olivia turned back, slipping into her office and closing the door behind her for privacy.

"Hello," she answered.

"Claire Roberts has been a victim before," Lauren said without preamble.

"She came to you? That's something, at least."

"Not when I'm trying to feed my child, it isn't," Lauren replied sharply. "She stood there, arms crossed, tapping her foot impatiently. Very distracting."

"So, what did she tell you?" Olivia asked.

"She mentioned a women's self-defense class. Apparently, she fought hard. Did you find ligature marks?"

Olivia wedged the phone between her ear and shoulder, flipping through the report again. "Yes. She told me that she managed to cut herself free. Said she was bound with a zip tie."

"So, she's already visited you?"

"She has, yes."

"Annoying. Simply annoying. I'm more than willing to help victims, but she was downright rude."

"How was she a victim before?"

"She was abducted when she was eight years old," Lauren explained. "She managed to escape. Afterward, she and her mother went to the police. I think that's when she started self-defense training."

"Poor girl," Olivia murmured.

"It explains her will to survive. Any DNA hits yet?"

"We're hopeful. She scratched her attacker, and we have Kyle. He's got bandages on his face and hand."

"Remember, if he doesn't willingly remove those bandages or give a DNA sample, you'll need a warrant. You'll need probable cause to get that warrant."

"I know," Olivia sighed. "We're not there yet, though."

"Patience," Lauren advised. "Every good profiler needs patience. Don't get discouraged. Every case, as tragic as it is, brings another opportunity to learn and brings you one step closer to solving the crime."

"I won't give up. I need to go, though. Danny's with Kyle in the interrogation room."

"Alright. We'll talk soon."

Olivia hung up, tucked the file under her arm, and headed for the room. Inside, Danny stood across from Kyle, who sat at the table, hands folded neatly in front of him.

"Did Danny offer you something to drink?" Olivia asked as she took a seat.

"Yes," Kyle replied with a polite smile. "I'm fine, though. What can I help you with?"

"Kyle, where were you last night between midnight and five this morning?" Olivia asked.

Kyle blinked. "It sounds like you're questioning me."

"I'm sorry, but we have to cover every base."

"I was home with Katie and Mike."

"Can she verify that?"

"I'm sure she can."

Olivia leaned in slightly. "What happened to your face and hand?"

"I was working in the garage," he replied. "I cut myself. Saw blades are not for the faint of heart. A piece of wood also flew up and hit me. I bandaged it. It was pretty deep."

Danny glanced at Kyle's hands, noticing several smaller cuts and bruises. "All those marks from woodworking, too?"

"Yeah. I'm still learning. It's been a rough hobby to pick up."

"Do you know anything about missing files from the archive?" Olivia asked.

"No. We have a system. I'm sure Amy went over that with you."

"She did, but I want to be thorough. Is there any chance someone from your department breached the system?"

"I doubt it. My team is experienced. They know the

protocols."

Olivia placed her hand on the file. "Kyle, we're going to need a sample of your DNA."

Kyle's smile faded. His mouth opened slightly, eyes darting between Olivia and Danny. "I don't understand."

"Please," Olivia said softly.

"You think I did this?"

"We're just trying to rule things out," Danny added, sitting down beside Olivia.

"I didn't do this. I've seen enough pain in my life. I would never hurt anyone like that."

"Then give us a DNA sample," Danny said.

"So we can clear you," Olivia added gently.

Kyle's jaw tightened. "I'm not saying anything else. I want to call my lawyer."

"Don't make this harder than it needs to be," Olivia pleaded.

"I'm done," Kyle said firmly. "With all due respect, Olivia, I know you're just doing your job. But I'm not saying anything else."

113

Later in the day, Danny sat in his office, scribbling notes for a preliminary report. The door creaked open, and Sue walked in, settling into a chair without a word. Danny glanced up briefly before returning his focus to his work.

"You and Olivia want to grab a bite? Rick's mom has the kids," Sue asked casually.

Danny didn't look up. "Why did you tell Olivia about the job in Dayton?"

"I didn't mean to. I thought you told her."

"She wants space now. And Henry showed his true colors, too. He told her he didn't want a relationship. Same thing she's been telling me. She freaked out, and now we're on hold." His voice lowered. "This has been a day from hell."

"I'm so sorry, Danny."

"You know I'm patient. I'd wait for that woman forever, but this… she keeps pushing me away."

"What did you tell her? That you'd give her space?"

"Yeah. I'm not going to force her. That would only drive her away."

Sue leaned in slightly. "Danny, I know you've been infatuated before, and I know you've been in love. Why is she different?"

He leaned back in his chair, staring at the ceiling for a moment. "She's the one. I've been looking for her my whole life."

Sue hesitated. "Are you sure it's not just physical? Sometimes it's easy to mix those feelings up."

"You know me better than that."

She sighed and propped her feet on the sofa's edge. "Yeah, I do. I'm reaching."

"You are," Danny said with a tired smile. "After everything with Donte, things shifted. I feel like there's a reason I'm in her life, and she's in mine. I just want to make sure she's okay."

Sue's voice softened. "You know I love Olivia, but I see what this is doing to you. It's not fair."

"She doesn't know what she wants. But at least Henry's off the table."

"And you want to be what's left?"

"No. I want to give her space to decide without any pressure from me."

"Are you sure she's the one?"

"I've never been so sure of anything. It's something that hits you deep, bone deep."

The sharp click of heels echoed down the hallway,

cutting through the room's tension. Olivia appeared in the doorway, her expression unreadable. Without a word, she grabbed the remote from Danny's desk and turned on the small television perched on his filing cabinet.

The reporter's voice filled the room. "Channel Ten has confirmed this is another crime scene linked to the Tic-Tac-Toe Killer. Seventeen-year-old Claire Roberts was discovered hanging from a rafter in this partially burned building. Sources say Kyle Armstrong was brought in for questioning by FCSO but was later released. Authorities seem focused on Armstrong, a supervisor at the county CPS office. We'll continue to update you on this developing story."

Silence weighed heavily in the room until Olivia broke it. "Who the hell leaked it?"

Danny rubbed his temple. "It makes me nervous."

"I talked to Claire's parents," Sue said. "They were both in the foster system. That's how they met. No connection to Mike or Holly Henson, though."

Danny clenched his jaw. "I'm sick of these dead ends."

"We're smarter than them," Olivia said firmly. "We'll figure this out."

114

At home, after Amelia was asleep and the house was quiet, Olivia sat on the living room floor, her legs crossed beneath her and her arms outstretched, palms up. She took time to reflect. She felt drained. The exchange between her and Henry, followed by the discussion with Danny, had left her exhausted.

As she quieted and became focused, she remembered what Validus had said. Suddenly, she realized that Henry's actions were the result of knowing she hadn't been faithful to him. He had put his defenses up again. She wondered if he truly cared deeply for her, but she had to go by what he told her. To protect herself, she would put her defenses up too.

She mulled over Henry's reaction. Another face entered her mind. Danny's. She smiled at the thought. In her mind, she could see the way his lips curved when he smiled, the way his skin felt beneath her fingers when they made love. She loved the way he looked at her when they merely talked. He was a beautiful soul beneath those good looks.

He protects you because we've put him in your life, she heard in her ear.

Her eyes stayed closed, her thoughts still on him. No matter what type of confirmation she received, she still wrestled with her own lack of confidence. She felt inadequate despite his consistent reassurance. Her defenses would eventually strangle any possibility of happiness. They would steal opportunities from her.

She felt fur brush against her knee and opened her eyes. Grinning, she caressed Nigel's head and ears. "You always know when to show up, huh, boy?" she said as she bent down, allowing him to lick her face. "You're such a good boy," she continued affectionately.

She remembered the hope Nigel had given her when she was in rehab. He had inspired her, and her decisions had led her to Danny, Sue, Lauren, and Nick. Most of all, they had fulfilled a calling in her life. Still, something was missing.

She wanted Danny. She wanted Henry. Now, the choice seemed easy. Yet she didn't want to choose Danny by default. She wanted to be sure. Knowing Henry was wounded by the competition and had likely put up walls made things harder for her. She refused to believe he didn't care. The only thing that gave her comfort was knowing that time would allow things to play out.

115

Danny lay in bed, unable to sleep. He gazed up at the ceiling, his hand resting across his chest. All he could see was Olivia's face. Then Amelia's face flickered in his mind. It was the beginning of October. He had been giving Olivia the space she requested. They hardly spent time together outside of work anymore. He still watched Amelia on Tuesdays and Thursdays while Olivia went to group, though. That gave him the chance to be with her.

His thoughts drifted to the job in Dayton. If Olivia didn't make a decision soon, he would have no choice but to leave, no matter how much it hurt. He couldn't bear being her partner if she ended up with Henry or fell in love with someone else. He knew he had a job to do, protecting her, but there was only so much his heart could take. He ached for her. He missed her. The smell of her perfume, the warmth of her cuddled against him, the way their legs intertwined as they lay together.

But it wasn't just the physical closeness he longed for. He missed Friday night pizza with her and Amelia. Their weekends with Rick and Sue. He didn't understand why she had isolated herself. It made him angry.

Amelia's face surfaced again in his thoughts. Rocking her to sleep felt like holding a piece of heaven. She was a gift. He had always wanted children. He had been in a few serious relationships, but none had been serious enough to discuss kids. And yet, here was Amelia, and she felt like his.

Danny knew what he felt for Olivia wasn't just a boyhood attraction. He knew the reason his heart was breaking. He truly and genuinely loved her. Amelia was the daughter he had always wanted. He had no idea how to make it all happen.

As he drifted toward sleep, the cell phone on his nightstand rang. He glanced at the clock. Three thirty in the morning. Taking the phone in hand, he saw Olivia's name on the screen.

"Hello," he answered, his voice deep with drowsiness.

"I'm so sorry to call this late," she said.

He heard Amelia crying in the background. His body tensed. "Olivia, what's going on?"

"Danny, Amelia's sick. Really sick. She's been throwing up for hours. I've been up with her all night. I can't leave to get anything. She needs something to rehydrate. She won't stop crying. I've rocked her, walked with her."

"I'll be right there. I'll stop at the store. Do you have stuff for the fever?"

"Yes. I've given it to her," she continued, her voice shaking with emotion, "but she keeps throwing it back up. She's never been this sick."

"Don't worry. I'm on my way."

After stopping at a twenty four hour convenience store to pick up rehydration juice, he took the interstate toward Olivia's house. Pulling into the driveway, he parked.

Turning the handle, he walked into the kitchen and announced himself, locking the door behind him. Amelia's cries were loud. He knew her, and she had never been like this. He understood why Olivia was so upset.

"We're in my room," Olivia called out.

Danny walked to the cabinet and got a sippy cup. He poured the grape flavored liquid into the cup, tightened the lid, and placed the jug into the fridge. Amelia's wails were sharp and unrelenting. He hurried to the bedroom.

Olivia sat on the bed, her eyes red from crying, hair disheveled. In her arms, Amelia squirmed and sobbed, her face flushed.

"Let me take her. See if I can do anything."

Olivia hesitated, then nodded. The moment Amelia saw him, her lips quivered, her tiny arms reaching out.

"Daddy," she croaked, her voice hoarse from crying.

Danny's heart clenched. "Aw, Monkey Girl, ya poor thing. Come here."

He took her gently into his arms, cradling her against his chest. He felt her stomach, hard and tense. Walking to the dresser, he picked up the sippy cup and held it to her lips. She resisted at first, but he rocked her, whispering soothing words.

He walked into the nursery and sat down in the rocking chair. "Come on, sweet girl, calm down," he said softly as he rocked her. "You got to drink this, baby."

Olivia walked in, sat down on the floor, and leaned her back against the wall. "She started throwing up at about ten. She went every half hour. She's never been this sick," she explained.

"It's probably just a virus. She'll feel like a million bucks tomorrow," he reassured her as Amelia finally took a sip from the cup.

Her breathing steadied as she gripped the cup tightly. "That's my girl," he whispered.

"You are so good with her. Thank you so much for doing this," Olivia said quietly.

"No problem. Happy to do it." He glanced at her. "You look like hell. I got this. Go to sleep."

"She called you Daddy," Olivia murmured, meeting his eyes.

Danny swallowed. "First time she's done that."

"You're the only man who's been a consistent part of her life besides my dad and my brother."

"Does it bother you?"

She smiled. "No."

Relief spread through him. Maybe the tide was turning. "You can't go to work tomorrow. I'll call Wallace. Seriously, get some rest."

"Thank you, Danny." She stood and walked toward him,

pressing a soft kiss to his forehead. "You can lay down with me when you're done."

"You sure?" he asked, careful to keep his voice quiet.

"I'm sure."

After making sure Amelia kept the liquid down and her fever had broken, Danny placed her gently in her crib. He tiptoed into Olivia's bedroom, watching her sleep peacefully. He hesitated. Sleeping beside her was too much temptation and too much heartache. Instead, he turned and went to the couch.

The next morning, Danny woke at eight and called Wallace. After explaining the situation, Wallace was understanding as always. With exhaustion still clinging to him, Danny lay back down and fell asleep again.

When he woke, he heard the two sweetest things in the world: the sound of Amelia's laughter and Olivia's voice. Then he heard Olivia's cell phone ring. Listening to her end of the conversation, he could tell she was talking about the case.

"Amy, what do you mean? Okay. So you have surveillance tapes? I can get a warrant. I will. Thank you so much."

He threw the comforter off and sat up. He ran his fingers through his hair. Drowsiness did not shake off easily as he stood to his feet.

Walking into Amelia's room, he saw Olivia on the floor

playing with her. When Amelia saw Danny standing in the doorway, she smiled. "Daddy play?" she asked.

"Whatcha playin', Monkey Girl?"

"Puzzles," she answered.

He walked in and sat down on the floor beside her. "You feel better this morning, Angel?" He touched her forehead.

"I better," she answered.

"What about you, Mommy? You get some rest?"

"Yes. A hot shower did wonders, too. Thank you again for coming over."

"Was that Amy from the archive?" Danny asked.

"Yes. I'll tell you about it later," Olivia answered.

"You girls had breakfast?" he asked.

"I eat," Amelia answered.

"She kept toast down. I didn't want to overload her stomach."

"Well, I'm starving. I'm going to make myself something, if that's okay."

"I can make something for you. It's the least I can do," Olivia said as she stood. "You can stay in here and play with her."

The smell of sausage drifted through the air as Danny played with Amelia. However, his grumbling stomach got the best of him, so he picked her up and carried her into the kitchen.

"I eat," Amelia said.

"She's hungry. That's a good sign," Danny said.

"You want some more toast, baby?" Olivia asked.

"Eat," she answered.

Olivia walked over and grabbed bread to make some more toast.

"So you going to tell me what Amy wanted?" Danny asked.

"She told me that Kyle came into the archive office with a large duffle bag. When she checked on the files from the search warrant, they were all there except for Henry's file."

"We can get a warrant for the surveillance. If Kyle is on it, we can question him again," Danny said.

"What about him lawyering up?"

"We can still make him squirm. I will call the judge today so we can pick up the warrant first thing tomorrow morning," Danny replied.

"That would be great. Then we can turn everything over to Forensics."

She walked to the skillet, took the sausage out, and put it on a plate. As she cracked the eggs, she continued. "Danny, why didn't you come to me last night?"

He shook his head and then stood. Leaning against the counter beside Olivia, he replied softly. "I just couldn't. We haven't spent much time together lately. I promised I would give you some space, so that is what I have been doing. Sleeping in the same bed is not giving you much space."

Olivia nodded. "I understand. I shouldn't have asked that of you."

"It's okay, but it's a good thing I'm a gentleman," he said quietly, laughing a little. He leaned over and whispered into her ear, "I could have easily taken advantage of the situation. So, if you ever wonder if I'm just hanging around for sex, you can think again."

Her eyes met his. "Listen, I'm going to eat breakfast and then I'm going to go on into work. I might be able to get that warrant today."

"You don't have to leave."

"If I stay here, I'm not sure I can follow through on the promise I've made to you."

"I don't mean to make this so difficult for you. I am sorting through things. If it makes you feel any better, the space has helped."

"I get it. I really do, but I need to separate from you. It just hurts too much."

Her eyes brimmed with tears. He thought his heart would snap in two. "Oh God, Livy, don't cry."

"I hurt everyone I care about," she said, her voice

shaking with emotion.

"No. You need to keep sorting through stuff. You'll be better for it. Don't worry about me. I'll be okay."

"I'm so sorry," she said as she brushed tears from her cheeks.

"Don't be. Please," he concluded as he leaned over and kissed her forehead. "And please don't cry. I don't think I can take that."

Later that day, Danny retrieved the warrant and the videotape. Unfortunately, it did not yield anything useful. The surveillance reset every twenty-four hours. So the investigation hit another dead end.

116

As Olivia sat on the nursery floor, she pulled the pink tights up over Amelia's diapered bottom. She was dressing her as a fairy princess for Halloween. The tutu and pink onesie sparkled with bling, and she knew the little plastic tiara would not last long, but it was worth a try.

The sound of the backdoor lock turning made Olivia look up. Sarah's voice followed. "Ladies, are we ready? It's almost six."

"We're done." Olivia met Amelia's big blue eyes. "Let's go show Aunt Sarah how beautiful you are."

"Mommy go?"

Hand in hand, they walked out of the nursery, down the hallway, and into the living room. Sarah's face lit up.

"Look at you!" she squealed. "Aren't you the prettiest princess? Hey, Mommy, give me your phone, and I'll take some pictures. I'm sure Mimi and Pap would love to see this."

"Daddy?" Amelia asked.

"We'll take pictures and send them to him, too," Olivia assured her.

"Daddy come?"

"No, sweetie. It's just going to be us. But we'll have fun,

I promise."

Amelia's face fell slightly, but the excitement of trick or treating quickly took over.

Sarah snapped dozens of photos before uploading them to messages, sending them to Robin, Matt, and Danny.

As they strolled through the neighborhood, they encountered witches and goblins, pirates and clowns, and many other colorful characters. Amelia smiled at everyone handing out candy, her sweet and outgoing nature shining through. Olivia felt a surge of pride.

As they approached another block, a familiar voice called her name. She turned and felt the color drain from her face. Kyle. She forced a smile.

"Kyle?" she asked. "What in the world are you doing here?"

"Well, since we live so far out in the country, Katie wanted to bring Mike into town. Henry always talks about how nice your neighborhood is, so Katie thought we'd come here."

"When did you talk to Henry?"

"A few weeks ago. Are you two not together anymore?"

"We're sort of taking a break," Olivia answered, studying Kyle's face. The bandage was gone, replaced by new skin with four visible scars forming a linear pattern. "Your face is healing," she blurted out.

"Yeah. And my hand." He stuffed both hands into his pockets. "I've gotten better at the woodworking thing. No more accidents."

She only nodded before glancing around. "Where are Katie and Mike?"

"Down the street, I think. They had me park the car. I was supposed to text them once I found a spot." Kyle's gaze dropped to Amelia. He crouched slightly and smiled. "And this must be Amelia. Hello there! Are you a fairy princess?"

The interaction made both Olivia and Sarah uneasy.

"Uh-huh," Amelia answered quietly.

Kyle straightened, meeting Olivia's wary eyes. "Henry was right. She's absolutely beautiful."

"Thank you," Olivia said, gripping Amelia's hand a little tighter. "Well, we've still got a lot of houses left, so we better keep going."

"Oh, I know. We're just getting started. It was good seeing you."

"Yeah. See ya," Olivia said before turning away.

Neighbor after neighbor handed out candy, the streets bustling with parents and children. At times, the crowd was overwhelming. As they turned onto Olivia's street, she smiled, relieved they were almost home.

Sarah walked a few steps ahead. Olivia heard her name again, this time it was her landlord. She turned, smiling in greeting. As they chatted, Olivia glanced down and saw Amelia sifting through her candy. Relaxing slightly, she refocused on her conversation, occasionally checking to make sure Amelia was still by her side.

As the conversation wrapped up, Olivia instinctively looked down again, only to find Amelia gone.

Her breath caught in her throat. Her eyes darted frantically. She scanned for Sarah, hoping Amelia had wandered to her, but she was nowhere in sight.

Her mouth went dry. Her heart pounded against her ribs. She spun around. "Amelia," she called, voice shaking.

Her landlord's face wrinkled in confusion.

"My daughter. She was right here." Her pulse thundered. "Amelia!" she shouted. "Amelia!" Her hands trembled. "Oh my God, Amelia!"

Panic surged through her veins as she rushed through the crowd, asking anyone if they had seen her daughter. Some were familiar neighbors, others were complete strangers. Desperately, she showed pictures on her phone.

No one had any answers.

Shaking, she dialed Sarah's number. The second she answered, Olivia's voice cracked. "I can't find her anywhere."

"We'll find her. Where are you?"

"I'm at the corner. Sarah, he's taken her."

"Who?"

"Kyle. I know he has her."

"Olivia, you're jumping to conclusions."

"I'm telling you. I know it was him."

"Don't move. I'm coming to get you."

By the time Sarah arrived, Olivia was hysterical, shaking and hyperventilating. When they got home, Olivia immediately called Danny. He arrived in less than fifteen minutes.

Walking through the back door, he spotted Sarah and Paul sitting on the couch, tense and on edge. He heard Olivia's frantic voice from the next room as she spoke on the phone, pacing with Nigel at her heels, whining.

Sarah met his eyes.

"What the hell happened?" Danny demanded. "She was so hysterical on the phone, I could barely understand her."

Olivia abruptly hung up and ran to him, throwing her arms around his neck and burying her face in his chest. She sobbed, unable to form words. He wrapped his arms around her, holding her tightly.

"Baby," he murmured, "you've got to calm down and talk to me. Where is Amelia?"

Olivia pulled away, her tear streaked face tilting up toward him. "She's gone. She's been taken."

Danny's hands cupped her face, his brow furrowed in confusion. "Taken? What do you mean, taken?"

"Kyle took her."

"Kyle?"

"We don't know that," Sarah interjected.

Danny turned back to Olivia. "How do you know it was Kyle?"

"He was here. He had no reason to be. He said he was with his wife and son, but we must have been all over the neighborhood, and I never once saw them. We were right there at the corner, just up the street." Her voice cracked, and fresh tears spilled onto his hands. "I know it was him. I just know it."

Danny pulled her close. Panic rose in his chest, but he forced himself to stay composed. "Have you called Sue? Reported her missing?"

Olivia was too overwhelmed to answer, so Sarah spoke up. "She called Sue and Wallace. Her parents are on their way. I called Lauren and Nick, and they're coming too."

"Has she called Henry?"

"No."

Danny pulled back slightly, his hands still framing Olivia's face. "Livy, listen to me. I need to go. I'm going to look for Amelia."

"Please, Danny."

"I'll be back. I promise. But I can't just stand here. I'll call Ma and Pop to come stay with you." His voice softened. "I will be back."

"Danny, find her. Please find her."

"I'll do everything I can," he assured her. "But, Livy, you have to keep it together. Think about what you'd do if this were someone else's kid. What steps would you take? I know you're looking at this as a mom, and I get that. I'm trying not to look at this as a dad. It's the only way I can do this." His voice wavered, his own eyes glassy with tears. "But I have to keep my head, and so do you. Think, Livy. Focus. Anything that proves Kyle took her, we need proof. Without it, we've got nothing."

She swallowed hard and nodded. "I know it was him."

"I believe you. But I need proof."

He kissed her softly. Then, before he could hesitate, he turned and walked out the back door.

117

Danny drove to Henry's apartment. It was almost 9 p.m. Amelia had been missing for over an hour. Every second lost was another second she was in danger. The longer it took to find her, the more likely it would be that they would recover a body, not a living child.

Convinced that Henry was involved, he stormed through the apartment building to Henry's door. Banging on it, he shouted, "Henry, it's Danny. Answer the damn door!"

When Henry finally cracked the door, his face twisted in irritation. "Detective Knight. What a wonderful surprise. What the hell are you doing here?"

Danny shoved the door open and stepped inside. "Where's Amelia?"

Henry's smirk vanished. "I would assume she's with Olivia?"

"She was taken tonight. By your friend Kyle."

Henry paled. "What? No. That's not possible. Danny, I don't know what you're talking about."

Danny quickly laid out what Olivia and Sarah had told him. As the weight of the situation sank in, Henry dropped into his chair, shock evident on his face.

"Oh my God," he whispered. "How's Olivia?"

"How do you think?" Danny snapped. "She's out of her mind. I need to know where Kyle would take Amelia."

Henry shook his head. "I don't know. Danny, I swear I have no idea."

Danny studied him for a moment before jerking his head toward the door. "Get up. You're coming with me."

"You can't arrest me."

"I'm not, you dumbass. Olivia needs something to calm her down, and you're a doctor. Now move."

"I don't keep meds here."

Danny rolled his eyes. "Of course you don't. Let's go."

118

When they pulled up to Olivia's house, Danny spotted multiple cars parked along the street, Sharon and Cecil's, the sheriff's cruiser, Rick and Sue's.

Henry and Danny got out of the vehicle and walked to the back door. The house was full of people. Dr. Meredith and Linda were even there. Danny had only met them once when he first started coming around. He knew the history with them and appreciated them coming to be with her.

Before Danny could go into the living room, Sue and Rick briskly walked to the kitchen, stopping both Henry and Danny.

"Anything?" Sue asked.

"He swears he's not involved," Danny said, jerking a thumb at Henry.

"I'm not," Henry protested.

"I think we can still secure a warrant to search Kyle's office based on Amy's interview with Olivia," Sue continued. "Amy gave a written statement. She said that she saw files sticking out of the bag. With that statement and with the fact that Kyle was in the proximity of where Amelia was taken, it'll be enough to search the office and possibly his home, but not the property. I know he has a lot of land, but the warrant will have to be specific to the files. If we find anything involving Amelia, we can use it and bring him in."

Danny nodded sharply. "Do it. And put a patrolman on this house and Kyle's."

As Sue and Rick headed out to make the calls, Henry muttered, "This is bad."

Danny shot him a glare. "No kidding. You know how bad. You've been here before."

Inside the living room, the tension was suffocating. Sharon sat on the couch, holding Olivia close. Cecil paced by the front door. Paul sat silently in the chair, while Wallace stood with his arms crossed. When he saw Danny, he stepped forward.

"We've got a team coming in to search the neighborhood," Wallace said.

"What about Nigel?"

"Rick's taking him."

Danny nodded. "We have to find her."

"We will, son. We will."

Then Olivia's tired, swollen eyes found him. She stood and rushed into his arms, clinging to him with the same desperate force as before.

"Did you find her?" she asked, her voice muffled against his chest.

"No, baby, but we're not giving up," he murmured, stroking her back, pressing a kiss to her forehead.

She pulled away slightly, her gaze landing on Henry. Her expression twisted with rage. "Why is he here?"

Henry stepped forward cautiously. "Danny thought I could help."

"Help?" Olivia asked, poison spouting from her mouth. "You never cared about Amelia. Hell, you're probably at the bottom of all of this, you and your best friend, Kyle."

"Olivia, you're not thinking clearly," Henry said carefully.

"Oh, I'm thinking just fine." Her voice shook with fury. "You disappeared for months, and now you want to play the hero?"

"Livy," Danny said, grabbing her shoulder, "I brought him here. He should be here. He lost his daughter, too. You're forgetting that. And he's right. You're not thinking clearly."

"Now you're on his side?" she bit out.

"Listen to me, he was at his apartment. He's not involved."

Her face crumpled. "I just want my daughter back," she sobbed as she dropped to her knees.

Danny knelt with her, pulling her close. She shook violently against him, her cries raw and gut-wrenching. Around the room, no one spoke.

Sue walked into the living room. "We got the warrant."

Olivia looked up from the floor, barely registering the words. "Warrant?"

Sue knelt in front of her. "We can search Kyle's office and home tonight."

"Thank you," Olivia whispered.

"Danny is coming with me and Rick," she continued. "Your family'll be here in just a few hours, and Nick and Lauren are on their way, too."

"We're going to get the warrants. I'll be back. I promise." Danny pressed a kiss to her lips before standing.

Olivia nodded, but the light in her eyes was fading, replaced by something hollow. He had to find Amelia before that emptiness consumed her completely.

119

The first place Danny, Sue, and Rick went after obtaining the warrant was the archive building. They were accompanied by Nigel and a few forensic team members. They seized Kyle's office computer, but an initial scan showed nothing promising. Nigel was given something with Amelia's scent, but he did not pick up anything in the building. Regardless, they tore the office apart.

By three in the morning, they descended on Kyle's house. The officer parked on the country road reported no traffic coming or going from the property since he took his post at ten o'clock.

When Danny pounded on the door, Katie answered. He shoved the warrant in her face and stepped inside, followed by Sue, Rick, and another forensic team. As the team tossed the downstairs, Katie stood with her arms folded, anger simmering beneath the surface.

"Where's your husband, Mrs. Armstrong?" Danny asked, scanning the room.

"He must have fallen asleep in his office. He does that sometimes," she answered. "And for God's sake, be quieter. I have a son who's asleep."

"Were you in Worthington tonight with your husband?"

"Worthington?"

"Yes. Were you in Worthington tonight, trick or

treating?"

"No. I took Mike to my parents' house in Dublin. What is going on?" she asked.

"Mrs. Armstrong, your husband was seen in Worthington tonight. He spoke to someone and claimed you and your son were there with him. But you're telling me you weren't. So my question to you is why would he lie, and where the hell is he?"

"I can assure you, I don't know. He told me he was working late. He said he had workers in the field and was staying to manage the midnight shift. He does that sometimes, for extra money or extra time off."

Sue approached.

"Kyle's story to Olivia doesn't check out," Danny said.

"Really?" Sue asked.

"Olivia? Olivia Gregory? Henry's girlfriend?" Katie interjected.

"Yes. Olivia Gregory. Her daughter went missing tonight, and one of the last people to see her was your husband. So we really need to find him," Danny said.

"He's probably at the office."

"Well, we've already been to the archive office, and another team checked the main office. He's not there," Danny continued.

544

Sue opened a file folder and pulled out photographs of the dead girls taken at autopsy by Bentley. "Do you know any of these girls, Mrs. Armstrong?"

Katie's face dropped, horror consuming her. "No. I don't. What is this?"

"These are the victims of the Tic Tac Toe Killer. We believe he had a partner. And right now, since Kyle is our prime suspect, that means you are being looked at as his accomplice."

"I don't believe it. Kyle would never do something like this. You don't know him the way I do."

"Yeah, yeah," Danny said as he threw his hand up dismissively.

Rick walked in and looked at Katie. "The safe in the library."

"What safe in the library?" she asked.

"We need the combination," he continued, ignoring her interruption.

"I do not know what you're talking about. There is no safe in the library."

"You live here and don't even know that there's a safe?" Sue scoffed. "Man, you are naive."

"Get one of the forensic guys to break it," Danny ordered.

"If we find anything in that safe that implicates Kyle, there's no saving him," Sue added. "So if you know something, you'd better tell us."

"I do not know anything. I swear."

A forensic team member entered the room. "Danny, you need to see this."

He and Sue followed him out the back door.

"What am I looking at, Hal?" Danny asked.

"There are boot prints," Sue interrupted. "They match the casts from the last couple of crime scenes. They're fresh." She turned to Hal. "Cast these."

"I'll get Nigel," Danny said, sprinting toward the driveway. He opened the hatch and pressed Amelia's shirt to the dog's nose. "Go find her, buddy," he said.

The dog leaped down, immediately pulling Danny forward. Flashlight in hand, Sue followed. They ran through the woods, the darkness stretching endlessly before them, until finally they came upon a small shack. Nigel dropped down, signaling he had the scent.

"Warrant?" Sue asked.

"Don't need it. The dog took us right to it. We have probable cause," Danny replied. He handed her the lead. "Take the dog," he said before calling into his radio. "Rick, I need you back here."

Sue stayed at the edge of the woods while Danny paced,

waiting for backup. His mind raced. What if he opened that door and found Amelia's body? What if the safe contained nothing useful?

Finally, Rick returned, weapon drawn. Danny switched on the flashlight attached to his gun.

"One," Danny started. "Two, three," he finished, kicking the door open.

The wood splintered, and the door collapsed inward. They swept the one room interior, but it was empty.

"Clear," Danny called.

Rick fumbled for a string hanging from the ceiling, finally finding it and pulling. A single bulb flickered to life, casting dim light over the panel covered walls and hardwood floors. A mattress sat in the center of the room. A wooden shelf held a large radio.

Danny frowned. "How the hell is there electricity here?" He stepped outside, searching the perimeter. No wires. It had to be underground, tapping into the main.

"Danny!" Sue shouted.

He rushed back in and saw Nigel lying on the floor in the corner.

"He's got her scent again," Sue said.

A blanket lay crumpled nearby, but nothing else.

"That's enough for me. Now if we could just find her,"

Danny muttered.

His radio crackled to life. Hal's voice came through, requesting his return to the house.

Danny radioed for a team to process the shack. Rick agreed to stay behind with Nigel.

Back at the house, Hal stood in the kitchen. "Come with me," he said.

Danny and Sue followed him upstairs to the library. The safe now stood open. Hal handed Danny a file and an envelope. "We've already processed the room and taken photographs, but we wanted to turn these over to you."

Danny pulled on a pair of gloves and took the file. It was tattered, its edges worn. It was Henry's juvenile file.

Setting it on the desk, he turned his attention to the envelope. As he opened it, his stomach twisted. Inside were photographs. Crime scene photos. Images of the dead girls. Kyle was the Tic Tac Toe Killer.

Danny had been so sure Kyle had a partner, but this was undeniable proof that Kyle had been working alone. "We've got to find him," Danny whispered.

He stormed downstairs, tossing the photos onto the kitchen island. Katie glanced at them, confusion etched across her face.

"Do you see these?" Danny snapped. "Your husband took these photos. He killed these girls. Now I need to find him, because he has my little girl."

"Your little girl?" Katie echoed.

"Yes, damn it. Now call your husband."

Shaking, she dialed his number. It went straight to voicemail. "He has it turned off," she said.

"Hal, ping it," Danny ordered.

"Got it," Hal said, dashing out of the house.

Danny turned to the patrolman. "Don't leave her side."

Then he leaned in close to Katie, his voice low and dangerous. "If I find out you've lied to me, and my little girl is dead, you won't have to worry about a jury. You'll have to worry about me. And God help you if Olivia gets ahold of you."

He spun on his heel and strode out the door.

At the forensic van, Hal was running a trace.

Danny's fists clenched. "Where the fuck is he?" His patience was gone. They were running out of time.

120

The progress made was the best in the case's history, but Sue, Rick, and Danny were returning without Amelia. By the time they arrived at Olivia's, it was close to 6:30 a.m. The three of them were exhausted, but there was no time to be tired. Danny dreaded bringing Olivia the news.

Pulling into the driveway, he noticed Robin and Matt's car, as well as Lauren and Nick's. Walking in through the back door, Danny found the house quiet, but Robin and Matt sat at the kitchen table drinking coffee. They both stood expectantly.

"Did you find her?" Robin whispered.

Pursing his lips, Danny dropped his head. "No, but we did find a lot of things that could help."

Robin's tears made him feel worthless.

"We're not done. There's still hope."

Matt simply patted him on the back. "We know you're doing all you can."

Danny's phone vibrated in his back pocket. He pulled it out and read the message from Hal. *No luck tracing the phone. It's a burner.*

"Damn it," Danny said softly.

"What?" Sue asked.

"The phone's a dead end," he answered quietly.

Wallace walked into the kitchen.

"Did you find anything in the neighborhood?" Rick asked.

"The dogs caught Amelia's scent all over, but she was trick or treating. They didn't find anything useful. I sent all of the volunteers and search officers home hours ago. What about you guys? Find anything?"

"We did," Rick answered. "Photos of the dead girls in a safe that not even the wife knew about. Nigel caught Amelia's scent in an outbuilding on the property, but not much else. No blood evidence or semen. We also found Henry's file in a safe."

No one realized that Henry stood in the doorway of the kitchen until he spoke. "My file?"

"Your juvenile file," Danny answered. "We've been looking for it, and Kyle was keeping it at his house."

Henry's mouth dropped. He walked to the kitchen table, sitting down in a vacant chair. His face turned the whitest shade of pale. "Dear God," he said, dropping his head.

"What's wrong?" Danny asked.

"This isn't about Olivia or Amelia. It's about me."

Olivia's cell phone rang from deeper inside the house. Danny hurried into the living area, searching for the phone. He found it in the nursery where Olivia was asleep. In her arms was one of Amelia's blankets. Sarah, Lauren, and Nick were lying on blankets and pillows nearby. Danny guessed they had been taking turns watching over Olivia. They must have been awakened by the ringing because they were now sitting up.

"Hello," Danny heard Olivia say. "Kyle? I don't understand. Please, Kyle, she's just a baby. Don't hurt her. Yes. Please let me talk to her. I need to know she's still alive."

Her face changed, and tears ran down her cheeks. Holding her hand to her chest, she sighed. "Hi, baby. Are you okay? Oh no, baby, don't cry, sweetie. Mommy will take care of it. I don't. Oh God," she said, her voice rising. "Kyle. Kyle. Kyle?"

She threw the phone to the floor, fell onto her pillow, and sobbed.

Danny ran to her. Taking her into his arms, he let her cry. "What did he say, Livy?"

"He has her. I told you."

"I know, I know. But what did he say?"

"He wants Henry and me to meet him in an abandoned warehouse on the outskirts of downtown. He told me he just wanted me and Henry. No cops or he'd kill her."

Henry stood silently.

"We can put snipers on the surrounding buildings," Nick said.

"My baby is with that monster," Olivia cried, her head resting on Danny's lap.

"I'm so sorry," Henry said. "This is my fault."

"How?" Danny asked, looking up at him.

"Why else would he keep my file?"

"But he already killed Mya," Danny objected. "He already took your child."

"It's deeper than that. He wants me. I changed his life. I took away the only people he knew as family. Even if they were two sadistic monsters, they were all he had."

"Lauren," Danny said, turning his attention toward her, "we didn't find any evidence of a team when we executed the warrant."

Her face twisted. "But the MO, the profile."

"I think your profile might be wrong," Danny concluded.

121

After everyone had time to gather themselves and settle down, it was time to put a strategy together. Danny, Sue, Rick, Lauren, Nick, Henry, Wallace, and Olivia gathered in the kitchen. Still shaking a little, Olivia drank tea to try to calm herself.

"So, here is what we're going to do," Sue began. "We're going to tap your phone, Olivia. You have to meet him at three p.m., right?"

"Yes," Olivia answered. "That's right. At the old Williams Industrial Park."

"I'll be on the roof of one of the buildings," Nick added. "SWAT will be on standby. You'll be covered if he tries anything."

Olivia nodded.

"The main concern is Amelia. We need her out of harm's way first," Nick continued. "Once she is, I'll have a clear shot."

"I'll have patrol cars in the area and an ambulance on standby as well," Wallace said. "Once we're all clear, I'll radio them in. Danny, you're going to stay hidden."

"No. I'm not putting her out there alone," Danny argued.

"Daniel," Lauren started, leaning across the table, "Kyle

has been very specific. He is going to follow through if we do not follow his rules. He requested Henry to be there. There is a reason why."

"Maybe he's going to kill her in front of us," Olivia said, putting her hand to her mouth and closing her eyes tightly.

"Don't think like that," Henry said, reaching over and touching Olivia's hand. "It's me he wants, not her. Just try to remember that."

"Maybe he'll kill all of us," Olivia added.

"I don't think so. Otherwise, he would have requested media attention. I think he wants an exchange. I just don't know if he will want you," Lauren said, looking at Olivia, "or you." She shifted her gaze to Henry. "So, Olivia, you're going to drive there with Henry. You're going to get out of the car and stay calm. You're going to get Amelia and follow his instructions. He needs to feel he's in control. Remember, he's been on a mission since the first kill. He's been playing a game, and he wants to win. You have to make him think he will win."

"I'll shoot him if he makes any sudden moves, but we want to be able to bring him in for questioning and arrest him. The evidence is there. He'll die anyway because he'll get the death penalty. There might be more victims somewhere else. We don't know enough right now. We can't learn anything if we aren't able to talk to him," Nick said, leaning against the counter with his arms crossed.

"What you need to do right now," Sue said as she walked to Olivia and knelt beside her, "is get some rest. Why don't you try to take a nap? Collect yourself. You need to be very clear and on your game for this."

"I can't rest."

"You know she's safe," Sue continued. "You talked to her. He's not going to harm her. She's leverage. Henry's right. He's the target. Amelia is just a means to an end."

Danny stood up and walked to Olivia, holding out his hand. "Come on, Livy. Try to rest. I'll go with you. We can both use the sleep."

He and Henry exchanged glances, and Henry nodded in approval.

The plan was set. If executed flawlessly, it would mean the difference between life and death.

122

- **Density of revelation**
This chapter delivers a large amount of truth in a short span. It works because it is climax, but it leaves little interpretive breathing room. That is acceptable here, but later chapters must slow deliberately to compensate.

- **Henry's self-blame framing**
His belief that his past "demands sacrifice" is powerful, but it places him in near-mythic guilt territory. The book later addresses this, which is essential. Without that later reckoning, this framing would feel unresolved.

Areas of concern (pressure points, not problems)

- **Reader endurance**
This chapter sits atop an already intense run. It succeeds because it resolves, not escalates. Post-chapter decompression is crucial and, based on later chapters, appropriately handled.

- **Interpretation risk**
Some readers may briefly interpret Henry's sacrifice as redemption-through-death logic. Later chapters must continue to dismantle that idea rather than affirm it. Book 3 does this, so the risk is managed.

- **Emotional asymmetry aftermath**
Olivia's gratitude toward Henry and continued bond could

risk romantic ambiguity if not followed by clear emotional boundaries later. The manuscript already trends toward that clarity, which protects this chapter.

123

Robin and Matt met them at the emergency room. The doctor admitted Amelia for observation, while Henry was rushed into emergency surgery to remove the bullet.

It was late when Olivia kissed Amelia's forehead and decided to check on Henry. Walking down the hallway, she stepped into the elevator, unable to believe it was finally over.

She exited on Henry's floor, making her way down the dimly lit corridor to his room. When she peeked inside, she was surprised to see him still awake.

"I figured you'd be asleep," she said softly, stepping in and sitting on the edge of his bed.

"No way. Do you see what they're giving me? Morphine." He nodded toward the IV with a smirk. "I'm not sleeping through this. It's the first opiate I've had since I got out of rehab. This is a legal way for me to get high," he joked.

She let out a breathy laugh, shaking her head. "Thank you for everything you did," she said, taking his hand in hers.

"I told you I had it figured out. I grew up with Kyle. I knew what he was thinking. Though I am ashamed I didn't figure out the tic-tac-toe thing."

"Did he play the game with you?"

"No. He played with Holly. I never even made the

connection." He paused. "Olivia, I'm sorry you got caught in the middle of this. Losing Mya was bad enough, but for him to try to make you suffer too…"

"We're all fine. No need to worry. It's over."

"When I get out of here, you owe me coffee."

A happy smile appeared on her lips. "I think I can manage that."

"You look exhausted."

"I am," she admitted, standing and walking over to the chair across the room. She flopped down, propping her feet up on a stool.

"You should go back up to Amelia's room. You need to be with her," he suggested.

"I can stay here a little longer and talk to you," she protested through a yawn.

After only a few more moments of conversation, she drifted off while sitting in the chair. She was awakened by the sound of Henry's voice in her ear.

"You are so beautiful when you sleep," he said quietly. "I don't think I've ever told you that."

Olivia stirred, her lips curling into a faint smile as she turned her head toward him. But Henry was not in his bed. He was kneeling beside her.

"I never deserved you," he said, but his lips did not

move.

Her eyes widened, her body freezing in place.

"You taught me so much. I always knew I was a temporary part of your life. Danny, he's the better man. Always has been," he said, his lips still not moving.

Olivia's breath caught in her throat. Her gaze snapped toward Henry's hospital bed. He lay as still as a statue. A man stood over him, his hands gripping the controls of the IV.

Her heart pounded as she reached for the gun strapped to her leg. Standing swiftly, she aimed. "Don't move," she said, her voice calm but firm.

The man, clad in blue scrubs and a lab coat, turned toward her. His face was hard, his hair streaked with gray.

"Step away from his bed," she ordered.

"It's too late to save him now," the man replied coldly.

"Who are you?"

He tilted his head, smirking. "Why, honey, I'm an old friend of Henry's. Name's Mike Henson."

The breath left Olivia's lungs. It all clicked into place. Kyle had sacrificed himself to protect Mike. He had been the true mastermind, lurking in the shadows all along.

Reaching for the nurse's alert button on the bed, she barely had time to react before Mike pulled out a gun of his own.

"No, no, no, sugar," he taunted. "Don't you touch that. I guess we're just gonna have to see who's the quicker shot, aren't we?"

"I don't understand," Olivia said, buying herself a moment.

Mike chuckled. "I've been working Kyle for years. That boy came to me after I got out of prison. We planned all of this. And now, here we are." His lips curled into a sick grin. "Looks like you lost after all. I'm just sorry Kyle didn't do what I told him to with your little girl. I kept telling him to break her in."

Rage ignited in Olivia's veins.

"He wouldn't do it though," Mike continued. "Said we weren't gonna damage the goods. I wanted to tear that little thing up."

"You son of a bitch," she roared, squeezing the trigger without hesitation.

She fired again. And again. And again.

Time moved in slow motion as the trauma set in. The gun clattered to the floor from her shaking hands.

Then, reality slammed back into her.

She turned to Henry.

Throwing herself over him, she began chest

compressions, her hands pressing against his unmoving body. "Come on, Henry," she begged. "Breathe. Please, just breathe."

Medical staff stormed into the room, pulling her away as they took over.

She backed up until her body hit the wall, sliding down to the cold tile floor. Her vision blurred, as if watching everything through a pane of dark glass. Nurses worked feverishly, calling out instructions, but all she heard was silence.

A presence settled beside her.

Henry.

Don't be sad, he said gently, though his lips never moved.

Her body trembled as fresh tears streamed down her cheeks. Knowing he was gone, knowing she had to help him cross over, hollowed her out. Her soul felt lost, and she cursed her gift.

I can't do this for you, she sobbed. *Not for you. Not like this.*

Yes, you can, he assured her. *It's what you do. It's your calling.* He reached out, brushing his fingers against her cheek, but she felt nothing. *You were the best thing that ever happened to me. I tried to protect you from me, too. If I had a second chance, I'd do things differently. I'd have forgiven you for sleeping with Danny. I never would have let you go.*

Her chest heaved. *Don't go.*

You know I have to. His eyes softened. *I can see Mya in the light. It's beautiful, Olivia. I see everything now. And nothing hurts. I don't regret my sacrifice.* He smiled faintly. *You know why?*

She shook her head, biting her lip to keep from sobbing.

Because you're going to live a long, beautiful life, he said. *One day, I'll just be a distant memory. And that's how it should be. You deserve something wonderful.*

I will never forget you, Henry, she whispered. *I'm so sorry.*

Shhh... He lifted a finger to her lips. *You have nothing to apologize for. You are an incredible, gifted woman. I was lucky to have spent even a fraction of time with you.*

The doctor's voice broke through the haze.

"Call it."

She lifted her head just in time to see the nurses pull off their gloves.

"Time of death, 2:46 a.m."

Henry exhaled deeply.

That's my cue.

She broke. Sobbing, she pulled her knees to her chest, clutching herself as though she might shatter into pieces.

Henry knelt one last time, his presence softer now, almost weightless.

I'll check in with you every now and then, he said. *But you'll never know I'm there.*

She choked on a sob.

Don't cry for me, Olivia. I know where I'm going. And I'm not afraid.

"I'll miss you," she whispered.

His final smile was full of peace. "I'll miss you too, gorgeous."

And then, he was gone.

Collapsing onto the cold floor, she cried until nothing was left but heartbreak.

124

Olivia sat in the front row at the graveside, her eyes fixed on Henry's casket. The minister spoke, his voice rising and falling with practiced reverence, but the words never reached her. Beside her sat Jim, Henry's medical team, and Michelle O'Dell. Behind them were Lauren, Danny, Nick, Sarah, Sue, Rick, and Wallace. More people than she expected had come to say goodbye.

As she glanced around, a small, bittersweet smile crossed her lips. Henry never knew how many lives he had touched. He would have been pleased to see this. So many people gathered, honoring him. Still, she couldn't shake the feeling of longing. Every now and then, she stole a glance around the cemetery, hoping just maybe she'd catch a glimpse of him. But Henry never appeared. Neither did Mya.

The ceremony ended, and people began to drift away, murmuring condolences and sharing quiet embraces. Yet Olivia remained. She stood rooted in place, watching as the casket was lowered into the earth. A gust of wind rustled through the bare trees, sending leaves swirling around her feet. The emptiness inside her felt vast, a hollow ache she had known before but never quite like this.

Then, a gentle warmth brushed against her fingers. She turned slightly and saw Danny standing beside her, his presence steady and certain.

"You're going to make it through this," he said softly. "You're the strongest woman I've ever met."

Henry's voice echoed in her memory. He is the better man. And in that moment, she understood. Henry had sacrificed himself, but Danny was her protector. That was his purpose. Some men gave their lives for love, but others stayed, bearing the weight of it every single day.

She slipped her hand fully into his, her gaze falling to the swirling leaves at their feet. "I do love you, Danny."

He didn't look at her right away, only nodded. "I know you do."

"I'm sorry it took so long to"

"Don't be." He turned to her then, his eyes filled with quiet certainty. "We're together now. That's all that matters."

She blinked against a fresh wave of tears. "You are the better man."

His lips curved into a small smile. "Then let's go start our life together."

A single tear slipped down her cheek, but this time, it wasn't from sorrow. She squeezed his hand, her grip firm. "That sounds like the beginning of something beautiful."

Epilogue

Olivia stood in her bedroom, packing the last of her things. Only a few boxes remained. She still couldn't believe she was moving. Yet relocating to the Dayton area wouldn't be much different from living in Worthington, except for the fact that this time, she wasn't doing it alone. It was the least she could do for Danny.

Not only was he embarking on a new adventure as an FBI field agent for Major Crimes, but Olivia was beginning her own journey as well. Lauren had generously offered to cover her undergraduate and graduate studies, allowing her to enroll in the clinical psychology program at Wright State. There, she would be studying directly under Lauren, working as a teaching assistant to help offset costs. Finally, she was taking real steps toward becoming a profiler.

Even Amelia's future was settled. She was enrolled at the daycare center on campus, ensuring child care was never an issue. And with Robin and Matt already living nearby, Olivia would be closer to them. Cecil and Sharon would remain in Columbus, but the drive was manageable, making regular visits easy. The same went for Sue, Rick, Sarah, and Paul.

Danny walked in, wiping sweat from his forehead. "How many more boxes?" he asked, resting his hand on the small of Olivia's back.

"A few," she answered.

"This is our last room, right?"

Nick appeared in the doorway. "How many more boxes?"

Danny smirked. "A few."

Lauren followed behind, holding Jason's hand while Amelia clung to the other. "How many more boxes?" she asked.

In perfect unison, they all replied, "A few."

Lauren laughed. "I'm heading out with the kids. They're talking about food. Anyone else hungry?"

They all shook their heads.

"Well, we better get moving," Danny said. "We're losing daylight, and I personally don't want to be unloading boxes all night."

Nick grinned. "That's just because you'd rather be doing the newlywed thing, huh?" He winked and nudged Danny with his elbow.

Danny shrugged. "I say we unload the bed first."

Lauren and Olivia exchanged amused smiles.

After a few more loads, Olivia found herself in the nursery, standing still amidst the empty space. Memories of the past rushed through her, everything that had brought her to this very moment. The long, rough road behind her had shaped her, tested her, and strengthened her. She had learned the value of loyalty and commitment. She had learned how to grieve without being consumed by loss. She had learned to let go and love with everything she had. Most of all, she had learned the immeasurable power of true friendship. And now, she would spend the rest of her life with her very best friend.

Lauren had been right all along. He was the one she couldn't breathe without.

She didn't know what adventures lay ahead, but she did know this. She could face anything as long as Danny, Amelia, and the people she loved were by her side. They were her strength, her anchor, her home.

Her new life was beginning. Her happily ever after had finally arrived. With an open heart and endless anticipation, she stepped forward, ready to embrace whatever came next. She and Danny would journey together, hand in hand, charging headfirst into the future, savoring every single moment.

ABOUT THE AUTHOR

Tracee Ford, known as the "Smart Mouth Writer," has been telling stories her whole life. She is an award-winning novelist whose work explores the intersection of love, belief, and the unseen forces that shape human lives.

Her debut novel, *The Fine Line*, received a Five Star Reader's Favorite Award. Her second novel, *Idolum*, was also honored by Reader's Favorite and nominated by the Paranormal Romance Guild for Best Romantic Suspense. *Through Glass Darkly* later earned first place for Best Paranormal Romance (General), and the *Between Worlds* series received additional recognition from the Paranormal Romance Guild.

Beyond fiction, Tracee has walked many creative paths as a playwright, director, and puppeteer. Her lifelong interest in the paranormal, paired with lived experience, informs her exploration of trauma, belief, and the quiet moments where ordinary life brushes up against something more.